W9-CNW-538

Hey kid . . . wanna be a *writer* . . . ?

"Kipling *is* complicated, complicated in the way Vergil is complicated—out of fashion, perhaps, and tending not to win favor with freshman English teachers—because the reasons Kipling is complicated have less to do with his grammar than with his skill at building sensory impression. That is what I sensed when I first read the poems, that, unlike my experience with certain poets highly in vogue, when you read Kipling, you're *there*. Kipling leads the hearer step by step through a series of impressions that evoke the senses in the correct viewpointed sequence, to build a total sensory impression that surpasses the language. This is why a thirteen-year-old read the books and the poetry without being asked to by an English teacher, this is why the adult writer considers Kipling a better poet than the ones they are teaching regularly in schools, and this is why Kipling is too complicated to teach to the average English class. Learn how Kipling plays sequence games with your senses and your opinions and you'll be a writer, my friend."

—C.J. Cherryh, from
"On Kipling and Weekday Afternoons"

DAVID DRAKE &
SANDRA MIESEL

HEADS TO THE STORM

HEADS TO THE STORM

This is a work of fiction. All the characters and events portrayed in this book are fictional, and any resemblance to real people or incidents is purely coincidental.

Copyright © 1989 by David Drake and Sandra Miesel

All rights reserved, including the right to reproduce this book or portions thereof in any form.

A Baen Books Original

Baen Publishing Enterprises
260 Fifth Avenue
New York, N.Y. 10001

ISBN: 0-671-69847-8

Cover art by David Hardy

First printing, November 1989

Distributed by
SIMON & SCHUSTER
1230 Avenue of the Americas
New York, N.Y. 10020

Printed in the United States of America

ACKNOWLEDGMENTS

"Why I Admire Rudyard Kipling"
by Gordon R. Dickson
copyright, ©, 1989, Gordon R. Dickson.

"Because Our Hearts Are Small"
by Gordon R. Dickson and Sandra Miesel
copyright, ©, 1989, Gordon R. Dickson and Sandra Miesel.

"Our First Death"
by Gordon R. Dickson
copyright, ©, 1955 Fantasy House, Inc.; copyright renewed 1983 by Gordon R. Dickson, reprinted by permission of the author.

"Introduction"
by Poul Anderson
copyright, ©, 1989, Poul Anderson.

"The Visitor"
by Poul Anderson
copyright, ©, 1974, Mercury Press, Inc.

"On Kipling and Weekday Afternoons"
by D.J. Cherryh
copyright, ©, 1989, C.J. Cherryh.

"The Haunted Tower"
by C.J. Cherryh
copyright, ©, 1981, C.J. Cherryh
appeared in *Sunfall* by C.J. Cherryh, reprinted by permission of the author.

"Late Have I Loved Thee, Kipling"
by Sandra Miesel
copyright, ©, 1989, Sandra Miesel.

"The Shadow Hart"
by Sandra Miesel
copyright, ©, 1985, Sandra Miesel
appeared in *Moonsinger's Friends* edited by Susan M. Shwartz, reprinted by permission of the author.

"Introduction"
by David Drake
copyright, ©, 1989, David Drake.

"The Barrow Troll"
by David Drake
copyright, ©, 1975, Stuart David Schiff.

"Introduction"
by Poul Anderson
copyright, ©, 1989, Poul Anderson.

"The Ballad of the Three Kings"
by Poul Anderson
copyright, ©, 1980, Poul Anderson
appeared in *The Westerfilk Songbook*, reprinted by permission of the author.

"Introduction"
by Gene Wolfe
copyright, ©, 1989, Gene Wolfe.

"Love, Among the Corridors"
by Gene Wolfe
copyright, ©, 1984, Gene Wolfe
appeared in *Interzone*, reprinted by permission of the author and the author's agent, Virginia Kidd.

"Introduction"
by Jerry Pournelle
copyright, ©, 1989, Jerry Pournelle.

"The Friggin Falcon"
by Theodore R. Cogswell
copyright, ©, 1981, Theodore R. Cogswell
appeared in *Placebos for the Orthodox* by Theodore R. Cogswell, reprinted by permission of the author's agents, Owlswick Literary Agency.

"The Writer as Showman and Bard: A Personal View of Rudyard Kipling"
by John Brunner
copyright, ©, 1989, Brunner Fact and Fiction, Ltd. Used by permission.

"Mowgli"
by John Brunner
appeared in *Authentic Science Fiction* Number 69
copyright, 1956, first serial rights only, Hamilton and Co. (Stafford), Ltd. copyright assigned, 1966, to Brunner Fact and Fiction, Ltd. by the author. United States copyright, ©, renewed,

1988. Used by permission of Brunner Fact and Fiction, Ltd. and its agents for the United States, Messrs. John Hawkins and Associates.

"Introduction"
by George R.R. Martin
copyright, ©, 1989, The Fevre River Packet Co. Used by permission.

"And Seven Times Never Kill Man"
by George R.R. Martin
copyright, ©, 1975, Condé Nast Publications, Inc. Used by permission of the author and The Fevre River Packet Co.

"East Is East"
by Sandra Miesel
copyright, ©, 1989, Sandra Miesel.

"The Burning of the Brain"
by Cordwainer Smith
copyright, ©, 1958, Quinn Publishing Co. Reprinted by permission of the author and the author's agents, Scott Meredith Literary Agency, Inc., 845 Third Avenue, New York, New York 10022.

"Big Friend of the World—Rudyard"
by Anne McCaffrey
copyright, ©, 1989, Anne McCaffrey.

"The Ship Who Sang"
by Anne McCaffrey
copyright, ©, 1961, Mercury Press, Inc. Reprinted by permission of the author and the author's agent, Virginia Kidd.

"Introduction"
by Roger Zelazny
copyright, ©, 1989, The Amber Corporation.

"Lucifer"
by Roger Zelazny
copyright, ©, 1964, Galaxy Publishing Corp. Used by permission of the author.

"Kipling"
by John Brunner
appeared in *Twentieth-Century Science-Fiction Writers*, ed. Curtis C. Smith. copyright, ©, 1981, Macmillan Press, Ltd. Used by permission of the author and the publishers, St. James Press, Chicago and London.

CONTENTS

To
Buck and Juanita Coulson:
Friends Indeed

Why I Admire Rudyard Kipling

Gordon R. Dickson

T. S. Eliot once said in the introduction to a collection of Kipling's poetry that most poets have to be supported against accusations of obscurity. In Kipling's case the need is to defend him against the baseless charge of writing jingles.

He did not write jingles. Anyone who believes that should be locked in a room and not let out until he or she has written at least a twenty-page paper on the various levels of meaning to be found in his poem "Sack of the Gods." But he makes his prose and his poetry seem to have been written with no effort.

They were not. They were carefully and deliberately constructed over as long a period as was necessary, and with the sort of conscious craftsmanship that places Kipling among the great literary artists of the language. It is ironic to remember that it was precisely Shakespeare's conscious craftsmanship that the critics of his own time held against him. True art, it was felt, came from the Muse—like Athene, fully formed from the head of Zeus—not from craftsmanship, which was workaday and inferior. Shakespeare was a master craftsman, not only of words and scenes, but of the way the stage can be put to use.

It is not possible, nor ever was, to ignore the involvement of craft in any greatly successful creative effort. Craft can make a pedestrian form of poetry or prose without art. But no art is possible in story or prose without craft being involved—conscious or unconscious—on the part of its creator. The measure of that truth is the influence (and Kipling, like Shakespeare, was a highly conscious craftsman) that a writer's craft has had upon generations of succeeding authors.

The end result is that, in his poetry as well as his prose, Kipling is a master of storytelling. And storytelling must be there, from the *Iliad* to the most recent verse that attempts to claim an audience, and in any piece of fiction that makes the same attempt.

Classics—real classics—are books you can find on library shelves that have been found in such places for a hundred or more years. Books, in other words, written in the environment of a time now past and gone, but in which the characters and the actions ring true to us even now because what they present of humanity is visceral, universal, basic to the human race, three thousand years ago as now.

It must always be remembered that it is not the words, the phrase, the scene by itself that makes for literary art. It is the overall conception of the writer. Christopher Marlowe, who was praised above Shakespeare when the two were contemporary, is hardly recognized by the majority of people who recognize the name of Shakespeare nowadays.

Marlowe has two pages of quotes in the fourteenth edition of *Bartlett's Familiar Quotations*. Shakespeare has eighty-four.

Kipling has five.

. . . So far.

Because Our Hearts Are Small

Gordon R. Dickson and Sandra Miesel

"Our First Death" contrasts a party of colonists and the new planet they are attempting to colonize. The heart-breaking bleakness of the alien landscape around them is more implied than described yet it is as much a "character" in the story as the moor in *Wuthering Heights*. In fact, it is the active enemy of the colonists, withering their lives because it reminds them how far they are from Earth and the flowery fields of home.

The Kipling connection here is the parallel to the British Raj. The English were acutely sensitive to the alienness of India. They proudly believed that they understood the "natives" even though events like the Sepoy Rebellion occasionally shook their confidence. But subconsciously, they knew they were not wanted and rather than admit this, they took out their hostility on the land itself, exaggerating its real perils to blame it for every ill that befell them.

British civil servants, who might wield the power of petty princes in India, would have been nothing more romantic than minor government clerks if they had stayed at home. Their ambivalent position created keen anxieties about social status and race. The English-born claimed precedence over the Indian-born and both looked down on the local people—especially those who imitated their conquerors too closely or carried mixed blood.

The women of the Raj rejected Indian ways even more forcefully than the men did. In defiance of good sense, they stubbornly tried to eat, drink, dress, and socialize in proper British fashion. Men and women alike blinded themselves to the exotic beauty around them. Many of them only came to appreciate India when they retired to England and drab obscurity.

Kipling, who was born in India but educated in England, was painfully aware of alienation throughout his life. He sought security in family, friends, and Inner Rings of Power. His fiction often explores miniature societies—a military unit, a work crew, the ladies of the Raj in summer retreat at Simla. He likes to place them under stress in hostile surroundings where they must close ranks or perish, for he knew such challenges well.

Exiled from India by his literary success, miserably out of place in his wife's native America, Kipling finally found the kind of home he had always longed for in "Sussex by the Sea." He came to love the English countryside with a convert's fervor: only an English oak was a proper oak. Precisely because he was an outsider, he looked on the Motherland's woods and fields and waters and found enchantment there.

Kipling celebrated his rediscovered heritage in *Puck of Pook's Hill* (1906) and *Rewards and Fairies* (1910). He even modeled the children in these books on his own John and Elsie, taking yet another opportunity to write about the youth with "quivering tenderness," as Lord Birkenhead put it.

Yet Kipling's happy and productive years in Sussex were bracketed between two deaths. His older daughter Josie died of pneumonia in New York in 1899; his son was blown to bits at Loos in 1915. He commemorated these tragedies in "They" (1904) and in much bitter poetry about World War I, but the scars struck so deep, he could not bear to mention them in his autobiographical *Something of Myself* (1937).

Nevertheless, Kipling and his family did have a chance to set down roots long enough to honor his pledge:

So to the land our hearts we give
Till the sure magic strike,
And Memory, Use, and Love make live
Us and our fields alike—

The characters in the following story have no such luck.

Our First Death

Gordon R. Dickson

Juny Vewlan died about 400 hours of the morning and we buried her that same day before noon at 1100 hours, because we had no means of keeping the body. She had not wanted to be cremated; and because she was our first and because some of her young horror at the thought of being done away with entirely had seeped into the rest of us during her illness (if you could call it illness—at any rate, as she lay dying), an exception was made in her case and we decided in full assembly to bury her.

As for the subsidiary reasons for this decision of ours, they were not actually clear to us at the time, nor yet indeed for a long time afterward. Certainly the fatherless, motherless girl had touched our hearts toward the end. Certainly the old man—her grandfather Gothrud Vewlan, who with his wife, Van Meyer and Kurt Meklin made up our four Leaders—caught us all up in the heartache of his own sorrow, as he stood feebly forth on the platform to ask of us this last favor for his dead grandchild. And certainly Kurt Meklin murmured against it, which was enough to dispose some of the more stiff-necked of us in its favor.

However—we buried her. It was a cold hard day, for winter had already set in on Our Planet. We carried her out over the unyielding ground, under the white and different sky, and lowered her down into the grave some of our men had dug for her. Beneath the transparent lid of her coffin, she looked younger than sixteen years—younger, in fact, than she had looked in a long time, with her dark hair combed back from around the small pointed face and her eyes closed. Her hands were folded in front of her. She had, Gothrud told us, also wished some flowers to hold in them; and none of us could imagine where she had got such an idea until one of the younger children came forward with an illustration from our library's *Snow White and the Seven Dwarfs*, showing Show White in *her* coffin with a bunch of flowers that never faded clasped in her hands. It was clear then, to some of us at least, that Juny had not been free from the dream of herself as a sort of captive—now sleeping—princess, merely putting in her time until the Prince her lover should arrive and carry her off.

But we had, of course, no flowers.

After she had been lowered into the grave and all of us had come up to look at her, Lydia Vewlan, Gothrud's wife and colony doctor as well as one of the Leaders, read some sort of service over her. Then, when all was finished, a cloth was laid over the transparent face of the plastic coffin and the earth was shoveled back. It had been dug out in chunks—a chunk to a spadeful; and the chunks had frozen in the bitter air, so that it was like piling angular rocks back upon the coffin, heavy purple rocks with the marblings of white shapes that were the embryos of strange plants frozen in hibernation. Because of their hard awkward shapes, they made quite a pile above the grave when they were all put back; and in fact it was not until the following summer was completely gone that the top of the grave was level again with the surrounding earth. By that time we had a small fence of white plastic pickets all around it; and it was part of the duty of the children in the colony to keep them scrubbed clean and free of the gray mold.

After the burial we all went back to the mess building for our noon meal. Outside, as we took our places at the tables, the midday wind sprang up and whistled around our metal huts and the stripped skeleton of the ship, standing apart at its distance on the landing spot and looking lonely and neglected in the bleak light from the white sky.

The Leaders of our colony sat at the head of the file of tables that stretched the length of the mess hut. Their table was just large enough for the four of them and was set a little apart from the rest so that they could discuss important matters in relative privacy. The other, large tables stretched away in order, with the ones at the far end with the small chairs and the low tops for the very young children—those who were just barely able to eat by themselves without supervision. These, the children, had as a group been unusually silent and solemn during the burial procedures, impressed by the emotions of their elders. But now, as they started to eat, their natural energy and exuberance began to break free of this restraint and show itself all the more noticeably for having been held down this long. In fact they began to pose quite a small disciplinary problem, and this necessitating the attentions of their elders, a diversion was created, which together with the warmth and the good effect of the hot food, bred a lightening of spirits among us adults as well. Our natural mood of optimism, which the Colonial Office had required in selecting us for a place on the immigration rosters, pressed down before by the awareness of death in our midst, began to rise again. And it continued to rise, like a warm tide throughout the length of the hut, until finally it reached the four who sat at the head table. But here it lapped unavailingly against the occupied minds of those who, twenty-four hours a day, breathed the constant atmosphere of responsibility for us all.

To talk and not be heard, they must lower their voices and lean their heads together. And this, while a perfectly natural action, had a tendency to impart an air of tenseness to their discussions. So they sat now, following the burial, in such an atmosphere of tenseness; and although the rest of us did not discover what they were then saying until long afterward—indeed until Maria Warna told us about it months later—there were those among us at the long tables who, glancing upward, noticed something perhaps graver than usual about their talking at that meal.

In particular, it had been Kurt Meklin—Kurt, with his old lined face thrust forward above his plate like some gray guardian of ancient privilege, who had been urging some point upon the other three all through the meal. But what it was, he had avoided stating openly, talking instead in half-hints, and obscure ambiguities, his black hard eyes sliding over to glance at Lydia, and then away again, and then back again. Until, finally, when the last plates had been removed and the coffee served, Lydia rose at last to the challenge and spoke out unequivocally.

"All right, Kurt!" she said—she, the strong old woman, meeting the clever old man eye to eye. "You've been hinting and hawing around ever since we got back from the burying. Now, what's wrong with it?"

"Well, now that you ask me, Lydia," said Kurt. "It's a question—a question of what she died of."

Gothrud, who had sat the whole meal with his head hanging and eating almost nothing, now suddenly raised his eyes and looked across at Kurt.

"What kind of a question's that?" demanded Lydia. "You saw me enter it on the records—death from natural causes."

"I'll tell you what she really died of," said Gothrud, suddenly.

"Well now," said Kurt, interrupting Gothrud, and with another of his side-glances at Lydia. "Do you think that's sufficient?"

"Sufficient? Why shouldn't it be sufficient?"

"Well now, of course, Lydia . . ." said Kurt. "I know nothing of doctoring myself, and we all know that the Colonial Office experts gave Our Planet a clean bill of health before they shipped our little colony out here. But I should think—just for the record, if nothing else—you'd have wanted to make an examination to determine the cause of death."

"I did."

"Naturally—but just a surface examination. Of course with the colony in a sentimental mood about the girl—eh, Van?"

Van Meyer, the youngest of them all, was turning his

coffee cup around and around between his thick fingers and staring at it. His heavy cheeks were slablike on either side of his mouth.

"Leave me out of it," he said, without looking up.

Lydia sniffed at him, and turned back to Kurt.

"Stop talking gibberish!" she commanded.

"Gibberish . . . sorry, Lydia," said Kurt. "I don't have the advantages of your medical education. A pharmacist really knows so little. But—it's just that I think you've left the record rather vague. *Natural causes* really doesn't tell us exactly what she died of."

"What she died of!" broke in Gothrud with sudden, low-voiced violence. "She died of a broken heart."

"Don't be a fool, Gothrud," said his wife, without looking at him. "And keep your voice down, you, Kurt. Do you want the whole colony to hear? Now, out with it. You sat with us and agreed to bury her. If you had any questions, you should have come out with them then."

"But I had to bend to the sentimentality of the colony," said Kurt. "It was best to let it go then. Later, I thought, later we can . . ." He fell silent, making a small, expressive gesture with his hand.

"Later we can do *what?*" grated Lydia.

"Why, I should think that naturally—as a matter of record—that in a case like this you'd want to do an autopsy on her."

"Autopsy!" The word jolted a little from Lydia's lips.

"Why, certainly," said Kurt, spreading his hands. "This way is much simpler than insisting on it in open Assembly. After curfew tonight, when everybody is in barracks—"

A low strangled cry from Gothrud interrupted him. From the moment in which the word *autopsy* had left Kurt's lips, he had been sitting in frozen horror. Now, it seemed, he managed at last to draw breath into his lungs to speak with.

"Autopsy!" he cried, in a thin, tearing, half-strangled whisper. "*Autopsy!* She didn't want to be touched! We agreed not to burn her; and now you'd—No—"

"Why, Gothrud—" said Kurt.

"Don't *Why Gothrud* me!" said Gothrud, his deep sunk

eyes at last flaming into violence. "A decision's been made by the colony. And none of you are going to set it aside."

"We are the Leaders," said Kurt.

"Leaders!" Gothrud laughed bitterly. "The ex-druggist—you, Kurt. The ex-nurse and—" He glanced at Van Meyer—"the ex-caterer's son, the ex-nothing."

Van Meyer held his cup and stared at it.

"And the ex-high school teacher," said Kurt, softly.

"Exactly!" said Gothrud, lifting his head to meet him stare for stare. "The ex-high school teacher. Me. As little an ex as the rest of you, Kurt, and as big a Leader right now. And a Leader that says you've got no right to touch my Juny to settle your two-bit intriguing and feed your egos—" He choked.

"Gothrud—" said Kurt. "Gothrud, you're overwrought. You—"

Gothrud coughed raspingly and went on. "I tell you—" He choked again, and had to stop.

Lydia spoke swiftly to him, in low, furious German. "Shut up! Will you kill yourself, old man?"

"That's being done for me," Gothrud answered her in English, and faced up to Kurt again. "You hear me!" he said. "We're nothings. Leaders, Great executives. Only none of us has been five miles from the landing spot. Only none of us organized this colony. None of us flew the ship, or assigned the work, or built the huts, or planned the plantings. All we did was sign the roster back on Earth, and polite young experts with twice our brains did it all for us. By what right are we Leaders?"

"We were elected!" snapped Kurt.

"Fools elected by fools!" Gothrud's head was beginning to swim from the violence of his effort in the argument. Through a gathering mist, he seemed to see Kurt's face ripple as if it were under water, and rippling, sneer at him. With a great effort, he gripped the edge of the table and went on.

"I tell you," he rasped, "that people have rights. That you won't—that you can't—that—"

His tongue had suddenly gone stubborn and refused to obey him. It rattled unintelligibly in his mouth and around him the room was being obscured by the white mist. Gothrud felt a sudden constriction in his throat; and, gasping abruptly for breath, he pushed back his chair and tried to stand up, clawing at his collar to loosen it.

Through the black specks that swarmed suddenly before his eyes, he was conscious of Van Meyer rising beside him and of Lydia's voice ordering the younger man to catch him before he fell.

"Come on, Gothrud," said the voice of Van Meyer, close to his ear. "You've been under too much of a strain. You better lie down. Come on, I'll help you."

Through the haze he was conscious of being half-assisted, half-carried from the dining room. There was a short space of confusion, and then things cleared for him, to allow him to find himself lying on his bunk in the room he shared with Lydia. Van Meyer, alone with him, stood over the washstand, filling a hypodermic syringe from a small frosted bottle of minimal, his gross bulk hunched over concentratedly with a sort of awkward and pathetic kindness.

"Feeling better?" he asked Gothrud.

"I'm all right," Gothrud answered. But the words came out thick and unnaturally. "What are you doing?"

"I'm going to give you a shot to make you sleep," said Van.

"Van—" said Gothrud. "Van—" Talking was really a tremendous effort. He swallowed desperately and went on. "*You* understand about Juny—don't you?"

"Why, yes, Gothrud."

"She shouldn't have come, you see. We made her—because she had no other family, Lydia and I. She never wanted to come. We talked her into it. She was just coming out of being a child—"

"Don't talk, Gothrud," said Van, struggling with the delicate plunger of the hypodermic. "You need to rest."

"—She was the only one that age. All the rest of us, adults or young children; and her in between, all alone. A whole lost generation, Van, in one lonely little girl."

"Now, Gothrud—"

"I tell you,'" cried Gothrud, struggling up onto one elbow, "we robbed her of every reason to live. She should have had love and fun and the company of young people her own age back on Earth. And we brought her here—to this desolate outpost of a world—"

Van Meyer had finally got the syringe properly filled. He came over to the bed with it and reached for Gothrud's arm when the older man sank back.

"That's why we owe it to her to leave her untouched the way she wanted," said Gothrud, in a low, feverish voice, as the needle went in. "But it's not that so much, Van. If it were for some good purpose, I wouldn't object. But it isn't. It's for Lydia—and Kurt. Van—" He grasped the younger man's arm as he started to turn away from the bunk, and held him, compelling Van Meyer to turn back.

"Van—" he said. "Things are going wrong here. You know that. It's Lydia. Married all those years back on Earth, and I never let myself see it. I watched her drive our son and daughter from our house. I watched her bend Juny to her way and bring her here with us. And Van" —his voice sunk to a whisper—"I never let myself see it until I got here, that awful hunger in her. It's power, she wants, Van, power. That's what she's always wanted, and now she sees a chance of getting it. Listen to me, Van, watch out for her. She did for Juny. It'll be me next, and then Kurt, and then—"

"Now, Gothrud—now just relax—" said Van, pulling his arm at last free from the older man's grasp, which now began to weaken as the drug took hold.

"Promise me you'll watch . . ." whispered Gothrud. "You must. I trust you, Van. You're weak, but there's nothing rotten in you. Kurt's no good. He's another like Lydia. Watch them. Promise—promise. . . ."

"I—I promise," said Van, and the minimal came in on Gothrud with a rush, like a great black wave that swept in and over him, burying him far beneath it, deep, and deep.

When Gothrud awoke, the room he shared with Lydia was in darkness; and through the single small, high window in the outer wall, with its reinforcing wire mesh patterning the glass, he saw the night sky—for a wonder momentarily free of clouds—and the bright stars of the

Cluster. Van Meyer's shot of minimal must have been a light one, for he had awakened clear-headed and, he felt quite sure, long before it had been planned for him to awaken. He felt positive in his own mind that they would have planned for him to sleep until morning; and only the unpredictable clock of his old body, ticking erratically, now fast and now slowing, running down toward final silence, had tricked them.

The illuminated clock-face on his bedside table read 21:20 and curfew was at 2100 hours. He fumbled into his clothes, got up, went over to the window and peered out, craning his neck. Yes, the colony was now completely lost in darkness, except for the small, yellow-gleaming windows of the Office Hut. Feverishly he turned and began to climb into his weather suit, struggling hastily into the bulky, overall-like outfit, zipping it tight and pulling the hood over his head. At the last minute, as he was going out the door, he remembered the diary; and, going back, dug through the contents of his locker until his fingers closed over the cylindrical thickness of it. He lifted it out, a faint hint of clean, light, young-girl's perfume reaching him from it momentarily. Then he stuffed it through the slit of his weather suit to an inside pocket; and went out the door.

The most direct route to the Office Hut led across the open compound. But as he started across this, leaning against the wind, an obscure fear made his feet turn away from the direct bulk of his destination and veer in the direction of the new grave. He went, chiding himself for his foolishness all the way, for although he knew now that the other three Leaders had held him in secret contempt for a long time, he was equally sure that they would not dare go directly against his wishes in this matter without consulting him.

So it was that when he came finally to Juny's grave and saw it gaping black and open under the stars, he could not at first bring himself to believe it. But when he did, all the strength went out of him and he fell on his knees beside the open trench. For a wild moment as he knelt there, he felt that, like a figure out of the Old Testament, he should pray—for guidance, or for a divine vengeance upon the desecrators of the grave of his grandchild. But all that came out of him were the crying reproaches of an old man: "Oh, God, why didn't you make me stronger? Why didn't you make me young again when this whole business of immigration was started? I could take a gun and—"

But he knew he would not take a gun; and if he did, the others would simply walk up and take it away from him. Because he could not shoot anybody. Not even for Juny could he shoot anybody. And after a while he wiped his eyes and got to his feet and went on toward the Office Hut, hugging one arm to his side, so that he could feel the round shape of the diary through all his heavy suit insulation.

When he came to the Office Hut, the door was locked. But he had his key in his pocket as always. His heart pounded and the entryway of the Hut seemed full of a soft mist lurking just at the edge of his vision. He leaned against the wall for a moment to rest, then painfully struggled out of his weather suit. When he had hung it up beside the others on the wall hooks, he opened the inner door of the Hut and went in.

The three were clustered around the long conference table at the far end of the office, Lydia with her dark old face looking darker and older even than usual above the white gown and gloves of surgery. They looked up at the sound of the opening door; and Van Meyer moved swiftly to block off Gothrud's vision of the table and came toward him.

"Gothrud!" he said. "What are you doing here?" And he put his hands on Gothrud's arms.

Gothrud struggled feebly to release himself and go around the younger man to the table, but was not strong enough.

"Let me go. Let me go!" he cried. "What have you done to her? Have you—"

"No, no," soothed Van Meyer. Still holding Gothrud's arms, he steered the older man over to a chair at one of the desks and sat him down in it. All the way across the room, he stayed between Gothrud and the conference table and when he had Gothrud in the chair, he pulled up another for himself and sat down opposite, so that the table was still hidden. Kurt and Lydia came over to stand behind him. All three looked at Gothrud.

Lydia's face was hard and bitter as jagged ice. The absorbent face mask around her neck, unfastened on one side and hanging by a single thread, somehow made her look, to Gothrud's eyes, not like a member of the profession of healing, but like some executioner, interrupted in the course of her duty.

"You!" she said.

Gothrud stared up at her, feeling a helpless fascination. "You—you mustn't—" he gasped.

"*Du!*" she broke out at him suddenly, in low voiced, furious German. "You old fool! Couldn't you stay in bed and keep out of trouble? Don't I have enough trouble on my hands with this one-time pill-peddler trying to undermine my authority, but I must suffer with you as well?"

"Lydia," he answered hoarsely, in the same language. "You can't do this thing. You mustn't let Kurt push you into it. It's a crime before God and man that you should even consider it."

"I consider—I consider the colony."

"No. You do not. You do not!" cried Gothrud in agony. "You think only of yourself. What harm will it do you if you tell the truth? It can't alter the facts. The colony will be upset for a little while, but then they will get over it. Isn't that better than living a lie and backing it up with an act of abomination?"

"Be silent!" snapped Lydia. "What I am doing, I am doing for the best of all concerned."

"I won't let you!" he cried. Changing swiftly into English, he swung away from her and appealed to the two men.

"Listen," he said. "Listen: you know there's no need for this—this autopsy. Colonial Office experts, men who *know*, certified this planet as clean. So it can't be any disease. And what would it benefit you to discover some physical frailty?"

"Ah? She was frail?" asked Kurt. "Something in the family?"

"No, she was not!" Lydia almost shouted. "Stop playing

the goose, Kurt." Suddenly regaining control of herself, she dropped her voice all at once to normal level again. "I'm surprised at you, Kurt, letting yourself be misled by a sick old man who never was able to look on the girl dispassionately."

"Dispassionately!" cried Gothrud, straining forward against Van Meyer's prisoning hands. "Did you look at Juny dispassionately? Did you bring her along to die out here, dispassionately, taking her away from everything that she longed for? I tell you—*I* tell you, she died of a broken heart! God— " He choked suddenly. "God forgive me for being so soft, so weak and flabby-soft that I let you have your way about her coming. Better an orphanage back on Earth, for her. Better the worst possible life, alive, back there, than this—to have her dead, so young, and wasted—wasted—"

He sobbed suddenly.

"Van," commanded Lydia, evenly, "take him back to Quarters."

"No!" shouted Gothrud, coming suddenly to his feet and with surprising strength pushing the younger man aside, so that he half-toppled in his chair and caught at a desk to keep from falling. Gothrud took two quick strides across to a recorder that perched on a nearby desk. Pulling the diary from his pocket, he snapped it onto the spindle and turned the playback on.

"She died of a broken heart—for all she wanted and couldn't have," cried Gothrud. "And here's your proof. Listen!"

"What are you doing?" snapped Kurt.

Gothrud turned blazing eyes upon him.

"This was her diary," he said. "Listen. . . ."

The speaker had begun to murmur words in the voice of a young girl. Gothrud reached out and turned up the volume. The sweet clear tones grew into words in the still air of the grim rectangular office, all plastic and metal about the four who listened.

". . . *and after that we flew out over Lake Michigan. The lake was all dark, but you could see the moon lighting a path on the water, all white and wonderful. And the lights went up the shore for miles. I just put my head on Davy's shoulder . . .*"

"Shut it off!" snapped Kurt, suddenly. "What are you trying to do, Gothrud?"

"Listen to her heart breaking," said Gothrud, his head a little on one side, attentively. "Listen and try to think of her dispassionately."

"You're out of your head, Gothrud!" said Lydia. "What odds is it, what the girl recorded back on Earth?"

"On Earth? On Earth?" echoed Gothrud. "She recorded it here, night by night, in her own room."

Before them the diary fell silent for a second and then took up with a new entry.

". . . *Month eight, fourth day: Today Walter took me to the Embassy ball. I wore my new formal all made out of yards of real night mist-lace. It was like walking in the center of a pink cloud. Walter has the high emotional index typical of such intense characters; and he was very jealous of me. He was afraid that I might take it into my head to turn around and go back to Our Planet and the colony. I let him worry for a little while, before I explained that I can never, never go back because of a clause the studio put in my contract that says I am not allowed to leave the Earth without studio permission which they will never give. And since I'm signed up with them for years and years . . .*"

Lydia's hand came down like a chopping knife on the cutoff, killing Juny's voice in mid-sentence.

"That's enough of that," she said. "Van, take him out."

"You heard," said Gothrud, staring at the two men. Van hesitated.

"Go on, Van!" snapped Lydia. Reluctantly, Van moved forward.

"Kurt—" cried Gothrud.

"It's up to Lydia," replied the druggist, tonelessly.

"Then we'll go ahead," said Lydia decisively, turning away.

"No, by heaven, you won't!" shouted Gothrud, fending off Van and taking a step forward. At the motion, the sudden familiar wave of dizziness swept over him, so that he staggered and was forced to cling to a nearby chair for support.

"All right," he said, fighting to clear his head. "If you won't stop—if you really won't stop—then I'll tell you. Lydia has no right. Lydia—"

"Be silent!" shouted Lydia in German, suddenly halting and wheeling about, her face deadly.

"No," said Gothrud in English. "No. Not any more. Listen, Kurt—and you too, Van. You know what kind of doctor Lydia is. A fourteen-day wonder. She was a registered nurse and the Colonial Office sent her to school for two weeks and gave her a medical diploma." He looked straight at Lydia, who stood frozen, her mouth half-open in an angry gape and her hands fisted by her side. "What you don't know, and what I've kept to myself all this time is that the diploma means nothing. Nothing."

"What's this?" said Kurt.

Gothrud laughed, chokingly.

"As if you haven't suspected, Kurt. Don't think I don't know why you suggested this autopsy. But all you had were suspicions. I know. I was at the school with her."

"I suspected nothing—"

Gothrud laughed hoarsely.

"Then you're a fool, Kurt. Who believes that a doctor can be made in two weeks when it takes eight years back on Earth? A two-week doctor would be prosecuted on Earth. But we little people who go out to colonize take what we can bring along with us. Us with our nurse-doctors, our druggist-Leaders, our handyman-engineers. Yes. Do you know what they taught us in those two weeks, Kurt—except that I didn't get a diploma for my part in it? Lydia learned how to attempt a forceps delivery, an appendectomy, and a tonsillectomy. They taught her the rudiments of setting broken bones and the proper methods for prescribing some two hundred common drugs."

He was still looking at Lydia as he spoke. She still had not moved, and her hands were still clenched, but her face had taken on an expression of complete serenity.

"This," said Gothrud, staring at her. "This woman who

has never held a scalpel in her hand in her life before is the trained specialist that you are expecting to make a professional examination of Juny's body."

Kurt turned to face Lydia.

"Lydia," he said. "Lydia, is this true?"

"Don't be ridiculous, Kurt," replied Lydia, calmly. "He's lying of course."

"How do we know it's not you who are lying?"

"Because I'm in complete control of my faculties. Gothrud's senile."

"Senile?" said Van.

"Of course. The first signs showed up in him some time back. I was hoping it would come on more slowly; but you've all noticed these fainting fits of his, and how he gets wrought up over every little thing. Poor Gothrud," she said, looking at him.

He stared back at her, so aghast at the depths of her perfidy that he could not even bring himself to speak.

"He's made this all up, of course," she went on. "The method by which I was trained was naturally top secret. I've been sworn to silence, of course, but I can tell you that the required information is fed directly to the brain. It's such a new and revolutionary method that it's being restricted to highly important Government Service, such as training key colonists like myself. That explains why the ordinary medical colleges don't know about it yet."

"Lydia," said Kurt. "You say this is true? You swear it's true? How can you prove it?"

"Proof?" she said airly. "Watch me do the autopsy."

Kurt's old eyelids closed down over his eyes until he seemed to look out through a narrow slit.

"All right, Lydia," he said. "That's just what we'll do."

A wordless cry broke from the lips of Gothrud. He snatched up a chair and took one step toward Lydia. Instantly Van Meyer jumped forward and caught him. Frantically, the old man struggled, his breath coming in short terrible gasps.

"Hold him, Van, while I give him a sedative!" cried Lydia—but before she could reach the hypodermic kit on the table across the room, Gothrud suddenly stopped struggling and stiffened. His eyes rolled upward until only the whites showed, for just a second before the lids dropped down over them. He sagged bonelessly. And Van Meyer, lowering him into a chair, snatched back his hands in horror, as if they had suddenly become covered with blood. But Lydia brusquely came across the room, pushed him aside, and bent over the motionless figure.

She took its pulse and rolled one eyelid back momentarily.

"That's all right," she said, stepping back. "Leave him alone. It's easier this way. Come on back to the table with me, both of you, I'll need your assistance."

But for a second, yet, she herself did not move; instead, standing, she stared down at the man she had lived with for more than 50 years. There was a particular glitter in her eye.

"Poor Gothrud," she said softly.

She turned away crisply and led the way back to the conference table, re-tying her face mask as she went.

"Stand over there, Kurt," she said. "You, Van, hand me that scalpel. That one, there." Her eyes jumped at him, as he hesitated. "Move, man! It's only a body."

They went to work. When Lydia was about half through, Gothrud came to himself a little in the chair and called out in a dazed voice to ask what they were doing.

"Don't answer," muttered Lydia, bent above her work. "Pay no attention to him."

They did not answer Gothrud. After a little while he called out again. And when they did not answer this time, either, he subsided in his chair and sat talking to himself and crying a little.

It was an unpleasant job. Van Meyer felt sick; but Kurt went about his duties without emotion, and Lydia was industriously and almost cheerfully busy about her part of it.

"Well," she said, at last. "Just as I suspected—nothing."

She untied her mask and frankly wiped a face upon which perspiration gleamed.

"Wrap her up," she said. "And then you can take her back out again." She glanced over to where her husband was. He had stopped talking to himself and was sitting up, staring at them with bright eyes. "Well, how are you, Gothrud?"

Gothrud did not answer, although he looked directly at her; and Van Meyer, standing beside her, stirred uncomfortably. Kurt sat down on a desk opposite her and mopped his face with a tissue. He produced one of the colony's few remaining cigarets and lighted it.

"And you didn't find anything?" he said sharply to Lydia.

She transferred her gaze from Gothrud to him.

"Not a thing," she said.

Kurt blinked his eyes and turned his head away. But Van Meyer continued to stare at her, uneasily and curiously.

"Lydia," he asked.

"What, Van?"

"What was it, then?"

"What was what?"

"I mean," he said. "Now that you've . . . seen her, what was it that made her die?"

"Nothing made her die," replied Lydia. "She just died. If I'm to write a more extensive report, I'll put down that death was due to heart failure—with general debility as a contributing factor."

In the silence that fell between them, the single word came sharp and clear from the old man seated across the room.

"Heart," said Gothrud.

"Yes," said Lydia, turning once more to face him. "If it makes you feel any better, Gothrud, it was her heart that killed her."

"Yes," repeated Gothrud. "Yes, her poor heart. Her heart that none of you understood. Lydia—"

"What?" she demanded sharply.

He stretched out his arms to her, his wrinkled fingers cupped and trembling.

"Her heart," he said. "Lydia. Give me the broken pieces."

The next day Gothrud was very weak and could not leave his bed. For three days Lydia looked after him alone; but it turned out to take too much of her time from the duties required of her by her colony positions, and on the fourth day they brought in Maria Warna from the unmarried women's barracks to stay with him and take care of him. And during the next few weeks he rambled a good deal in his talk, so that, one way or another, he told Maria everything. And eventually, later, she told it to the rest of us. But that was a long time after when things were different.

Gothrud lingered for a few days more than three weeks and finally died. He was cremated, as was everyone else who died after that. That was the same week that the last of the tobacco and cigarets were used up; and those of us who smoked had a hard time getting used to doing without them.

Introduction

Poul Anderson

So pervasive is Kipling's influence that often those on whom it works are unaware of it. Certainly I had never thought of this story in any such terms, and was surprised when David Drake told me that he did. I am not much given to introspection, but insights like his are worth exploring.

To the best of my recollection, I had had a dream that stayed in my memory, which dreams seldom do. In it, I found myself visiting a little girl who lived by herself in a big house. When I told my wife about it, she suggested a context that would make it a story. Ordinarily I would have first-drafted a piece of that length in one day, two at the most. This took a week, because I could only bear to write a couple of pages at a time. There must be something in it, because two different men, both rather on the macho side, have admitted to me that it made them cry.

The story employs telepathy and deals with the relationship of father and daughter. Kipling's work does one or the other on occasion. Of course, neither theme is unique to him, nor shows that he was even in my unconscious mind. However—

In the year of the writing, Karen's and my daughter Astrid had turned seventeen, a charming young lady on whom we looked with affection and pride. Nevertheless, I wistfully remembered, and always shall, how it was when she was small. No doubt every normal father of a girl does likewise. Love and joy carry their price, a part of which is the dread of loss. That had forever haunted the back of my awareness, and therefore "The Visitor" raises it.

Karen and I were lucky, and still are. (Astrid has now given us a grandchild—our first, we hope.) Kipling was not. His Josephine was only six when she died. Knowing this, I cannot read the second poem of the two in *Just So Stories* that the collected verse gives the common title "Merrow Down" without a stinging in the eyes.

I scarcely think we were in any kind of rapport across time, as happens in his magnificent "Wireless." Both of us being human, we had shared a universe of experience and feelings. He helped determine which out of these I would try to work with and, within the limits of my ability, *how* I would, as he did for so many others among the writers who came after him.

The Visitor

POUL ANDERSON

As we drove up between lawns and trees, Ferrier warned me, "Don't be shocked at his appearance."

"You haven't told me anything about him," I answered. "Not to mention."

"For good reason," Ferrier said. "This can never be a properly controlled experiment, but we can at least try to keep down the wild variables." He drummed fingers on the steering wheel. "I'll say this much. He's an important man in his field, investment counseling and brokerage."

"Oh, you mean he's a partner in—Why, I've done some business with them myself. But I never met him."

"He doesn't see clientele. Or very many people ever. He works the research end. Mail, telephone, teletype, and reads a lot."

"Why aren't we meeting in his office?"

"I'm not ready to explain that." Ferrier parked the car and we left it.

The hospital stood well out of town. It was a tall clean block of glass and metal which somehow fitted the Ohio countryside rolling away on every side, green, green, and green, here and there a white-sided house, red-sided barn, blue-blooming flax field, motley of cattle, to break the corn and woodlots, fence lines and toning telephone wires. A warm wind soughed through birches and flickered their leaves; it bore scents of a rose bed where bees quemed.

Leading me up the stairs to the main entrance, Ferrier

said, "Why, there he is." A man in a worn and outdated brown suit waited for us at the top of the flight.

No doubt I failed to hide my reaction, but no doubt he was used to it, for his handclasp was ordinary. I couldn't read his face. Surgeons must have expended a great deal of time and skill, but they could only tame the gashes and fill in the holes, not restore an absolute ruin. That scar tissue would never move in human fashion. His hair did, a thin flutter of gray in the breeze; and so did his eyes, which were blue behind glasses. I thought they looked trapped, those eyes, but it could be only a fancy of mine.

When Ferrier had introduced me, the scarred man said, "I've arranged for a room where we can talk." He saw a bit of surprise on me and his tone flattened. "I'm pretty well known here." His glance went to Ferrier. "You haven't told me what this is all about, Carl. But"—his voice dropped—"considering the place—"

The tension in my friend had hardened to sternness. "Please, let me handle this my way," he said.

When we entered, the receptionist smiled at our guide. The interior was cool, dim, carbolic. Down a hall I glimpsed somebody carrying flowers. We took an elevator to the uppermost floor.

There were the offices, one of which we borrowed. Ferrier sat down behind the desk, the scarred man and I took chairs confronting him. Though steel filing cabinets enclosed us, a window at Ferrier's back stood open for summer to blow in. From this level I overlooked the old highway, nowadays a mere picturesque side road. Occasional cars flung sunlight at me.

Ferrier became busy with pipe and tobacco. I shifted about. The scarred man waited. He had surely had experience in waiting.

"Well," Ferrier began. "I apologize to both you gentlemen. This mysteriousness. I hope that when you have the facts, you'll agree it was necessary. You see, I don't want to predispose your judgments or . . . or imaginations. We're dealing with an extraordinarily subtle matter."

He forced a chuckle. "Or maybe with nothing. I give no promises, not even to myself. Parapsychological phenomena at best are"—he paused to search—"fugitive."

"I know you've made a hobby of them," the scarred man said. "I don't know much more."

Ferrier scowled. He got his pipe going before he replied: "I wouldn't call it a hobby. Can serious research only be done for an organization? I'm convinced there's a, well, a reality involved. But solid data are damnably hard to come by." He nodded at me. "If my friend here hadn't happened to be in on one of my projects, his whole experience might as well never have been. It'd have seemed like just another dream."

A strangeness walked along my spine. "Probably that's all it was," I said low. "Is."

The not-face turned toward me, the eyes inquired; then suddenly hands gripped tight the arms of the chair, as they do when the doctor warns he must give pain. I didn't know why. It made my voice awkward:

"I don't claim sensitivity, I can't read minds or guess Rhine cards, nothing of that sort works for me. Still, I do often have pretty detailed and, uh, coherent dreams. Carl's talked me into describing them on a tape recorder, first thing when I wake up, before I forget them. He's trying to check on Dunne's theory that dreams can foretell the future." Now I must attempt a joke. "No such luck, so far, or I'd be rich. However, when he learned about one I had a few nights ago—"

The scarred man shuddered. "And you happened to know *me*, Carl," broke from him.

The lines deepened around Ferrier's mouth. "Go on," he directed me, "tell your story, quick," and cannonaded smoke.

I sought from them both to the serenity beyond these walls, and I also spoke fast:

"Well, you see, I'd been alone at home for several days. My wife had taken our kid on a visit to her mother. I won't deny, Carl's hooked me on this ESP. I'm not a true believer, but I agree with him the evidence justifies looking further, and into curious places, too. So I was in bed, reading myself sleepy with . . . Berdyaev, to be exact, because I'd been reading Lenau earlier, and he's wild, sad, crazy, you may know he died insane; nothing to go to sleep on. Did he linger anyhow, at the bottom of my mind?"

* * *

I was in a formlessness which writhed. Nor had it color, or heat or cold. Through it went a steady sound, whether a whine or drone I cannot be sure. Unreasonably sorrowful, I walked, though there was nothing under my feet, no forward or backward, no purpose in travel except that I could not weep.

The monsters did when they came. Their eyes melted and ran down the blobby heads in slow tears, while matter bubbled from within to renew that stare. They flopped as they floated, having no bones. They wavered around me and their lips made gibbering motions.

I was not afraid of attack, but a horror dragged through me of being forever followed by them and their misery. For now I knew that the nature of hell lies in that it goes on. I slogged, and they circled and rippled and sobbed, while the single noise was that which dwelt in the nothing, and time was not because none of this could change.

Time was reborn in a voice and a splash of light. Both were small. She was barely six years old, I guessed, my daughter's age. Brown hair in pigtails tied by red bows, and a staunch way of walking, also reminded me of Alice. She was more slender (elven, I thought) and more neat than my child—starched white flowerbud-patterned dress, white socks, shiny shoes, no trace of dirt on knees or tip-tilted face. But the giant teddy bear she held, arms straining around it, was comfortably shabby.

I thought I saw ghosts of road and tree behind her, but could not be certain. The mourning was still upon me.

She stopped. Her own eyes widened and widened. They were the color of earliest dusk. The monsters roiled. Then: "Mister!" she cried. The tone was thin but sweet. It cut straight across the hum of emptiness. "Oh, Mister!"

The tumorous beings mouthed at her. They did not wish to leave me, who carried some of their woe. She dropped the bear and pointed. "Go 'way!" I heard. "Scat!" They shivered backward, resurged, clustered close. "Go 'way, I want!" She stamped her foot, but silence responded and I felt the defiance of the monsters. "All right," she said grimly. "Edward, you make them go."

The bear got up on his hind legs and stumped toward me. He was only a teddy, the fur on him worn off in patches by much hugging, a rip in his stomach carefully mended. I never imagined he was alive the way the girl and I were; she just sent him. Nevertheless he had taken a great hammer, which he swung in a fingerless paw, and become the hero who rescues people.

The monsters flapped stickily about. They didn't dare make a stand. As the bear drew close, they trailed off sullenly crying. The sound left us too. We stood in an honest hush and a fog full of sunglow.

"Mister, Mister, Mister!" The girl came running, her arms out wide. I hunkered down to catch her. She struck me in a tumult and joy exploded. We embraced till I lifted her on high, made to drop her, caught her again, over and over, while her laughter chimed.

Finally, breathless, I let her down. She gathered the bear under an elbow, which caused his feet to drag. Her free hand clung to mine. "I'm so glad you're here," she said. "Thank you, thank you. Can you stay?"

"I don't know," I answered. "Are you all by yourself?"

"Yes. 'Cept for Edward and—" Her words died out. At the time I supposed she had the monsters in mind and didn't care to speak of them.

"What's your name, dear?"

"Judy."

"You know, I have a little girl at home, a lot like you. Her name's Alice."

Judy stood mute for a while and a while. At last she whispered, "Could she come play?"

My throat wouldn't let me answer.

Yet Judy was not too dashed. "Well," she said, "I didn't 'spect you, and you came." Happiness rekindled in her and caught in me. Could my presence be so overwhelmingly enough? Now I felt at peace, as though every one of the rat-fears which ride in each of us had fled me. "Come on to my house," she added, a shy invitation, a royal command.

We walked. Edward bumped along after us. The mist vanished and we were on a lane between low hedges. Elsewhere reached hills, their green a palette for the emerald or silver of coppices. Cows grazed, horses galloped, across miles. Closer, birds flitted and sparkled, a robin redbreast, a chickadee, a mockingbird who poured brook-trills from a branch, a hummingbird bejeweled among bumblebees in a surge of honeysuckle. The air was vivid with odors, growth, fragrance, the friendly smell of the beasts. Overhead lifted an enormous blue where clouds wandered.

This wasn't my country. The colors were too intense, crayon-brilliant, and a person could drown in the scents. Birds, bees, butterflies, dragonflies somehow seemed gigantic, while cattle and horses were somehow unreachably far off, forever cropping or galloping. The clouds made real castles and sailing ships. Yet there was rightness as well as brightness. I felt—maybe not at home, but very welcome.

Oh, infinitely welcome.

Judy chattered, no, caroled. "I'll show you my garden an' my books an', an' the whole house. Even where Hoo Boy lives. Would you push me in the swing? I only can pump myself. I pretend Edward is pushing me, an' he says, 'High, high, up in the sky, Judy fly, I wonder why,' like Daddy would, but it's only pretend, like when I play with my dolls or my Noah's ark animals an' make them talk. Would you play with me?" Wistfulness crossed her. "I'm not so good at making up ad-*ven*tures for them. Can you?" She turned merry again and skipped a few steps. "We'll have dinner in the living room if you make a fire. I'm not s'posed to make fire, I remember Daddy said, 'cept I can use the stove. I'll cook us dinner. Do you like tea? We have lots of different kinds. You look, an' tell me what kind you want. I'll make biscuits an' we'll put butter an' maple syrup on them like Grandmother does. An' we'll sit in front of the fire an' tell stories, okay?" And on and on.

The lane was now a street, shaded by big old elms; but it was empty save for the dappling of the sunlight, and the houses had a flatness about them, as if nothing lay behind their fronts. Wind mumbled in leaves. We reached a gate in a picket fence, which creaked when Judy opened it.

The lawn beyond was quite real, aside from improbably

tall hollyhocks and bright roses and pansies along the edges. So was this single house. I saw where paint had peeled and curtains faded, the least bit, as will happen to any building. (Its neighbors stood flawless.) A leftover from the turn of the century, it rambled in scale-shaped shingles, bays, turrets, and gingerbread. The porch was a cool cavern that resounded beneath our feet. A brass knocker bore the grinning face of a gnome.

Judy pointed to it. "I call him Billy Bungalow because he goes bung when he comes down low,' she said. "Do you want to use him? Daddy always did, an' made him go a lot louder than I can. Please. He's waited such a long time." I have too, she didn't add.

I rattled the metal satisfactorily. She clapped her hands in glee. My ears were more aware of stillness behind the little noise. "Do you really live alone, brighteyes?" I asked.

"Sort of," she answered, abruptly going solemn.

"Not even a pet?"

"We had a cat, we called her Elizabeth, but she died an' . . . we was going to get another."

I lifted my brows. "We?"

"Daddy an' Mother an' me. C'mon inside!" She hastened to twist the doorknob.

We found an entry where a Tiffany window threw rainbows onto hardwood flooring. Hat rack and umbrella stand flanked a coat closet, opposite a grandfather clock which broke into triumphant booms on our arrival: for the hour instantly was six o'clock of a summer's evening. Ahead of us swept a staircase; right and left, doorways gave on a parlor converted to a sewing room, and on a living room where I glimpsed a fine stone fireplace. Corridors went high-ceilinged beyond them.

"Such a big house for one small girl," I said. "Didn't you mention, uh, Hoo Boy?"

Both arms hugged Edward close to her. I could barely hear: "He's 'maginary. They all are."

It never occurred to me to inquire further. It doesn't in dreams.

"But *you're* here, Mister!" Judy cried, and the house was no longer hollow.

She clattered down the hall ahead of me, up the stairs,

through chamber after chamber, basement, attic, a tiny space she had found beneath the witch-hat roof of a turret and assigned to Hoo Boy; she must show me everything. The place was bright and cheerful, didn't even echo much as we went around. The furniture was meant for comfort. Down in the basement stood shelves of jelly her mother had put up and a workshop for her father. She showed me a half-finished toy sailboat he had been making for her. Her personal room bulged with the usual possessions of a child, including books I remembered well from years agone. (The library had a large collection too, but shadowy, a part of that home which I cannot catalog.) Good pictures hung on the walls. She had taken the liberty of pinning clippings almost everywhere, cut from the stacks of magazines which a household will accumulate. They mostly showed animals or children.

In the living room I noticed a cabinet-model radio-phonograph, though no television set. "Do you ever use that?" I asked.

She shook her head. "No, nothing comes out of it anymore. I sing for myself a lot." She put Edward on the sofa. "You stay an' be the lord of the manor," she ordered him. "I will be the lady making dinner, an' Mister will be the faithful knight bringing firewood." She went timid. "Will you, please, Mister?"

"Sounds great to me," I smiled, and saw her wriggle for delight.

"Quick!" She grabbed me anew and we ran back to the kitchen. Our footfalls applauded.

The larder was well stocked. Judy showed me her teas and asked my preference. I confessed I hadn't heard of several kinds; evidently her parents were connoisseurs. "So'm I," Judy said after I explained that word. ""Then I'll pick. An' you tell me, me an' Edward, a story while we eat, okay?"

"Fair enough," I agreed.

She opened a door. Steps led down to the backyard. Unlike the closely trimmed front, this was a wilderness of assorted toys, her swing, and fever-gaudy flowers. I had to laugh. "You do your own gardening, do you?"

She nodded. "I'm not very expert. But Mother promised I could have a garden here." She pointed to a shed at the far end of the grounds. "The firewood's in that. I got to get busy." However firm her tone, the fingers trembled which squeezed mine. "I'm so happy," she whispered.

I closed the door behind me and picked a route among her blossoms. Windows stood wide to a mild air full of sunset, and I heard her start singing.

"The little red pony ran over the hill
And galloped and galloped away—"

The horses in those meadows came back to me, and suddenly I stood alone, somewhere, while one of them who was my Alice fled from me for always; and I could not call out to her.

After a time, walking became possible again. But I wouldn't enter the shed at once; I hadn't the guts, when Judy's song had ended, leaving me here by myself. Instead, I brushed on past it for a look at whatever might lie behind for my comfort.

That was the same countryside as before, but long-shadowed under the falling sun and most quiet. A blackbird sat on a blackberry tangle, watched me and made pecking motions. From the yard, straight southward through the land, ran a yellow brick road.

I stepped onto it and took a few strides. In this light the pavement was the hue of molten gold, strong under my feet; here was the kind of highway which draws you ahead one more mile to see what's over the next hill, so you may forget the pony that galloped. After all, don't yellow brick roads lead to Oz?

"Mister!" screamed at my back. "No, stop, stop!"

I turned around. Judy stood at the border. She shuddered inside the pretty dress as she reached toward me. Her face was stretched quite out of shape. "Not yonder, Mister!"

Of course I made haste. When we were safely in the yard, I held her close while the dread went out of her in a burst of tears. Stroking her hair and murmuring, at last I dared ask, "But where does it go?"

She jammed her head into the curve of my shoulder and gripped me. "T-t-to Grandmother's."

"Why, is that bad? You're making us biscuits like hers, remember?"

"We can't *ever* go there," Judy gasped. Her hands on my neck were cold.

"Well, now, well, now." Disengaging, while still squatted to be at her height, I clasped her shoulder and chucked her chin and assured her the world was fine; look what a lovely evening, and we'd soon dine with Edward, but first I'd better build our fire, so could she help me bring in the wood? Secretly through me went another song I know, Swedish, the meaning of it:

"Children are a mysterious folk, and they live in a wholly strange world—"

Before long she was glad once more. As we left, I cast a final glance down the highway, and then caught a breath of what she felt: less horror than unending loss and grief, somewhere on that horizon. It made me be extra jocular while we took armloads of fuel to the living room.

Thereafter Judy trotted between me and the kitchen, attending to her duties. She left predictable chaos, heaped dishes, scorched pan, strewn flour, smeared butter and syrup and Lord knows what else. I forbore to raise the subject of cleanup. No doubt we'd tackle that tomorrow. I didn't mind.

Later we sat cross-legged under the sofa where Edward presided, ate our biscuits and drank our tea with plenty of milk, and laughed a great deal. Judy had humor. She told me of a Fourth of July celebration she had been at, where there were so many people "I bet just their toes weighed a hundred pounds." That led to a picnic which had been rained out, and—she must have listened to adult talk—she insisted that in any properly regulated universe, Samuel Gompers would have invented rubber boots. The flames whirled red, yellow, blue, and talked back to the ticking, booming clock; shadows played tag across walls; outside stood a night of gigantic stars.

"Tell me another story," she demanded and snuggled into my lap, the calculating minx. Borrowing from what I had done for Alice, I spun a long yarn about a girl named

Judy, who lived in the forest with her friends Edward T. Bear and Billy Bungalow and Hoo Boy, until they built a candy-striped balloon and departed on all sorts of explorations; and her twilight-colored eyes got wider and wider.

They drooped at last, though. "I think we'd better turn in," I suggested. "We can carry on in the morning."

She nodded. "Yesterday they said today was tomorrow," she observed, "but today they know better."

I expected that after those fireside hours the electrics would be harsh to us; but they weren't. We went upstairs, Judy on my right shoulder, Edward on my left. She guided me to a guest room, pattered off, and brought back a set of pajamas. "Daddy wouldn't mind," she said.

"Would you like me to tuck you in?" I asked.

"Oh—" For a moment she radiated. Then the seriousness came upon her. She put finger to chin, frowning, before she shook her head. "No, thanks. I don't think you're s'posed for that."

"All right." My privilege is to see Alice to her bed; but each family has its own tradition. Judy must have sensed my disappointment, because she touched me and smiled at me, and when I stooped she caught me and breathed,

"You're really real, Mister. I love you," and ran down the hall.

My room resembled the others, well and unpretentiously furnished. The wallpaper showed willows and lakes and Chinese castles which I had seen in the clouds. Gauzy white curtains, aflutter in easy airs, veiled away those lantern-big stars. Above the bed Judy had pinned a picture of a galloping pony.

I thought of a trip to the bathroom, but felt no need. Besides, I might disturb my hostess; I had no doubt she brushed her teeth, being such a generally dutiful person. Did she say prayers too? In spite of Alice, I don't really understand little girls, any more than I understand how a mortal could write *Jesu Joy of Man's Desiring*. Boys are different; it's true about the slugs and snails and puppy dogs' tails. I've been there and I know.

I got into the pajamas, lay down in the bed and the breeze, turned off the light, and was quickly asleep.

Sometimes we remember a night's sleep. I spent this one being happy about tomorrow.

Maybe that was why I woke early, in a clear, shadowless gray, cool as the air. The curtains rippled and blew, but there was no sound whatsoever.

Or . . . a rustle? I lay half awake, eyes half open and peace behind them. Someone moved about. She was very tall, I knew, and she was tidying the house. I did not try, then, to look upon her. In my drowsiness, she might as well have been the wind.

After she had finished in this chamber, I came fully to myself, and saw how bureau and chair and the bulge of blankets that my feet made were strangers in the dusk which runs before the sun. I swung legs across bedside, felt hardwood under my soles. My lungs drank odors of grass. Oh, Judy will snooze for hours yet, I thought, but I'll go peek in at her before I pop downstairs and start a surprise breakfast.

When dressed, I followed the hallway to her room. Its door wasn't shut. Beyond, I spied a window full of daybreak.

I stopped. A woman was singing.

She didn't use real words. You often don't, over a small bed. She sang well-worn nonsense,

> "Cloddledy loldy boldy boo,
> Cloddledy lol-dy bol-dy boo-oo,"

to the tenderest melody I have ever heard. I think that tune was what drew me on helpless, till I stood in the entrance.

And she stood above Judy. I couldn't truly see her: a blue shadow, maybe? Judy was as clear to me as she is this minute, curled in a prim nightgown, one arm under her cheek (how long the lashes and stray brown hair), the other around Edward, while on a shelf overhead, Noah's animals kept watch.

The presence grew aware of me.

She turned and straightened, taller than heaven. Why have you looked? she asked me in boundless gentleness. Now you must go, and never come back.

No, I begged. Please.

When even I may do no more than this, she sighed, you cannot stay or ever return, who looked beyond the Edge.

I covered my eyes.

I'm sorry, she said; and I believe she touched my head as she passed from us.

Judy awakened. "Mister—" She lifted her arms, wanting me to come and be hugged, but I didn't dare.

"I have to leave, sweetheart," I told her.

She bolted to her feet. "No, no, no," she said, not loud at all.

"I wish I could stay awhile," I answered. "Can you guess how much I wish it?"

Then she knew. "You . . . were awful kind . . . to come see me," she got out.

She went to me with the same resolute gait as when first we met, and took my hand, and we walked downstairs together and forth into the morning.

"Will you say hello to your daughter from me?" she requested once.

"Sure," I said. Hell, yes. Only how?

We went along the flat and empty street, toward the sun. Where a blackbird perched on an elm bough, and the leaves made darkness beneath, she halted. "Good-bye, you good Mister," she said.

She would have kissed me had I had the courage. "Will you remember me, Judy?"

"I'll play with my remembering of you. Always." She snapped after air; but her head was held bravely. "Thanks again. I do love you."

So she let me go, and I left her. A single time I turned around to wave. She waved back, where she stood under the sky all by herself.

The scarred man was crying. He wasn't skilled in it; he barked and hiccoughed.

Surgically, Ferrier addressed him. "The description of the house corresponds to your former home. Am I correct?"

The hideous head jerked a nod.

"And you're entirely unfamiliar with the place," Ferrier declared to me. "It's in a different town from yours."

"Right," I said. "I'd no reason before today to suppose

I'd had anything more than a dream." Anger flickered. "Well, God damn your scientific caution, now I want some explanations."

"I can't give you those," Ferrier admitted. "Not when I've no idea how the phenomenon works. You're welcome to what few facts I have."

The scarred man toiled toward a measure of calm. "I, I, I apologize for the scene," he stuttered. "A blow, you realize. Or a hope?" His gaze ransacked me.

"Do you think we should go see her?" Ferrier suggested.

For reply, the scarred man led us out. We were silent in corridor and elevator. When we emerged on the third floor, the hospital smell struck hard. He regained more control over himself as we passed among rubber-tired nurses and views of occupied beds. But his gesture was rickety that, at last, beckoned us through a certain doorway.

Beyond lay several patients and a near-total hush. Abruptly I understood why he, important in the world, went ill-clad. Hospitals don't come cheap.

His voice grated: "Telepathy, or what? The brain isn't gone; not a flat EEG. Could you—" That went as far as he was able.

"No," I said, while my fingers struggled with each other. "It must have been a fluke. And since, I'm forbidden."

We had stopped at a cluster of machinery. "Tell him what happened," Ferrier said without any tone whatsoever.

The scarred man looked past us. His words came steady if a bit shrill. "We were on a trip, my wife and daughter and me. First we meant to visit my mother-in-law in Kentucky."

"You were southbound, then," I foreknew. "On a yellow brick road." They still have that kind, here and there in our part of the country.

"A drunk driver hit our car," he said. "My wife was killed. I became what you see. Judy—" He chopped a hand toward the long white form beneath us. "That was nineteen years ago," he ended.

On Kipling and Weekday Afternoons

C. J. Cherryh

Certain passages of Kipling evoke the smells of leather and ink and paper—*The Jungle Book* and the poems about the Middle East in particular—and being thirteen and downtown in a moderate-sized town and waiting for a ride home with my dad, because I went to school about eight blocks away and I had to catch rides home, either (I forget) because I couldn't afford the bus every day (not impossible in those days) or because my school schedule and an occasional run past the municipal library kept me too late for the regular city bus that took my friends home.

All of which is probably an improbable introduction to a story like this, except for the fact that I had a better time than kids are supposed to, pent up in a government office for an hour every afternoon—I used to sit and draw and mess with the office equipment, equipment you only see nowadays in vintage movies. I learned to type on a truly vintage Underwood, in those hours. You know, the kind of machine that not only isn't electric, you have to bash the keys from about one to two inches above the keyboard to even make the type contact the paper . . .

. . . which stood me in good stead, you can see.

And when the fingers had had it or when somebody was using the machine I got to use when no one else was, I used to park myself in one of those government-issue genuine oak interview chairs and sit there reading Kipling, *not* because anybody had assigned it to me. I had just hunted it out of the library mostly because of *The Jungle Book*, which I had seen in film, and I was at that age when running off to live with wolves seems rather more attractive than squidging past juvenile gangs in school hallways. I liked the poetry better: since I was a pretty good artist, with thoughts even of *doing* art for a living to support my writing, I used to love things that gave me ideas for sketches.

Kipling did—only not, after the initial try at a few tigers, from *The Jungle Book*. I liked the stuff about Arab chieftains and horses and mediaeval knights and horses . . .

Well, I was in my romantic phase, and Kipling hit me hard, for the first time since my early infatuation with radio science fiction. I was writing then. My learning to type had a secret purpose. And Kipling had an odd effect on me—an initial reaction of *I can do that*, and an *I want to do that*, and then a niggling suspicion that anyone who made it look that easy was really complicated.

Kipling *is* complicated, I can say after several decades more, complicated in the way Vergil is complicated—out of fashion, perhaps, and tending not to win favor with freshman English teachers—because the reasons Kipling is complicated have less to do with his grammar than with his skill at building sensory impression. That is what I sensed when I first read the poems, that, unlike my experience with certain poets highly in vogue, when you read Kipling, you're *there*. Kipling leads the hearer step by step through a series of impressions that evoke the senses in the correct viewpointed sequence, to build a total sensory impression that surpasses the language. This is why a thirteen-year-old read the books and the poetry without being asked to by an English teacher, this is why the adult writer considers Kipling a better poet than the ones they are teaching regularly in schools, and this is why Kipling is too complicated to teach to the average English class. Learn how Kipling plays sequence games with your senses and your opinions and you'll be a writer, my friend.

The Haunted Tower

C. J. CHERRYH

There were ghosts in old London, that part of London outside the walls and along the river, or at least the townsfolk outside the walls believed in them: mostly they were attributed to the fringes of the city, and the unbelievers inside the walls insisted they were manifestations of sunstruck brains, of senses deceived by the radiations of the dying star and the fogs which tended to gather near the Thames. Ghosts were certainly unfashionable for a city management which prided itself on technology, which confined most of its bulk to a well-ordered cube (geometrically perfect except for the central arch which let the Thames flow through) in which most of the inhabitants lived precisely ordered lives. London had its own spaceport, maintained offices for important offworld companies, and it thrived on trade. It pointed at other cities in its vicinity as declined and degenerate, but held itself as an excellent and enlightened government: since the Restoration and the New Mayoralty, reason reigned in London, and traditions were cultivated only so far as they added to the comfort of the city and those who ruled it. If the governed of the city believed in ghosts and other intangibles, well enough; reliance on astrology and luck and ectoplasmic utterances made it less likely that the governed would seek to analyze the governors upstairs.

There were some individuals who analyzed the nature of

things, and reached certain conclusions, and who made their attempts on power.

For them the Tower existed, a second cube some distance down the river, which had very old foundations and very old traditions. The use of it was an inspiration on the part of the New Mayoralty, which studied its records and found itself a way to dispose of unwanted opinion. The city was self-contained. So was the Tower. What disappeared into the Tower only rarely reappeared . . . and the river ran between, a private, unassailable highway for the damned, so that there was no untidy publicity.

Usually the voyagers were the fallen powerful, setting out from that dire river doorway of the city of London.

On this occasion one Bettine Maunfry came down the steps toward the rusty iron boat and the waters of old Thames. She had her baggage (three big boxes) brought along by the police, and though the police were grim, they did not insult her, because of who she had been, and might be again if the unseen stars favored her.

She boarded the boat in a state of shock, sat with her hands clenched in her lap and stared at something other than the police as they loaded her baggage aboard and finally closed the door of the cabin. This part of the city was an arch above the water, a darksome tunnel agleam with lights which seemed far too few; and she swallowed and clenched her hands the more tightly as the engines began to chug their way downriver toward the daylight which showed at the end.

They came finally into the wan light of the sun, colors which spread themselves amber and orange across the dirty glass of the cabin windows. The ancient ruins of old London appeared along the banks, upthrust monoliths and pillars and ruined bits of wall which no one ever had to look at but those born outside—as she had been, but she had tried to forget that.

In not so long a time there was a smooth modern wall on the left side, which was the wall of the Tower, and the boat ground and bumped its way to the landing.

Then she must get out again, and, being frightened and unsteady, she reached out her hand for the police to help her across the narrow ramp to the shore and the open gate of that wall. They helped her and passed her on to the soldier/warders, who brought her within the gates; she stood on stones which were among the most ancient things in all of ancient London, and the steel gates, which were not at all ancient, and very solid, gaped and hissed and snicked shut with ominous authority. The chief warder, a gray-haired man, led her beyond the gatehouse and into the interior of the Tower which, to her surprise, was not a building, but a wall, girding many buildings, many of them crumbling brick and very, very old-seeming. Guards followed with her baggage as she walked this strange, barren courtyard among the crumbling buildings.

"What are these stones?" she asked of the older man who led the way, proper and militarily slim. "What are they?"

But he would not answer her, as none of them spoke to her. They escorted her to the steps of a modern tower, which bestraddled ancient stones and made them a part of its structure, old brick with gleaming steel. The older man showed her through the gateway and up the steps, while the others followed after. It was a long climb—no lift, nothing of the sort; the lights were all shielded and the doors which they passed were all without handles.

Third level; the chief warder motioned her through a doorway just at the top of the stairs, which led to a hall ending in a closed door. She found the guards pushing her luggage past her into that short corridor, and when she did not move, the chief warder took her arm and put her through the archway, himself staying behind. "Wait," she cried, "wait," but no one waited and no one cared. The door shut. She wept, she beat at the closed door with her fists, she kicked the door and kicked it again for good measure, and finally she tried the door at the other end of the hall, pushed the only door switch she had, which let her into a grim, one-room apartment, part brick and part steel, a bed which did not look comfortable, thinly mattressed; a bathroom at least separate of the single room, a window, a wall console: she immediately and in panic pushed buttons there, but it was dead, quite dead. Tears streamed down her face and she wiped them with the back of her hand and snuffled because there was no one to see the inelegance.

She went to the window then and looked out, saw the courtyard and in it the guards who had brought her heading to the gates; and the gates opening on the river and closing again.

Fear came over her, dread that perhaps she was alone in this place and the stones and the machines might be all there was. She ran to the panel and punched buttons and pleaded, and there was nothing; then she grew anxious that the apartment door might close on its own. She scurried out into the short hallway and dragged her three cases in and sat down on the thin mattress and cried.

Tears ran out after a time; she had done a great deal of crying and none of it had helped, so she sat with her hands in her lap and hoped earnestly that the screen and the phone would come on and it would be Richard, his honor Richard Collier the mayor, to say he had frightened her enough, and he had.

The screen did not come on. Finally she began to snuffle again and wiped her eyes and realized that she was staying at least . . . at least a little time. She gathered her clothes out of the boxes and hung them; laid out her magazines and her books and her knitting and sewing and her jewelry and her cosmetics and all the things she had packed. . . . At least they had let her pack. She went into the bath and sat down and repaired her makeup, painting on a perfectly insouciant face, and finding in this mundane act a little comfort.

She was not the sort of person who was sent to the Tower; she was only a girl, (though thirty) the Mayor's girl. She was plain Bettine Maunfry. His Honor's wife knew about her and had no resentments; it just could not be that Marge had turned on her; she was not the first girl his Honor had had, and not the only even at the moment. Richard was jealous, that was all, angry when he had found out there might be someone else, and he had power and he was using it to frighten her. It had to be. Richard had other girls and a wife, and there was no reason for him to be jealous. He had no right to be jealous. But he was; and he was vindictive. And because he was an important man, and she was no one, she was more frightened now than she had ever been in her life.

The Tower was for dangerous criminals. But Richard had been able to do this and get away with it, which she would never have dreamed; it was all too cruel a joke. He had some kind of power and the judges did what he wanted; or he never even bothered to get a court involved.

The tears threatened again, and she sniffed and stared without blinking at her reflected image until the tears dried. Her face was her defense, her beauty her protection. She had always known how to please others. She had worked all her life at it. She had learned that this was power, from the time she was a tiny girl, that she must let others have control of things, but that she could play on them and get them to do most things that she wanted. *I like people*, was the way she put it, in a dozen variants; all of which meant that as much as she hated technical things she liked to know all about different types of personalities; it sounded altruistic, and it also gave her power of the kind she wanted. Most of the time she even believed in the altruism . . . until a thing like this, until this dreadful grim joke. This time it had not worked, and none of this should be happening.

It would still work, if she could get face-to-face with Richard, and not Richard the Lord Mayor. She tested a deliberate and winning smile in the mirror, perfect teeth, a bewitching little twitch of a shoulder.

Downy lashes rimming blue eyes, a mouth which could pout and tremble and reflect emotions like the breathing of air over water, so fine, so responsive, to make a man like His Honor feel powerful . . . that was all very well: she knew how to do that. He *loved* her . . . after a possessive fashion; he had never said so, but she fed his middle-aged vanity, and that was what was hurt; that had to be it, that she had wounded him more than she had thought and he had done this, to show her he was powerful.

But he would have to come, and see how chastened she was and then he would feel sorry for what he had done, and they would make up and she would be back safe in the city again.

He would come.

She changed to her lounging gown, with a very deep neckline, and went back and combed her dark masses of hair just so, just perfect with the ruby gown with the deep plunge and the little bit of ruby glitter paler than the blood-red fabric. . . . He had given that to her. He would remember that evening when he saw her wearing it.

She waited. The silence here was deep, so, so deep. Somewhere in this great building there should be *someone* else. It was night outside the window now, and she looked out and could not bear to look out again, because it was only blackness, and reminded her she was alone. She wished that she could curtain it; she might have hung something over it, but that would make the place look shabby, and she lived by beauty. Survived by it. She sat down in the chair and turned on the light and read her magazines, articles on beauty and being desirable which now, while they had entertained her before, seemed shatteringly *important*.

Her horoscope was good; it said she should have luck in romance. She tried to take this for hopeful. She was a Pisces. Richard had given her this lovely charm which she wore about her neck; the fish had real diamond eyes. He laughed at her horoscopes, but she knew they were right.

They must be this time. *My little outsider*, he called her, because like most who believed in horoscopes, she came from outside; but she had overcome her origins. She had been a beautiful child, and because her father had worked Inside, she had gotten herself educated . . . was educated, absolutely, in all those things proper for a girl, nothing serious or studious, nothing of expertise unless it was in Working With People, because she knew that it was just not smart at all for a girl to be too obviously clever . . . modesty got a girl much further . . . that and the luck of being beautiful, which let her cry prettily. Her childish tantrums had gotten swift comfort and a chuck under the chin, while her brothers got spanked, and that was the first time she had learned about *that* kind of power, which she had always had. It was luck, and that was in the stars. And her magazines told her how to be even more pleasing and pleasant and that she succeeded in what she thought she did. That it worked was self-evident: a girl like her, from the outside, and a receptionist in His Honor the Mayor's office, and kept by him in style people Outside could not imagine. . . .

Only there were bad parts to it too, and being here was one, that she had never planned for—

A door opened somewhere below. Her heart jumped. She started to spring up and then thought that she should seem casual and then that she should not, that she should seem anxious and worried, which was why Richard had sent her here. Perhaps she should cry. Perhaps it was Richard. It *must* be Richard.

She put the magazine away and fretted with her hands, for once in her life not knowing what to do with them, but even this was a pretty gesture and she knew that it was.

The door opened. It was the military warden, with dinner.

"I can't eat," she said. It seemed upon the instant that intense depression was the ploy to use. She turned her face away, but he walked in and set it on the table.

"That's your business," he said, and started to leave.

"Wait." He stopped and she turned her best pleading look on him . . . an older man and the kind who could be intensely flattered by beauty . . . flattered, if she seemed vulnerable, and she put on that air. "Please. Is there any word . . . from Richard?"

"No," he said, distressingly impervious. "Don't expect any."

"Please. Please tell him that I want to talk to him."

"If he asks."

"Please. My phone doesn't work."

"Not supposed to. It doesn't work for all prisoners. Just those with privileges. You don't have any."

"*Tell* him I want to see him. Tell him. It's his message. Won't *he* decide whether he wants to hear it?"

That got through. She saw the mouth indecisive. The man closed the door; she heard the steps going away. She clutched her hands together, finding them shaking.

And she ignored the food, got out her magazine again and tried to read, but it hardly occupied her mind. She dared not sit on the bed and prop her knees up and read; or sit down to eat; it was too informal, too unlovely. She started to run her hand through her hair, but that would disarrange it. She fretted back and forth across the floor, back and forth, and finally she decided she could put on her negligee and if His Honor walked in on her that was to the better.

She took out not the bright orange one, but the white, lace-trimmed, transparent only here and there, innocent; innocence seemed precious at the moment. She went to the mirror in the bath, wiped off the lipstick and washed her face and did it all over again, in soft pinks and rosy blushes; she felt braver then. But when she came out again to go to bed, there was that black window, void and cold and without any curtain against the night. It was very lonely to sleep in this place. She could not bear to be alone.

And she had slept alone many a night until Tom had come into her life. Tom Ash was a clerk in the Mayor's office in just the next office over from hers; and he was sweet and kind . . . after all, she was beautiful, and still young, only thirty, and seven years she had given to Richard, who was not handsome, though he was attractive after the fashion of older, powerful men; but Tom was . . . Tom was handsome, and a good lover and all those things romances said she was due, and he loved her moreover. He had said so.

Richard did not know about him. Only suspected. Tom had got out the door before Richard arrived, and there was no way in the world Richard could know who it was; more to the point, Richard had asked who it was.

And if Richard had power to put her here despite all the laws he had power to put Tom here too, and maybe to do worse things.

She was not going to confess to Richard, that was all. She was not going to confess, or she would tell him some other name and let Richard try to figure it all out.

Richard had no proof of anything.

And besides, he did not own her.

Only she liked the good things and the pretty clothes and the nice apartment Tom could never give her. Even her jewelry . . . Richard could figure out a way to take that back. Could blacklist her so she could never find a job, so that she would end up outside the walls, exiled.

She was reading a romance about a woman who had gotten herself into a similar romantic triangle, and it was all too very much like her situation. She was almost afraid to find out how it ended. Light reading. She had always liked light reading, about real, *involved* people, but of a sudden it was much too dramatic and involved her.

But it had to have a happy ending; all such stories did, which was why she kept reading them, to assure herself that she would, and that beautiful women could go on being clever and having happy endings.

Whoever *wanted* tragedy?

She grew weary of reading, having lost the thread of it many times, and arranged the pillows, and having arranged herself as decorously as she could, pushed the light switch by the head of the bed and closed her eyes.

She did sleep a time, more exhausted than she had known, and came to herself with the distinct impression that there had been someone whispering nearby, two someones, in very light voices.

Children, of all things; children in the Tower.

She opened her eyes, gaped upon candlelight, and saw to her wonder two little boys against the brick wall, boys dressed in red and blue brocades, with pale faces, tousled hair and marvelous bright eyes.

"Oh," said one, "she's awake."

"Who are you?" she demanded.

"She's beautiful," said the other. "I wonder if she's nice."

She sat bolt upright, and they held each other as if *she* had frightened them . . . they could hardly be much more than twelve . . . and stared at her wide-eyed.

"Who *are* you?" she asked.

"I'm Edward," said one; "I'm Richard," said the other.

"And how did you get in here?"

Edward let go Richard's arm, pointed vaguely down. "We live here," said young Edward, and part of his hand seemed to go right through the wall.

Then she realized what they must be if they were not a dream, and the hair rose on the back of her neck and she drew the sheet up to cover her, for they *were* children, and she was little covered by the gown. They were quaint and somewhat wise-eyed children, in grown-up clothes which seemed old and dusty.

"How did you get here?" Richard echoed her own question. ""Who sent you here? Are you Queen?"

"Richard Collier. The Lord Mayor."

"Ah," said Edward. "A Richard sent us here too. He's supposed to have murdered us both. But he didn't, you know."

She shook her head. She did not know. She never bothered with history. She kept clinging to the idea that they were a dream, some old school lesson come out of her subconscious, for while she believed in ghosts and horoscopes, her mind was reeling under the previous shocks.

"We always come first," said Edward. "I am a king, you know."

"First? What *are* you? What are you doing here?"

"Why, much the same as everyone else," young Edward laughed, and his eyes, while his face was that of a child, now seemed fearsomely old. "We live here, that's all. What's your name?"

"Bettine."

"Bettine? How strange a name. But most are strange now. And so few come here, after all. Do you think he will let you go?"

"Of course he'll let me go."

"Very few ever leave. And no one leaves . . . lately."

"You're dead," she cried. "Go away. Go away."

"We've been dead longer than you've been alive," said Richard.

"Longer than this London's stood here," said Edward. "I liked my London better. It was brighter. I shall always prefer it. Do you play cards?"

She sat and shivered, and Richard tugged at Edward's sleeve.

"I think we should go," said Richard. "I think she's about to be afraid."

"She's very pretty," said Edward. "But I don't think it's going to do her any good."

"It never does," said Richard.

"I go first," said Edward, "being King."

And he vanished, right through the wall; and Richard followed; and the candle glow went out, leaving dark.

Bettine sat still, and held the bedclothes about her, and finally reached for the light button, feverishly, madly, and blinked in the white glare that showed nothing wrong, nothing at all wrong. But there was a deathly chill in the air.

She had dreamed. This strange old place gave her nightmares. It had to be that. Tears ran from her eyes. She shivered and finally she got up and picked at her cold dinner because she wanted something to take her mind off the solitude. She would not look up at the window over the table, not while there was night outside.

She would have shadows beneath her eyes in the morning, and she would not be beautiful, and she had to be. At last she gathered the courage to go back to bed, and lay wrapped in her nightrobe and shivering, in the full light, which she refused to turn out.

She tried the phone again in the morning, and it still refused to work. She found everything saner with the daylight coming in through the window again and the room seemed warmer because of it. She bathed and washed her hair and dried it, brushing it meticulously. It had natural curl and she fashioned it in ringlets and tried it this way and that about her face.

Suddenly the door open on the short hallway closed; she sprang up and looked toward it in consternation, heard footsteps downstairs and dithered about in panic, finally flung on a dress and fluffed her hair and while she heard footsteps coming up the long stairs, leaned near the mirror in the bath and put on her makeup with swift, sure strokes, not the full job, which she had no time for, but at least the touch of definition to the eyes, the blush to lips and cheeks. . . .

It was Richard come to see her, come to ask if she had had enough, and she had, oh, she had. . . .

The far-side door opened. She ran to the door on her side, waited, hands clasped, anxious, meaning to appear anxious and contrite and everything and anything that he should want.

Then the outer door closed again; and hers opened. She rushed to meet her visitor.

There was only a breakfast tray, left on the floor, and the door closed, the footsteps receding.

"Come back!" she cried, wept, wailed.

The steps went on, down the stairs.

She stood there and cried a good long time; and then because she found nothing else to do, she gathered up the tray. She had to bend down to do it, which disarranged her hair and upset her and humiliated her even with no one to see it. She was angry and frightened and wanted to throw the tray and break all the things in sight; but that would make a terrible mess of food and she reckoned that she would have to live in it if she did that, or clean it up herself, so she spared herself such labor and carried it meekly back to the table. She was sick to her stomach, and there was the old food tray which was smelling by now, and the new one which brought new, heavy aromas. She considered them both with her stomach tight with fear and her throat so constricted with anger and frustration that she could not swallow her breaths, let alone the food.

She carried the old tray to the anteroom and set it on the floor, and suddenly, with inspiration, began to search through her belongings for paper . . . she *had* brought some, with the sewing kit, because she made patterns for her embroideries and for her knitting. She searched through the needles and the yarns and found it at the bottom, found the pen, sat down at the desk and chewed the pen's cap, trying to think.

"Richard," she wrote, not "Dearest Richard," which she thought might not be the right approach to an angry man. "I am frightened here. I must see you. Please. Bettine."

That was right, she thought. To be restrained, to be calm, and at the same time dissuade him from doing worse to frighten her. Pathos. That was the tone of it. She folded it up, and with a clever impulse, stitched thread through it to seal it, so that the jailer should not be getting curious without making it obvious. "To His Honor Richard Collier," she wrote on the outside, in the beautiful letters she had practiced making again and again. And then she took it and set it in the supper tray, out in the hall, so that it should leave with the dishes and whoever got it would have to think what to do with it. And throwing away a letter to the Mayor was not a wise thing to do.

She sniffed then, satisfied, and sat down and ate her breakfast, which did fill a little bit of the loneliness in her stomach, and made her feel guilty and miserable afterward, because she had eaten too much; she would get fat, that was what they wanted, feeding her all that and leaving her nothing to do but eat; she would soon be fat and unlovely if there was nothing to do here but eat and pace the floor.

And maybe she would be here a long time. That began to penetrate her with a force it had not until now. A second day in this place . . . and how many days; and she would run out of things to read and to do . . . she set the second tray in the hall too, to be rid of the smell of the food, and punched buttons trying to close the door from inside; the whole console was complicated, and she started punching buttons at random. There were controls she did not know; she punched buttons in different combinations and only succeeded in getting the lights out in a way in which she could not get them on again, not from any combination of buttons until finally she punched the one by the bed. That frightened her, that she might cut off the heating or lose the lighting entirely and be alone in the dark when the sun should go down. She stopped punching buttons, knowing nothing of what she was doing with them, although when she had been in school there had been a course in managing the computers . . . but that was something the other girls did, who had plain long faces and fastened their hair back and had flat bodies and thought of nothing but studying and working. She hated them. Hated the whole thing. Hated prisons that could be made of such things.

She picked up her knitting and thought of Tom, of his eyes, his body, his voice . . . he *loved* her; and Richard did not perhaps, but used her because she was beautiful, and one had to put up with that. It brought things. Would buy her way out of here. Richard might be proud and angry and have his feelings hurt, but ultimately he would want his pride salved, and she could do that, abundantly, assuring him that she was contrite, which was all she had to do, ultimately.

It was Tom she daydreamed of, wondering where he was and if he was in the Tower too. Oh, surely, surely not; but the books she read seemed so frighteningly real, and dire things happened for jealousy. She began to think of Tom in that kind of trouble, while her hands plied the colored yarns, knitting click, click, click, measuring out the time, stitch by stitch and row by row. Women did such things and went on doing them while the sun died because in all of women's lives there were so many moments that would kill the mind if one thought about them, which would suck the heart and the life out of one, and engrave lines in the face and put gray in the hair if ever one let one's mind work; but there was in the rhythm and the fascination of the stitches a loss of thought, a void, a blank, that was only numbers and not even that, because the mind did not need to count, the fingers did, the length of a thread against the finger measured evenly as a ruler could divide it, the slight difference in tension sensed finely as a machine could sense, the exact *number* of stitches keeping pattern without really the need to count, but something inward and regular as the beat of a heart, as the slow passing of time which could be frozen in such acts, or speeded past.

So the day passed; and click, click, click the needles went, using up the yarn, when she did not read; and she wound more and knitted more, row upon row, not thinking.

There was no noon meal; the sun began to fade, and the room grew more chill. I shall have to ask for more yarn someday, she thought with surprising placidity, and realized what that thought implied and refused to think anymore. At last she heard the steps coming up to the door and this time she refused to spring up and expect it to be Richard. She went right on with her knitting, click, click, while the steps came up and opened the door and closed it again.

Then quite calmly she went out and retrieved the new tray, saw with a little surge of hope that the message and the trays had gone. So, she thought; so, it will get to him; and she sat down and had her dinner, but not all of it. She took the tray out to the anteroom after, and went back and prepared herself for bed.

The light faded from the window, and the outside became black again; again she avoided looking toward it, because it so depressed her, and made the little room on the third level so lonely and so isolated.

And again she went to bed with the light on, because she was not willing to suffer more such illusions . . . they *were* illusions, and she put her mind from them all day long. She *believed* in supernatural things, but it had stopped being something which happened to someone else, and something which waited to happen to her, which was not shivery-entertaining, not in the least. It rather made her fear she was losing touch with things and losing control of her imagination, and she refused to have that happen.

She put on her white negligee again, reckoning that she just could be summoned out of bed by a phone call . . . after all, the message *could* be carried to His Honor Richard Collier direct. But it was more likely that it would go to his office instead, and that the call would come tomorrow, so she could relax just a bit and get some sleep, which she really needed. She was not actually afraid this second night, and so long as lights were on, there was no likelihood that she would have silly dreams about dead children.

Dead children. She shuddered, appalled that such a dream could have come out of her own imagination; it was not at all the kind of thing that a girl wanted to think about.

Tom . . . now *he* was worth thinking about.

She read her story; and the woman in the story had problems *not* direr than hers, which made her own seem worse and the story seem trivial; but it was going to be a happy ending. She was sure that it would, which would cheer her up.

Would they give her more books, she wondered, when these ran out? She thought that in the morning she would put another note on the tray and ask for books for herself; and maybe she should not, because that would admit to the jailer that she thought she was staying; and *that* would get to Richard too, who would ask how she was bearing up. She was sure that he would ask.

No. She would not ask for things to indicate a long stay here. They might give them to her, and she could not bear that.

Again she found she was losing the thread of the story, and she laid the book down against the side of the bed. She tried to think of Tom and could not, losing the thread of him too. She dreamed only the needles, back and forth, in and out, click.

The light dimmed . . . to candlelight; she felt it dim through her closed lids; and she cracked a lid very carefully, her muscles rigid and near to shivering. The dream was back; she heard the children laughing together.

"Well," said Edward's voice, "Hello, Bettine."

She looked; she had to, not knowing how near they were, afraid they might touch her. They were standing against the bricks again, both of them, solemn-faced like boys holding some great joke confined for the briefest of moments.

"Of course we're back," said the boy Richard. "How are you, lady Bettine?"

"Go away," she said; and then the least little part of her heart said that she did not really want them to go. She blinked and sat up, and there was a woman walking toward her out of the wall, who became larger and larger as the boys retreated. The newcomer was beautiful, in an ancient mode, wearing a golden brocade gown. The visitor dipped a curtsy to the boy king Edward, who bowed to her. "Madam," the boy-king said; and "Majesty," said the stranger, and turned curious eyes on *her*. "She is Bettine," said Edward. "Be polite, Bettine: Anne is one of the queens."

"Queen Anne?" asked Bettine, wishing that she knew a little more of the ancient Tower. If one was to be haunted, it would be at least helpful to know by whom; but she had paid very little attention to history—there was so much of it.

"Boleyn," said the queen, and spread her skirts and sat on the end of her bed, narrowly missing her feet, very forthright for a dream. "And how are you, my dear?"

"Very well, thank you, Majesty."

The boys laughed. "She only half believes in us, but she plays the game, doesn't she? They don't have queens now."

"How pretty she is," said the queen. "So was I."

"I'm not staying here," Bettine said. It seemed important in this web of illusions to have that clear. "I don't really believe in you entirely. I'm dreaming this anyway."

"You're not, my dear, but there, there, believe what you like." The queen turned, looked back; the children had gone, and another was coming through, a handsome man in elegant brocade. "Robert Devereaux," said Anne. "Robert, her name is Bettine."

"Who is he?" Bettine asked. "Is he the king?"

The man named Robert laughed gently and swept a bow; "I might have been," he said. "But things went wrong."

"Earl of Essex," said Anne softly, and stood up and took his hand. "The boys said that there was someone who believed in us, all the same. How nice. It's been so long."

"You make me very nervous," she said. "If you were real I think you'd talk differently; something old. You're just like me."

Robert laughed. "But we aren't like the walls, Bettine. We do change. We listen and we learn and we watch all the passing time."

"Even the children," said Anne.

"You died here."

"Indeed we did. And the same way."

"Murdered?" she asked with a shiver.

Anne frowned. "Beheaded, my dear. Quite a few had a hand in arranging it. I was maneuvered, you see; and how should I know we were spied on?"

"You and Essex?"

"Ah, no," said Robert. "*We* weren't lovers, then."

"Only now," said Anne. "We met . . . posthumously on my part. And how are you here, my dear?"

"I'm the Mayor's girl," Bettine said. It was good to talk, to have even shadows to talk to. She sat forward, embracing her knees in her arms. Suddenly the tears began to flow, and she daubed at her eyes with the sheet, feeling a little silly to be talking to ectoplasms, which all the fashionable folk denied existed; and yet it helped. "We quarreled and he put me here."

"Oh dear," said Anne.

"Indeed," said Lord Essex, patting Anne's hand. "That's why the boys said we should come. It's very like us."

"You died for love?"

"Politics," said Anne. "So will you."

She shook her head furiously. This dream of hers was not in her control, and she tried to drag things her own way. "But it's a silly quarrel. And I don't die. They don't kill people here, they don't."

"They do," Anne whispered. "Just like they did."

"Well," said Essex, "not axes, any more. They're much neater than they were."

"Go away," Bettine cried. "Go away, go away, go away."

"You'd do well to talk with us," said Anne. "We could make you understand what you're really up against. And there's really so much you don't seem to see, Bettine."

"Don't think of love," said Essex. "It's not love, you know, that sends people here. It's only politics. I know that. And Anne does. Besides, you don't sound like someone in love, do you? You don't sound like someone in love, Bettine."

She shrugged and looked down, expecting that they would be gone when she looked up. "There *is* someone I love," she said in the faintest of whispers when she saw they were not gone.

Anne snorted delicately. "That's not worth much here. Eternity is long, Bettine. And there's love and love, Bettine." She wound insubstantial fingers with the earl's. "You mustn't think of it being love. That's not the reason you're here. Be wise, Bettine. These stones have seen a great deal come and go. So have we; and you don't have the face of one who loves."

"What do *you* know?" she cried. "You're nothing. I know *people*, believe me. And I know Richard."

"Good night, Bettine," Anne said.

"Good night," Essex said very softly and patiently, so that she did not seem to have ruffled either of them at all. And the children were back, who bowed with departing irony and faded. The lights brightened.

She flounced down among the bedclothes sulking at such depressing ideas and no small bit frightened, but not of the ghosts—of her situation. Of things they said. There was a chill in the air, and a whiff of dried old flowers and spices . . . the flowers, she thought, was Anne; and the spice must be Essex. Or maybe it was the children Edward and Richard. The apparitions did not threaten her; they only spoke her fears. That was what they really were, after all. Ectoplasms, indeed. She burrowed into the covers and punched out the lights, having dispensed with fear of ghosts; her eyes hurt and she was tired. She lay down with utter abandon, which she had really not done since she came, burrowed among the pillows and tried not to think or dream at all.

In the morning the phone came on and the screen lit up.

"Bettine," said Richard's voice, stern and angry.

She sprang up out of the covers, went blank for a moment and then assumed one of her bedroom looks, pushed her thick masses of hair looser on her head, stood up with a sinuous twist of her body and looked into the camera, moue'd into a worried frown, a tremble, a look near tears.

"Richard. Richard, I was so afraid. Please." Keep him feeling superior, keep him feeling great and powerful, which was what she was *for* in the world, after all, and how she lived. She came and stood before the camera, leaned there. "I want out of here, Richard. I don't understand this place." Naïveté always helped, helplessness: and it was, besides, truth. "The jailer was terrible." Jealousy, if she could provoke it. "Please, let me come back. I never meant to do anything wrong . . . what is it I've *done*, Richard?"

"Who was he?"

Her heart was beating very fast. Indignation now; set him off balance. "No one. I mean, it was just a small thing and he wasn't anyone in particular, and I never did anything like that before, Richard, but you left me alone and what's a girl to do, after all? Two weeks and you hadn't called me or talked to me—?"

"What's the *name*, Bettine? And where's the grade-fifty file? Where is it, Bettine?"

She was the one off balance. She put a shaking hand to her lips, blinked, shook her head in real disorganization. "I don't know anything about the file." This wasn't it, this wasn't what it was supposed to be about. "Honestly, Richard, I don't know. What file? Is *that* what this is? That you think I *stole* something? Richard, I never, I never stole anything."

"Someone got into the office. Someone who didn't belong there, Bettine; and you have the key, and I do, and that's a pretty limited range, isn't it? My office. My private office. Who did that, Bettine?"

"I don't know," she wailed, and pushed her hair aside—the pretty gestures were lifelong-learned and automatic. "Richard, I've gotten caught in something I don't understand at all, I don't understand, I don't, and I never let anyone in there." (But Tom had gotten in there; *he* could have, any time, since he was in the next office.) "Maybe the door . . . maybe I left it open and I shouldn't have, but, Richard, I don't even know what was in that file, I swear I don't."

"Who was in your apartment that night?"

"I—it wasn't connected to that, it wasn't, Richard, and I wish you'd understand that. It wasn't anything, but that I was lonely and it was a complete mistake, and now if I gave you somebody's name then it would get somebody in trouble who just never was involved; I mean, I might have been careless, Richard, I guess I was; I'm terribly sorry about the file, but I did leave the door open sometimes, and you were gone a lot. I mean . . . it was possible someone could have gotten in there, but you never told me there was any kind of trouble like that. . . ."

"The access numbers. You understand?"

"I don't. I never saw that file."

"Who was in your apartment?"

She remained silent, thinking of Tom, and her lip trembled. It went on trembling while Richard glared at her, because she could not make up her mind what she ought to do and what was safe. She could *handle* Richard. She was sure that she could.

And then he blinked out on her.

"Richard!" she screamed. She punched buttons in vain. The screen was dead. She paced the floor and wrung her hands and stared out the window.

She heard the guard coming, and her door closed and the outer door opened for the exchange of the tray. Then the door gave back again and she went out into the anteroom after it. She carried the tray back and set it on the table, finally went to the bath and looked at herself, at sleep-tangled hair and shadowed eyes and the stain of old cosmetic. She was appalled at the face she had shown to Richard, at what she had been surprised into showing him. She scrubbed her face at once and brushed her hair and put slippers on her bare feet, which were chilled to numbness on the tiles.

Then she ate her breakfast, sparingly, careful of her figure, and dressed and sat and sewed. The silence seemed twice as heavy as before. She hummed to herself and tried to fill the void. She sang—she had a beautiful voice, and she sang until she feared she would grow hoarse, while the pattern grew. She read some of the time, and, bored, she found a new way to do her hair; but then she thought after she had done it that if Richard should call back he might not like it, and it was important that he like the way she looked. She combed it back the old way, all the while mistrusting this instinct, this reliance on a look which had already failed.

So the day passed, and Richard did not call again.

They wanted Tom. There was the chance that if she did give Richard Tom's name it could be the right one, because it was all too obvious who *could* have gotten a file out of Richard's office, because there had been many times Richard had been gone and Tom had followed her about her duties, teasing her.

Safest not to ask and not to know. She was determined not to. She resented the thing that had happened—politics—politics. She hated politics.

Tom . . . was someone to love. Who loved her; and Richard had reasons which were Richard's, but it came down to two men being jealous. And Tom, being innocent, had no idea what he was up against . . . Tom could be hurt, but Richard would never hurt her; and while she did not tell Richard, she still had the power to perplex him. While he was perplexed he would do nothing.

She was not totally confident . . . of Tom's innocence, or of Richard's attitude. She was not accustomed to saying no. She was not accustomed to being put in difficult positions. Tom should not have asked it of her. He should have known. It was not fair what he did, whatever he had gotten himself involved in—some petty little record-juggling—to have put her in this position.

The pattern grew, delicate rows of stitches, complex designs which needed no thinking, only seeing, and she wept sometimes and wiped at her eyes while she worked.

Light faded from the window. Supper came and she ate, and this night she did not prepare for bed, but wrapped her night robe about her for warmth and sat in the chair and waited, lacking all fear, expecting the children, looking forward to them in a strangely keen longing, because they were at least company, and laughter was good to hear in this grim place. Even the laughter of murdered children.

There began to be a great stillness. And not the laughter of children this time, but the tread of heavier feet, the muffled clank of metal. A grim, shadowed face materialized in dimming light.

She stood up, alarmed, and warmed her chilling hands before her lips. "Edward," she cried aloud. "Edward, Richard . . . are you there?" But what was coming toward her was taller and bare of face and arm and leg, bronze elsewhere, and wearing a *sword*, of all things. She wanted the children; wanted Anne or Robert Devereaux, any of the others. This one . . . was different.

"Bettine," he said in a voice which echoed in far distances. "Bettine."

"I don't think I like you," she said.

The ghost stopped with a little clank of armor, kept fading in and out. He was young, even handsome in a foreign way. He took off his helmet and held it under his arm. "I'm Marc," he said. "Marcus Atilius Regulus. They said I should come. Could you see your way, Bettine, to prick your finger?"

"Why should I do that?"

"I am oldest," he said. "Well—almost, and of a different persuasion, and perhaps it is old-fashioned, but it would make our speaking easier."

She picked up her sewing needle and jabbed her cold finger, once and hard, and the blood welled up black in the dim light and fell onto the stones. She put the injured finger in her mouth, and stared quite bewildered, for the visitor was very much brighter, and seemed to draw a living breath.

"Ah," he said. "Thank you with all my heart, Bettine."

"I'm not sure at all I should have done that. I think you might be dangerous."

"Ah, no, Bettine."

"Were you a soldier, some kind of knight?"

"A soldier, yes; and a knight, but not the kind you think of. I think you mean of the kind born to this land. I came from Tiberside. I am Roman, Bettine. We laid some of the oldest stones just . . ." he lifted a braceletted arm, rather confusedly toward one of the steel walls. "But most of the old work is gone now. There are older levels; all the surly ones tend to gather down there. Even new ones, and some that never were civilized, really, or never quite accepted being dead, all of them—" he made a vague and deprecating gesture. "But we don't get many now, because there hasn't been anyone in here who could believe in us . . . in so very long . . . does the finger hurt?"

"No." She sucked at it and rubbed the moisture off and looked at him more closely. "I'm not sure *I* believe in you."

"You're not sure you don't, and that's enough."

"Why are you here? Where are the others?"

"Oh, they're back there."

"But why you? Why wouldn't they come? I expected the children."

"Oh. They're there. Nice boys."

"And why did *you* come? What has a soldier to do with me?"

"I—come for the dead. I'm the psychopomp."

"The what?"

"Psychopomp. Soul-guider. When you die."

"But I'm not going to die," she wailed, hugging her

arms about her and looking without wanting to at the ancient sword he wore. "There's a mistake, that's all. I've been trying to explain to the others, but they don't understand. We're civilized. We don't go around killing people in here, whatever *used* to happen. . . ."

"Oh, they *do*, Bettine; but we don't get them, because they're very stubborn, and they believe in nothing, and they can't see us. Last month I lost one. I almost had him to see me, but at the last he just couldn't; and he slipped away and I'm not sure where. It looked hopelessly drear. I try with all of them. I'm glad you're not like them."

"But you're wrong. I'm not going to die."

He shrugged, and his dark eyes looked very sad.

"I can get out of here," she said, unnerved at his lack of belief in her. "If I have to, there's always a way. I can just tell them what they want to know and they'll let me go."

"And," he said.

"It's true."

His young face, so lean and serious, looked sadder still. "Oh Bettine."

"It *is* true; what do *you* know?"

"Why haven't you given them what they want before now?"

"Because. . . ." She made a gesture to explain and then shook her head. "Because I think I can get out of it without doing that."

"For pride? Or for honor?"

It sounded like something *he* should say, after all, all done up in ancient armor and carrying a sword. "You've been dead a long time," she said.

"Almost the longest of all. *Superbia*, we said. That's the wrong kind of pride; that's being puffed up and too important and not really seeing things right. And there's *exemplum.* That's a thing you do because the world needs it, like setting up something for people to look at, a little marker, to say Marcus Regulus stood here."

"And what if no one sees it? What good is it then, if I never get out of here? There's being brave and being stupid."

He shook his head very calmly. "An *exemplum* is an

exemplum even if no one sees it. They're just markers, where someone was."

"Look outside, old ghost. The sun's going out and the world's dying."

"Still," he said, "*exempla* last . . . because there's nothing anyone can do to erase them."

"What, like old stones?"

"No. Just moments. Moments are the important thing. Not every moment, but more than some think."

"Well," she said, perplexed and bothered. "Well, that's all very well for men who go around fighting ancient wars, but I don't fight anyone. I don't like violence at all, and I'll do what I can for Tom but I'm not brave and there's a limit."

"Where, Bettine?"

"The next time Richard asks me, that's where. I want out of here."

He looked sad.

"Stop that," she snapped. "I suppose you think you're superior."

"No."

"I'm just a girl who has to live and they can take my job away and I can end up outside the walls starving, that's what could happen to me."

"Yes, sometimes *exempla* just aren't quick. Mine would have been. And I failed it."

"You're a soldier. I'm a woman."

"Don't you think about honor at all, Bettine?"

"You're out of date. I stopped being a virgin when I was thirteen."

"No. *Honor*, Bettine."

"I'll bet you were some kind of hero, weren't you, some old war hero?"

"Oh no, Bettine. I wasn't. I ran away. That's why I'm the psychopomp. Because the old Tower's a terrible place; and a good many of the dead do break down as they die. There were others who could have taken the job: the children come first, usually, just to get the prisoners used to the idea of ghosts, but I come at the last . . . because I know what it is to be afraid, and what it is to want to run. I'm an Atilius Regulus, and there were heroes in my house, oh, there was a great one . . . I could tell you the story. I will, someday. But in the same family there was myself, and they were never so noble after me. *Exemplum* had something to do with it. I wish I could have left a better one. It came on me so quickly . . . a moment; one lives all one's life to be ready for moments when they come. I used to tell myself, you know, that if mine had just—crept up slowly, then I should have thought it out; I always did think. But I've seen so much, so very much, and I know human beings, and do you know . . . quick or slow in coming, it was what I *was* that made the difference, thinking or not; and I just wasn't then what I am now."

"Dead," she said vengefully.

He laughed silently. "And eons wiser." Then his face went sober. "O Bettine, courage comes from being ready whenever the moment comes, not with the mind . . . I don't think anyone ever is. But what you *are* . . . can be ready."

"What happened to you?"

"I was an officer, you understand. . . ." He gestured at the armor he wore. "And when the Britons got over the rampart . . . I ran, and took all my unit with me—I didn't think what I was doing; *I* was getting clear. But a wise old centurion met me coming his way and ran me through right there. The men stopped running then and put the enemy back over the wall, indeed they did. And a lot of men were saved and discipline held. So I was an *exemplum,* after all; even if I was someone else's. It hurt. I don't mean the wound—those never do quite the way you think, I can tell you that—but I mean really hurt, so that it was a long long time before I came out in the open again—after the Tower got to be a prison. After I saw so many lives pass here. Then I decided I should come out. May I touch you?"

She drew back, bumped the chair, shivered. "That's not how you. . . ?"

"O no. *I* don't take lives. May I touch you?"

She nodded mistrustingly, kept her eyes wide open as he drifted nearer and a braceletted hand came toward her face, beringed and masculine and only slightly transparent. It was like a breath of cool wind, and his young face grew wistful. Because she was beautiful, she thought, with a little rush of pride, and he was young and very handsome and very long dead.

She wondered. . . .

"Warmth," he said, his face very near and his dark eyes very beautiful. "I had gone into my melancholy again . . . in all these last long centuries, that there was no more for me to do, no souls for me to meet, no special one who believed, no one at all. I thought it was all done. Are there more who still believe?"

"Yes," she said. And started, for there were Anne and Essex holding hands within the brickwork or behind it or somewhere; and other shadowy figures. The children were there, and a man who looked very wet, with a slight reek of alcohol, and more and more and more, shadows which went from brocades to metals to leather to furs and strange helmets.

"Go away," she cried at that flood, and fled back, overturning the tray and crowding into the corner. "Get out of here. I'm not going to die. I'm not brave and I'm not going to. Let someone else do the dying. I don't want to die."

They murmured softly and faded; and there came a touch at her cheek like a cool breeze.

"Go away!" she shrieked, and she was left with only the echoes. "I'm going mad," she said then to herself, and dropped into the chair and bowed her head into her hands. When she finally went to bed she sat fully dressed in the corner and kept the lights on.

Breakfast came, and she bathed and dressed, and read her book, which began to come to its empty and happy ending. She threw it aside, because her life was not coming out that way, and she kept thinking of Tom, and crying, not sobs, just a patient slow leaking of tears, which made her makeup run and kept her eyes swollen. She was not powerful. She had lost all illusion of that. She just wanted out of this alive, and to live and to forget it. She tried again to use the phone and she could not figure out the keyboard which she thought might give her access to *someone*, if she knew anything about such systems, and she did not.

For the first time she became convinced that she was in danger of dying here, and that instead, Tom was going to, and she would be in a way responsible. She was no one, no one against all the anger that swirled about her. She was quite, quite helpless; and not brave at all, and nothing in her life had ever prepared her to be. She thought back to days when she was a child, and in school, and all kinds of knowledge had been laid out in front of her. She had found it useless . . . which it was, to a ten-year-old girl who thought she had the world all neatly wrapped around her finger. Who thought at that age that she knew all the things that were important, that if she went on pleasing others that the world would always be all right.

Besides, the past was about dead people and she liked living ones; and learning about science was learning that the world was in the process of ending, and there was no cheer in that. She wanted to be Bettine Maunfry who had all that she would ever need. Never think, never think about days too far ahead, or things too far to either side, or understand things, which made it necessary to decide, and prepare.

Moments. She had never wanted to imagine such moments would come. There was no time she could have looked down the long currents of her life, which had *not* been so long after all, and when she could have predicted that Bettine Maunfry would have gotten herself into a situation like this. People were supposed to take care of her. There had always been someone to take care of her. That was what it was being female and beautiful and young. It was just not supposed to happen this way.

Tom, she thought. O Tom, now what do I do, what am I supposed to do?

But of course the doing was hers.

To him.

She had no idea what her horoscope or his was on this date, but she thought that it must be disaster, and she fingered the little fishes which she wore still in her décolletage for His Honor Richard Collier to see.

And she waited, to bend as she had learned to bend;

only . . . she began to think with the versatility of the old Bettine . . . never give up an advantage. *Never*.

She went in and washed her face and put on her makeup again, and stopped her crying and repaired all the subtle damages of her tears.

She dressed in her handsomest dress and waited.

And toward sundown the call came.

"Bettine," His Honor said. "Have you thought better of it, Bettine?"

She came and faced the screen and stood there with her lips quivering and her chin trembling because weakness worked for those who knew how to use it.

"I might," she said.

"There's no 'might' about it, Bettine," said Richard Collier, his broad face suffused with red. "Either you do or you don't."

"When you're here," she said, "when you come here and see me yourself, I'll tell you."

"Before I come."

"No," she said, letting the tremor become very visible. "I'm *afraid*, Richard; I'm afraid. If you'll come here and take me out of here yourself, I promise I'll tell you anything I know, which isn't much, but I'll tell you. I'll give you his name, but he's not involved with anything besides that he had a silly infatuation and I was lonely. But I won't tell anything if you don't come and get me out of here. This has gone far enough, Richard. I'm frightened. Bring me home."

He stared at her, frowning. "If I come over there and you change your mind, Bettine, you can forget any favors you think I owe you. I won't be played with. You understand me, girl?"

She nodded.

"All right," he said. "You'll tell me his name, and you'll be thinking up any other detail that might explain how he could have gotten to that office, and you do it tonight. I'm sure there's some sense in that pretty head, there's a girl. You just think about it, Bettine, and you think hard, and where you want to be. Home, with all the comforts . . . or where you are, which isn't comfortable at all, is it, Bettine?"

"No," she said, crying. She shook her head. "No. It's not comfortable, Richard."

"See you in the morning, Bettine. And you can pack, if you have the right name."

"Richard—" But he had winked out, and she leaned there against the wall shivering, with her hands made into fists and the feeling that she was very small indeed. She did not want to be in the Tower another night, did not want to face the ghosts, who would stare at her with sad eyes and talk to her about honor, about things that were not for Bettine Maunfry.

I'm sorry, she thought for them. I won't be staying and dying here after all.

But Tom would. That thought depressed her enormously. She felt somehow responsible, and that was a serious burden, more serious than anything she had ever gotten herself into except the time she had thought for ten days that she was pregnant. Maybe Tom would—lie to them; maybe Tom would try to tell them she was somehow to blame in something which was not her fault.

That frightened her. But Tom loved her. He truly did. Tom would not hurt her by anything he would say, being a man, and braver, and motivated by some vaguely different drives, which had to do with pride and being strong, qualities which she had avoided all her life.

She went through the day's routines, such of the day as was left, and packed all but her dress that Richard said matched her eyes. She put that one on, to sit up all the night, because she was determined that Richard should not surprise her looking other than beautiful, and it would be like him to try that mean trick. She would simply sleep sitting up and keep her skirts from wrinkling, all propped with pillows: that way she could both be beautiful and get some sleep.

And she kept the lights on because of the ghosts, who were going to feel cheated.

Had he really died that way, she wondered of the Roman, the young Roman, who talked about battles from forgotten ages. Had he really died that way or did he only make it up to make her listen to him? She thought about battles which might have been fought right where this building stood, all the many, many ages.

And the lights faded.

The children came, grave and sober, Edward and then Richard, who stood and stared with liquid, disapproving eyes.

"I'm sorry," she said shortly. "I'm going to be leaving."

The others then, Anne and Robert, Anne with her heart-shaped face and dark hair and lovely manners, Essex tall and elegant, neither looking at her quite the way she expected—not disapproving, more as if they had swallowed secrets. "It was politics after all," asked Anne, "wasn't it, Bettine?"

"Maybe it was," she said shortly, hating to be proved wrong. "But what's that to me? I'm still getting out of here."

"What if your lover accuses you?" asked Essex. "Loves do end."

"He won't," she said. "He wouldn't. He's not likely to."

"*Exemplum*," said a mournful voice. "O Bettine, is this yours?"

"Shut up," she told Marc. He was hardest to face, because his sad, dark gaze seemed to expect something special of her. She was instantly sorry to have been rude; he looked as if his heart was breaking. He wavered, and she saw him covered in dust, the armor split, and bloody, and tears washing down his face. She put her hands to her face, horrified.

"You've hurt him," said Anne. "We go back to the worst moment when we're hurt like that."

"O Marc," she said, "I'm sorry. I don't want to hurt you. But I want to be *alive*, you understand . . . can't you remember that? Wouldn't you have traded anything for that? And you had so much . . . when the sun was young and everything was new. O Marc, do you blame me?"

"There is only one question," he said, his eyes melting-sad. "It's your moment, Bettine. Your moment."

"Well, I'm not like you; I never was; never will be. What good is being right and dead? And what's right? Who's to know? It's all relative. Tom's not that wonderful,

I'll have you to know. And neither's Richard. And a girl gets along the best she can."

A wind blew, and there was a stirring among the others, an intaken breath. Essex caught at Anne's slim form, and the children withdrew to Anne's skirts. "It's *her*," said young Edward. "*She's* come."

Only Marc refused the panic which took the others; bright again, he moved with military precision to one side, cast a look back through the impeding wall where a tiny figure advanced.

"She didn't die here," he said quietly. "But she has many ties to this place. She is one of the queens, Bettine, a great one. And very seldom does *she* come out."

"For me?"

"Because you are one of the last, perhaps."

She shook her head, looked again in bewilderment as Anne and Robert and young Richard bowed; and Edward inclined his head. Marc only touched his heart and stepped further aside. "Marc," Bettine protested, not wanting to lose him, the one she trusted.

"Well," said the visitor, a voice like the snap of ice. She seemed less woman than small monument, in a red and gold gown covered with embroideries and pearls, and ropes of pearls and pearls in crisp red hair; she had a pinched face out of which two eyes stared like living cinder. "Well?"

Bettine bowed like the others; she thought she ought. The Queen paced slowly, diverted herself for a look at Essex, and a slow nod at Anne. "Well."

"My daughter," said Anne. "The first Elizabeth."

"Indeed," said the Queen. "And Marc, good evening. Marc, how do you fare? And the young princes. Quite a stir, my dear, indeed quite a stir you've made. I have my spies; no need to reiterate."

"I'm not dying," she said. "You're all mistaken. I've told them I'm not dying. I'm going back to Richard."

The Queen looked at Essex, offered her hand. Essex kissed it, held it, smiled wryly. "Didn't you once say something of the kind?" asked the Queen.

"He did," said Anne. "It was, after all, your mistake, daughter."

"At the time," said Elizabeth. "But it was very stupid of you, Robert, to have relied on old lovers as messengers."

Essex shrugged, smiled again. "If not that year, the next. We were doomed to disagree."

"Of course," Elizabeth said. "There's love and there's power; and we all three wanted that, didn't we? And you . . ." Again that burning look turned on Bettine. "What sort are you? Not a holder. A seeker after power?"

"Neither one. I'm the Lord Mayor's girl and I'm going home."

"The Lord Mayor's girl." Elizabeth snorted. "The Lord Mayor's girl. I have spies, I tell you; all London's haunted. I've asked questions. The fellow gulled you, this Tom Ash. Ah, he himself's nothing; he works for others. He needs the numbers, that's all, for which he's paid. And with that list in others' hands your precious Lord Mayor's in dire trouble. Revolution, my dear, the fall of princes. Are you so blind? Your Lord Mayor's none so secure, tyrant that he is . . . if not this group of men, this year, then others, next. They'll have him; London town's never cared for despots, crowned or plain. Not even in its old age has it grown soft-witted. Just patient."

"I don't want to hear any of it. Tom loved me, that's all. Whatever he's involved in . . ."

Elizabeth laughed. "I was born to power. Was it accident? Ask my mother here what she paid. Ask Robert here what he paid to try for mine, and how I held it all the same . . . no hard feelings, none. But do you think your Lord Mayor gained his by accident? You move in dark waters, with your eyes *shut*. You've wanted power all your life, and you thought there was an easy way. But you don't have it, because you don't understand what you want. If they gave you all of London on a platter, you'd see only the baubles. You'd look for some other hands to put the real power in; you're helpless. You've trained all your life to be, I'll warrant. I know the type. Bettine. What name is that? Abbreviated and diminished. *E-liz-a-beth* is our name, in fine round tones. You're tall; you try to seem otherwise. You dress to please everyone else; I pleased *Elizabeth*, and others copied me. If I was fond, it was that I liked men, but by all reason, I never handed my crown to one, no. However painful the decision . . . however many the self-serving ministers urging me this way and that, I did my own thinking; yes, Essex, even with you. Of course I'd hesitate, of course let the ministers urge me, of course I'd grieve—I'm not unhuman—but at the same time they could seem heartless and I merciful. And the deed got done, didn't it, Robert?"

"Indeed," he said.

"You were one of my favorites; much as you did, I always liked you; loved you, of course, but liked you, and there weren't as many of those. And you, Mother, another of the breed. But this modern bearer of my name—you have none of it, no backbone at all."

"I'm not in your class," Bettine said. "It's not fair."

"Whine and whimper. You're a born victim. I could make you a queen and you'd be a dead one in a fortnight."

"I just want to be comfortable and I want to be happy."

"Well, look at you."

"I will be again. I'm not going to be dead; I'm going to get out of this."

"Ah. You want, want, want; never look to see how things *are*. You spend all your life reacting to what others do. Ever thought about getting in the first stroke? No, of course not. I'm Elizabeth. You're just Bettine."

"I wasn't born with your advantages."

Elizabeth laughed. "I was a bastard . . . pardon me, Mother. And what were you? Why aren't *you* the Mayor? Ever wonder that?"

Bettine turned away, lips trembling.

"Look at me," said the Queen.

She did so, not wanting to. But the voice was commanding.

"Why did you?"

"What?"

"Look at me."

"You asked."

"Do you do everything people ask? You're everyone's victim, that's all. The Mayor's girl. You choose to be, no getting out of it. You *choose*, even by choosing not to choose. You'll go back and you'll give His Honor what he wants, and you'll go back to your apartment . . . maybe."

"What do you mean maybe?"

"Think, my girl, think. Girl you are; you've spent your whole majority trying to be nothing. I think you may achieve it."

"There's the Thames," said Essex.

"It's not what they take from you," said Anne, "it's what you give up."

"The water," said Edward, "is awfully cold; so I've heard."

"What do you know? You didn't have any life."

"But I did," said the boy, his eyes dancing. "I had my years . . . like you said, when the sun was very good."

"I had a pony," said Richard. "Boys don't, now."

"Be proud," said Elizabeth.

"I know something about you," Bettine said. "You got old and you had no family and no children, and I'm sure pride was cold comfort then."

Elizabeth smiled. "I hate to disillusion you, my dear, but I *was* happy. Ah, I shed a few tears, who doesn't in a lifetime? But I had exactly what I chose; and what I traded I knew I traded. I did precisely as I wanted. Not always the story book I would have had it, but for all that, within my circumstances, precisely as I chose, for all my life to its end. I lived and I was curious; there was nothing I thought foreign to me. I saw more of the world in a glance than you've wondered about lifelong. I was ahead of my times, never caught by the outrageously unanticipated; but your whole life's an accident, isn't it, little Elizabeth?"

"*Bettine,*" she said, setting her chin. "My *name* is Bettine."

"Good," laughed the Queen, slapping her skirted thigh. "Excellent. Go *on* thinking; and straighten your back, woman. Look at the eyes. Always look at the eyes."

The Queen vanished in a little thunderclap, and Essex swore and Anne patted his arm. "She was never comfortable," Anne said. "I would have brought her up with gentler manners."

"If I'd been your son—" said Essex.

"If," said Anne.

"They'll all be disturbed downstairs," said young Edward. "They *are*, when she comes through."

They faded . . . all but Marc.

"They don't change my mind," said Bettine. "The Queen was rude."

"No," said Marc. "Queens aren't. She's just what she is."

"Rude," she repeated, still smarting.

"Be what you are," said Marc, "I'll go. It's your moment."

"Marc?" She reached after him, forgetting. Touched nothing. She was alone then, and it was too quiet. She would have wanted Marc to stay. Marc understood fear.

Be what she was. She laughed sorrowfully, wiped at her eyes, and went to the bath to begin to be beautiful, looked at eyes which had puffed and which were habitually reddened from want of sleep. And from crying. She found herself crying now, and did not know why, except maybe at the sight of Bettine Maunfry as she was, little slim hands that had never done anything and a face which was all sex and a voice that no one would ever obey or take seriously . . . just for games, was Bettine. In all this great place which had held desperate criminals and fallen queens and heroes and lords, just Bettine, who was going to do the practical thing and turn in Tom who had never loved her, but only wanted something.

Tom's another, she thought with curiously clear insight, a *beautiful* person who was good at what he did, but it was not Tom who was going to be important, he was just smooth and good and all hollow, nothing behind the smiling white teeth and clear blue eyes. If you cracked him it would be like a china doll, nothing in the middle.

So with Bettine.

"I love you," he had protested. As far as she had known, no one had ever really loved Bettine Maunfry, though she had sold everything she had to keep people pleased and smiling at her all her life. She was not, in thinking about it, sure what she would do *if* someone loved her, or if she would know it if he did. She looked about at the magazines with the pictures of eyes and lips and the articles on how to sell one's soul.

Articles on love.

There's love and love, Anne had said.

Pleasing people. Pleasing everyone, so that they would please Bettine. Pretty children got rewards for crying and boys got spanked. While the world was pacified, it would not hurt Bettine.

Eyes and lips, primal symbols.

She made up carefully, did her hair, added the last items to her packing.

Except her handwork, which kept her sane. Click, click. Mindless sanity, rhythms and patterns. There was light from the window now. Probably breakfast would arrive soon, but she was not hungry.

And finally came the noise of the doors, and the steps ascending the tower.

Richard Collier came. He shut the door behind him and looked down at her frowning; and she stood up in front of the only window.

Look them in the eyes, the Queen had said. She looked at Richard that way, the Queen's way, and he evidently did not like it.

"The name," he said.

She came to him, her eyes filling with tears in spite of herself. "I don't want to tell you," she said. "It would hurt somebody; and if you trusted me you'd let me straighten it out. I can get your file back for you."

"You leave that to me," Richard said. "The name, girl, and no more—"

She had no idea why she did it. Certainly Richard's expression was one of surprise, as if he had calculated something completely wrong. There was blood on her, and the long needle buried between his ribs, and he slid down to lie on the floor screaming and rolling about, or trying to. It was a very soundproof room; and no one came. She stood and watched, quite numb in that part of her which ought to have been conscience; if anything feeling mild vindication.

"Bettine," she said quietly, and sat down and waited for him to die and for someone who had brought him to the tower to miss him. Whoever had the numbers was free to use them now; there would be a new order in the city; there would be a great number of changes. She reckoned that if she had ordered her life better she might have been better prepared, and perhaps in a position to escape. She was not. She had not planned. It's not the moments that can be planned, the Roman would say; it's the lives . . . that lead to them.

And did London's life . . . lead to Bettine Maunfry? She suspected herself of a profound thought. She was even proud of it. Richard's eyes stared blankly now. There had not been a great deal of pain. She had not wanted that, particularly, although she would not have shrunk from it. In a moment, there was not time to shrink.

There was power and there was love, and she had gotten through life with neither. She did not see what one had to do with the other; nothing, she decided, except in the sense that there really never had been a Bettine Maunfry, only a doll which responded to everyone else's impulses. And there had been nothing of her to love.

She would not unchoose what she had done; that was Elizabeth's test of happiness. She wondered if Richard would.

Probably not, when one got down to moments; but Richard had not been particularly smart in some things.

I wonder if I could have been Mayor, she thought. Somewhere I decided about that, and never knew I was deciding.

There was a noise on the stairs now. They were coming. She sat still, wondering if she should fight them too, but decided against it. She was not, after all, insane. It was politics. It had to do with the politics of His Honor the Mayor and of one Bettine, a girl, who had decided not to give a name.

They broke in, soldiers, who discovered the Mayor's body with great consternation. They laid hands on her and shouted questions.

"I killed him," she said. They waved rifles at her, accusing her of being part of the revolution.

"I led my own," she said.

They looked very uncertain then, and talked among themselves and made calls to the city. She sat guarded by rifles, and they carried the Mayor out, poor dead Richard. They talked out the murder and wondered that she could have had the strength to drive the needle so deep. Finally—incredibly—they questioned the jailer as to what kind of prisoner she was, as if they believed that she had been more than the records showed, the imprisoned leader of some cause, the center of the movement they had been hunting. They talked about more guards. Eventually she had them, in great number, and by evening, all the Tower was ringed with soldiery, and heavy guns moved into position, great batteries of them in the inner court. Two days later she looked out the window and saw smoke where outer London was, and knew there was riot in the town.

The guards treated her with respect. Bettine Maunfry, they called her when they had to deal with her, not girl, and not Bettine. They called on her—of all things, to issue a taped call for a cease-fire.

But of her nightly companions . . . nothing. Perhaps they were shy, for at night a guard stood outside in the anteroom. Perhaps, after all, she was a little mad. She grieved for their absence, not for Richard and not for Tom, living in this limbo of tragic comedy. She watched the city burn and listened to the tread of soldiers in the court, and watched the gun crews from her single window. It was the time before supper, when they left her a little to herself—if a guard at the stairside door was privacy; they had closed off the anteroom as they usually did, preparing to deliver her dinner.

"Quite a turmoil you've created."

She turned from the window, stared at Marc in amazement. "But it's daytime."

"I *am* a little faded," he said, looking at his hand, and looked up again. "How are you, Bettine?"

"It's ridiculous, isn't it?" She gestured toward the courtyard and the guns. "They think I'm dangerous."

"But you are."

She thought about it, how frightened they were and what was going on in London. "They keep asking me for names. Today they threatened me. I'm not sure I'm *that* brave, Marc, I'm really not."

"But you don't know any."

"No names," she said. "Of course I don't. So I'll be counted as brave, won't I?"

"The other side needs a martyr, and you're it, you know that."

"How does it go out there? Do the Queen's spies tell her?"

"Oh, it's violent, quite. If I were alive I'd be out there; it's a business for soldiers. The starships are hanging off just waiting. The old Mayor was dealing under the table in favoring a particular company, and the company that supported him had its offices wrecked. . . . others just standing by waiting to move in and give support to the rebels, to outmaneuver their own rivals. The ripple goes on to stars you've never seen."

"That's amazing."

"You're not frightened."

"Of course I'm frightened."

"There was a time a day ago when you might have ended up in power; a mob headed this way to get you out, but the troops got them turned."

"We'll it's probably good they didn't get to me. I'm afraid I wouldn't know what to do with London if they gave it to me. Elizabeth was right."

"But the real leaders of the revolution have come into the light now; they use your name as a cause. It's the spark they needed so long. Your name is their weapon."

She shrugged.

"They've a man inside the walls, Bettine . . . do you understand me?"

"No. I don't."

"I couldn't come before; it was still your moment . . . these last few days. None of us could interfere. It wouldn't be right. But I'm edging the mark . . . just a little. I always do. Do you understand me now, Bettine?"

"I'm going to die?"

"He's on his way. It's one of the revolutionaries . . . not the loyalists. The revolution needs a martyr; and they're afraid you *could* get out. They can't have their own movement taken away from their control by some mob. You'll die, yes. And they'll claim the soldiers killed you to stop a rescue. Either way, they win."

She looked toward the door, bit her lip. She heard a door open, heard steps ascending; a moment's scuffle.

"I'm here," Marc said.

"Don't you have to go away again? Isn't this . . . something I have to do?"

"Only if you wish."

The inner door opened. A wild-eyed man stood there, with a gun, which fired, right for her face. It *hurt*. It seemed too quick, too ill-timed; she was not ready, had not said all she wanted to say.

"There are things I wanted to do," she protested.

"There always are."

She had not known Marc was still there; the place was undefined and strange.

"Is it over? Marc, I wasn't through. I'd just figured things out."

He laughed and held out his hand. "Then you're ahead of most."

He was clear and solid to her eyes; it was the world which had hazed. She looked about her. There were voices, a busy hum of accumulated ages, time so heavy the world could scarcely bear it.

"I could have done better."

The hand stayed extended, as if it were important. She reached out hers, and his was warm.

"Till the sun dies," he said.

"Then what?" It was the first question.

He told her.

Late Have I Loved Thee, Kipling

Sandra Miesel

Most of the contributors to this book reminisce about first falling in love with Kipling through the *Just So Stories* and *The Jungle Books*. So did I. Indeed, I still have the handsome Victorian edition of the first *Jungle Book* bound in olive green silk. My father gave me it when I was eight.

But what should have subsequently flowered into a life-long affair got sidetracked in my case. No sooner had I happily finished the local library's copy of *Kim* than our collie ate it. It took a long time to save up the replacement cost of a book on an allowance of twenty-five cents a week.

It would be too melodramatic to say that the incident traumatized me against Kipling but I didn't begin reading him again until after I'd grown up and entered the world of SF. (Patience, gentle reader, it took St. Augustine a while to return to the fold, too.) Here I found myself in the company of ardent Kipling admirers, in particular the two writers who have influenced me most, Poul Anderson and Gordon Dickson. Through them, I began to feel the hand of Kipling at second remove. But I still wasn't ready for direct contact. I can remember arguing this very point with Poul and Gordy at a convention in the summer of 1975. All I was willing to admit was that Kipling's poetry made rousing "filksongs." But although I stubbornly continued to avoid Kipling's prose, I bought and dutifully read the *Collected Poems* so that I could quote the Master's words like everyone around me.

The stalemate might have continued indefinitely.

Then I saw John Huston's wonderful film, *The Man who Would Be King*, surely the finest and most faithful screen treatment Kipling has yet received. So I read the original story. And tracked down the hymn that is its *leitmotiv*. And wrote my own filksong in the same meter about Gordy's novella "Lost Dorsai" (which was itself inspired by Kipling's "Guns of the Fore and Aft"). And sold my first story "The Shadow Hart" which was written in honor of Andre Norton (who loves Kipling's historical fantasies) but inspired by Poul Anderson's treatments of the legend of King Valdemar and the Wild Hunt. And went on to read a *lot* more Kipling. And surrendered at long last to the faith I had formerly fled "down the nights and down the days."

I'm even passing it on. This month I persuaded my older daughter to accompany me to a showing of *The Man Who Would Be King*. She agreed strictly out of filial piety—and unspoken threats of bodily harm. But she quickly fell under the spell of the film's raffish heroes and laughed even harder at them than I did. But she wasn't expecting the comedy to turn tragic. Nervous breathing betrayed her anxiety as Peachy and Danny's royal dreams faded. Their doom left her sighing with real grief. "But I *loved* those guys. . . ."

Later, at home, she finally paid attention to the grim sepia picture that hangs over my side of her parents' bed. It's an etching by turn-of-the century artist William Strang illustrating the final scene of "The Man Who Would Be King," the moment when Peachy reveals Danny's mummified head.

Now she's eager to read the original story.

So as each generation gives way to the next, Kipling continues to win an audience. His art has a durable beauty "ever ancient, ever new."

The Shadow Hart

Sandra Miesel

After the hart, the bier . . .

She rubbed the crusted pot harder as if to scour that hateful saying from her mind. Hateful saying, fateful saying. Scrub harder. Amaze the cook with the strength still left in these aged arms. Finish before the hearth fire fails.

Back and forth on the whitewashed kitchen wall, her shadow plunged like a wounded beast. But, by the luck of the hunt, no venison graced the good *herremand*'s table this Yuletide, no hated flesh to tear nor bones to shatter. *O God, give me a hart to break as a hart has broken—* Revenge denied, denied, as when she raged to grow black wings and feed on that cursed brute's heart. If only she had the right Words!

Had she all the right Words her kindred knew, her man would not have died while hunting, most surely would not have died unshriven in the wildwood, borne home like bloody meat. Wearily, she tapped out the last of the cleansing sand and wiped the vessel with a greasy rag. Some in this blond country still misliked her dark looks and the Finnish lilt in her speech. Yet if she were in truth the witch they signed against behind her back, she would have cast a better lot for herself. What sorceress culled table leavings for her master's dogs?

But at least she was earning her bread. Better to drag out her days as a wretched serving maid than a beggar. The folk here were decent, the holder of this garth no harsher than needful. She was glad of this shelter this six months past. For scarcely was her lover under the earth when that *beengjerd* wife of his had turned her out to starve. It was a grim blessing that she left no living child to suffer the widow's wrath.

She threw on her cloak and hoisted the bucket of scraps. Since the feasting had gone on so late, the farmyard curs would be hungrier than usual. No sooner was she out the door than the barking began. They smelled the food—and her fear.

Although she had a way with most animals, tame or wild, dogs terrified her. The mere sight of flashing fangs was enough to set old scars aching, for it stirred memories of a half-naked child dodging among the fir trees with a baying pack in hot pursuit. She had been carried off to Estland as a slave and when she tried to escape, her master had set his hounds on her. But for some barely remembered Words from home, the brutes would have torn her apart.

At least the dogs here were stoutly chained tonight. She could see them now beside the byre, leaping blots on the frost-rimed earth. Best to quiet them before someone remarked their frenzy. Ere she spoke, a chill breeze stirred. The dogs cowered in sudden silence, cringing back against the log wall. Brushed by the same terror, she tossed them their scraps with trembling hands. Then as she turned to face the bitter wind, three long notes on a distant horn pierced her to the heart.

She ran. Heedless of her footing, she sped across the rutted yard, skidded on a pool of frozen slops, and slammed into a gatepost near the kitchen door. After catching her breath, she carefully closed the wicket behind her and left the bucket in its proper place. Rubbing her bruises, she limped off to the women's bower in the house yard. She hoped the few roisterers still out and couples seeking private nooks would be too intent on their own pleasures to pay any heed.

But once abed, she could not sleep, either that night or the next. Why should something so faint as that ghostly horn keep her wakeful when the snorings and rustlings of her fellow servants caused scant unease?

She remembered other beds and the sole mate who had shared them with her. Whether in snug wall boxes fragrant with herbs or a saddle blanket spread within some sheltering thicket, she had slept at her darling's side in every district ruled by Denmark's Crown. As sheriff, castellan, counselor, he was ever King Valdemar's loyal man. Did he follow his liege still in the Land of Darkness where the river of poison wends its way and—*Christ have mercy!* Such heathen nightmare should have died decades ago in the ashes of Estland when the Dane lords came to harry that earthly hell. Herself was all she had to give the knight who delivered her from slave yoke and rebel peasant's knife.

She burrowed deeper under covers that could not keep the cold at bay. Her jab at a hungry flea nearly woke the woman next to her. After a moment's pause, she cracked the creature and flicked it away. She used to seek far braver game. In times gone by, she rode to the hounds with her love and joined her strength to his to take the panting hart. Then he would call her his hunt queen and give her the gristly deercross cut from the slain beast's heart. Every day seemed summer and dusk stretched eager arms toward dawn, until he was forced to marry a woman hard as Fimbulwinter. *In summer course the hart, but in winter the hind.*

And yet the bond sealed in youth endured though youth itself did not. Years after lust had flickered out they still clung together for warmth. She sobbed for a gray head's weight upon her shriveled breasts. That night and the next, gory antlers haunted her dreams.

Then on the last day of the year, fresh snow fell. Shrouded stillness without made feasting all the merrier within. The heaping platters of pickled fish, pork and white flour pastries were even heavier than those at Christmas. Her shoulders ached from pouring so many pitchers of beer to wet throats dried out by songs and laughter.

When her stint was done, there was no place left for her at the long plank table flanking the central hearth. Instead, she sat on the opposite wall bench, well away from the other servants, and ate from a wooden plate on her lap. She gazed along a row of ruddy, glistening faces all the way to the carven high seat where the *herremand* and his lady presided, little soberer than their household. But if any of these jolly folk should chance to stare at her, would they see aught save a smudge of shadow?

She left them to their noisy joy and their New Year's hope.

Afterward, well-muffled and booted against the cold, she walked up to the main road. The rutted track from the garth was already trodden but the empty fields alongside it shone wonderfully white beneath the moonlit sky. From the positions of the stars, she reckoned the time to be midnight. Powers were abroad this festive night of time's rebirth, this miracle season when the sun began her slow return. She might see alder trees strolling like men or wolves trooping off to watch the woods' fairy brand their prey for the coming year. Or else she might meet the Elf-King out seeking his annual tribute of horseshoes. No, the king she meant to see was neither of earth nor of heaven. She brushed the snow from a roadside stump and sat down to wait.

She had scarcely begun her watch when a fierce southwestern wind sprang up. The force of it shook trees free of clinging snow and rattled bare boughs like bones. As she pulled her cloak tighter about her, the wind brought the horn call she expected to hear. She crossed herself, squared her shoulders, and stepped up to the roadway to challenge the huntsmen in passage.

At first all she spied in the distance was a roiling blur. With more than thirty leagues to cover before cockcrow—all the way to the edge of Sjaelland and back—they had to course at a furious pace. Then she beheld what few are born with eyes to see—the Wild Hunt in full career. Men and mounts alike were pale as mist and followed storm-black hounds whose eyes were wheels of flame.

She would have fled that horrid belling pack but her surging panic ebbed once the chief huntsman came into view. She dared to hail this shade as the liege he used to be. One wave of his regal hand slowed headlong gallop to dreamy glide. Clearer sight proved legend true. With a broad hat clapped on his fur-trimmed hood, King Valdemar Atterdag looked just as he did when last seen alive. And with the same crisp courtesy of old, he acknowledged her salute. Among the grim company he led past, she recognized Stig Anderssen, Peder Iron-Beard, and other royal intimates of yesteryear. But if the accursed men in their turn knew her, they gave no sign.

Had the one she sought escaped his comrades' doom? Desire warred with dread as she scanned each somber face. But fate is the hunter no quarry can elude. Last in line—*O merciful God*—rode her lost love.

Her lips froze shut. Still, he heard the name her heart alone could speak. He harkened to her and turned his steed aside. Almost smiling, he bent down as if to bear her away on his saddlebow just as he had a lifetime ago. But his welcoming arm passed straight through her body like a blade of ice.

She fainted under a blizzard of plunging hooves. By the time she came to her senses, the Hunt had gone, leaving not so much as a hoofprint behind.

She rubbed the blood back into her numbed flesh and smeared away tears with her fists. *O God, how can you be so cruel and command us to be kind?* Whyfor did her man deserve this end: for too much faithfulness to a king or too little to a wife? No just lord forced his folk to share in punishment that was solely his nor just judge impose so harsh a sentence for so common a fault. *Stand accused!* Righteous anger flared. She would get justice of both king and God. Whatever the cost, she would wrest her lover free. Wrath warmed her all the way to bed and heavy, dreamless sleep.

The morrow was a Holy Day, to celebrate Christ's first shedding of blood. She and the rest of the household heard Mass in the nearest village. But while neighbors lingered in the churchyard to wish each other New Year's luck, she slipped away unnoticed. Determined to plead her case in the right court, she set out on foot for Sorø Abbey, site of King Valdemar's tomb.

Snow on the road lengthened the short journey. Despite bright sunshine, the cold bit deep through layers of garb. She again had cause to be glad that, when her lover's widow turned her out last summer with only the clothes on her back, she had had the wit to dress beforehand in every warm garment she possessed. Where the woods were thick, she went warily, though the blessed bells of Sorø should suffice to keep the trolls roundabout pent up in their hollow hills.

Before sunset she found refuge in the Abbey's guest-house. Although she had to share supper with a greedy clutch of paupers and vagabonds, she did not begudge them the chance to eat their fill.

Afterward, she begged leave to enter the monastic church for Compline, the final office of the day. Only a few others availed themselves of this opportunity to stand in the frigid nave while a choir of white-robed monks chanted behind the roodscreen.

As she prayed, she could see her frosty breath—the community did not stint on candles. Banks of huge tapers banished darkness back to the plain brick walls. Above these flickering lights, the wooden Image on the Cross seemed to bleed and writhe. She thought of stags at bay and looked aside. Her gaze kept wandering to the wall niche where the dead king lay. His effigy gleamed icy white atop his huge black tomb.

The service ended. The monks filed out. She lingered alone in the darkened church. Only now did she venture to inspect the object of her quest. The fully armored figure seemed to float on its polished marble slab while watchful rows of pale apostles and prelates stared out of nothing-ness below. At the west end, figures of the king and his queen knelt with prayerbooks in their hands to receive Christ's benediction. By rights, the other end ought to show Valdemar and a different lady quite otherwise en-gaged. She laughed bitterly and dared to stroke the stone lion supporting the king's feet. Unearthly chill burnt through her mittened fingers straight to the bone.

She drew back with a cry. Was she a fool to have come? Although others had witnessed the king at chase and gone unscathed, how many dared to trouble him at his rest? She tried to pray but could not. Instead she paced uneas-ily to and fro, shivering worse with each step. This build-ing held cold as an oven did heat. It might be as long as two hours until midnight. The red sanctuary lamp glowed overhead like the watchful eye of God. If only it hung lower, she would be tempted to warm her stiff fingers over its flame. In happier times she used to carry a hollow metal ball with a hot coal inside for winter comfort. But there were crueller deaths than freezing; Valdemar's queen had roasted his leman alive in the bathhouse.

She pounded her hands together and stamped her feet as she walked her sentry round. The moonlit shadow of the rood crept across her path. She flinched when this shadow touched her own—shades of St. Eustace's cross-bearing hart, the quarry that suffered itself to be hunted to save its hunter's soul.

As twelve o'clock struck, she turned to find the king suddenly there.

"Hear me, Dane-King," she called, and fell to her knees.

"I listen better when petitioners do not fawn—as you whom I knew in life should recall." Valdemar gave a wry smile. "My rank is but an illusion now in all events."

Awkwardly, she faced the ghost of majesty.

"Make haste, woman. The Hunt gathers."

"Why must *he* ride with you, sir—the good lord I loved?"

"One Lord alone is truly good. And was I so very wicked in my day?" Ice crystals sparkled in his thick moustache. "I was a lawgiver, a conquerer, a builder. As pilgrim to Jerusalem, I kept a whole night's vigil at St. Sepulchre's. But I cursed God when my Tovelil was murdered: '*Keep your heaven*,' I cried, '*and leave me the earth that holds her grave*.' I spoke my own doom, and I must serve it."

"And did you condemn your courtiers as well?"

"When sin was shared, so also should expiation be."

"Then share it with your lady and let my love go!"

"Which of the two would I sooner have beside me?" His eyes narrowed, glinting. "That choice lies in other hands. Meanwhile every evening brings another night." He sighed. "Till Doomsday dawns, our company cannot grow less. Our hunting changes not by the season or the century—a chase with never a beast in view."

"No remedy at all?" she screamed. "Where then is justice, on earth or in high heaven?"

"There—or nowhere." He pointed to the rood and took

his leave. "Would you have me late to my appointed torment?"

His spurred boots made not a sound as he strode away.

She stumbled back to the guesthouse and slept, grateful for the warmth of other human bodies around her. In her dreams, she fled naked through a wintry forest pursued by unseen foes until at the heart of the wood, she reached a fountain of blood that burned. Here was everlasting refuge and healing for all wounds.

She awoke knowing the price to be paid for his freedom: if fate was a hunter, so was love. And what hunts may itself be hunted.

Leaving Sorø Abbey as soon as it was light, she returned to the *herregaard*. Ere her master could scold her for her absence overnight, she gave notice. He railed at her ingratitude and offered blows, but she had heard and felt worse, delivered in hotter rage. Her decision stood. She took the waybread he grudgingly gave and set off the next morning on her eastward journey.

Her strides left deep footprints in snow the Wild Hunt's headlong gallop could not mark. Had King Valdemar built this road he now was doomed to ride? Memory failed. No matter. She had the scent; she knew the trail. There would be no denying the prize she sought.

Three days' trek in deepening cold and rising fever brought her through wildwood and hamlets arranged like shield-rings to shut that selfsame wildwood out. She passed Ringsted Abbey where other Dane-Kings slept in hallowed peace and circled proud Roskilde town with the twin green spires of its cathedral reigning on the heights.

The highroad vanished. But she found a once-familiar track despite encroaching brambles. She could smell the sea and a nearby lake. By Epiphany Eve she reached her goal, the empty royal manor at Gurre. Tove's toy castle stood barred and shuttered. Moss stained its red brick walls. Dark feathers on the snow and piercing cries proclaimed that hawks now roosted in the bower of Tovelil, Valdemar's dove.

She would not have forced entry into the place even if her dwindling strength had permitted. Instead she cut some pine boughs with her belt knife to make herself a rude bed at the foot of a huge birch tree nearby. It had been a gathering point for royal hunts in gladder days when she had ridden with her love behind Tove and the king—black whore shadowing white. Here she meant to rest until the sky turned round to midnight.

Huddled in her makeshift nest, she pressed her burning cheek against the smooth birchbark and wept for the body she used to clasp. Her tears ebbed, the sobbing passed, and she slept.

Her dream was bitter as her vigil. She saw the summer sky rain swords that stabbed great bleeding wounds into the blooming earth. From that seeding grew a whole steel forest where every leaf and branch was a blade. She fled their clashing, whirring edges over caltrop grass through stands of jabbing spears. The wind's teeth ripped her half-flayed hide, and the chilling torrent that should have hidden her scent washed flesh away from bone.

She awoke sweating and trembling despite the frosty air. Her glazed eyes could not judge the hour from the few stars still visible between scudding clouds. A gale blowing up from the southwest moaned like the baying of hounds. If the pack were already uncoupled, then it must be past midnight.

She was too weary to be brave. Every long year of her age lay heavy upon her. Only her love's sore need held her to the course. She fairly panted for a last sip of water but her flask was empty. And yet the fate she chose promised honor as well as pain. If Christ Himself did not shrink from playing the wounded hart, why should she? *O Lord, once quarry for man's sake, be with me now.*

No drum had she, nor staff, nor fabulous regalia. Let keen desire serve in their stead. Fixing her eyes on the Nail Star overhead, she braced her back against the birch, stretched wide her arms, and summoned the powers that coursed in her blood. She sang. The lost Words came flooding back. In seven steps her spirit climbed the Tree that upholds the heavens like a mighty pillar. She touched the very point on which the sky-roof hangs. . . .

Darkness flowed down the white bark. One heartbreaking moment later, it shied away from a new-made corpse and sprang into the forest. It wore antlers, hooves, and hide, and woman's form nevermore.

All have faded into shadow—woods and manor, Hunt and prey. They are phantoms faint as drawings on vellum that never felt the colorist's brush. Like an old book read again page by timeworn page, their course runs nightly from Sorø to Gurre, from Unharbouring to Bay. The hart cannot count how many hunters give chase or recall why the number should matter. Its doom is to offer sport until the final stroke that sounds its death.

Alas, how long that horn call echoes . . .

Introduction

David Drake

Many of Kipling's short stories—and many of the best-known of his short stories—were set in the historical past. When you're reading a vivid evocation of life on the slave benches of a Greek galley, or doctrinal squabbles in the early Christian church, it's easy to forget that Kipling's own formal schooling ended when his was sixteen years old. He wasn't a trained historian, any more than he was a trained writer.

And partly for that reason, he was frequently in error in his descriptions of historical settings.

I won't say, "but of course that doesn't matter," because it *does* matter to me, and it certainly mattered to Kipling himself. One of the characters in *Puck of Pook's Hill* is Parnesius, *A Centurion of the Thirtieth*. The Thirtieth Legion, Ulpia Victrix, was never formally stationed in Britain. Kipling's satisfaction when a correspondent showed him proof that elements of the Thirtieth *were* in Britain is quite evident in his autobiography *Something of Myself*.

So that time the experts were wrong and Kipling was right, either because he'd made a logical conjecture based on his knowledge of British Army practice—or because he was lucky. The important thing is that he really cared that his facts be correct, even though he was writing fiction and not a history text.

There were other times when he was dead wrong, because he wasn't a trained historian and therefore didn't realize that past practice differed from that of more recent times. A good example is the one I mentioned above, Kipling's brilliant flashes from the life of a Greek galley slave in "The Finest Story in the World."

The problem is that the Greeks (and the Romans after them) used free oarsmen rather than slaves to power their galleys. This isn't a matter of conjecture: it's solidly documented fact, known to anybody who's read Thucydides (to pick one of many readily-accessible sources). For Lew Wallace, who was a bad general, a bad governor, and a bad writer, to make such an error is hardly surprising; but why did *Kipling* get it wrong?

Very simply, because Kipling didn't know there was a question. Universally in Renaissance times, and well into the Nineteenth Century among the Barbary pirates, galleys were rowed by slaves or condemned prisoners. Kipling assumed the same practice held true in the Classical period; and that assumption was false.

My taste when I'm writing, like that of Kipling and in large measure because of Kipling's influence, runs to historical settings. I've had more formal schooling than Kipling did, but I'm certainly not an academic historian. In any case, the settings that I've used range far wider than would be considered within the competence of any single historian or archeologist.

Therefore, I make mistakes.

One of those mistakes occurred in "The Barrow Troll." Sandra (the other name on the cover, who happens to be a medievalist) tells me that rosaries weren't in use by Christians during the time at which the story is set (about the middle of the Eleventh Century). I was going to correct the error—and I *will* correct it in later appearances—but I decided to leave it as originally written for just this once.

My mistake points up several of the lessons Kipling's stories taught me about writing historical fiction. First, that it's important to care about getting things right. People who don't care—in any business, and certainly in the business of writing—are bad craftsmen, and that's something neither Kipling nor I could stomach.

Second, that the story remains more important than the accuracy of its background. I know that Kipling was wrong about galley slaves, but "The Finest Story in the World" remains one of my favorites among the body of the work. Likewise, "The Barrow Troll" doesn't stand or fall on what I knew about medieval religious paraphernalia (though it gripes my soul that I didn't know enough).

Third, that unless you're a specialist in the field, you're apt to make mistakes which are obvious to a specialist—*but*, that you can't wait to write a story until you have a specialist's knowledge in every aspect of it. Kipling's three tales of Parnesius the Centurion are stunningly effective for what the author *did* know about . . . and most particularly, for what the author knew about men and soldiers. That would remain true even if he'd blown it with his speculation about where the Thirtieth was stationed.

But boy, was he ever (rightly!) proud to have been correct. . . .

The Barrow Troll

DAVID DRAKE

Playfully, Ulf Womanslayer twitched the cord bound to his saddlehorn. "Awake, priest? Soon you can get to work."

"My work is saving souls, not being dragged into the wilderness by madmen," Johann muttered under his breath. The other end of the cord was around his neck, not that of his horse. A trickle of blood oozed into his cassock from the reopened scab, but he was afraid to loosen the knot. Ulf might look back. Johann had already seen his captor go into a berserk rage. Over the Northerner's right shoulder rode his axe, a heavy hooked blade on a four foot shaft. Ulf had swung it like a willow-wand when three Christian traders in Schleswig had seen the priest and tried to free him. The memory of the last man in three pieces as head and sword arm sprang from his spouting torso was still enough to roil Johann's stomach.

"We'll have a clear night with a moon, priest; a good night for our business." Ulf stretched and laughed aloud, setting a raven on a fir knot to squawking back at him. The berserker was following a ridge line that divided wooded slopes with a spine too thin-soiled to bear trees. The flanking forests still loomed above the riders. In three days, now, Johann had seen no man but his captor, nor even a tendril of smoke from a lone cabin. Even the route they were taking to Parmavale was no mantrack but an accident of nature.

"So lonely," the priest said aloud.

Ulf hunched hugely in his bearskin and replied, "You soft folk in the south, you live too close anyway. Is it your Christ-god, do you think?"

"Hedeby's a city," the German priest protested, his fingers toying with his torn robe, "and my brother trades to Uppsala. . . . But why bring me to this manless waste?"

"Oh, there were men once, so the tale goes," Ulf said. Here in the empty forest he was more willing for conversation than he had been the first few days of their ride north. "Few enough, and long enough ago. But there were farms in Parmavale, and a lordling of sorts who went a-viking against the Irish. But then the troll came and the men went, and there was nothing left to draw others. So they thought."

"You Northerners believe in trolls, so my brother tells me," said the priest.

"Aye, long before the gold I'd heard of the Parma troll," the berserker agreed. "Ox broad and stronger than ten men, shaggy as a denned bear."

"Like you," Johann said, in a voice more normal than caution would have dictated.

Blood fury glared in Ulf's eyes and he gave a savage jerk on the cord. "You'll think me a troll, priestling, if you don't do just as I say. I'll drink your blood hot if you cross me."

Johann, gagging, could not speak nor wished to.

With the miles the sky became a darker blue, the trees a blacker green. Ulf again broke the hoof-pummeled silence, saying, "No, I knew nothing of the gold until Thora told me."

The priest coughed to clear his throat. "Thora is your wife?" he asked.

"Wife?" Ho!" Ulf brayed, his raucous laughter ringing like a demon's. "Wife? She was Hallstein's wife, and I killed her with all her house about her! But before that, she told me of the troll's hoard, indeed she did. Would you hear that story?"

Johann nodded, his smile fixed. He was learning to recognize death as it bantered under the axehead.

"So," the huge Northerner began. "There was a bonder, Hallstein Kari's son, who followed the king to war but left his wife, that was Thora, behind to manage the stead. The first day I came by and took a sheep from the herdsman. I told him if he misliked it to send his master to me."

"Why did you do that?" the fat priest asked in surprise.

"Why? Because I'm Ulf, because I wanted the sheep. A woman acting a man's part, it's unnatural anyway.

"The next day I went back to Hallstein's stead, and the flocks had already been driven in. I went into the garth around the buildings and called for the master to come out and fetch me a sheep." The berserker's teeth ground audibly as he remembered. Johann saw his knuckles whiten on the axe helve and stiffened in terror.

"Ho!" Ulf shouted, bringing his left hand down on the shield slung at his horse's flank. The copper boss rang like thunder in the clouds. "She came out," Ulf grated, "and her hair was red. 'All our sheep are penned,' says she, 'but you're in good time for the butchering.' And from out the hall came her three brothers and the men of the stead, ten in all. They were in full armor and their swords were in their hands. And they would have slain me, Ulf Otgeir's son, *me*, at a woman's word. Forced me to run from a woman!"

The berserker was snarling his words to the forest. Johann knew he watched a scene that had been played a score of times with only the trees to witness. The rage of disgrace burned in Ulf like pitch in a pine faggot, and his mind was lost to everything except the past.

"But I came back," he continued, "in the darkness, when all feasted within the hall and drank their ale to victory. Behind the hall burned a log fire to roast a sheep. I killed the two there, and I thrust one of the logs half-burnt up under the eaves. Then at the door I waited until those within noticed the heat and Thora looked outside.

" 'Greetings, Thora,' I said. 'You would not give me mutton, so I must roast men tonight.' She asked me for speech. I knew she was fey, so I listened to her. And she told me of the Parma lord and the treasure he brought back from Ireland, gold and gems. And she said it was cursed that a troll should guard it, and that I must needs have a mass priest, for the troll could not cross a Christian's fire and I should slay him then."

"Didn't you spare her for that?" Johann quavered, more fearful of silence than he was of misspeaking.

"Spare her? No, nor any of her house," Ulf thundered back. "She might better have asked the flames for mercy, as she knew. The fire was at her hair. I struck her, and never was woman better made for an axe to bite—she cleft like a waxen doll, and I threw the pieces back. Her brothers came then, but one and one and one through the doorway, and I killed each in his turn. No more came. When the roof fell, I left them with the ash for a headstone and went my way to find a mass priest—to find you, priestling." Ulf, restored to good humor by the climax of his own tale, tweaked the lead cord again.

Johann choked onto his horse's neck, nauseated as much by the story as by the noose. At last he said, thick-voiced, "Why do you trust her tale if she knew you would kill her with it or not?"

"She was fey," Ulf chuckled, as if that explained everything. "Who knows what a man will do when his death is upon him? Or a woman," he added more thoughtfully.

They rode on in growing darkness. With no breath of wind to stir them, the trees stood as dead as the rocks underfoot.

"Will you know the place?" the German asked suddenly. "Shouldn't we camp now and go on in the morning?"

"I'll know it," Ulf grunted. "We're not far now—we're going down hill, can't you feel?" He tossed his bare haystack of hair, silvered into a false sheen of age by the moon. He continued, "The Parma lord sacked a dozen churches, so they say, and then one more with more of gold than the twelve besides, but also the curse. And he brought it back with him to Parma, and there it rests in his barrow, the troll guarding it. That I have on Thora's word."

"But she hated you!"

"She was fey."

They were into the trees, and looking to either side Johann could see hill slopes rising away from them. They were in a valley, Parma or another. Scraps of wattle and daub, the remains of a house or a garth fence, thrust up to the right. The firs that had grown through it were generations old. Johann's stubbled tonsure crawled in the night air.

"She said there was a clearing," the berserker muttered, more to himself than his companion. Johann's horse stumbled. The priest clutched the cord reflexively as it tightened. When he looked up at his captor, he saw the huge Northerner fumbling at his shield's fastenings. For the first time that evening, a breeze stirred. It stank of death.

"Others have been here before us," said Ulf needlessly.

A row of skulls, at least a score of them, stared blank-eyed from atop stakes rammed through their spinal openings. To one, dried sinew still held the lower jaw in a ghastly rictus; the others had fallen away into the general scatter of bones whitening the ground. All of them were human or could have been. They were mixed with occasion glimmers of buttons and rust smears. The freshest of the grisly trophies was very old, perhaps decades old. Too old to explain the reek of decay.

Ulf wrapped his left fist around the twin handles of his shield. It was a heavy circle of linden wood, faced with leather. Its rim and central boss were of copper, and rivets of bronze and copper decorated the face in a serpent pattern.

"Good that the moon is full," Ulf said, glancing at the bright orb still tangled in the fir branches. "I fight best in the moonlight. We'll let her rise the rest of the way, I think."

Johann was trembling. He joined his hands about his saddle horn to keep from falling off the horse. He knew Ulf might let him jerk and strangle there, even after dragging him across half the northlands. The humor of the idea might strike him. Johann's rosary, his crucifix—everything he had brought from Germany or purchased in Schleswig save his robe—had been left behind in Hedeby when the berserker awakened him in his bed. Ulf had jerked a noose to near-lethal tautness and whispered that he needed a priest, that this one would do, but that there were others should this one prefer to feed crows. The disinterested bloodlust in Ulf's tone had been more terrifying than the threat itself. Johann had followed in silence to the waiting horses. In despair, he wondered again if a quick death would not have been better than this lingering one that had ridden for weeks a mood away from him.

"It looks like a palisade for a house," the priest said aloud in what he pretended was a normal voice.

"That's right," Ulf replied, giving his axe an exploratory heft that sent shivers of moonlight across the blade. "There was a hall here, a big one. Did it burn, do you think?" His knees sent his roan gelding forward in a shambling walk past the line of skulls. Johann followed of necessity.

"No, rotted away," the berserker said, bending over to study the post holes.

"You said it was deserted a long time," the priest commented. His eyes were fixed straight forward. One of the skulls was level with his waist and close enough to bite him, could it turn on its stake.

"There was time for the house to fall in, the ground is damp," Ulf agreed. "But the stakes, then, have been replaced. Our troll keeps his front fence new, priestling."

Johann swallowed, said nothing.

Ulf gestured briefly. "Come on, you have to get your fire ready. I want it really holy."

"But we don't sacrifice with fires. I don't know how—"

"Then learn!" the berserker snarled with a vicious yank that drew blood and a gasp from the German. "I've seen how you Christ-shouters love to bless things. You'll bless me a fire, that's all. And if anything goes wrong and the troll spares you—I won't, priestling. I'll rive you apart if I have to come off a stake to do it!"

The horses walked slowly forward through brush and soggy rubble that had been a hall. The odor of decay grew stronger. The priest himself tried to ignore it, but his horse began to balk. The second time he was too slow with a heel to its ribs, and the cord nearly decapitated him. "Wait!" he wheezed. "Let me get down."

Ulf looked back at him, flat-eyed. At last he gave a brief crow-peck nod and swung himself out of the saddle. He looped both sets of reins on a small fir. Then, while Johann dismounted clumsily, he loosed the cord from his saddle and took it in his axe hand. The men walked forward without speaking.

"There . . . ," Ulf breathed.

The barrow was only a black-mouthed swell in the ground, its size denied by its lack of features. Such trees as had tried to grow on it had been broken off short over a period of years. Some of the stumps had wasted into crumbling depressions, while from others the wood fibers still twisted raggedly. Only when Johann matched the trees on the other side of the tomb to those beside him did he realize the scale on which the barrow was built: its entrance tunnel would pass a man walking upright, even a man Ulf's height.

"Lay your fire at the tunnel mouth," the berserker said, his voice subdued. "He'll be inside."

"You'll have to let me go—"

"I'll have to nothing!" Ulf was breathing hard. "We'll go closer, you and I, and you'll make a fire of the dead trees from the ground. Yes. . . ."

The Northerner slid forward in a pace that was cat soft and never left the ground a finger's breadth. Strewn about them as if flung idly from the barrow mouth were scraps and gobbets of animals, the source of the fetid reek that filled the clearing. As his captor paused for a moment, Johann toed one of the bits over with his sandle. It was the hide and paws of something chisel-toothed, whether rabbit or other was impossible to say in the moonlight and state of decay. The skin was in tendrils, and the skull had been opened to empty the brains. Most of the other bits seemed of the same sort, little beasts, although a rank blotch on the mound's slope could have been a wolf hide. Whatever killed and feasted here was not fastidious.

"He stays close to hunt," Ulf rumbled. Then he added, "The long bones by the fence; they were cracked."

"Umm?"

"For marrow."

Quivering, the priest began gathering broken-off trees, none of them over a few feet high. They had been twisted off near the ground, save for a few whose roots lay bare in wizened fists. The crisp scales cut Johann's hands. He did not mind the pain. Under his breath he was praying that God would punish him, would torture him, but at least would save him free of this horrid demon that had snatched him away.

"Pile it there," Ulf directed, his axe head nodding toward the stone lip of the barrow. The entrance was corbelled out of heavy stones, then covered over with dirt and sods. Like the beast fragments around it, the opening was dead and stinking. Biting his tongue, Johann dumped his pile of brush and scurried back.

"There's light back down there," he whispered.

"Fire?"

"No, look—it's pale, it's moonlight. There's a hole in the roof of the tomb."

"Light for me to kill by," Ulf said with a stark grin. He looked over the low fireset, then knelt. His steel sparked into a nest of dry moss. When the tinder was properly alight, he touched a pitchy faggot to it. He dropped his end of the cord. The torchlight glinted from his face, white and coarse-pored where the tangles of hair and beard did not cover it. "Bless the fire, mass-priest," the berserker ordered in a quiet, terrible voice.

Stiff-featured and unblinking, Johann crossed the brushwood and said, "In nomine Patris, et Filii, et Spiritus Sancti, Amen."

"Don't light it yet," Ulf said. He handed Johann the torch. "It may be," the berserker added, "that you think to run if you get the chance. There is no Hell so deep that I will not come for you from it."

The priest nodded, white-lipped.

Ulf shrugged his shoulders to loosen his muscles and the bear hide that clothed them. Axe and shield rose and dipped like ships in a high sea.

"Ho! Troll! Barrow fouler! Corpse licker! Come and fight me, troll!"

There was no sound from the tomb.

Ulf's eyes began to glaze. He slashed his axe twice across the empty air and shouted again, "Troll! I'll spit on your corpse, I'll lay with your dog mother. Come and fight me, troll, or I'll wall you up like a rat with your filth!"

Johann stood frozen, oblivious even to the drop of pitch that sizzled on the web of his hand. The berserker bellowed again, wordlessly, gnashing at the rim of his shield so that the sound bubbled and boomed in the night.

And the tomb roared back to the challenge, a thunderous BAR BAR BAR even deeper than Ulf's.

Berserk, the Northerner leaped the brush pile and ran down the tunnel, his axe thrust out in front of him to clear the stone arches.

The tunnel sloped for a dozen paces into a timber-vaulted chamber too broad to leap across. Moonlight spilled through a circular opening onto flags slimy with damp and liquescence. Ulf, maddened, chopped high at the light. The axe burred inanely beneath the timbers.

Swinging a pair of swords, the troll leapt at Ulf. It was the size of a bear, grizzled in the moonlight. Its eyes burned red.

"Hi!" shouted Ulf and blocked the first sword in a shower of sparks on his axehead. The second blade bit into the shield rim, shaving a hand's length of copper and a curl of yellow linden from beneath it. Ulf thrust straight-armed, a blow that would have smashed like a battering ram had the troll not darted back. Both the combatants were shouting; their voices were dreadful in the circular chamber.

The troll jumped backward again. Ulf sprang toward him and only the song of the blades scissoring from either side warned him. The berserker threw himself down. The troll had leaped onto a rotting chest along the wall of the tomb and cut unexpectedly from above Ulf's shield. The big man's boots flew out from under him and he struck the floor on his back. His shield still covered his body.

The troll hurtled down splay-legged with a cry of triumph. Both bare feet slammed on Ulf's shield. The troll was even heavier than Ulf. Shrieking, the berserker pistoned his shield arm upward. The monster flew off, smashing against the timbered ceiling and caroming down into another of the chests. The rotted wood exploded under the weight in a flash of shimmering gold. The berserker rolled to his feet and struck over-arm the same motion. His lunge carried the axehead too far, into the rock wall in a flower of blue sparks.

The troll was up. The two killers eyed each other, edging sideways in the dimness. Ulf's right arm was numb to the shoulder. He did not realize it. The shaggy monster leaped with another double flashing and the axe moved too slowly to counter. Both edges spat chunks of linden as they withdrew. Ulf frowned, backed a step. His boot trod on a ewer that spun away from him. As he cried out, the troll grinned and hacked again like Death the Reaper. The shield-orb flattened as the top third of it split away. Ulf snarled and chopped at the troll's knees. It leaped above the steel and cut left-handed, its blade nocking the shaft an inch from Ulf's hand.

The berserker flung the useless remainder of his shield in the troll's face and ran. Johann's torch was an orange pulse in the triangular opening. Behind Ulf, a sword-edge went *sring!* as it danced on the corbels. Ulf jumped the brush and whirled. "Now!" he cried to the priest, and Johann hurled his torch into the resin-jeweled wood.

The needles crackled up in the troll's face like a net of orange silk. The flames bellied out at the creature's rush but licked back caressingly over its mats of hair. The troll's swords cut at the fire. A shower of coals spit and crackled and made the beast howl.

"Burn, dog-spew!" Ulf shouted. "Burn, fish-guts!"

The troll's blades rang together, once and again. For a moment it stood, a hillock of stained gray, as broad as the tunnel arches. Then it strode forward into the white heart of the blaze. The fire bloomed up, its roar leaping over the troll's shriek of agony. Ulf stepped forward. He held his axe with both hands. The flames sucked down from the motionless troll, and as they did the shimmering arc of the axehead chopped into the beast's collarbone. One sword dropped and the left arm slumped loose.

The berserker's axe was buried to the helve in the troll's shoulder. The faggots were scattered, but the troll's hair was burning all over its body. Ulf pulled at his axe. The troll staggered, moaning. Its remaining sword pointed down at the ground. Ulf yanked again at his weapon and it slurped free. A thick velvet curtain of blood followed it. Ulf raised his dripping axe for another blow, but the troll tilted toward the withdrawn weapon, leaning forward, a smouldering rock. The body hit the ground, then flopped so that it lay on its back. The right arm was flung out at an angle.

"It was a man," Johann was whispering. He caught up a brand and held it close to the troll's face. "Look, look!" he demanded excitedly, "It's just an old man in bearskin. Just a man."

Ulf sagged over his axe as if it were a stake impaling him. His frame shuddered as he dragged air into it. Neither of the troll's swords had touched him, but reaction had left him weak as one death-wounded. "Go in," he wheezed. "Get a torch and lead me in."

"But . . . why—" the priest said in sudden fear. His eyes met the berserker's and he swallowed back the rest of his protest. The torch threw highlights on the walls and flags as he trotted down the tunnel. Ulf's boots were ominous behind him.

The central chamber was austerely simple and furnished only with the six chests lining the back of it. There was no corpse, nor even a slab for one. The floor was gelatinous with decades' accumulation of foulness. The skidding tracks left by the recent combat marked paving long undisturbed. Only from the entrance to the chests was a path, black against the slime of decay, worn. It was toward the broken container and the objects which had spilled from it that the priest's eyes arrowed.

"Gold," he murmured. Then, "Gold! There must—the others—in God's name, there are five more and perhaps all of them—"

"Gold," Ulf grated terribly.

Johann ran to the nearest chest and opened it one-handed. The lid sagged wetly, but frequent use had kept it from swelling tight to the side panels. "Look at this crucifix!" the priest marveled. "And the torque, it must weigh pounds. And Lord in heaven, this—"

"Gold," the berserker repeated.

Johann saw the axe as it started to swing. He was turning with a chalice ornamented in enamel and pink gold. It hung in the air as he darted for safety. His scream and the dull belling of the cup as the axe divided it were simultaneous, but the priest was clear and Ulf was off balance. The berserker backhanded with force enough to drive the peen of his axehead through a sapling. His strength was too great for his footing. His feet skidded, and this time his head rang on the wall of the tomb.

Groggy, the huge berserker staggered upright. The priest was a scurrying blur against the tunnel entrance. "Priest!" Ulf shouted at the suddenly empty moonlight. He thudded up the flags of the tunnel. "Priest!" he shouted again.

The clearing was empty except for the corpse. Nearby, Ulf heard his roan whicker. He started for it, then paused. The priest—he could still be hiding in the darkness. While Ulf searched for him, he could be rifling the barrow, carrying off the gold behind his back. "Gold," Ulf said again. No one must take his gold. No one ever must find it unguarded.

"I'll kill you!" he screamed into the night. "I'll kill you all!"

He turned back to his barrow. At the entrance, still smoking, waited the body of what had been the troll.

Introduction

Poul Anderson

These lines were never a conscious imitation of Kipling. They were just dashed off for my own amusement, many years ago. If I had any particular intent, it was to gibe at self-righteousness.

In those days Gordon Dickson and I were young bachelors living in Minneapolis. He had taken up balladeering as a hobby and had already written a few fine songs with science fiction or fantasy motifs. He composed the melodies too, and sang them with guitar accompaniment. This was simply in our circle of friends. Sometimes it was only the two of us singing. He did that well, and managed to endure my voice.

As I recall, he dropped around to my place with his guitar and I showed him this piece. He was much taken by it and promptly set about developing a tune. That went so fast that we were able to call on Marvin Larson, another enthusiast, the same evening and render it for him. Marv exclaimed that this was like finding a new "Lord Randall," but doubtless the music stirred him more than the words. Ted Cogswell, who also created songs for the hell of it, likewise enjoyed "Three Kings." Soon he and Gordy were belting it out, among others, at science fiction conventions. The custom of what is now called filk singing was getting started, although it was then unorganized, amateurish, and a lot of fun. This lay has been in the repertoire ever since.

As said, it was not meant as a Kipling pastiche, but his influence is obvious. "The Ballad of the 'Clampherdown' " had had an amusingly similar fate, being itself a satire that got taken seriously and set to music. Otherwise I do not venture to compare my verse to his.

The Ballad of the Three Kings

Poul Anderson

Three kings rode out on the road to hell,
And ravens flew on the gale.
The night wind rang like an iron bell
And hissed with sleet and hail.
Three kings rode out where the night wind runs,
And onto death's highway:
The King of the Britons, the King of the Huns,
And the King of Norroway.

And the King of the Britons was crowned with gold
And rode a stallion white.
"Oh, all men gang when they are told,
But I go not in fright.
A goodly king, who loved his folk,
And guarded them with the rod,
With stakes and gallows, against themselves,
Will surely go to God."

And the King of the Huns was capped with steel,
And rode a stallion red.
"Oh, truly proud my fathers feel
Of me who crowned my head
Halfway across a world in pain,
Which mightily I did win;
And I go home to my fathers' fane,
And not to the evil djinn."

And the King of Norway was helmed with wings,
And rode a stallion gray.
"Oh, fiercely glad my heart now sings;
Odin guests me today.
I died in bed, aye, but I hung
Full many a screaming thrall
On Odin's tree. With runes on tongue,
I gang now to his hall."

Three kings rode down to the depths of hell,
And the bloody-breasted hound
Howled as they rode where black rivers fell,
Icy beneath the ground.
Three kings a final judgment won
From the high gods' lips that day:
The Devil took the Briton, the djinn took the Hun,
and Hel took Norroway!

Introduction

Gene Wolfe

When I listened to the *Just So Stories* (and for many years after), I didn't know that they had a precursor, "The Children of the Zodiac." It is a work in which Kipling did what Poe is justly celebrated for doing over and over: he invented a whole new *kind* of story, the modern literary myth or antiallegory. It is an updating of a type that has not been popular for the last thousand years, in part because it is so often confused with the sort of story that Hans Christian Andersen and Oscar Wilde wrote so well—the kind of story that Jane Yolen does brilliantly today.

It is characteristically said of the Andersen-Wilde-Yolen story that though intended for adults, it is enjoyed immensely by children; sometimes it is actually true. But it is never true, I think, of the literary myth. It is not to the child in us that it appeals, but to the savage. At one time or another, one must have lived among wolves as Mowgli did, and Romulus.

Nor is it favored by the academic critics, who are forever confusing it with its mirror twin. In allegory, we say, "What if a giant were despair?" Then we have the giant wrestle our hero, and so on. It has always seemed an obvious idea to me and a rather stupid one, since a giant is much more interesting than despair. Furthermore this obvious and rather stupid idea blinds many of those same people to the true nature of classical myth. They discover, for example, that Eros "is" eroticism, and when they have congratulated one another on that brilliant discovery for twenty years and more, they also discover that Eros doesn't always behave as they "know" he should (in being Aphrodite's son instead of her father, for example) and solemnly inform us that the mythmakers of the classical age lacked their own insight.

But what Kipling (and the ancients) really said was much more interesting: "What if love were a woman?"

Love, Among The Corridors

A Fable

Gene Wolfe

Her own footfalls echoed after her, reverberating from stone floor to ceiling of stone, so that she felt herself pursued, though she knew herself to be the pursuer. The ticking of the clocks told the footsteps of time.

The walls were lined with pictures and carvings, with dusty furniture and old vases bellied like the cupids on a valentine. She looked at all and walked on. She could not bear to think of where she had begun to walk (for that was nothingness) or where she went (for that was to the grave).

When it had grown late, and all the windows of the palace were darkened by more than ivy, she saw, among the other statues and figures, a Harlequin cast of bronze standing upon a marble pedestal. There was nothing about him, perhaps, to take her interest, and yet take it he did; and with one small, white hand, she touched him.

At once it seemed the sun had broken through the ivy and the evening. An aureate ray pierced the window nearest the statue and touched it too, so that she saw immediately that, cobwebbed though it was, it was not a statue at all but a living Harlequin, dominoed and costumed as in the old plays.

When the sunlight had faded—as it did in an instant—

the ruddy glow of health remained in the Harlequin's cheeks and the light of life in his eyes.

He moved and sneezed at the dust, raising a great, gray cloud of it; then sneezing again, leaped from his pedestal. She started back in fear.

"What is your name?" he said, wiping his nose upon his sleeve.

And she, "Amor . . ."

"I too. But who are you, and how came you to walk in this palace?"

Taking courage, she told him, "That is the question no one can answer. Rather, recount to me how you, who appeared but an image a moment ago, are now a man."

"By stepping down," he said. "At least, that is how it seems to me when I reflect upon it. For a long time—oh, very long, longer than your whole dear life, I feel sure—I stood . . ." He hesitated.

"Why, right up there, wasn't it? Right up on that stone block, that seems so ordinary now. Ten thousand times, at least, I watched the sun come in at those windows and go out, and Night come with her cats and wolves. Many a hundred walkers have I seen go up and down this corridor before yourself, my darling. It seems to me now that at any moment I might have stepped down, and yet I did not, nor even thought on it. And now it seems to me that I might mount up again and pose as I did before, and yet that would be too laborious for me to stand. But tell me more; who are you, and who are your father and mother?"

"My name you know," Amor said. "But let me confess at once, lest you should discover it in time after, that I was born out of wedlock. The noble Chivalry was my father, and Poetry my mother."

"Ah, brave old Chivalry." Harlequin cocked his head, finding as other men do that to concentrate his thoughts it was needful to make them run to one side. "I saw him often, long since, but not for many a year now."

"He is dead," Amor sighed. "And I, a neglectful daughter, ought to have said 'my late father' and not spoken as I did."

"What? Brave Chivalry late? But Chivalry cannot be late, or else 'tis not Chivalry."

"How truly you speak. No, that poor body cannot be my noble father, ever so light of step, even when he was stiff of knee. It is—what it is. But Chivalry was never so."

"As for Poetry," continued Harlequin. "She still lives, I believe; but she is old and crank and ill."

"I feared it might be thus. It has been so very long since last I saw her."

"Then you are alone in the world," Harlequin said, and made her a deep bow. "But not entirely alone, for you have me."

"And you," Amor said. "You are alone also."

"Indeed, I hope not."

She took him by the hand. "My dear friend—"

Fearing her words: "Your touch thrills me still. It was your touch, beloved Amor, that called me to life. I came down from that block of stone to feel your touch. There is true magic in your touch, I swear!"

"How could my touch kindle anything to life?"

He kissed her hand. "I cannot say—and yet I know it brought life to me."

"Shall we make trial of it?" Amor inquired doubtfully. "If it were so, I might— I even might— Shall I touch another?"

"Oh, not another!" Harlequin gasped.

"Not another such as you, dear friend, for there is no other such as you. But should I not touch something else? Perhaps the dragon on that vase?"

"But suppose your touch effectual. We would have a dragon between us. Would that not be horrible?"

"And if it were not—"

"That would be more horrible still."

"What then? There is a painted mask upon that wall."

"Friend to you, he would prove a false friend. No, touch . . ."

"What?"

"Touch . . ."

"Yes?"

"The entire palace!"

"Everything? I cannot touch it all at once."

"You did not touch me all at once, but only in a single spot."

"I'll try," she said; and while Harlequin watched, she knelt upon the floor, embraced a column, and blew a kiss to the ceiling.

Nothing occurred.

"I knew it could not be," she said.

"I knew it could." He hung his head.

She took his hand again, and together they wandered down the many and dividing corridors that led to the grave.

"It worked for me," he said.

"I know it did."

And the marble was white no longer, but flushed with rose.

She said, "It would have been a wondrous thing."

"It was, for me." And later, "It will always be."

As their footsteps echoed the ticking of the clocks in the benighted corridors, a new wind fluttered the candle flames and whispered to the dry stones there of rain in spring.

"It was joy even to fancy it," she said, "though it was only for a moment."

"It is true," he told her.

A daisy pushed its golden eye from between two blocks of marble. Harlequin nearly trod on it. "It's true! Amor, you can, you do! You did! Oh, Amor, don't you see? It only took longer because the palace is so huge."

"I do?" she asked. Then whispered, "I *did*." And with trembling hand touched her own heart.

Introduction

Jerry Pournelle

I first met Ted Cogswell at the 1962 World Science Fiction Convention in Chicago. World SF Cons were much smaller affairs in those days; I think there were all of 340 people attending. It was also where I met H. Beam Piper. Both friendships lasted for life.

Came the dawn Ted and I and a dozen others were in Robert Heinlein's penthouse suites in Chicago's Pick-Congress Hotel watching the sun rise over Lake Michigan. In those days science fiction didn't pay very much, and Mr. Heinlein was the only writer who made enough to afford an actual suite. Or maybe he was Guest of Honor and got it free. I can't recall.

Back then Ted was part of a group that included Gordon Dickson, Poul Anderson, and a few others, all devoted to getting together at World Conventions, drinking somewhat too much beer, and singing what they were pleased to call "the Old Songs." I don't know what the membership criteria were: certainly not the ability to carry a tune, since I can't do that, and neither can Poul. (In my case volume makes up for what I lack in tunefulness.) In any event, we became a foursome at SF conventions, or, more likely, a threesome since it wasn't too often that all four of us had enough money at the same time.

When we did get together, one characteristic we all shared was a love for Kipling. We used to recite Kipling poems at each other. We also made up tunes to sing them to;

I still like Poul Anderson's music for "The Legionnaires' Marching Song" better than Leslie Fish's version (*The Undertaker's Horse*, a collection of Kipling poems set to music and performed by Leslie Fish; tape published by Off Centaur).

We also performed some classics. *Die Beiden Grenadieren*, "John Henry", whole rafts of Scots border ballads, "The Ballad of Eskimo Nell" . . . and, of course, "The Friggin' Falcon," which I first heard in Chicago in Robert's suite in 1962, and memorized a couple of years later when I managed to get Ted aside at a convention. I think it cost me two pitchers of beer, and it was worth every dime.

Some years later I was, for my sins, elected to follow Poul Anderson as President of the Science Fiction Writers of America, and I persuaded Ted to publish "The Friggin' Falcon" in the SFWA Forum. Alas, Ted's memory was getting rotten: although he'd written the poem, he'd forgotten some of the lines, and substituted "she knifed him 'till his tripes fell out" for the classic "his smiling face rolled on the floor". There were a few other aberrations. Ted had spent some years in Mexico—where, among other things, he acquired Mrs. George Rae Cogswell, a charming lady just about as strong-willed as he was; the story of how they spent their wedding night in a Mexican jail should I suppose someday be told. Anyway, down there he didn't often get a chance to perform "The Friggin' Falcon," which probably accounts for his memory lapses.

Niven and I later included "The Friggin' Falcon" in *Lucifer's Hammer*: it's the song Harry the Mailman sings as he's trying to let the householders know he's not a burglar. Of course we paid Ted for the right to do that. Not a lot; probably the price of a good dinner, which I hope he enjoyed.

He probably did. He enjoyed darned near everything he did. Herewith, then from Brigadier General Theodore Cogswell, US Podiatric Corps. (Ret.), "The Friggin' Falcon," which may be the only theologically correct scatological ballad ever written.

The Friggin Falcon

THEODORE R. COGSWELL

I was walking out one evening
  By the friggin reservoir,
A-wishing that I had a quid
  To pay my friggin score.
My head it was a-aching
  And my throat was parched and dry,
So I went and sent a little prayer
  A-winging to the sky.

Then there came a friggin falcon
  And he walked upon the waves,
And I said, "A friggin miracle!"
  And sang a couple staves
Of a friggin churchy ballad
  I learned at my mother's knee;
But then the friggin bird took off
  And went and splattered me.

I dropped upon my friggin knees
  And bowed my friggin head
And said three friggin aves
  For all the friggin dead,
And then I rose up to my feet
  And said another ten.
The friggin bird burst into flame
  And shat on me again.

The falcon blazed up in the sky
  Just like a friggin sun
And seared my friggin eyelids shut.
  And when the job was done,
He whooshed across the friggin sky
  Just like a shooting star.
I ran to see the friggin priest;
  He bummed my last cigar.

I showed him where the burning bird
  Had fouled my Sunday clothes
And how its guano crowned my head.
  The bastard held his nose.
So I went to see the bishop,
  But the friggin bishop said,
"Go home and sleep it off, you sod,
  And wash your friggin head."

But I came upon a friggin wake
  For a lousy friggin swine
By the name of Jock O'Leary,
  And I touched his head with mine.
Jock opened up his bleary eyes
  And sat up in his bed.
His wife pulled out a forty-four
  And shot him in the head.

Then I lost my friggin temper
  And let out a friggin yell,
"Blow one more hole in poor old Jock,
  And I'll see you burn in hell!"
She flopped upon her friggin knees
  And started in to pray.
"You sod," says she, "it's forty years
  I've waited for this day."

Now the Good Lord sends his blessings down
  In a friggin curious way,
And when he's marked a man for love,
  That love is there to stay.
But the way you got to use that love

Is a friggin queer affair:
There ain't no point to raising stiffs
And there ain't no point to prayer.

And this I know because I've got
An ever-flowing sign,
For every time I wash my hair
The water turns to wine.
And I give it free to working blokes
To brighten their poor lives
So they don't kick no dogs around
Or beat up on their wives.

For there ain't no point to miracles
Like walking on the sea.
They crucified the Son of God,
But they don't muck with me.
For I leave the friggin blind alone
And the dying and the dead,
But every day at four o'clock
I wash my friggin head.

The Writer as Showman and Bard: A Personal View of Rudyard Kipling

John Brunner

I can't remember my first encounter with Kipling's work, but I suspect it may well have occurred when I discovered *Just So Stories*. Certainly I was delighted with two of them in particular, the pair called "How the First Letter was Written" and "How the Alphabet was Made", and set about inventing alphabets of my own in the margins of my *Mickey Mouse Weekly*. (If this is correct I must have been about six.)

Next? Most likely, I suppose, *The Jungle Book*, though it was much later when I found *The Second Jungle Book*, and for a long time I imagined there were only three Mowgli stories. (Trivia question: there's an extra one that isn't in either of the *Jungle Books*—what's it called?)

By then I was reading whatever I could lay hands on, and because my father and his father before him had amassed a nearly complete set of Kipling, and I had already enjoyed so much of his work, I worked my way through more or less his entire output. Naturally I came across much that I was too young to understand—I especially recall being baffled by *The Naulahka* and "The Light that Failed", and I don't suppose I got the point of "The Brushwood Boy", either—but I was entranced by his vivid descriptions of India, by his talking animals, by the way he breathed life into machines, into steamers and locomotives, and by his ability to make the past seem as real as today, in *Puck of Pook's Hill* and (my favorite) *Rewards and Fairies*.

As for my first reading of "With the Night Mail" . . . !

And the magic still works. Often, when I go back to re-read the work of someone who impressed me mightily when I was a kid, I find there was little substance beneath the veneer of elegant words. Yet only a few months ago I took down from my shelves, one by one, every volume of Kipling that I possess, and read them all again after a lapse of—how long? Twenty years, perhaps, in some cases—and it felt like meeting old and dear friends. Over and over I found myself saying under my breath, "Oh, so *that's* what that story was called!"

Why is his work so durable, when so many of the ideals he admired have been proved hollow, when so many of the dreams and ambitions he celebrated have been tarnished with the passing of the years?

First and foremost, he was a superb and painstaking craftsman. I have often said, and I still believe, he was the most completely equipped writer of short stories ever to tackle that form in the richest of all languages. For the sake of a single project he soaked himself in everything that Chaucer ever wrote until he could compose in Chaucer's own style (this is "Dayspring Mishandled," of course), and not content with that made the resulting pastiche into an acrostic. And who else could have made his readers believe, if only for as long as it takes to read "Proofs of Holy Writ," that Shakespeare and Jonson might have acted as consultants for the King James Bible?

His craftsmanship aside, though, there are two other factors that in my view justify continued admiration. On the one hand, he perfectly understood the show-business adage, "Make 'em laugh, make 'em cry!" He could, and he did. He is often depicted as rather a humorless person, but who could make that absurd mistake after being reduced, as I have been more than once, to helpless laughter by "The Village that Voted the Earth was Flat"? As to crying, surely only a reader with a heart of silicon could fail to be moved by the understated tragedy of "Without

Benefit of Clergy", and by those stories where he trespassed close to sentimentality but with so sure a footing he never crossed its edge, like "The Miracle of Purun Bhagat."

And then, of course, there's his poetry. I read all of that, too, not long ago. (Incidentally, some of it is very funny; I particularly like "Natural Theology.") You know T. S. Eliot was a great admirer of his? At one time almost the only collection of Kipling's verse in print in Britain was one that Eliot insisted on editing for Faber & Faber, of which firm he was a director at the time.

And the word that kept coming into my mind as I turned the 800-plus pages of the definitive edition was *bard*.

My Collins dictionary says: "one of an ancient Celtic order of poets who recited verses about the exploits, often legendary, of their tribes." That's about right, isn't it? That's what Kipling did, not all the time, but pretty often—with the qualification that he didn't confine himself, as might perhaps have been expected, to the exploits of one tribe, to wit the British. He far transcended any such limitation, and I'm not just thinking of minor masterpieces like "Harp Song of the Dane Women." No, I'm thinking of the way he put words into the mouths of monkeys . . . and seals . . . and dogs . . .

And indirectly, as this collection proves, into the minds of fellow writers, long after he himself was dead.

Mowgli

John Brunner

Dr. Corrigan looked up and had the momentary impression that the consulting room was crowded. The new arrival was not quite big enough to have to stoop to miss the ceiling, but it seemed as if he was stooping anyway—bending down to catch the clamor of dwarfs.

He was about six feet seven or eight tall, Dr. Corrigan judged, and probably weighed in the region of three hundred pounds, tidily distributed over a massive frame of bones. Two-octave hands—Dr. Corrigan was an amateur musician and measured hands against an imaginary piano keyboard. Conservatively dressed in a specially tailored suit—well, it would have to be—of dark blue; he would certainly have left an overcoat and hat, and possibly a walking stick, in the anteroom. His face was definitely red-skinned, and the color went well with his shiny black hair. Big Chief——?

"Good morning," said Dr. Corrigan, before his snap judgments ran away with him. "Mr. Norway?"

"Jack Norway—that's right." His voice was bass-baritone and a little hesitant.

"Won't you sit down?"

The stranger gingerly accepted the chair facing the desk, but it was stronger than it looked.

"And what can I do for you?" Dr. Corrigan went on.

The giant shrugged. "I don't know yet," he said, in a voice which held a hint of mockery mingled with desperation. "However, if anyone is in a position to help me, you are. You're about the best psychiatrist in the country."

Dr. Corrigan looked properly modest, but it was no news to him that he was so regarded. "Perhaps you can give me some idea of the nature of the trouble which led you to seek psychiatric advice, then."

"Maybe if I give you the dope about myself you'll get a glimmering. I have a shrewd notion I'm handing you a unique case; if you don't find it so, you've previously discovered, by chance, what I've spent most of my life looking for."

"Very well," Dr. Corrigan agreed. He reached for a fresh note pad and scribbled the name and the date at the top of the first sheet. "Your age, Mr. Norway?"

"Around sixty-five," said the giant dryly. Corrigan's pen stopped halfway down the first digit, and he looked up. That was absurd; the man didn't look older than thirty, at the most. Why, he himself was only fifty-nine.

"Are you sure of that?" he said, a little testily, and knew as he spoke that the question was futile.

"No," said the giant cheerfully. "Only, if I'm not sixty-five, I'm older."

"How is it you don't know, then?"

"No birth certificate, doctor. I was a foundling."

Source of the trouble? Corrigan felt glad that it promised to be so simple. He made a note of the fact and said: "Profession?"

"Mentalist."

"I'm sorry?"

"Mentalist. Faker-fakir. Swami. Medium. Telepath. Take your choice—I've done all of them."

Not so stable a personality, then. "That sounds interesting. What exactly do you do?"

"Comfort distraught old women, mostly. I can assure you it's irrelevant."

Another note. "Your parents would be dead, then, by now?" Corrigan suggested.

"Highly unlikely."

"Oh, come now, Mr. Norway." Corrigan smiled, removed his glasses and polished them. "Surely it's improbable that they would have survived till now if"—he could not help stressing that word slightly—"you are sixty-five."

"I disagree. I have it on the authority of a number of excellent doctors that my physical condition is that of an average man half my age. I expect to live to be over a hundred." He spoke with calm certainty. "Maybe more. I doubt whether such unusual longevity could be other than a strongly inherited characteristic."

Let it ride, decided Dr. Corrigan. However, a number of questions had posed themselves: (a) had he proof of his age or was it a fantasy? (b) if he had proof, how did he look so youthful? (c) what had he in particular which had brought him from the obscurity of anonymous birth to his present obvious affluence, when he could afford to call on the most expensive psychiatric advice?

"I can read minds," said Norway flatly. A tiny gleam of sweat shone on his forehead, as though it had cost him great effort to make the admission. "Before the war, you might have seen me on the halls as Norway the Mysterious; since, you may have run across my name in connection with less—reputable undertakings."

"Really?" said Dr. Corrigan, with professional imperturbability. "Are you reading my mind now?"

"I'll need to get to know you a little better before I can do that. With a stranger, I only get flashes. I think I started to develop the power too late for full effectiveness—as if I had learnt to talk too late and never got it under control."

Dr. Corrigan's agile mind had already mapped out a sequence of investigation. An unusual delusion, true, but almost certainly traceable to obvious causes, and more amenable to confrontation with reality than some. Whether lack of parental background was responsible, or whether it had been adequately replaced by whoever had adopted the foundling, and the cause was to be sought in some other maladjustment such as failure to accept his abnormal physical development, remained to be decided.

"I think I can help you, Mr. Norway," he said smoothly.

"But I haven't told you what I want you to do yet," the giant pointed out. "I have *not* come here to be persuaded that I can't read minds. I may say that the talent has so far earned me some hundreds of thousands—I don't want to throw away my livelihood, do I? In any case, it will present itself as incontrovertible fact soon after you commence analysis. What I want to find out is why the talent isn't any better than it is—whether it would be possible to remove the mental inhibitions which act as a brake on it, or whether the fault lies in the minds of the other people I come across."

Dr. Corrigan was hard put to it not to stare. Norway sounded so completely self-assured. He took out a silver cigarette case to cover the momentary loss of poise and offered it across the desk.

"Thank you, I can't smoke," said the other, shaking his head.

"Do you mind if I do?"

"Not at all."

"You said," Dr. Corrigan realised suddenly, "you *can't* smoke. That's an odd way to put it, isn't it?"

"Not at all. It's true. I'm allergic to one of the constituents of tobacco smoke. I don't know which it is—not the nicotine, one of the tars. I have a number of allergies. Caffeine's another; I can't drink tea or coffee."

Dr. Corrigan applied the flame of his gold and enamel lighter and breathed a delicate puff of grey smoke. "You were a foundling, you say, Mr. Norway. When and where?"

"Sixty-five years and a few months ago. I don't know how old I was at the time. I was found by a Mrs. Norway—courtesy title, if you follow me—in a field. She was with a circus which camped there overnight. She and her man had no children, so they took me in. Mother Norway said she thought I was about eight or ten months old then, but in view of my slow development later, I think I might have been as much as three or four years old."

"Why, precisely?"

"Fact that I didn't walk till I was going on five, and didn't get to talking till I was going on seven. They assumed I was subnormal at first, but I came on fast enough eventually. Mother Norway said it was just as if I simply didn't get the idea—as if I didn't know how to work my vocal cords."

Dr. Corrigan looked Norway straight in the face. "You certainly seem to have got over your early handicap," he suggested with a slight smile.

"Oh, it wasn't a handicap. Just all-round slowness of development. For instance, I didn't reach physical adolescence till I was past twenty; it was less than fifteen years ago that I had to start shaving daily, though the rest of my bodily processes are perfectly normal, thank you."

Dr. Corrigan inscribed a short note on the pad to the effect that Norway's claims were possible but unlikely. He looked up. "You spent your entire childhood with the circus, did you? Not a very settled life, I imagine."

"I got very little education, if that's what you mean. But, of course, it depends on what you mean by childhood. When Pa Norway died, he left me a little money—he was an auguste, incidentally. I left the circus then. I was around twenty, but I looked at least six years younger." He took out a wallet. "This was me then."

He handed over a photograph taken on a beach in summer; either it had been staged, which was ridiculous, or Norway's double had been walking around in about 1912, or his claims were true. Dr. Corrigan remembered the era to which the fashions shown in the picture belonged. His tentative acceptance of Norway's claims regarding himself went up.

"And——?" he prompted.

"I decided to educate myself. I also decided to make a lot of money. I've done both."

"I see. When was it you developed this power to—uh—read minds?"

"I can't put a finger on it. I remember the first time I consciously noticed it. I was about ten. I'd been crying all night with a raging tooth-ache, but there was no sign of a rotten tooth in my jaw. There couldn't very well have been; I'd just lost all my milk teeth, and I never grew a second set. These are false. Well, it turned out that one of the performing dogs who were my special pets among the animals *did* have a bad tooth. The trainer found it and knocked it out, and my pain stopped, too."

This, thought Dr. Corrigan, is going to be a very interesting case, if only for the entertainment value. He tapped ash from his cigarette . "Well, Mr. Norway, I'm willing to undertake full-scale analysis. Do you live in London?"

"The teepee is in Chelsea." Norway gave the address at dictation speed.

"Teepee?" said Dr. Corrigan in a gently inquiring tone, pressing blotting paper down over the words.

"For the benefit of my more gullible clients I am the reincarnation of Chief Standing Horse, a well-known Plains Indian, and, therefore, in constant touch with the spirit world." A humourless smile accompanied the words.

"Amusing." Dr. Corrigan shuffled through his appointment book. "Shall we make the first visit—Tuesday next?"

"Morning, please. I'm busy in the afternoon."

"Ten o'clock." Dr. Corrigan closed the book, and the giant rose and took his leave. The psychiatrist watched him go with a faint lifting of his eyebrows. A *very* interesting case!

Ten a.m. Tuesday; Norway was prompt. Dr. Corrigan gave him a quick white smile and took out his pen as he sat down. "Have you ever taken a word-association test, Mr. Norway?" he inquired. "I like to start an analysis with a few of the standard tests like that, before going on to more direct questioning—just to give me a rough idea of your mental orientation, shall I say?"

Norway shrugged. "I can't vouch for the success of it," he said. "I'm afraid I may start to take the answers you expect from your mind, in which case you'll find evidence for anything you like from an Œdipus complex to racial memory of the amœba stage of evolution."

"We'll take that chance," smiled Corrigan. "Now, if you'll just relax——"

For about five minutes it went very smoothly. Corrigan kept nodding as he received characteristic response patterns for the simpler words, and the outline he had sketched was filled in. Then——

"Life," said Corrigan.

"Long," answered Norway.

"Love."

"Something rather complex—wait a second. Marriage of true minds, that's it."

"Are you married, incidentally, Mr. Norway?"

"Not officially, shall we say? And no children."

Corrigan dismissed it. He resumed: "Home."

"Big."

Unexpected, that. Was it a true subconscious association? Perhaps a baby's view of the comparatively enormous size of a room? "Child."

"Idiot—father—tall—pain—I'm sorry, Dr. Corrigan, but this is getting you nowhere. I had to take those next few words out of your mind because you wouldn't stop poking them at me."

Dr. Corrigan almost gaped. Then he collected himself. Clever noting of the way those key words recurred could account for it, but they were due next, and in that order. He masked his surprise carefully.

"Why did you associate *child* with *idiot?*" he inquired blandly.

"When I was about four or five, it must have been, I overheard my adopted parents quarrelling. Pa Norway said something about her having foisted an idiot on him." He passed his hand across his forehead, puzzled. "I wasn't within earshot," he muttered. "How did I know that? It never struck me before."

The second session. Dr. Corrigan adjusted his spectacles patiently and looked at the length of Norway's massive body stretched out on his couch—fortunately, the couch was *just* long enough. "How far back can you remember, Mr. Norway? Last time you mentioned something which happened when you were four years old. What's the first thing you clearly recollect?"

"Clearly? Well, aside from sort of indefinite memories of warmth and pain and hunger—chiefly hunger; the circus folk weren't all that well off—I guess that would be the earliest."

"You are back then," said Corrigan authoritatively. "You are aged four. Where are you?"

In a caravan—naturally. Indistinct and confused associations of temperature, lighting and smell, especially smell, but whether from that particular episode or from several was uncertain. He narrowed it down to the smell from an animal truck parked nearby. *Idiot* seemed to have importance; it was the key word of the scene. Closer questioning produced—

"Well, I don't really know. Yes, I do at that. Untidiness. That's as near as I can get. What was in Pa Norway's mind was so repulsive, with overtones of mental sloppiness, that I just didn't want to be one. An idiot, I mean. I think I must have started to want to talk then."

"If you couldn't already talk, how did you know the meaning of *idiot?*"

Norway sounded surprised. "Well, isn't it obvious? I must have been trying to make my mind serve instead of my ears up till then. I probably hadn't even been able to distinguish between voices and background noise; I remember being angry and hurt when Mother Norway failed to answer my mental signals of pain and distress when I was very small."

Note: he always refers to his adopted parents with the addition of their surname. Early awareness of difference between himself and them. Classic fantasy? Prince among beggars, waiting for his father, the king, to claim him?

Norway was continuing. "My ears have remained pretty useless. I've been tone-deaf all my life. Just can't enjoy music, though I was surrounded by it all the time at the circus. I went to a dianetic auditor when that was the fad—you remember? The man I tried had got some rather unexpected results. He tried to turn on audio, as they call it, in my memory, but he spent a hundred and thirty hours trying and said in the end that it just wasn't there."

That gave two fruitful lines. It also gave a key to an earlier stage. Armed with his new knowledge of the background, Corrigan began again. This time he started on the "mental signals of distress." How far back did that delusion really go? Wasn't it sure to be rooted in the sense of difference? Compensation for lack of normal hearing?

Fifth session. Very promising. Corrigan leaned back and looked at the ceiling of the room, listening to the fascinating flow of Norway's voice. Even discounting his claim that he had not learnt to speak until he was seven, he had absorbed and retained a fantastic amount of visual and verbal evidence of his early childhood. They were far past the superficialities of environment. Corrigan could have drawn the inside of the Norways' van down to the last pot hanging on the wall; he knew all the various acts and artists who had held jobs with the circus over a period of three years. It had been incongruous at first to hear the memory of a child of four or five discussing the reflexes of animals in terms of human emotion, with an insight which would have done credit to Konrad Lorenz, but he had got used to it.

He threw out something else. The prince-changeling fantasy was obviously there, and very markedly. The sense of being separated from his fellows had been foremost in Norway's mind even at the pre-adolescent stage, and had grown and become more subtle with the years. What was the palace like? Corrigan wanted to know in effect. Had he any recollection of his true origin other than wild imaginings?

"It was a big and shining place," said Norway sleepily. "It went on for ever in all directions, and it lasted for ages."

Corrigan sat up. *What* was that?

But the elusive reference had gone. Norway was helpful, but he was scratching around in a level of his mind which was normally out of reach.

"The shining place?" he repeated thoughtfully. "That's the nearest way I can put it. I've had the concept since I was very small, I'm sure. I must have christened it after I learnt to talk. I remember the dianeticist turned it on in those words, but precisely what it was like I can't recall now. It seemed to be infinite—not just big, but infinite. And all colours! As if—well, as if you could look at white light and see it as white, but also at the same time see it was made up of the colours of the rainbow, with every subtle gradation perfectly clear."

A markedly un-childish idea. A child's idea of grandeur is more usually measured in terms of visible size and tangible wealth. How had that affected his later life? Perhaps there are clues to it in after years. How about his career as a professional mentalist?

Norway was helpful again, but this was ordinary memory, not stimulated submerged recollection. Corrigan listened. The choice of a career had apparently come from his friendship with a conjurer at the circus, whose "magical" powers seemed to have impressed the odd youth greatly.

Oh, it was there, all right. But it wasn't an ordinary version of the fantasy. This had differences as marked as those between other people and Norway's conception of himself.

Seventh session. Now it was plain, Corrigan thought. He waited until Norway had been started off on another mental exploration of the circus as it had been. There were wolves in the menagerie which accompanied the circus; he keyed in a reference to them. The sequence was clear—feral child! Outcast! Superior being struggling to make his way under difficulties through the folkways of a savage species, defeating their manœuvres with ease, achieving what they called success but never fulfilling his own misty idea of his destiny.

It was the deepest and most far-reaching variant of the classic pattern he had ever run across, but now he knew what it was, he could confidently start digging for the cause.

Though it was likely a retarded child in a circus would never have learnt to read in time for the actual *Jungle Book* to have rooted itself in his thoughts, the reference to wolves might establish a conscious connection on a later level of memory. Let the patient cure himself—the most significant concept in all psycho-analysis.

But wolves did not trigger the response. Dr. Corrigan took the slim red-bound volume from his pocket and laid it on the desk, with the embossed design of an elephant's head uppermost. The movement disturbed Norway; he sat up and turned to face the other.

"You think you know!" he said excitedly. "It's right in the front of your mind." He closed his eyes. "In the book? *The Jungle Book*, it's called . . ." He opened his eyes again and smiled. "Oh, not a bad guess, doctor! I haven't read the book, but I get the idea of it."

Dr. Corrigan shrugged. "If you can see my explanation—" he began.

"Why don't I admit that I think of myself as a human being among wolves, and that it's nonsense? Well, I'll admit the first part—and thank you. You've given me the clue I was after. I grew out of that 'fantasy' too long ago to have remembered it for myself. It had gone all misty."

"I'm glad you said that," Dr. Corrigan nodded. "Now, if you'll lie down again, we'll see if we can show you the source of it—"

"The source is in the shining place, Dr. Corrigan. I don't think I could explain what that is, but—well, it's *here*, only it's a long way away unless you can find the right direction to get to it—" Norway was choosing his words with great care, and finding them inadequate.

"Come now, Mr. Norway—"

"I won't need your help much longer. Now I know that much, I can do the rest for myself. Just sit still and I can take what I need from your mind. I can read you pretty thoroughly now I know you about as well as one human being"—the words were flavoured with contempt—"ever can get to know another."

Dr. Corrigan shrugged and made to get out of his chair. Norway stood up, his face menacing. "I said *sit still!*" he thundered from his immense stature, and Dr. Corrigan froze. What—how—*why?* Why this sudden lapse into violence and threats? Premature identification of the psychiatrist with the source of his trouble—?

Norway was watching him. He remained still, not even attempting to reach for the emergency bell on the side of the desk. A sort of cool breeze was running through his brain, and unconsciously he reached up to brush it away.

Perhaps a minute ticked by before Norway threw back his head, a smile of ineffable delight on his face, and *shouted.* His lips were still, and no sound smote Corrigan's ears for all the volume of that enormous cry. It went out to echo and re-echo down the corridors of space-time, a plea without words such as a lost toddler might give to alarm its mother.

It was heard.

* * *

But Mowgli is fiction. There have been children lost, brought up by animals, and found again by their own kind. There have been skinny, dirty, scarred beasts, their elbows calloused from running on all fours, incapable of using their hands except as paws, of learning to talk in a human tongue, of recognising their own kind—and they are the same.

Their "rescuers" have brought them back to waste for a while, refusing to eat cooked meat or to sleep in a bed or to trust a locked door, or to accept the warmth of fire; cringing from those helpful, well-meaning, stupid humans who cannot see that they are not human. They are animals.

The hearer of the cry knew the meaning of mercy; he also knew the limitations of his powers. The mistake had been made too long ago to rectify, except in a single way. He took that course.

With the aftermath of Norway's shout still ringing in his head, Dr. Corrigan felt the room fill with the presence of forces beyond human understanding; he felt his mind stretch like a balloon to contain things it was never meant to contain. He understood for a moment what Norway had meant by the light in the shining place, and covered his eyes.

When he looked again, he saw Jack Norway stiffened to the maximum of his great height, frozen for a timeless second.

Then he relaxed; his limbs folded like a jointed doll, like a child falling asleep. He slid to the floor and lay still. Completely still.

It was over.

Introduction

George R.R. Martin

I first discovered Kipling in the early seventies, when I was living in Chicago and working as a VISTA volunteer. How I managed to avoid him throughout my childhood is hard to say, but I managed it somehow, and I might have kept on managing it if my roommate at the time hadn't just happened to have a paperback copy of *The Jungle Book* lying about.

I certainly would never have sought out Kipling on my own, at least not then. The thing you have to remember is that it was the early seventies, that is to say, the tail end of the sixties, and I was just out of college, a conscientious objector, very much into the antiwar movement and all other movements of the day. I knew a lot about Kipling for someone who'd never read him. I knew that he was racist, sexist, imperialist, in the habit of glorifying war, and all-around politically incorrect.

What I didn't know was what a good writer he was.

That is, I didn't know it until that day I picked up my friend's copy of *The Jungle Book*, out of idle curiosity, and found I couldn't put it down. I'd known that Mowgli was the inspiration for Tarzan, of course, but since I'd always found Burroughs unreadable and Tarzan insipid, that hadn't made much of an impression. Mowgli was a different matter. On the worst day he ever had, Kipling could write rings around E. R. B. and all his like, as I soon discovered.

Mowgli was the start, but soon after I sought out the

poems, the *Just So Stories*, and all the rest, and I'm glad I did. He's still not politically correct, and I don't suppose he ever will be, although I found that most of his supposed sins had been vastly overstated. Like all of us, he was a product of his times, be they the 1890s or the 1960s.

But that's not important. What matters is the work he left behind him, and the work is superb. He knew a lot about humanity, and he could make his words sing.

And my story? I wrote it in 1974, not long after I stumbled over *The Jungle Book*, and it was the title—from what is perhaps my favorite poem in the book—that inspired the story. In a way it's an homage to Kipling; in another, it's an answer. I don't know if Rudyard would have agreed with me, but that's okay. I still don't always agree with him, but his people and places and words still live in my memory and talk to me, and in the end that's what really counts.

And Seven Times Never Kill Man

George R.R. Martin

Ye may kill for yourselves,
and your mates,
and your cubs as they need,
and ye can;

But kill not for pleasure of killing,
and seven times never kill Man!
—Rudyard Kipling.

Outside the walls the Jaenshi children hung, a row of small gray-furred bodies still and motionless at the ends of long ropes. The oldest among them, obviously, had been slaughtered before hanging; here a headless male swung upside down, the noose around the feet, while there dangled the blast-burned carcass of a female. But most of them, the dark hairy infants with the wide golden eyes, most of them had simply been hung. Toward dusk, when the wind came swirling down out of the ragged hills, the bodies of the lighter children would twist at the ends of their ropes and bang against the city walls, as if they were alive and pounding for admission.

But the guards on the walls paid the thumping no mind as they walked their relentless rounds, and the rust-streaked metal gates did not open.

"Do you believe in evil?" Arik neKrol asked Jannis Ryther as they looked down on the City of the Steel

Angels from the crest of a nearby hill. Anger was written across every line of his flat yellow-brown face, as he squatted among the broken shards of what once had been a Jaenshi worship pyramid.

"Evil?" Ryther murmured in a distracted way. Her eyes never left the redstone walls below, where the dark bodies of the children were outlined starkly. The sun was going down, the fat red globe that the Steel Angels called the Heart of Bakkalon, and the valley beneath them seemed to swim in bloody mists.

"Evil," neKrol repeated. The trader was a short, pudgy man, his features decidedly mongoloid except for the flame-red hair that fell nearly to his waist. "It is a religious concept, and I am not a religious man. Long ago, when I was a very child growing up on ai-Emerel, I decided that there was no good or evil, only different ways of thinking." His small, soft hands felt around in the dust until he had a large, jagged shard that filled his fist. He stood and offered it to Ryther. "The Steel Angels have made me believe in evil again," he said.

She took the fragment from him wordlessly and turned it over in her hands. Ryther was much taller than neKrol, and much thinner; a hard bony woman with a long face, short black hair, and eyes without expression. The sweat-stained coveralls she wore hung loosely on her spare frame.

"Interesting," she said finally, after studying the shard for several minutes. It was as hard and smooth as glass, but stronger; colored a translucent red, yet so very dark it was almost black. "A plastic?" she asked, throwing it back to the ground.

NeKrol shrugged. "That was my very guess, but of course it is impossible. The Jaenshi work in bone and wood and sometimes metal, but plastic is centuries beyond them."

"Or behind them," Ryther said. "You say these worship pyramids are scattered all through the forest?"

"Yes, as far as I have ranged. But the Angels have smashed all those close to their valley, to drive the Jaenshi away. As they expand, and they *will* expand, they will smash others."

Ryther nodded. She looked down into the valley again,

and as she did the last sliver of the Heart of Bakkalon slid below the western mountains and the city lights began to come on. The Jaenshi children swung in pools of soft blue illumination, and just above the city gates two stick figures could be seen working. Shortly they heaved something outward, a rope uncoiled, and then another small dark shadow jerked and twitched against the wall. "Why?" Ryther said, in a cool voice, watching.

NeKrol was anything but cool. "The Jaenshi tried to defend one of their pyramids. Spears and knives and rocks against the Steel Angels with lasers and blasters and screechguns. But they caught them unaware, killed a man. The Proctor announced it would not happen again." He spat. "Evil. The children trust them, you see."

"Interesting," Ryther said.

"Can you do anything?" neKrol asked, his voice agitated. "You have your ship, your crew. The Jaenshi need a protector, Jannis. They are helpless before the Angels."

"I have four men in my crew," Ryther said evenly. "Perhaps four hunting lasers as well." That was all the answer she gave.

NeKrol looked at her helplessly. *"Nothing?"*

"Tomorrow, perhaps, the Proctor will call on us. He has surely seen the *Lights* descend. Perhaps the Angels wish to trade. She glanced again into the valley. "Come, Arik, we must go back to your base. The trade goods must be loaded."

Wyatt, Proctor of the Children of Bakkalon on the World of Corlos, was tall and red and skeletal, and the muscles stood out clearly on his bare arms. His blue-black hair was cropped very short, his carriage was stiff and erect. Like all the Steel Angels, he wore a uniform of chameleon cloth (a pale brown now, as he stood in the full light of day on the edge of the small, crude spacefield), a mesh-steel belt with hand-laser and communicator and screechgun, and a stiff red Roman collar. The tiny figurine that hung on a chain about his neck—the pale child Bakkalon, nude and innocent and bright-eyed, but holding a great black sword in one small fist—was the only sign of Wyatt's rank.

Four other Angels stood behind him: two men, two

women, all dressed identically. There was a sameness about their faces, too; the hair always cropped tightly, whether it was blond or red or brown, the eyes alert and cold and a little fanatic, the upright posture that seemed to characterize members of the military-religious sect, the bodies hard and fit. NeKrol, who was soft and slouching and sloppy, disliked everything about the Angels.

Proctor Wyatt had arrived shortly after dawn, sending one of his squad to pound on the door of the small gray prefab bubble that was neKrol's trading base and home. Sleepy and angry, but with a guarded politeness, the trader had risen to greet the Angels, and had escorted them out to the center of the spacefield, where the scarred metal teardrop of the *Lights of Jolostar* squatted on three retractable legs.

The cargo ports were all sealed now; Ryther's crew had spent most of the evening unloading neKrol's trade goods and replacing them in the ship's hold with crates of Jaenshi artifacts that might bring good prices from collectors of extraterrestrial art. No way of knowing until a dealer looked over the goods; Ryther had dropped neKrol only a year ago, and this was the first pickup.

"I am an independent trader, and Arik is my agent on this world," Ryther told the Proctor when she met him on the edge of the field. "You must deal through him."

"I see," Proctor Wyatt said. He still held the list he had offered Ryther, of goods the Angels wanted from the industrialized colonies on Avalon and Jamison's World. "But neKrol will not deal with us."

Ryther looked at him blankly.

"With good reason," neKrol said. "I trade with the Jaenshi, you slaughter them."

The Proctor had spoken to neKrol often in the months since the Steel Angels had established their city-colony, and the talks had all ended in arguments; now he ignored him. "The steps we took were needed," Wyatt said to Ryther. "When an animal kills a man, the animal must be punished, and other animals must see and learn, so that beasts may know that man, the seed of Earth and child of Bakkalon, is the lord and master of them all."

NeKrol snorted. "The Jaenshi are not beasts, Proctor,

they are an intelligent race, with their own religion and art and customs, and they . . ."

Wyatt looked at him. "They have no soul. Only the children of Bakkalon have souls, only the seed of Earth. What mind they may have is relevant only to you, and perhaps them. Soulless, they are beasts."

"Arik has shown me the worship pyramids they build," Ryther said. "Surely creatures that build such shrines must have souls."

The Proctor shook his head. "You are in error in your belief. It is written clearly in the Book. We, the seed of Earth, are truly the children of Bakkalon, and no others. The rest are animals, and in Bakkalon's name we must assert our dominion over them."

"Very well," Ryther said. "But you will have to assert your dominion without aid from the *Lights of Jolostar*, I'm afraid. And I must inform you, Proctor, that I find your actions seriously disturbing, and intend to report them when I return to Jamison's World."

"I expected no less," Wyatt said. "Perhaps by next year you will burn with love of Bakkalon, and we may talk again. Until then, the world of Corlos will survive." He saluted her, and walked briskly from the field, followed by the four Steel Angels.

"What good will it do to report them?" neKrol said bitterly, after they had gone.

"None," Ryther said, looking off toward the forest. The wind was kicking up the dust around her, and her shoulders slumped, as if she were very tired. "The Jamies won't care, and if they did, what could they do?"

NeKrol remembered the heavy red-bound book that Wyatt had given him months ago. "And Bakkalon the pale child fashioned his children out of steel," he quoted, "for the stars will break those of softer flesh. And in the hand of each new-made infant He placed a beaten sword, telling them, 'This is the Truth and the Way.' " He spat in disgust. "That is their very creed. And we can do nothing?"

Her face was empty of expression now. "I will leave you two lasers. In a year, make sure the Jaenshi know how to use them. I believe I know what sort of trade goods I should bring."

* * *

The Jaenshi lived in clans (as neKrol thought of them) of twenty to thirty, each clan divided equally between adults and children, each having its own home-forest and worship pyramid. They did not build; they slept curled up in trees around their pyramid. For food, they foraged; juicy blue-black fruits grew everywhere, and there were three varieties of edible berries, a hallucinogenic leaf, and a soapy yellow root the Jaenshi dug for. NeKrol had found them to be hunters, as well, though infrequently. A clan would go for months without meat, while the snuffling brown bushogs multiplied all around them, digging up roots and playing with the children. Then suddenly, when the bushog population had reached some critical point, the Jaenshi spearmen would walk among them calmly, killing two out of every three, and that week great hog roasts would be held each night around the pyramid. Similar patterns could be discerned with the white-bodied tree slugs that sometimes covered the fruit trees like a plague, until the Jaenshi gathered them for a stew, and with the fruit-stealing pseudomonks that haunted the higher limbs.

So far as neKrol could tell, there were no predators in the forests of the Jaenshi. In his early months on their world, he had worn a long force-knife and a hand-laser as he walked from pyramid to pyramid on his trade route. But he had never encountered anything even remotely hostile, and now the knife lay broken in his kitchen, while the laser was long lost.

The day after the *Lights of Jolostar* departed, neKrol went armed into the forest again, with one of Ryther's hunting lasers slung over his shoulder.

Less than two kilometers from his base, neKrol found the camp of the Jaenshi he called the waterfall folk. They lived up against the side of a heavily-wooded hill, where a stream of tumbling blue-white water came sliding and bouncing down, dividing and rejoining itself over and over, so the whole hillside was an intricate glittering web of waterfalls and rapids and shallow pools and spraying wet curtains. The clan's worship pyramid sat in the bottommost pool, on a flat gray stone in the middle of the eddies; taller than most Jaenshi, coming up to neKrol's chin, looking infinitely heavy and solid and immovable, a three-sided block of dark, dark red.

NeKrol was not fooled; he had seen other pyramids sliced to pieces by the lasers of the Steel Angels and shattered by the flames of their blasters; whatever powers the pyramids might have in Jaenshi myth, whatever mysteries might lie behind their origin, it was not enough to stay the swords of Bakkalon.

The glade around the pyramid-pool was alive with sunlight when NeKrol entered, and the long grasses swayed in the light breeze, but most of the waterfall folk were elsewhere. In the trees perhaps, climbing and coupling and pulling down fruits, or ranging through the forests on their hill. The trader found only a few small children riding on a bushog in the clearing when he arrived. He sat down to wait, warm in the sunlight.

Soon the old talker appeared.

He sat down next to neKrol, a tiny shriveled Jaenshi with only a few patches of dirty gray-white fur left to hide the wrinkles in his skin. He was toothless, clawless, feeble; but his eyes, wide and golden and pupilless as those of any Jaenshi, were still alert, alive. He was the talker of the waterfall folk, the one in closest communion with the worship pyramid. Every clan had a talker.

"I have something new to trade," neKrol said, in the soft slurred speech of the Jaenshi. He had learned the tongue before coming here, back on Avalon. Tomas Chung, the legendary Avalonian linguist, had broken it centuries before, when the Kleronomas Survey brushed by this world. No other human had visited the Jaenshi since, but the maps of Kleronomas and Chung's language-pattern analysis both remained alive in the computers at the Avalon Institute for the Study of Non-Human Intelligence.

"We have made you more statues, have fashioned new woods," the older talker said. "What have you brought? Salt?"

NeKrol undid his knapsack, laid it out, and opened it. He took out one of the bricks of salt he carried, and laid it before the old talker. "Salt," he said. "And more." He laid the hunting rifle before the Jaenshi.

"What is this?" the old talker asked.

"Do you know of the Steel Angels?" neKrol asked.

The other nodded, a gesture neKrol had taught him. "The godless who run from the dead valley speak of them. They are the ones who make the gods grow silent, the pyramid breakers."

"This is a tool like the Steel Angels use to break your pyramids," neKrol said. "I am offering it to you in trade."

The old talker sat very still. "But we do not wish to break pyramids," he said.

"This tool can be used for other things," neKrol said. "In time, the Steel Angels may come here, to break the pyramid of the waterfall folk. If by then you have tools like this, you can stop them. The people of the pyramid in the ring-of-stone tried to stop the Steel Angels with spears and knives, and now they are scattered and wild and their children hang dead from the walls of the City of the Steel Angels. Other clans of the Jaenshi were unresisting, yet now they too are godless and landless. The time will come when the waterfall folk will need this tool, old talker."

The Jaenshi elder lifted the laser and turned it curiously in his small withered hands. "We must pray on this," he said. "Stay, Arik. Tonight we shall tell you, when the god looks down on us. Until then, we shall trade." He rose abruptly, gave a swift glance at the pyramid across the pool, and faded into the forest, still holding the laser.

NeKrol sighed. He had a long wait before him; the prayer assemblies never came until sundown. He moved to the edge of the pool and unlaced his heavy boots to soak his sweaty, calloused feet in the crisp cold waters.

When he looked up, the first of the carvers had arrived; a lithe young Jaenshi female with a touch of auburn in her body fur. Silent (they were all silent in neKrol's presence, all save the talker), she offered him her work.

It was a statuette no larger than his fist, a heavy-breasted fertility goddess fashioned out of the fragrant, thin-veined blue wood of the fruit trees. She sat cross-legged on a triangular base, and three thin slivers of bone rose from each corner of the triangle to meet above her head in a blob of clay.

NeKrol took the carving, turned it this way and that, and nodded his approval. The Jaenshi smiled and vanished, taking the salt brick with her. Long after she was gone, neKrol continued to admire his acquisition. He had traded all his life, spending ten years among the squid-faced gethsoids of Aath and four with the stick-thin Fyndii, traveling a trader's circuit to a half-dozen stone age planets that had once been slaveworlds of the broken Hrangan Empire; but nowhere had he found artists like the Jaenshi. Not for the first time, he wondered why neither Kleronomas nor Chung had mentioned the native carvings. He was glad they hadn't, though, and fairly certain that once the dealers saw the crates of wooden gods he had sent back with Ryther, the world would be overrun by traders. As it was, he had been sent here entirely on speculation, in hopes of finding a Jaenshi drug or herb or liquor that might move well in stellar trade. Instead he'd found the art, like an answer to a prayer.

Other workmen came and went as the morning turned to afternoon and the afternoon to dusk, setting their craft before him. He looked over each piece carefully, taking some and declining others, paying for what he took in salt. Before full darkness had descended, a small pile of goods sat by his right hand; a matched set of redstone knives, a gray deathcloth woven from the fur of an elderly Jaenshi by his widow and friends (with his face wrought upon it in the silky golden hairs of a pseudomonk), a bone spear with tracings that reminded neKrol of the runes of Old Earth legend; and statues. The statues were his favorites, always; so often alien art was alien beyond comprehension, but the Jaenshi workmen touched emotional chords in him. The gods they carved, each sitting in a bone pyramid, wore Jaenshi faces, yet at the same time seemed archetypically human: stern-faced war gods, things that looked oddly like satyrs, fertility goddesses like the one he had bought, almost-manlike warriors and nymphs. Often neKrol had wished that he had a formal education in extee anthropology, so that he might write a book on the universals of myth. The Jaenshi surely had a rich mythology, though the talkers never spoke of it; nothing else could explain the carvings. Perhaps the old gods were no longer worshipped, but they were still remembered.

By the time the Heart of Bakkalon went down and the

last reddish rays ceased to filter through the looming trees, neKrol had gathered as much as he could carry, and his salt was all but exhausted. He laced up his boots again, packed his acquisitions with painstaking care, and sat patiently in the poolside grass, waiting. One by one, the waterfall folk joined him. Finally the old talker returned.

The prayers began.

The old talker, with the laser still in his hand, waded carefully across the night-dark waters, to squat by the black bulk of the pyramid. The others, adults and children together, now some forty strong, chose spots in the grass near the banks, behind neKrol and around him. Like him, they looked out over the pool, at the pyramid and the talker outlined clearly in the light of a new-risen, oversized moon. Setting the laser down on the stone, the old talker pressed both palms flat against the side of the pyramid, and his body seemed to go stiff, while all the other Jaenshi also tensed and grew very quiet.

NeKrol shifted restlessly and fought a yawn. It was not the first time he'd sat through a prayer ritual, and he knew the routine. A good hour of boredom lay before him; the Jaenshi did silent worship, and there was nothing to be heard but their steady breathing, nothing to be seen but forty impassive faces. Sighing, the trader tried to relax, closing his eyes and concentrating on the soft grass beneath him and the warm breeze that tossed his wild mane of hair. Here, briefly, he found peace. How long would it last, he mused, should the Steel Angels leave their valley . . .

The hour passed, but neKrol, lost in meditation, scarce felt the flow of time. Until suddenly he heard the rustlings and chatter around him, as the waterfall folk rose and went back into the forest. And then the old talker stood in front of him, and laid the laser at his feet.

"No," he said simply.

NeKrol started. "What?" But you *must*. Let me show you what it can do . . ."

"I have had a vision, Arik. The god has shown me. But also he has shown me that it would not be a good thing to take this in trade."

"Old talker, the Steel Angels will come . . ."

"If they come, our god shall speak to them," The Jaenshi

elder said, in his purring speech, but there was finality in the gentle voice, and no appeal in the vast liquid eyes.

"For our food, we thank ourselves, none other. It is ours because we worked for it, ours because we fought for it, ours by the only right that is: the right of the strong. But for that strength—for the might of our arms and the steel of our swords and the fire in our hearts—we thank Bakkalon, the pale child, who gave us life and taught us how to keep it."

The Proctor stood stiffly at the centermost of the five long wooden tables that stretched the length of the great mess hall, pronouncing each word of the grace with solemn dignity. His large veined hands pressed tightly together as he spoke, against the flat of the upward-jutting sword, and the dim lights had faded his uniform to an almost-black. Around him, the Steel Angels sat at attention, their food untouched before them; fat boiled tubers, steaming chunks of bushog meat, black bread, bowls of crunchy green neograss. Children below the fighting age of ten, in smocks of starchy white and the omnipresent mesh-steel belts, filled the two outermost tables beneath the slit-like windows; toddlers struggled to sit still under the watchful eyes of stern nine-year-old houseparents with hardwood batons in their belts. Further in, the fighting brotherhood sat, fully armed, at two equally long tables, men and women alternating, leather-skinned veterans sitting next to ten-year-olds who had barely moved from the children's dorm to the barracks. All of them wore the same chameleon cloth as Wyatt, though without his collar, and a few had buttons of rank. The center table, less than half the length of the others, held the cadre of the Steel Angels; the squadfathers and squadmothers, the weapons-masters, the healers, the four fieldbishops, all those who wore the high, stiff crimson collar. And the Proctor, at its head.

"Let us eat," Wyatt said at last. His sword moved above his table with a whoosh, describing the slash of blessing, and he sat to his meal. The Proctor, like all the others, had stood single-file in the line that wound past the kitchen to the mess hall, and his portions were no larger than the least of the brotherhood.

There was a clink of knives and forks, and the infrequent clatter of a plate, and from time to time the thwack of a baton, as a houseparent punished some transgression of discipline by one of his charges; other than that, the hall was silent. The Steel Angels did not speak at meals, but rather meditated on the lessons of the day as they consumed their spartan fare.

Afterwards, the children—still silent—marched out of the hall, back to their dormitory. The fighting brotherhood followed, some to chapel, most to the barracks, a few to guard duty on the walls. The men they were relieving would find late meals still warm in the kitchen.

The officer core remained; after the plates were cleared away, the meal became a staff meeting.

"At ease," Wyatt said, but the figures along the table relaxed little, if at all. Relaxation had been bred out of them by now. The Proctor found one of them with his eyes. "Dhallis," he said, "you have the report I requested?"

Fieldbishop Dhallis nodded. She was a husky middle-aged woman with thick muscles and skin the color of brown leather. On her collar was a small steel insignia, an ornamental memory-chip that meant Computer Services. "Yes, Proctor," she said, in a hard, precise voice. "Jamison's World is a fourth-generation colony, settled mostly from Old Poseidon. One large continent, almost entirely unexplored, and more than twelve thousand islands of various sizes. The human population is concentrated almost entirely on the islands, and makes its living by farming sea and land, aquatic husbandry, and heavy industry. The oceans are rich in food and metal. The total population is about seventy-nine million. There are two large cities, both with spaceports: Port Jamison and Jolostar." She looked down at the computer printout on the table. "Jamison's World was not even charted at the time of the Double War. It has never known military action, and the only Jamie armed forces are their planetary police. It has no colonial program and has never attempted to claim political jurisdiction beyond its own atmosphere."

The Proctor nodded. "Excellent. Then the trader's threat

to report us is essentially an empty one. We can proceed. Squadfather Walman?"

"Four Jaenshi were taken today, Proctor, and are now on the walls," Walman reported. He was a ruddy young man with a blond crewcut and large ears. "If I might, sir, I would request discussion of possible termination of the campaign. Each day we search harder for less. We have virtually wiped out every Jaenshi youngling of the clans who originally inhabited Sword Valley."

Wyatt nodded. "Other opinions?"

Fieldbishop Lyon, blue-eyed and gaunt, indicated dissent. "The adults remain alive. The mature beast is more dangerous than the youngling, Squadfather."

"Not in this case," Weaponsmaster C'ara DaHan said. DaHan was a giant of a man, bald and bronze-colored, the chief of Psychological Weaponry and Enemy Intelligence. "Our studies show that, once the pyramid is destroyed, neither full-grown Jaenshi nor the immature pose any threat whatsoever to the children of Bakkalon. Their social structure virtually disintegrates. The adults either flee, hoping to join some other clan, or revert to near-animal savagery. They abandon the younglings, most of whom fend for themselves, in a confused sort of way and offer no resistance when we take them. Considering the number of Jaenshi on our walls, and those reported slain by predators or each other, I strongly feel that Sword Valley is virtually clean of the animals. Winter is coming, Proctor, and much must be done. Squadfather Walman and his men should be set to other tasks."

There was more discussion, but the tone had been set; most of the speakers backed DaHan. Wyatt listened carefully, and all the while prayed to Bakkalon for guidance. Finally he motioned for quiet.

"Squadfather," he said to Walman, "tomorrow collect all the Jaenshi—both adults and children—that you can, but do not hang them if they are unresisting. Instead, take them to the city, and show them their clanmates on our walls. Then cast them from the valley, one in each direction of the compass." He bowed his head. "It is my hope that they will carry a message, to all the Jaenshi, of the price that must be paid when a beast raises hand or claw or blade against the seed of Earth. Then, when the spring comes and the children of Bakkalon move beyond Sword Valley, the Jaenshi will peacefully abandon their pyramids and quit whatever lands men may require, so the glory of the pale child might be spread."

Lyon and DaHan both nodded, among others. "Speak wisdom to us," Fieldbishop Dhallis said then.

Proctor Wyatt agreed. One of the lesser-ranking squad-mothers brought him the Book, and he opened it to the Chapter of Teachings.

"In those days much evil had come upon the seed of Earth," the Proctor read, "for the children of Bakkalon had abandoned Him to bow to softer gods. So their skies grew dark and upon them from above came the Sons of Hranga with red eyes and demon teeth, and upon them from below came the vast Horde of Fyndii like a cloud of locusts that blotted out the stars. And the worlds flamed, and the children cried out, 'Save us! Save us!'

"And the pale child came and stood before them, with His great sword in His hand, and in a voice like thunder He rebuked them. 'You have been weak children,' He told them, 'for you have disobeyed. Where are your swords? Did I not set swords in your hands?

"And the children cried out, 'We have beaten them into plowshares, oh Bakkalon!'

"And He was sore angry. 'With plowshares, then, shall you face the Sons of Hranga! With plowshares shall you slay the Horde of Fyndii!" And He left them, and heard no more their weeping, for the Heart of Bakkalon is a Heart of Fire.

"But then one among the seed of Earth dried his tears, for the skies did burn so bright that they ran scalding on his cheeks. And the bloodlust rose in him and he beat his plowshare back into a sword, and charged the Sons of Hranga, slaying as he went. Then others saw, and followed, and a great battle-cry rang across the worlds.

"And the pale child heard, and came again, for the sound of battle is more pleasing to his ears than the sound of wails. And when He saw, He smiled. 'Now you are my children again,' He said to the seed of Earth. 'For you had turned against me to worship a god who calls himself a lamb, but did you not know that lambs go only to the slaughter? Yet now your eyes have cleared, and again you are the Wolves of God!'

"And Bakkalon gave them all swords again, all His children and all the seed of Earth, and He lifted his great black blade, the Demon-Reaver that slays the soulless, and swung it. And the Sons of Hranga fell before His might, and the great Horde that was the Fyndii burned beneath His gaze. And the children of Bakkalon swept across the worlds."

The Proctor lifted his eyes. "Go, my brothers-in-arms, and think on the Teachings of Bakkalon as you sleep. May the pale child grant you visions!"

They were dismissed.

The trees on the hill were bare and glazed with ice, and the snow—unbroken except for their footsteps and the stirrings of the bitter-sharp north wind—gleamed a blinding white in the noon sun. In the valley beneath, the City of the Steel Angels looked preternaturally clean and still. Great snowdrifts had piled against the eastern walls, climbing halfway up the stark scarlet stone; the gates had not opened in months. Long ago, the children of Bakkalon had taken their harvest and fallen back inside the city, to huddle around their fires. But for the blue lights that burned late into the cold black night, and the occasional guard pacing atop the walls, neKrol would hardly have known that the Angels still lived.

The Jaenshi that neKrol had come to think of as the bitter speaker looked at him out of eyes curiously darker than the soft gold of her brothers. "Below the snow, the god lies broken," she said, and even the soothing tones of the Jaenshi tongue could not hide the hardness in her voice. They stood at the very spot where neKrol had once taken Ryther, the spot where the pyramid of the people of the ring-of-stone once stood. NeKrol was sheathed head to foot in a white thermosuit that clung too tightly, accenting every unsightly bulge. He looked out on Sword Valley from behind a dark blue plastifilm in the suit's cowl. But the Jaenshi, the bitter speaker, was nude, covered only by the thick gray fur of her winter coat. The strap of the hunting laser ran down between her breasts.

"Other gods beside yours will break unless the Steel Angels are stopped," neKrol said, shivering despite his thermosuit.

The bitter speaker seemed hardly to hear. "I was a child when they came, Arik. If they had left our god, I might be a child still. Afterwards, when the light went out and the glow inside me died, I wandered far from the ring-of-stone, beyond our own home forest, knowing nothing, eating where I could. Things are not the same in the dark valley. Bushogs honked at my passing, and charged me with their tusks, other Jaenshi threatened me and each other. I did not understand and I could not pray. Even when the Steel Angels found me, I did not understand, and I went with them to their city, knowing nothing of their speech. I remember the walls, and the children, many so much younger than me. Then I screamed and struggled; when I saw those on the ropes, something wild and godless stirred to life inside me." Her eyes regarded him, her eyes like burnished bronze. She shifted in the ankle-deep snow, curling a clawed hand around the strap of her laser.

NeKrol had taught her well since the day she had joined him, in the late summer when the Steel Angels had cast her from Sword Valley. The bitter speaker was by far the best shot of his six, the godless exiles he had gathered to him and trained. It was the only way; he had offered the lasers in trade to clan after clan, and each had refused. The Jaenshi were certain that their gods would protect them. Only the godless listened, and not all of them; many—the young children, the quiet ones, the first to flee—many had been accepted into other clans. But others, like the bitter speaker, had grown too savage, had seen too much; they fit no longer. She had been the first to take the weapon, after the old talker had sent her away from the waterfall folk.

"It is often better to be without gods," neKrol told her. "Those below us have a god, and it has made them what they are. And so the Jaenshi have gods, and because they trust, they die. You godless are their only hope."

The bitter speaker did not answer. She only looked down on the silent city, besieged by snow, and her eyes smoldered.

And neKrol watched her, and wondered. He and his six were the hope of the Jaenshi, he had said; if so, was there hope at all? The bitter speaker, and all his exiles, had a madness about them, a rage that made him tremble. Even if Ryther came with the lasers, even if so small a group could stop the Angels' march, even if all that came to pass—what then? Should all the Angels die tomorrow, where would his godless find a place?

They stood, all quiet, while the snow stirred under their feet and the north wind bit at them.

The chapel was dark and quiet. Flameglobes burned a dim, eerie red in either corner, and the rows of plain wooden benches were empty. Above the heavy altar, a slab of rough black stone, Bakkalon stood in holograph, so real he almost breathed; a boy, a mere boy, naked and milky white, with the wide eyes and blond hair of innocent youth. In his hand, half again taller than himself, was the great black sword.

Wyatt knelt before the projection, head bowed and very still. All through the winter his dreams had been dark and troubled, so each day he would kneel and pray for guidance. There was none else to seek but Bakkalon; he, Wyatt, was the Proctor, who led in battle and in faith. He alone must riddle his visions.

So daily he wrestled with his thoughts, until the snows began to melt and the knees of his uniform had nearly worn through from long scraping on the floor. Finally, he had decided, and this day he had called upon the senior collars to join him in the chapel.

Alone they entered, while the Proctor knelt unmoving, and chose seats on the benches behind him, each apart from his fellows. Wyatt took no notice; he prayed only that his words would be correct, his vision true. When they were all there, he stood and turned to face them.

"Many are the worlds on which the children of Bakkalon have lived," he told them, "but none so blessed as this, our Corlos. A great time is on us, my brothers-in-arms.

The pale child has come to me in my sleep, as once he came to the first Proctors in the years when the brotherhood was forged. He has given me visions."

They were quiet, all of them, their eyes humble and obedient; he was their Proctor, after all. There could be no questioning when one of higher rank spoke wisdom or gave orders. That was one of the precepts of Bakkalon, that the chain of command was sacred and never to be doubted. So all of them kept silence.

"Bakkalon Himself has walked upon this world. He has walked among the soulless and the beasts of the field and told them our dominion, and this he has said to me: that when the spring comes and the seed of Earth moves from Sword Valley to take new land, all the animals shall know their place and retire before us. This I do prophesy!

"More, we shall see miracles. That too the pale child has promised me, signs by which we will know His truth, signs that shall bolster our faith with new revelation. But so too shall our faith be tested, for it will be a time of sacrifices, and Bakkalon will call upon us more than once to show our trust in Him. We must remember His Teachings and be true, and each of us must obey Him as a child obeys the parent and a fighting man his officer: that is, swiftly and without question. For the pale child knows best.

"These are the visions He has granted me, these are the dreams that I have dreamed. Brothers, pray with me."

And Wyatt turned again and knelt, and the rest knelt with him, and all the heads were bowed in prayer save one. In the shadows at the rear of the chapel where the flameglobes flickered but dimly, C'ara DaHan stared at his Proctor from beneath a heavy beetled brow.

That night, after a silent meal in the mess hall and a short staff meeting, the Weaponsmaster called upon Wyatt to go walking on the walls. "Proctor, my soul is troubled." he told him. "I must have counsel from he who is closest to Bakkalon." Wyatt nodded, and both donned heavy nightcloaks of black fur and oil-dark metal cloth, and together they walked the red-stone parapets beneath the stars.

Near the guardhouse that stood above the city gates,

DaHan paused and leaned out over the ledge, his eyes searching the slow-melting snow for long moments before he turned them on the Proctor. "Wyatt," he said at last, "my faith is weak."

The Proctor said nothing, merely watched the other, his face concealed by the hood of his nightcloak. Confession was not a part of the rites of the Steel Angels; Bakkalon had said that a fighting man's faith ought never to waver.

"In the old days," C'ara DaHan was saying, "many weapons were used against the children of Bakkalon. Some, today, exist only in tales. Perhaps they never existed. Perhaps they are empty things, like the gods the soft men worship. I am only a Weaponsmaster; such knowledge is not mine.

"Yet there is a tale, my Proctor—one that troubles me. Once, it is said, in the long centuries of war, the Sons of Hranga loosed upon the seed of Earth foul vampires of the mind, the creatures men called soul-feeds. Their touch was invisible, but it crept across kilometers, farther than a man could see, farther than a laser could fire, and it brought madness. Visions, my Proctor, visions! False gods and foolish plans were put in the minds of men, and . . ."

"Silence." Wyatt said. His voice was hard, as cold as the night air that crackled around them and turned his breath to steam.

There was a long pause. Then, in a softer voice, the Proctor continued. "All winter I have prayed, DaHan, and struggled with my visions. I am the Proctor of the Children of Bakkalon on the World of Corlos, not some new-armed child to be lied to by false gods. I spoke only after I was sure. I spoke as your Proctor, as your father in faith and your commanding officer. That you would question me, Weaponsmaster, that you would doubt—this disturbs me greatly. Next will you stop to argue with me on the field of battle, to dispute some fine point of my orders?"

"Never, Proctor," DaHan said, kneeling in penance in the packed snow atop the walkway.

"I hope not. But, before I dismiss you, because you are my brother in Bakkalon, I will answer you, though I need not and it was wrong of you to expect it. I will tell you this; the Proctor Wyatt is good officer as well as a devout man. The pale child has made prophecies to me, and has predicted that miracles will come to pass. All these things we shall see with our very eyes. But if the prophecies should fail us, and if no signs appear, well, our eyes will see that too. And then I will know that it was not Bakkalon who sent the visions, but only a false god, perhaps a soul-feed of Hranga. Or do you think a Hrangan can work miracles?"

"No," DaHan said, still on his knees, his great bald head downcast. "That would be heresy."

"Indeed, said Wyatt. The Proctor glanced briefly beyond the walls. The night was crisp and cold and there was no moon. He felt transfigured, and even the stars seemed to cry the glory of the pale child, for the constellation of the Sword was high upon the zenith, the Soldier reaching up toward it from where he stood on the horizon.

"Tonight you will walk guard without your cloak," the Proctor told DaHan when he looked down again. "And should the north wind blow and the cold bite at you, you will rejoice in the pain, for it will be a sign that you submit to your Proctor and your god. As your flesh grows bitter numb, the flame in your heart must burn hotter."

"Yes, my Proctor," DaHan said. He stood and removed his night-cloak, handing it to the other. Wyatt gave him the slash of blessing.

On the wallscreen in his darkened living quarters the taped drama went through its familiar measured paces, but neKrol, slouched in a large cushioned recliner with his eyes half-closed, hardly noticed. The bitter speaker and two of the other Jaenshi exiles sat on the floor, golden eyes rapt on the spectacle of humans chasing and shooting each other amid the vaulting tower cities of ai-Emerel; increasingly they had begun to grow curious about other worlds and other ways of life. It was all very strange, neKrol thought; the waterfall folk and the other clanned Jaenshi had never shown any such interest. He remembered the early days, before the coming of the Steel Angels in their ancient and soon-to-be-dismantled warship, when he had set all kinds of trade goods before the Jaenshi talkers; bright bolts of glittersilk from Avalon, glowstone jewelry from High Kavalaan, duralloy knives and solar generators and steel powerbows, books from a dozen worlds, medicines and wines—he had come with a little of everything. The talkers took some of it, from time to time, but never with any enthusiasm; the only offering that excited them was salt.

It was not until the spring rains came and the bitter speaker began to question him that neKrol realized, with a start, how seldom any of the Jaenshi clans had ever asked him *anything*. Perhaps their social structure and their religion stifled their natural intellectual curiosity. The exiles were certainly eager enough, especially the bitter speaker. NeKrol could answer only a small portion of her questions of late, and even then she always had new ones to puzzle him with. He had begun to grow appalled with the extent of his own ignorance.

But then, so had the bitter speaker; unlike the clanned Jaenshi—did the religion make *that* much difference?—she would answer questions as well, and neKrol had tried quizzing her on many things that he'd wondered at. But most of the time she would only blink in bafflement, and begin to question herself.

"There are no stories about our gods," she said to him once, when he'd tried to learn a little of Jaenshi myth. "What sort of stories could there be? The gods live in the worship pyramids, Arik, and we pray to them and they watch over us and light our lives. They do not bounce around and fight and break each other like your gods seem to do."

"But you had other gods once, before you came to worship the pyramids," neKrol objected. "The very ones your carvers did for me." He had even gone so far as to unpack a crate and show her, though surely she remembered, since the people of the pyramid in the ring-of-stone had been among the finest craftsmen.

Yet the bitter speaker only smoothed her fur, and shook her head. "I was too young to be a carver, so perhaps I was not told," she said. "We all know that which we need to know, but only the carvers need to do these things, so perhaps only they know the stories of these old gods."

Another time he had asked her about the pyramids, and

had gotten even less. "Build them?" she had said. "We did not build them, Arik. They have always been, like the rocks and the trees." But then she blinked. "But they are *not* like the rocks and the trees, are they?" And, puzzled, she went away to talk to the others.

But if the godless Jaenshi were more thoughtful than their brothers in the clans, they were also more difficult, and each day neKrol realized more and more the futility of their enterprise. He had eight of the exiles with him now—they had found two more, half dead from starvation, in the height of winter—and they all took turns training with the two lasers and spying on the Angels. But even should Ryther return with the weaponry, their force was a joke against the might the Proctor could put in the field. The *Lights of Jolostar* would be carrying a full arms shipment in the expectation that every clan for a hundred kilometers would now be roused and angry, ready to resist the Steel Angels and overwhelm them by sheer force of numbers; Jannis would be blank-faced when only neKrol and his ragged band appeared to greet her.

If in fact they did. Even that was problematical; he was having much difficulty keeping his guerrillas together. Their hatred of the Steel Angels still bordered madness, but they were far from a cohesive unit. None of them liked to take orders very well, and they fought constantly, going at each other with bared claws in struggles for social dominance. If neKrol had not warned them, he suspected they might even duel with the lasers. As for staying in good fighting shape, that too was a joke. Of the three females in the band, the bitter speaker was the only one who had not allowed herself to be impregnated. Since the Jaenshi usually gave birth in litters of four to eight, neKrol calculated that late summer would present them with an exile population explosion. And there would be more after that, he knew; the godless seemed to copulate almost hourly, and there was no such thing as Jaenshi birth control. He wondered how the clans kept their population so stable, but his charges didn't know that either.

"I suppose we sexed less," the bitter speaker said when he asked her, "but I was a child, so I would not really know. Before I came here, there was never the urge. I was just young, I would think." But when she said it, she scratched herself and seemed very unsure.

Sighing, neKrol eased himself back in the recliner and tried to shut out the noise of the wallscreen. It was all going to be very difficult. Already the Steel Angels had emerged from behind their walls, and the powerwagons rolled up and down Sword Valley turning forest into farmland. He had gone up into the hills himself, and it was easy to see that the spring planting would soon be done. Then, he suspected, the children of Bakkalon would try to expand. Just last week one of them—a giant "with no head fur," as his scout had described him—was seen up in the ring-of-stone, gathering shards from the broken pyramid. Whatever that meant, it could not be for the good.

Sometimes he felt sick at the forces he had set in motion, and almost wished that Ryther would forget the lasers. The bitter speaker was determined to strike as soon as they were armed, no matter what the odds. Frightened, neKrol reminded her of the hard Angel lesson the last time a Jaenshi had killed a man; in his dreams he still saw children on the walls.

But she only looked at him, with the bronze tinge of madness in her eyes, and said, "Yes, Arik. I remember."

Silent and efficient, the white-smocked kitchen boys cleared away the last of the evening's dishes and vanished. "At ease," Wyatt said to his officers. Then: "The time of miracles is upon us, as the pale child foretold.

"This morning I sent three squads into the hills to the southeast of Sword Valley, to disperse the Jaenshi clans on lands that we require. They reported back to me in early afternoon, and now I wish to share their reports with you. Squadmother Jolip, will you relate the events that transpired when you carried out your orders?"

"Yes, Proctor." Jolip stood, a white-skinned blond with a pinched face, her uniform hanging slightly loose on a lean body. "I was assigned a squad of ten to clear out the so-called cliff clan, whose pyramid lies near the foot of a low granite cliff in the wilder part of the hills. The information provided by our intelligence indicated that they were one of the smaller clans, with only twenty-odd adults, so I dispensed with heavy armor. We did take a class five blastcannon, since the destruction of the Jaenshi pyramids is slow work with sidearms alone, but other than that our armament was strictly standard issue.

"We expected no resistance, but recalling the incident at the ring-of-stone, I was cautious. After a march of some twelve kilometers through the hills to the vicinity of the cliff, we fanned out in a semicircle and moved in slowly, with screechguns drawn. A few Jaenshi were encountered in the forest, and these we took prisoner and marched before us, for use as shields in the event of an ambush or attack. That, of course, proved unnecessary.

"When we reached the pyramid by the cliff, they were waiting for us. At least twelve of the beasts, sir. One of them sat near the base of the pyramid with his hands pressed against its side, while the others surrounded him in a sort of a circle. They all looked up at us, but made no other move."

She paused a minute, and rubbed a thoughtful finger up against the side of her nose. "As I told the Proctor, it was all very odd from that point forward. Last summer, I twice led squads against the Jaenshi clans. The first time, having no idea of our intentions, none of the soulless were there; we simply destroyed the artifact and left. The second time, a crowd of the creatures milled around, hampering us with their bodies while not being actively hostile: They did not disperse until I had one of them screeched down. And, of course, I studied the reports of Squadfather Allor's difficulties at the ring-of-stone.

"This time, it was all quite different. I ordered two of my men to set the blastcannon on its tripod, and gave the beasts to understand that they must get out of the way. With hand signals, of course, since I know none of their ungodly tongue. They complied at once, splitting into two groups and, well, lining up, on either side of the line-of-fire. We kept them covered with our screechguns, of course, but everything seemed very peaceful.

"And so it was. The blaster took the pyramid out neatly, a big ball of flame and then sort of a thunder as the thing exploded. A few shards were scattered, but no one was injured, as we had all taken cover and the Jaenshi seemed unconcerned. After the pyramid broke, there was a sharp ozone smell, and for an instant a lingering bluish fire—perhaps an afterimage. I hardly had time to notice them, however, since that was when the Jaenshi all fell to their knees before us. All at once, sirs. And then they pressed their heads against the ground, prostrating themselves. I thought for a moment that they were trying to hail us as gods, because we had shattered their god, and I tried to tell them that we wanted none of their animal worship, and required only that they leave these lands at once. But then I saw that I had misunderstood, because that was when the other four clan members came forward from the trees atop the cliff, and climbed down, and gave us the statue. Then the rest got up. The last I saw, the entire clan was walking due east, away from Sword Valley and the outlying hills. I took the statue and brought it back to the Proctor." She fell silent but remained standing, waiting for questions.

"I have the statuette here," Wyatt said. He reached down beside his chair and set it on the table, then pulled off the white cloth covering he had wrapped around it.

The base was a triangle of rock-hard blackbark, and three long splinters of bone rose from the corners to make a pyramid-frame. Within, exquisitely carved in every detail from soft blue wood, Bakkalon the pale child stood, holding a painted sword.

"What does this mean?" Fieldbishop Lyon asked, obviously startled.

"Sacrilege!" Fieldbishop Dhallis said.

"Nothing so serious," said Gorman, Fieldbishop for Heavy Armor. "The beasts are simply trying to ingratiate themselves, perhaps in the hope that we will stay our swords."

"None but the seed of Earth may bow to Bakkalon," Dhallis said. "It is written in the Book! The pale child will not look with favor on the soulless!"

"Silence, my brothers-in-arms!" the Proctor said, and the long table abruptly grew quiet again. Wyatt smiled a thin smile. "This is the first of the miracles of which I spoke this winter in the chapel, the first of the strange happenings that Bakkalon told to me. For truly he has walked this world, our Corlos, so even the beasts of the fields know his likeness! Think on it, my brothers. Think on this carving. Ask yourselves a few simple questions. Have any of the Jaenshi animals ever been permitted to set foot in this holy city?"

"No, of course not," someone said.

"Then clearly none of them have seen the holograph that stands above our altar. Nor have I often walked among the beasts, as my duties keep me here within the walls. So none could have seen the pale child's likeness on the chain of office that I wear, for the few Jaenshi who have seen my visage have not lived to speak of it—they were those I judged, who hung upon our city walls. The animals do not speak the language of the Earthseed, nor have any among us learned their simple beastly tongue. Lastly, they have not read the Book. Remember all this, and wonder; how did their carvers know what face and form to carve?"

Quiet; the leaders of the children of Bakkalon looked back and forth among themselves in wonderment.

Wyatt quietly folded his hands. "A miracle. We shall have no more trouble with the Jaenshi, for the pale child has come to them."

To the Proctor's right, Fieldbishop Dhallis sat rigidly. "My Proctor, my leader in faith," she said, with some difficulty, each word coming slowly, "surely, *surely*, you do not mean to tell us that these, these *animals*—that they can worship the pale child, that he accepts their worship!"

Wyatt seemed calm, benevolent; he only smiled. "You need not trouble your soul, Dhallis. You wonder whether I commit the First Fallacy, remembering perhaps the Sacrilege of G'hra when a captive Hrangan bowed to Bakkalon to save himself from an animal's death, and the False Proctor Gibrone proclaimed that all who worship the pale child must have souls." He shook his head. "You see, I read the Book. But no, Fieldbishop, no sacrilege has transpired. Bakkalon *has* walked among the Jaenshi, but surely has given them only truth. They have seen him in all his armed dark glory, and heard him proclaim that they are animals, without souls, as surely as he would proclaim. Accordingly, they accept their place in the order of the universe, and retire before us. They will never kill a man again. Recall that they did not bow to the statue they carved, but rather gave the statue to *us*, the seed of Earth, who alone can rightfully worship it. When they did prostrate themselves, it was at *our* feet, as animals to men, and that is as it should be. You see? They have been given truth."

Dhallis was nodding. "Yes, my Proctor. I am enlightened. Forgive my moment of weakness."

But halfway down the table, C'ara DaHan leaned forward and knotted his great knuckled hands, frowning all the while. "My Proctor," he said heavily.

"Weaponsmaster?" Wyatt returned. His face grew stern.

"Like the Fieldbishop, my soul has flickered briefly with worry, and I too would be enlightened, if I might?"

Wyatt smiled. "Proceed," he said, in a voice without humor.

"A miracle this thing may be indeed," DaHan said, "but first we must question ourselves, to ascertain that it is not the trick of a soulless enemy. I do not fathom their stratagem, or their reasons for acting as they have, but I do know of one way that the Jaenshi might have learned the features of our Bakkalon."

"Oh?"

"I speak of the Jamish trading base, and the red-haired trader Arik neKrol. He is an Earthseed, an Emereli by his looks, and we have given him the Book. But he remains without a burning love of Bakkalon, and goes without arms like a godless man. Since our landing he has opposed us, and he grew most hostile after the lesson we were forced to give the Jaenshi. Perhaps he put the cliff clan up to it, told them to do the carving, to some strange ends of his own. I believe that he *did* trade with them."

"I believe you speak truth, Weaponsmaster. In the early months after landing, I tried hard to convert neKrol. To no avail, but I did learn much of the Jaenshi beasts and of the trading he did with them." The Proctor still smiled. "He traded with one of the clans here in Sword Valley, with the people of ring-of-stone, with the cliff clan and that of the far fruit tangle, with the waterfall folk, and sundry clans further east."

"Then it is his doing," DaHan said. "A trick!"

All eyes moved to Wyatt. "I did not say that. NeKrol,

whatever intentions he might have, is but a single man. He did not trade with all the Jaenshi, nor even know them all." The Proctor's smile grew briefly wider. "Those of you who have seen the Emereli know him for a man of flab and weakness; he could hardly walk as far as might be required, and he has neither aircar nor power sled."

"But he *did* have contact with the cliff clan," DaHan said. The deep-graven lines on his bronze forehead were set stubbornly.

"Yes, he did," Wyatt answered. "But Squadmother Jolip did not go forth alone this morning. I also sent out Squadfather Walman and Squadfather Allor, to cross the waters of the White Knife. The land there is dark and fertile, better than that to the east. The cliff clan, who are southeast, were between Sword Valley and the White Knife, so they had to go. But the other pyramids we moved against belonged to far-river clans, more than thirty kilometers south. They have never seen the trader Arik neKrol, unless he has grown wings this winter."

Then Wyatt bent again, and set two more statues on the table, and pulled away their coverings. One was set on a base of slate, and the figure was carved in a clumsy broad manner; the other was finely detailed soaproot, even to the struts of the pyramid. But except for the materials and the workmanship, the later statues were identical to the first.

"Do you see a trick, Weaponsmaster?" Wyatt asked.

DaHan looked, and said nothing, for Fieldbishop Lyon rose suddenly and said, "I see a miracle," and others echoed him. After the hubbub had finally quieted, the brawny Weaponsmaster lowered his head and said, very softly, "My Proctor. Read wisdom to us."

"The lasers, speaker, the *lasers!*" There was a tinge of hysterical desperation in neKrol's tone. "Ryther is not back yet, and that is the very point. We must wait."

He stood outside the bubble of the trading base, bare-chested and sweating in the hot morning sun, with the thick wind tugging at his tangled hair. The clamor had pulled him from a troubled sleep. He had stopped them just on the edge of the forest, and now the bitter speaker had turned to face him, looking fierce and hard and most unJaenshi-like with the laser slung across her shoulders, a bright blue glittersilk scarf knotted around her neck, and fat glowstone rings on all eight of her fingers. The other exiles, but for the two that were heavy with child, stood around her. One of them held the other laser, the rest carried quivers and powerbows. That had been the speaker's idea. Her newly-chosen mate was down on one knee, panting; he had run all the way from the ring-of-stone.

"No, Arik," the speaker said, eyes bronze-angry. "Your lasers are now a month overdue, by your own count of time. Each day we wait, and the Steel Angels smash more pyramids. Soon they may hang children again."

"Very soon," neKrol said. "Very soon, if you attack them. Where is your very hope of victory? Your watcher says they go with two squads and a powerwagon—can you stop them with a pair of lasers and four powerbows? Have you learned to think here, or not?"

"Yes," the speaker said, but she bared her teeth at him as she said it. "Yes, but that cannot matter. The clans do not resist, so we must."

From one knee, her mate looked up at neKrol. "They . . . they march on the waterfall," he said, still breathing heavily.

"The waterfall!" the bitter speaker repeated. "Since the death of winter, they have broken more than twenty pyramids, Arik, and their powerwagons have crushed the forest and now a great dusty road scars the soil from their valley to the riverlands. But they had hurt no Jaenshi yet this season, they had let them go. And all those clans-without-a-god have gone to the waterfall, until the home forest of the waterfall folk is bare and eaten clean. Their talkers sit with the old talker and perhaps the waterfall god takes them in, perhaps he is a very great god. I do not know these things. But I *do* know that now the bald Angel has learned of the twenty clans together, of a grouping of half-a-thousand Jaenshi adults, and he leads a powerwagon against them. Will he let them go so easy this time, happy with a carved statue? Will *they* go, Arik, will they give up a second god as easily as a first?" The speaker blinked. "I fear they will resist with their silly claws. I fear the bald

Angel will hang them even if they do not resist, because so many in union throws suspicion in him. I fear many things and know little, but I know *we* must be there. You will not stop us, Arik, and we cannot wait for your long-late lasers."

And she turned to the others and said, "Come, we must run," and they had faded into the forest before neKrol could even shout for them to stay. Swearing, he turned back to the bubble.

The two female exiles were leaving just as he entered. Both were close to the end of their term, but they had powerbows in their hands. neKrol stopped short. "You too!" he said furiously, glaring at them. "Madness, it is the very stuff of madness!" They only looked at him with silent golden eyes, and moved past him toward the trees.

Inside, he swiftly braided his long red hair so it would not catch on the branches, slipped into a shirt, and darted toward the door. Then he stopped. A weapon, he must have a weapon! He glanced around frantically and ran heavily for his storeroom. The powerbows were all gone, he saw. What then, what? He began to rummage, and finally settled for a duralloy machete. It felt strange in his hand and he must have looked most unmartial and ridiculous, but somehow he felt he must take something.

Then he was off, toward the place of the waterfall folk.

NeKrol was overweight and soft, hardly used to running, and the way was nearly two kilometers through lush summer forest. He had to stop three times to rest, and quiet the pains in his chest, and it seemed an eternity before he arrived. But still he beat the Steel Angels; a powerwagon is ponderous and slow, and the road from Sword Valley was longer and more hilly.

Jaenshi were everywhere. The glade was bare of grass and twice as large as neKrol remembered it from his last trading trip, early that spring. Still the Jaenshi filled all of it, sitting on the ground, staring at the pool and the waterfall, all silent, packed together so there was scarcely room to walk among them. More sat above, a dozen in every fruit tree, some of the children even ascending to the higher limbs where the pseudomonks usually ruled alone.

On the rock at the center of the pool, with the waterfall behind them as a backdrop, the talkers pressed around the pyramid of the waterfall folk. They were closer together than even those in the grass, and each had his palms flat against the sides. One, thin and frail, sat on the shoulders of another so that he too might touch. NeKrol tried to count them and gave up; the group was too dense, a blurred mass of gray-furred arms and golden eyes, the pyramid at their center, dark and unmovable as ever.

The bitter speaker stood in the pool, the waters ankle-deep around her. She was facing the crowd and screeching at them, her voice strangely unlike the usual Jaenshi purr; in her scarf and rings, she looked absurdly out of place. As she talked, she waved the laser rifle she was holding in one hand. Wildly, passionately, hysterically, she was telling the gathered Jaenshi that the Steel Angels were coming, that they must leave at once, that they should break up and go into the forest and regroup at the trading base. Over and over again she said it.

But the clans were stiff and silent. No one answered, no one listened, no one heard. In full daylight, they were praying.

NeKrol pushed his way through them, stepping on a hand here and a foot there, hardly able to set down a boot without crunching Jaenshi flesh. He was standing next to the bitter speaker, who still gestured wildly, before her bronze eyes seemed to see him. Then she stopped. "Arik," she said, "the Angels are coming, and *they will not listen.*"

"The others," he panted, still short on breath. "Where are they?"

"The trees," the bitter speaker replied, with a vague gesture. "I sent them up in the trees. Snipers, Arik, such as we saw upon your wall."

"Please," he said. "Come back with me. Leave them, leave them. You told them. I told them. Whatever happens, it is their doing, it is the fault of their fool religion."

"I cannot leave," the bitter speaker said. She seemed confused, as so often when neKrol had questioned her back at the base. "It seems I should, but somehow I know I must stay here. And the others will *never* go, even if I did. They feel it much more strongly. We must be here.

To fight, to talk." She blinked. "I do not know *why*, Arik, but we must."

And before the trader could reply, the Steel Angels came out of the forest.

There were five of them at first, widely spaced; then shortly five more. All afoot, in uniforms whose mottled dark greens blended with the leaves, so that only the glitter of the mesh-steel belts and matching battle helmets stood out. One of them, a gaunt pale woman, wore a high red collar; all of them had hand-lasers drawn.

"You!" the blond woman shouted, her eyes finding Arik at once, as he stood with his braid flying in the wind and the machete dangling uselessly in his hand. "Speak to these animals! Tell them they must leave! Tell them that no Jaenshi gathering of this size is permitted east of the mountains, by order of the Proctor Wyatt, and the pale child Bakkalon. Tell them!" And then she saw the bitter speaker, and started. "And take the laser from the hand of that animal before we burn both of you down!"

Trembling, neKrol dropped the machete from limp fingers into the water. "Speaker, drop the gun," he said in Jaenshi, "*please*. If you ever hope to see the far stars. Let loose the laser, my friend, my child, this very now. And I will take you when Ryther comes, with me to ai-Emerel and further places." The trader's voice was full of fear; the Steel Angels held their lasers steady, and not for a moment did he think the speaker would obey him.

But strangely, meekly, she threw the laser rifle into the pool. NeKrol could not see to read her eyes.

The Squadmother relaxed visibly. "Good," she said. "Now, talk to them in their beastly talk, tell them to leave. If not, we shall crush them. A powerwagon is on its way!" And now, over the roar and tumble of the nearby waters, neKrol could hear it; a heavy crunching as it rolled over trees, rending them into splinters beneath wide duramesh treads. Perhaps they were using the blastcannon and the turret lasers to clear away boulders and other obstacles.

"We have told them," neKrol said desperately. "Many times we have told them, but they do not hear!" He gestured all about him; the glade was still hot and close with Jaenshi bodies and none among the clans had taken the slightest notice of the Steel Angels or the confrontation. Behind him, the clustered talkers still pressed small hands against their god.

"Then we shall bare the sword of Bakkalon to them," the Squadmother said, "and perhaps they will hear their own wailing!" She holstered her laser and drew a screechgun, and neKrol, shuddering, knew her intent. The screechers used concentrated high-intensity sound to break down cell walls and liquefy flesh. It effects were psychological as much as anything; there was no more horrible death.

But then a second squad of the Angels were among them, and there was a creak of wood straining and snapping, and from behind a final grove of fruit trees, dimly, neKrol could see the black flanks of the powerwagon, its blastcannon seemingly trained right at him. Two of the newcomers wore the scarlet collar—a red-faced youth with large ears who barked orders to his squad, and a huge, muscular man with a bald head and lined bronze skin. NeKrol recognized him; the Weaponsmaster C'ara DaHan. It was DaHan who laid a heavy hand on the Squadmother's arm as she raised her screechgun. "No," he said. "It is not the way."

She holstered the weapon at once. "I hear and obey."

DaHan looked at neKrol. "Trader," he boomed, "is this your doing?"

"No," neKrol said.

"They will not disperse," the Squadmother added.

"It would take us a day and a night to screech them down," DaHan said, his eyes sweeping over the glade and the trees, and following the rocky twisted path of the waterwall up to its summit. "There is an easier way. Break the pyramid and they go at once." He stopped then, about to say something else; his eyes were on the bitter speaker.

"A Jaenshi in rings and cloth," he said. "They have woven nothing but deathcloth up to now. This alarms me."

"She is one of the people of the ring-of-stone," neKrol said quickly. "She has lived with me."

DaHan nodded. "I understand. You are truly a godless man, neKrol, to consort so with soulless animals, to teach them to ape the ways of the seed of Earth. But it does not matter." He raised his arm in signal; behind him, among the trees, the blastcannon of the powerwagon moved slightly to the right. "You and your pet should move at once." DaHan told neKrol. "When I lower my arm, the Jaenshi god will burn and if you stand in the way, you will never move again."

"The *talkers!*" neKrol protested, "the blast will—" and he started to turn to show them. But the talkers were crawling away from the pyramid, one by one.

Behind him, the Angels were muttering. "A miracle!" one said hoarsely. "Our child! Our Lord!" cried another.

neKrol stood paralyzed. The pyramid on the rock was no longer a reddish slab. Now it sparkled in the sunlight, a canopy of transparent crystal. And below that canopy, perfect in every detail, the pale child Bakkalon stood smiling, with his Demon-Reaver in his hand.

The Jaenshi talkers were scrambling from it now, tripping in the water in their haste to be away. neKrol glimpsed the old talker, running faster than any despite his age. Even he seemed not to understand. The bitter speaker stood open-mouthed.

The trader turned. Half of the Steel Angels were on their knees, the rest had absent-mindedly lowered their arms and they froze in gaping wonder. The Squadmother turned to DaHan. "It *is* a miracle," she said. "As Proctor Wyatt has foreseen. The pale child walks upon this world."

But the Weaponsmaster was unmoved. "The Proctor is not here and this is no miracle," he said in a steely voice. "It is a trick of some enemy, and I will not be tricked. We will burn the blasphemous thing from the soil of Corlos." His arm flashed down.

The Angels in the powerwagon must have been lax with awe; the blastcannon did not fire. DaHan turned in irritation. "It is no miracle!" he shouted. He began to raise his arm again.

Next to neKrol, the bitter speaker suddenly cried out. He looked over with alarm, and saw her eyes flash a brilliant yellow-gold. "The god!" she muttered softly. "The light returns to me!"

And the whine of powerbows sounded from the trees around them, and two long bolts shuddered almost simultaneously in the broad back of C'ara DaHan. The force of the shots drove the Weaponsmaster to his knees, smashed him against the ground.

"*RUN!*" neKrol screamed, and he shoved the bitter speaker with all his strength, and she stumbled and looked back at him briefly, her eyes dark bronze again and flickering with fear. Then, swiftly, she was running, her scarf aflutter behind her as she dodged toward the nearest green.

"Kill her!" the Squadmother shouted. "Kill them all!" And her words woke Jaenshi and Steel Angels both; the children of Bakkalon lifted their lasers against the suddenly-surging crowd, and the slaughter began. neKrol knelt and scrabbled on the moss-slick rocks until he had the laser rifle in his hands, then brought it to his shoulder and commenced to fire. Light stabbed out in angry bursts; once, twice, a third time. He held the trigger down and the bursts became a beam, and he sheared through the waist of a silver-helmeted Angel before the fire flared in his stomach and he fell heavily into the pool.

For a long time he saw nothing; there was only pain and noise, the water gently slapping against his face, the sounds of high-pitched Jaenshi screaming, running all around him. Twice he heard the roar and crackle of the blastcannon, and more than twice he was stepped on. It all seemed unimportant. He struggled to keep his head on the rocks, half out of the water, but even that seemed none too vital after a while. The only thing that counted was the burning in his gut.

Then, somehow, the pain went away, and there was a lot of smoke and horrible smells but not so much noise, and neKrol lay quietly and listened to the voices.

"The pyramid, Squadmother?" someone asked.

"It *is* a miracle," a woman's voice replied. "Look, Bakkalon stands there yet. And see how he smiles! We have done right here today!"

"What should we do with it?"

"Lift it aboard the powerwagon. We shall bring it back to Proctor Wyatt."

Soon after the voices went away, and neKrol heard only the sound of the water, rushing down endlessly, falling and tumbling. It was a very restful sound. He decided he would sleep.

The crewman shoved the crowbar down between the slats and lifted. The thin wood hardly protested at all before it gave. "More statues, Jannis," he reported, after reaching inside the crate and tugging loose some of the packing material.

"Worthless," Ryther said, with a brief sigh. She stood in the broken ruins of neKrol's trading base. The Angels had ransacked it, searching for armed Jaenshi, and debris lay everywhere. But they had not touched the crates.

The crewman took his crowbar and moved on to the next stack of crated artifacts. Ryther looked wistfully at the three Jaenshi who clustered around her, wishing they could communicate a little better. One of them, a sleek female who wore a trailing scarf and a lot of jewelry and seemed always to be leaning on a powerbow, knew a smattering of Terran, but hardly enough. She picked up things quickly, but so far the only thing of substance she had said was, "Jamson' World. Arik take us. Angels kill." That she had repeated endlessly until Ryther had finally made her understand that, yes, they would take them. The other two Jaenshi, the pregnant female and the male with the laser, never seemed to talk at all.

"Statues again," the crewman said, having pulled a crate from atop the stack in the ruptured storeroom and pried it open.

Ryther shrugged; the crewman moved on. She turned her back on him and wandered slowly outside, to the edge of the spacefield where the *Lights of Jolostar* rested, its open ports bright with yellow light in the gathering gloom of dusk. The Jaenshi followed her, as they had followed her since she arrived; afraid, no doubt, that she would go away and leave them if they took their great bronze eyes off her for an instant.

"Statues," Ryther muttered, half to herself and half to the Jaenshi. She shook her head. "Why did he do it?" she asked them, knowing they could not understand. "A trader of his experience? You could tell me, maybe, if you knew what I was saying. Instead of concentrating on deathcloths and such, on real Jaenshi art, why did Arik train you people to carve alien versions of human gods? He should have known no dealer would accept such obvious frauds. Alien art is *alien.*" She sighed. "My fault, I suppose. We should have opened the crates." She laughed.

The bitter speaker stared at her. "Arik deathcloth. Gave."

Ryther nodded, abstractly. She had it now, hanging just above her bunk; a strange small thing, woven partly from Jaenshi fur and mostly from long silken strands of flame red hair. On it, gray against the red, was a crude but recognizable caricature of Arik neKrol. She had wondered at that, too. The tribute of a widow? A child? Or just a friend? What *had* happened to Arik during the year the *Lights* had been away? If only she had been back on time, then . . . but she'd lost three months on Jamison's World, checking dealer after dealer in an effort to unload the worthless statuettes. It had been middle autumn before the *Lights of Jolostar* returned to Corlos, to find neKrol's base in ruins, the Angels already gathering in their harvests.

And the Angels—when she'd gone to them, offering the hold of unwanted lasers, offering to trade, the sight on those blood-red city walls had sickened even her. She had thought she'd gone prepared, but the obscenity she encountered was beyond any preparation. A squad of Steel Angels found her, vomiting, beyond the tall rusty gates, and had escorted her inside, before the Proctor.

Wyatt was twice as skeletal as she remembered him. He had been standing outdoors, near the foot of a huge platform-altar that had been erected in the middle of the city. A startlingly lifelike statue of Bakkalon, encased in a glass pyramid and set atop a high redstone plinth, threw a long shadow over the wooden altar. Beneath it, the squads of Angels were piling the newly-harvested neograss and wheat and the frozen carcasses of bushogs.

"We do not need your trade," the Proctor told her. "The World of Corlos is many-times-blessed, my child, and Bakkalon lives among us now. He has worked vast miracles, and shall work more. Our faith is in Him." Wyatt gestured toward the altar with a thin hand. "See? In tribute we burn our winter stores, for the pale child has promised that this year winter will not come. And He has taught us to cull ourselves in peace as once we were culled in war, so the seed of Earth grows ever stronger. It is a time of great new revelation!" His eyes had burned as he spoke to her; eyes darting and fanatic, vast and dark yet strangely flecked with gold.

As quickly as she could. Ryther had left the City of the Steel Angels, trying hard not to look back at the walls. But when she had climbed the hills, back toward the trading base, she had come to the ring-of-stone, to the broken pyramid where Arik had taken her. Then Ryther found that she could not resist, and powerless she had turned for a final glance out over Sword Valley. The sight had stayed with her.

Outside the walls the Angel children hung, a row of small white-smocked bodies still and motionless at the end of long ropes. They had gone peacefully, all of them, but death is seldom peaceful; the older ones, at least, died quickly, necks broken with a sudden snap. But the small pale infants had the nooses round their waists, and it had seemed clear to Ryther that most of them had simply hung there till they starved.

As she stood, remembering, the crewman came from inside neKrol's broken bubble. "Nothing," he reported. "All statues." Ryther nodded.

"Go?" the bitter speaker said. "Jamson' World?"

"Yes," she replied, her eyes staring past the waiting *Lights of Jolostar*, out toward the black primal forest. The Heart of Bakkalon was sunk forever. In a thousand thousand woods and a single city, the clans had begun to pray.

East Is East

Sandra Miesel

The man the science fiction field knew as "Cordwainer Smith" (1913–66) lived in a wider world as Paul Linebarger, internationally renowned Professor of Asiatic Politics at Johns Hopkins University. Linebarger also wrote the classic text *Psychological Warfare* (1948), refining its principles while serving in the United States Army during World War II and the Korean conflict: few scholars have been better acquainted with the practical consequences of abstract theories.

China dominated Linebarger's youth much as India did Kipling's. His godfather was Sun Yat-sen, founder of the Chinese Republic, and his father, a former Federal judge in the Philippines, was legal advisor to the Nationalist Chinese Council of State. Moving in these circles as his father's secretary gave Linebarger the "punctilio found only in traditional societies."

Linebarger found the formalities of classical Chinese civilization congenial. In later years, he had both his calling cards and his silk ties inscribed with his name phonetically rendered in ideographs as "Mr. Forest of Incandescent Bliss." Yet he had also witnessed the chaos and disruption of a young nation at war: "I grew up in a household where soldiers of fortune were common visitors, where secret messages were received and dispatched, where men left black satchels full of money in the front hall, much to my mother's consternation."

Though Linebarger, like Kim, could have boasted of having "two sides to his head," his horizons were even broader than those of Kipling's hero. Besides his experiences in China and education in America, Linebarger also lived in Germany, studied in England, and taught in Australia. Like Kipling, he had a special love of French literature. He was a voracious reader who never forgot what he read. ("I still remember Daddy declaiming 'Gunga Din' from memory," recalls his elder daughter.)

First-hand knowledge of alienness stood Linebarger in good stead as a science fiction writer. He had a gift for making the fantastic seem matter of fact: why shouldn't a faster-than-light starship look like Mount Vernon? His sympathies transcended the boundaries of class and species to encompass all that lives—or imitates living. He lavished special tenderness on his Underpeople, genetically modified animals enslaved by humans, who slowly win their freedom.

Since Linebarger's fiction faithfully reflects his real-life concerns, politics is by no means absent from his universe. The authority that comes to govern hundreds of human-colonized worlds is called The Instrumentality of Mankind, an imperium of excellence beyond Kipling's fondest dreams. (Its cool competence led A. J. Budrys to compare it with the Aerial Board of Control in Kipling's "As Easy as ABC.") But although the Lords and Ladies of the Instrumentality are all-powerful regulators, they eventually deregulate their subjects, freeing them to take their chances as responsible individuals. There is no room here for "a strong man ruling alone."

Among Linebarger's favorite themes were searches—for personal love, racial liberation, and universal meaning. Mental manipulations, whether by drugs, surgery, conditioning, or technology play major parts in these processes. In contrast to Kipling, who suffered from depression but resisted introspection, Linebarger found psychoanalysis and the sciences of the mind to be valuable sources of insight. Furthermore, all these quests are suffused by the author's Christian faith, here called The Old Strong Religion. Linebarger, unlike the agnostic Kipling, was a devout High Church Anglican.

Death closed Linebarger's SF career far too soon, leaving only glimpses of a marvelous vision. Yet it is clear that he was not unscrolling a conventionally neat future history. Instead he was recounting legends drawn from a loosely connected cycle of traditions stretching across 13,000 years. His direct narrative voice hints at adventures yet untold (or as Kipling would say, "That is a story for next time") and makes cross-references so that each episode may illuminate others. Though a frankly unrealistic writer, Linebarger achieves the illusion that his cosmos and characters continue to exist whether his books be open or closed.

When I read the original magazine publication of "The Burning of the Brain" at sixteen, I found the story puzzling and grotesque. After re-reading it for this project, I see it as a wry comment on youth, age, and the follies of the heart. (But then, I also have a better understanding now of the mother-daughter tensions Kipling satirizes in "My Rival.")

Australian critic John Foyster said that the literary reputation of "Cordwainer Smith" could rest on the last two sentences of this story. No fair peeking, Gentle Reader. Take it straight from the top.

The Burning of The Brain

Cordwainer Smith

I. Dolores Oh

I tell you, it is sad, it is more than sad, it is fearful—for it is a dreadful thing to go into the Up-and-Out, to fly without flying, to move between the stars as a moth may drift among the leaves on a summer night.

Of all the men who took the great ships into planoform none was braver, none stronger, than Captain Magno Taliano.

Scanners had been gone for centuries and the jonasoidal effect had become so simple, so manageable, that the traversing of light-years was no more difficult to most of the passengers of the great ships than to go from one room to the other.

Passengers moved easily.

Not the crew.

Least of all the captain.

The captain of a jonasoidal ship which had embarked on an interstellar journey was a man subject to rare and overwhelming strains. The art of getting past all the complications of space was far more like the piloting of turbulent waters in ancient days than like the smooth seas which legendary men once traversed with sails alone.

Go-Captain on the *Wu-Feinstein*, finest ships of its class, was Magno Taliano.

Of him it was said, "He could sail through hell with the

muscles of his left eye alone. He could plow space with his living brain if the instruments failed . . ."

Wife to the Go-Captain was Dolores Oh. The name was Japonical, from some nation of the ancient days. Dolores Oh had been once beautiful, so beautiful that she took men's breath away, made wise men into fools, made young men into nightmares of lust and yearning. Wherever she went men had quarreled and fought over her.

But Dolores Oh was proud beyond all common limits of pride. She refused to go through the ordinary rejuvenescence. A terrible yearning a hundred or so years back must have come over her. Perhaps she said to herself, before that hope and terror which a mirror in a quiet room becomes to anyone.

"Surely I am me. There must be a *me* more than the beauty of my face, there must be a something other than the delicacy of skin and the accidental lines of my jaw and my cheekbone.

"What have men loved if it wasn't me? Can I ever find out who I am or what I am if I don't let beauty perish and live on in whatever flesh age gives me?"

She had met the Go-Captain and had married him in a romance that left forty planets talking and half the ship lines stunned.

Magno Taliano was at the very beginning of his genius. Space, we can tell you, is rough—rough like the wildest of storm-driven waters, filled with perils which only the most sensitive, the quickest, the most daring of men can surmount.

Best of them all, class for class, age for age, out of class, beating the best of his seniors, was Magno Taliano.

For him to marry the most beautiful beauty of forty worlds was a wedding like Heloise and Abelard's or like the unforgettable romance of Helen America and Mr. Grey-no-more.

The ships of the Go-Captain Magno Taliano became more beautiful year by year, century by century.

As ships became better he always obtained the best. He maintained his lead over the other Go-Captains so overwhelmingly that it was unthinkable for the finest ship of mankind to sail out amid the roughness and uncertainties of two-dimensional space without himself at the helm.

Stop-Captains were proud to sail space beside him. (Though the Stop-Captains had nothing more to do than to check the maintenance of the ship, its loading and unloading when it was in normal space, they were still more than ordinary men in their own kind of world, a world far below the more majestic and adventurous universe of the Go-Captains.)

Magno Taliano had a niece who in the modern style used a place instead of a name: she was called "Dita from the Great South House."

When Dita came aboard the *Wu-Feinstein* she had heard much of Dolores Oh, her aunt by marriage who had once captivated the men in many worlds. Dita was wholly unprepared for what she found.

Dolores greeted her civilly enough, but the civility was a sucking pump of hideous anxiety, the friendliness was the driest of mockeries, the greeting itself an attack.

What's the matter with the woman? thought Dita.

As if to answer her thought, Dolores said aloud and in words: "It's nice to meet a woman who's not trying to take Taliano from me. I love him. Can you believe that? Can you?"

"Of course," said Dita. She looked at the ruined face of Dolores Oh, at the dreaming terror in Dolores's eyes, and she realized that Dolores had passed all limits of nightmare and had become a veritable demon of regret, a possessive ghost who sucked the vitality from her husband, who dreaded companionship, hated friendship, rejected even the most casual of acquaintances, because she feared forever and without limit that there was really nothing to herself, and feared that without Magno Taliano she would be more lost than the blackest of whirlpools in the nothing between the stars.

Magno Taliano came in.

He saw his wife and niece together.

He must have been used to Dolores Oh. In Dita's eyes Dolores was more frightening than a mud-caked reptile raising its wounded and venomous head with blind hunger and blind rage. To Magno Taliano the ghastly woman who stood like a witch beside him was somehow the beautiful girl he had wooed and had married one-hundred-sixty-four years before.

He kissed the withered cheek, he stroked the dried and stringy hair, he looked into the greedy terror-haunted eyes as though they were the eyes of a child he loved. He said, lightly and gently,

"Be good to Dita, my dear."

He went on through the lobby of the ship to the inner sanctum of the planoforming room.

The Stop-Captain waiting for him. Outside on the world of Sherman the scented breezes of that pleasant planet blew in through the open windows of the ship.

Wu-Feinstein, finest ship of its class, had no need for metal walls. It was built to resemble an ancient, prehistoric estate named Mount Vernon, and when it sailed between the stars it was encased in its own rigid and self-renewing field of force.

The passengers went through a few pleasant hours of strolling on the grass, enjoying the spacious rooms, chatting beneath a marvelous simulacrum of an atmosphere-filled sky.

Only in the planoforming room did the Go-Captain know what happened. The Go-Captain, his pinlighters sitting beside him, took the ship from one compression to another, leaping hotly and frantically through space, sometimes one light-year, sometimes a hundred light-years, jump, jump, jump, jump until the ship, the light touches of the captain's mind guiding it, passed the perils of millions upon millions of worlds, came out at its appointed destination and settled as lightly as one feather resting upon others, settled into an embroidered and decorated countryside where the passengers could move as easily away from their journey as if they had done nothing more than to pass an afternoon in a pleasant old house by the side of a river.

II. The Lost Locksheet

Magno Taliano nodded to his pinlighters. The Stop-Captain bowed obsequiously from the doorway of the planoforming room. Taliano looked at him sternly, but with robust friendliness. With formal and austere courtesy he asked,

"Sir and colleague, is everything ready for the jonasoidal effect?"

The Stop-Captain bowed even more formally. "Truly ready, sir and master."

"The locksheets in place?"

"Truly in place, sir and master."

"The passengers secure?"

"The passengers are secure, numbered, happy and ready, sir and master."

Then came the last and most serious of questions. "Are my pinlighters warmed with their pin-sets and ready for combat?"

"Ready for combat, sir and master." With these words the Stop-Captain withdrew. Magno Taliano smiled to his pinlighters. Through the minds of all of them were passed the same thought.

How could a man that pleasant stay married all those years to a hag like Dolores Oh? How could that witch, that horror, have ever been a beauty? How could that beast have ever been a woman, particularly the divine and glamorous Dolores Oh whose image we still see in four-di every now and then?

Yet pleasant he was, though long he may have been married to Dolores Oh. Her loneliness and greed might suck at him like a nightmare, but his strength was more than enough strength for two.

Was he not the captain of the greatest ship to sail between the stars?

Even as the pinlighters smiled their greetings back to him, his right hand depressed the golden ceremonial lever of the ship. This instrument alone was mechanical. All other controls in the ship had long since been formed telepathically or electronically.

Within the planoforming room the black skies became visible and the tissue of space shot up around them like boiling water at the base of a waterfall. Outside that one room the passengers still walked sedately on scented lawns.

From the wall facing him, as he sat rigid in his Go-

Captain's chair, Magno Taliano sensed the forming of a pattern which in three or four hundred milliseconds would tell him where he was and would give him the next clue as to how to move.

He moved the ship with the impulses of his own brain, to which the wall was a superlative complement.

The wall was a living brickwork of locksheets, laminated charts, one-hundred-thousand charts to the inch, the wall preselected and preassembled for all imaginable contingencies of the journey which, each time afresh, took the ship across half-unknown immensities of time and space. The ship leapt, as it had before.

The new star focused.

Magno Taliano waited for the wall to show him where he was, expecting (in partnership with the wall) to flick the ship back into the pattern of stellar space, moving it by immense skips from source to destination.

This time nothing happened.

Nothing?

For the first time in a hundred years his mind knew panic.

It couldn't be nothing. Not *nothing*. Something had to focus. The locksheets always focused.

His mind reached into the locksheets and he realized with a devastation beyond all limits of ordinary human grief that they were lost as no ship had ever been lost before. By some error never before committed in the history of mankind, the entire wall was made of duplicates of the same locksheet.

Worst of all, the Emergency Return sheet was lost. They were amid stars none of them had ever seen before, perhaps as little as five-hundred-million miles, perhaps as far as forty parsecs.

And the locksheet was lost.

And they would die.

As the ship's power failed coldness and blackness and death would crush in on them in a few hours at the most. That then would be all, all of the *Wu-Feinstein*, all of Dolores Oh.

III. The Secret Of The Old Dark Brain

Outside of the planoforming room of the *Wu-Feinstein* the passengers had no reason to understand that they were marooned in the nothing-at-all.

Dolores Oh rocked back and forth in an ancient rocking chair. Her haggard face looked without pleasure at the imaginary river that ran past the edge of the lawn. Dita from the Great South House sat on a hassock by her aunt's knees.

Dolores was talking about a trip she had made when she was young and vibrant with beauty, a beauty which brought trouble and hate wherever it went.

". . . so the guardsman killed the captain and then came to my cabin and said to me. 'You've got to marry me now. I've given up everything for your sake,' and I said to him, 'I never said that I loved you. It was sweet of you to get into a fight, and in a way I suppose it is a compliment to my beauty, but it doesn't mean that I belong to you the rest of my life. What do you think I am, anyhow?"

Dolores Oh sighed a dry, ugly sigh, like the crackling of subzero winds through frozen twigs. "So you see, Dita, being beautiful the way you are is no answer to anything. A woman has got to be herself before she finds out what she is. I know that my lord and husband, the Go-Captain, loves me because my beauty is gone, and with my beauty gone there is nothing but *me* to love, is there?"

An odd figure came out on the verandah. It was a pinlighter in full fighting costume. Pinlighters were never supposed to leave the planoforming room, and it was most extraordinary for one of them to appear among the passengers.

He bowed to the two ladies and said with the utmost courtesy.

"Ladies, will you please come into the planoforming room? We have need that you should see the Go-Captain now."

Dolores's hand leapt to her mouth. Her gesture of grief was as automatic as the striking of a snake. Dita sensed that her aunt had been waiting a hundred years and more for disaster, that her aunt had craved ruin for her husband the way that some people crave love and others crave death.

Dita said nothing. Neither did Dolores, apparently at second thought, utter a word.

They followed the pinlighter silently into the planoforming room.

The heavy door closed behind them.

Magno Taliano was still rigid in his Captain's chair.

He spoke very slowly, his voice sounding like a record played too slowly on an ancient parlophone.

"*We are lost in space, my dear,*" said the frigid, ghostly, voice of the Captain, still in his Go-Captain's trance. "*We are lost in space and I thought that perhaps if your mind aided mine we might think of a way back.*"

Dita started to speak.

A pinlighter told her: "Go ahead and speak, my dear. Do you have any suggestion?"

"Why don't we just go back? It would be humiliating, wouldn't it? Still it would be better than dying. Let's use the Emergency Return Locksheet and go on right back. The world will forgive Magno Taliano for a single failure after thousands of brilliant and successful trips."

The pinlighter, a pleasant enough young man, was as friendly and calm as a doctor informing someone of death or of a mutilation. "The impossible has happened, Dita from the Great South House. All the locksheets are wrong. They are all the same one. And not one of them is good for emergency return."

With that the two women knew where they were. They knew that space would tear into them like threads being pulled out of a fiber so that they would either die bit by bit as the hours passed and as the material of their bodies faded away a few molecules here and a few there. Or, alternatively, they could die all at once in a flash if the Go-Captain chose to kill himself and the ship rather than to wait for a slow death. Or, if they believed in religion, they could pray.

The pinlighter said to the rigid Go-Captain, "We think we see a familiar pattern at the edge of your own brain. May we look in?"

Taliano nodded very slowly, very gravely.

The pinlighter stood still.

The two women watched. Nothing visible happened, but they knew that beyond the limits of vision and yet before their eyes a great drama was being played out. The minds of pinlighters probed deep into the mind of the frozen Go-Captain, searching amid the synapses for the secret of the faintest clue to their possible rescue.

Minutes passed. They seemed like hours.

At last the pinlighter spoke. "We can see into your mid-brain, Captain. At the edge of your paleocortex there is a star pattern which resembles the upper left rear of our present location."

"The pinlighter laughed nervously. "We want to know can you fly the ship home on your brain?"

Magno Taliano looked with deep tragic eyes at the inquirer. His slow voice came out at them once again since he dared not leave the half-trance which held the entire ship in stasis. *"Do you mean can I fly the ship on a brain alone? It would burn out my brain and the ship would be lost anyhow . . ."*

"But we're lost, lost, lost," screamed Dolores Oh. Her face was alive with hideous hope, with a hunger for ruin, with a greedy welcome of disaster. She screamed at her husband, "Wake up, my darling, and let us die together. At least we can belong to each other that much, that long, forever!"

"Why die?" said the pinlighter softly. "You tell him, Dita."

Said Dita, "Why not try, sir and uncle?"

Slowly Magno Taliano turned his face toward his niece. Again his hollow voice sounded. *"If I do this I shall be a fool or a child or a dead man but I will do it for you."*

Dita had studied the work of the Go-Captains and she knew well enough that if the paleocortex was lost the personality became intellectually sane, but emotionally crazed. With the most ancient part of the brain gone the fundamental controls of hostility, hunger and sex disappeared. The most ferocious of animals and the most brilliant of men were reduced to a common level—a level of infantile friendliness in which lust and playfulness and gentle, unappeasable hunger become the eternity of their days.

Magno Taliano did not wait.

He reached out a slow hand and squeezed the hand of Dolores. Oh. "*As I die you shall at last be sure I love you.*"

Once again the women saw nothing. They realized they had been called in simply to give Magno Taliano a last glimpse of his own life.

A quiet pinlighter thrust a beam-electrode so that it reached square into the paleocortex of Captain Magno Taliano.

The planoforming room came to life. Strange heavens swirled about them like milk being churned in a bowl.

Dita realized that her partial capacity of telepathy was functioning even without the aid of a machine. With her mind she could feel the dead wall of the locksheets. She was aware of the rocking of the *Wu-Feinstein* as it leapt from space to space, as uncertain as a man crossing a river by leaping from one ice-covered rock to the other.

In a strange way she even knew that the paleocortical part of her uncle's brain was burning out at last and forever, that the star patterns which had been frozen in the locksheets lived on in the infinitely complex pattern of his own memories, and that with the help of his own telepathic pinlighters he was burning out his brain cell by cell in order for them to find a way to the ship's destination. This indeed was his last trip.

Dolores Oh watched her husband with a hungry greed surpassing all expression.

Little by little his face became relaxed and stupid.

Dita could see the midbrain being burned blank, as the ship's controls with the help of the pinlighters searched through the most magnificent intellect of its time for a last course into harbor.

Suddenly Dolores Oh was on her knees, sobbing by the hand of her husband.

A pinlighter took Dita by the arm.

"We have reached destination," he said.

"And my uncle?"

The pinlighter looked at her strangely.

She realized he was speaking to her without moving his lips—speaking mind-to-mind with pure telepathy.

"Can't you see it?"

She shook her head dazedly.

The pinlighter thought his emphatic statement at her once again.

"As your uncle burned out his brain, you picked up his skills. Can't you sense it? You are a Go-Captain yourself and one of the greatest of us."

"And he?"

The pinlighter thought a merciful comment at her.

Magno Taliano had risen from his chair and was being led from the room by his wife and consort, Dolores Oh. He had the amiable smile of an idiot, and his face for the first time in more than a hundred years trembled with shy and silly love.

Big Friend of the World—Rudyard

Anne McCaffrey

If you are expecting a scholarly presentation of the various postures, attitudes, intolerances or prejudices of Rudyard Kipling, or the effect his writing style had on the *Dragonriders of Pern*, turn past this essay.

I refuse to parse, prod or pickle Mr. Kipling. He's too close a friend, too early an influence, too great a jewel in my memory to dare at this point in time. It'd be like dissecting a parent!

My mother began kipling us—or maybe it was my father, the Colonel—with the *Just So Stories*—as good read-aloud-to-their-children mothers do. "Oh best beloved," or "Hear and attend and listen" were magic words that shut me and my brothers up in the only form of truce we knew as siblings. Mother tried other childish tales on us: Peter Rabbit bored us stupid after "Mowgli's Brothers". I knew every whisker and hair of Rikki Tikki Tavi's smooth pelt though I didn't see a mongoose until I went to Australia in 1980. (I bloody knew what they were, and that snakes travel in mated pairs . . . I'll get back to that.)

"The Cat Who Walked By Himself" has always been my special tale—I'm one of those myself, and that story became a talisman when I could read for myself, and was rejected (for very laudable reasons) by my peer group. I, me, myself, Anne McCaffrey was a cat who walked by herself, and I often walked in the Wild Wet Woods and climbed the Wild Wet Trees (and fell out often enough to learn not to climb wet trees.) Mother had a habit of reading us "The Elephant's Child" when we exhibited an excess of curiosity. She did a marvelous nose-held-by-a-crocodile voice!

My father, who often referred affectionately to his wife as "The White Man's Burden," was not to be left out of this family brainwashing. The Colonel had a parade-ground voice that projected beautifully through the halls of our house—or the streets of our town. He "declaimed" Kipling. He even managed a properly cockney accent when needed. And he had rhythm! We used to clap to "*Boots, Boots, Boots/Slogging Up and Down Again/And There's No Discharge in the War.*" I used to shiver with awe at his final ringing *You're a better man than I am, Gunga Din* and who needed Sam Jaffe! My father's notion of entertaining sick children was to start at one end of *Barrack Room Ballads* and come out the other—if we were sick enough, he launched into *Departmental Ditties*: "For they're hanging Danny Deever in the Morning!" "Please to step in front, sir, when there's trouble in the wind," "Fuzzy-Wuzzy who broke a British Square," and "Mandalay"! The Colonel could be counted on to read "Toomai of the Elephants" or "Rikki" if Mother wouldn't.

We graduated from *Just So Stories* to the two *Jungle Books*, and clammered for more, utterly betrayed that Mowgli grew up and Kipling wrote no more about him and the Law of the Jungle. My brothers went on to *Puck of Pook's Hill* and *Stalky & Company* but they hadn't the same appeal for me somehow as Bagheera and Shere Khan. So I'd get lost in the poetry, more a girl's thing (in the dim dark dense '30s) anyhow. In my teens, I read my way through all the other volumes.

The Kipling edition my family owned was bound in red calf, with gold leaf trim, and the swastika of *Indian* origin. They were lovely books to hold, not too large, but the type was clear and the illustrations were the original J. Lockwood Kipling and the Drakes. They eventually fell apart from use, but the smell of calf leather, the soft feel of the covers, the size of the books are indelibly part of my early years and my discovery of Rudyard Kipling.

None of that edition survived our usage, though I've

most of *Departmental Ditties* packaged in plastic as a keepsake. Mac used to reread *Kim* but then, living in Thailand for nearly 25 years, he was closer to Kipling-land than I've ever got. Keve has a set and it's like seeing old friends waiting for me in the shelves.

All three of us found *Kim* on our own, and I've been back on the Grand Trunk Road on a yearly basis, just for the magic Kipling wrought in that tale—and for reassurance when the Russians invaded Afghanistan—finally. (Not that that maneuver has accomplished a damned thing—even as Kipling maintained.) That novel proves the point that good storytelling rises above its origins and becomes timeless. It's even survived some bad Hollywood presentations.

What Kipling gave me, Anne McCaffrey, was the lilt of storytelling at a very early age, an appreciation of wry humor and great wit, a rhythm for ballad, a sense of rhyme, and a hunger for stories just like the ones that enthralled me as a child. He zapped me *into* the jungle with a dirty little clever boy named Mowgli, cavorting with wolf cubs and poor-mouthing a tiger from the safety of a tree. He handed me a view of a world totally different to Upper Montclair, New Jersey, and I *believed* in it. I learned from Kipling the flow of words, and their bedazzlement. (Poor guy—he had to hand write everything with a scratchy ink-pen nib! Drying his hand off to keep from smudging the paper he was writing on, whisking flies and mosquitoes and whatever away without breaking concentration, and hoping his publisher would send the money in time to pay his more pressing debts. Don't *ever* try to tell another writer *why* people write what they do!)

One of the first educational shocks I had was that Kipling was *not* considered a great writer by otherwise perfectly sensible English teachers and college English professors. In fact, he wasn't considered a writer at all—a hack, a (nasty word then) journalist, yellow in fact, a begetter of popular doggerel at best. A Raj, an imperialist, a . . . whatever. I don't even want to repeat all the unfair adjectives and scurrilous criticisms. He's had the last laugh. So many of the writers considered "worthy" during his lifetime are totally forgotten.

It wasn't until I entered the science fiction milieu that I

could be comfortable with my secret passion for Kipling, my reverence for his abilities. One of the most reassuring discussions I had in 1959 was with James Blish and his high opinion of Kipling! So many SF writers could see his sterling merit as a storyteller that I felt vindicated. We folks know Storytellers when we reads 'em!

I said I'd return to it—Kipling wasn't just an entertaining writer: he could be instructive and reported accurately, trustworthily. One summer at a Girl Scout Camp, the unit I lived in was infested by rattlesnakes during a long wet spell. Our counselor had hysterics after one rattler was killed not far from her tent so she refused to believe that there could possibly be another! I could. I'd read Kipling. She didn't listen to me so I ended up hunting down the second one, the larger female, and killed it by chopping off its head with an axe. Kipling had also remarked that it took a long time for a snake to know it was dead. Rather comforting for a twelve-year old.

That was the same summer in which I wrote, costumed, directed and produced a play based on *The Butterfly That Stamped*, a story I have quoted on numerous occasions! Kipling's ineffably quotable.

Kipling also spoke to me when he wrote:

I go to concerts, parties, balls
What profit is in these
I sit alone against the wall,
and strive to look at ease
The incense that is mine by right
They burn before her shrine
But that's because I'm seventeen
and SHE is forty-nine.

(I even remembered it fondly when I became forty-nine!) I used to recite that poem as a monologue piece, trying out for other dramatic shows all during high school and college. Actually, as I was often a wallflower, I could recite it with considerable and appropriate emotion. Unfortunately, Kipling wrote more for the male voice, like my father's, than soprano. A shame that! That didn't keep me from knowing most of his poetry by heart.

Later, that vast pool of quotables came into daily use when I was working as a copywriter for Liberty Music Shops, writing radio commercials. Until my boss balked at repeating one more line of Kipling.

When I had children, I read Kipling aloud to them—well, until TV invaded. Still, they did know how Disney perverted *The Jungle Book*, but wasn't George Sanders' voice perfect for Shere Khan?

I'll get a last bit of Kiplingesque whimsy in—remember "A General Summary:"

> *Who shall doubt the secret hid*
> *Beneath Cheops' pyramid*
> *Is that the contractor did*
> *Cheops out of several millions?*

Seems that there is now a scanner sensitive enough to detect a hidden room in Cheops' pyramid that was only suspected before. Wonder if Kipling *knew* what was in it? Or, good writer that he was, put *that* in as a reader hook? But wasn't it clever of Rudyard?

The Ship Who Sang

ANNE McCAFFREY

She was born a thing and as such would be condemned if she failed to pass the encephalograph test required of all newborn babies. There was always the possibility that though the limbs were twisted, the mind was not, that though the ears would hear only dimly, the eyes see vaguely, the mind behind them was receptive and alert.

The electro-encephalogram was entirely favorable, unexpectedly so, and the news was brought to the waiting, grieving parents. There was the final, harsh decision: to give their child euthanasia or permit it to become an encapsulated "brain," a guiding mechanism in any one of a number of curious professions. As such, their offspring would suffer no pain, live a comfortable existence in a metal shell for several centuries, performing unusual service to Central Worlds.

She lived and was given a name, Helva. For her first three vegetable months she waved her crabbed claws, kicked weakly with her clubbed feet and enjoyed the usual routine of the infant. She was not alone for there were three other such children in the big city's special nursery. Soon they all were removed to Central Laboratory School where their delicate transformation began.

One of the babies died in the initial transferral but of Helva's "class," seventeen thrived in the metal shells. Instead of kicking feet, Helva's neural responses started her wheels; instead of grabbing with hands, she manipulated mechanical extensions. As she matured, more and more neural synapses would be adjusted to operate other mechanisms that went into the maintenance and running of a space ship. For Helva was destined to be the "brain" half of a scout ship, partnered with a man or a woman, whichever she chose, as the mobile half. She would be among the elite of her kind. Her initial intelligence tests registered above normal and her adaptation index was unusually high. As long as her development within her shell lived up to expectations, and there were no side-effects from the pituitary tinkering, Helva would live a rewarding, rich and unusual life, a far cry from what she would have faced as an ordinary, "normal" being.

However, no diagram of her brain patterns, no early I.Q. tests recorded certain essential facts about Helva that Central must eventually learn. They would have to bide their official time and see, trusting that the massive doses of shell-psychology would suffice her, too, as the necessary bulwark against her unusual confinement and the pressures of her profession. A ship run by a human brain could not run rogue or insane with the power and resources Central had to build into their scout ships. Brain ships were, of course, long past the experimental stages. Most babes survived the techniques of pituitary manipulation that kept their bodies small, eliminating the necessity of transfers from smaller to larger shells. And very, very few were lost when the final connection was made to the control panels of ship or industrial combine. Shell people resembled mature dwarfs in size whatever their natal deformities were, but the well-oriented brain would not have changed places with the most perfect body in the Universe.

So, for happy years, Helva scooted around in her shell with her classmates, playing such games as Stall, Power-Seek, studying her lessons in trajectory, propulsion techniques, computation, logistics, mental hygiene, basic alien psychology, philology space history, law, traffic, codes: all the et ceteras that eventually became compounded into a reasoning, logical, informed citizen. Not so obvious to her, but of more importance to her teachers, Helva ingested the precepts of her conditioning as easily as she absorbed her nutrient fluid. She would one day be grateful to the patient drone of the sub-conscious-level instruction.

Helva's civilization was not without busy, do-good associations, exploring possible inhumanities to terrestrial as well as extraterrestrial citizens. One such group got all incensed over shelled "children" when Helva was just turning fourteen. When they were forced to, Central Worlds shrugged its shoulders, arranged a tour of the Laboratory Schools and set the tour off to a big start by showing the members case histories, complete with photographs. Very few committees ever looked past the first few photos. Most of their original objections about "shells" were overridden by the relief that these hideous (to them) bodies *were* mercifully concealed.

Helva's class was doing Fine Arts, a selective subject in her crowded program. She had activated one of her microscopic tools which she would later use for minute repairs to various parts of her control panel. Her subject was large—a copy of the Last Supper—and her canvas, small—the head of a tiny screw. She had tuned her sight to the proper degree. As she worked she absentmindedly crooned, producing a curious sound. Shell people used their own vocal cords and diaphragms but sound issued through microphones rather than mouths. Helva's hum then had a curious vibrancy, a warm, dulcet quality even in its aimless chromatic wanderings.

"Why, what a lovely voice you have," said one of the female visitors.

Helva "looked" up and caught a fascinating panorama of regular, dirty craters on a flaky pink surface. Her hum became a gurgle of surprise. She instinctively regulated her "sight" until the skin lost its cratered look and the pores assumed normal proportions.

"Yes, we have quite a few years of voice training, madam," remarked Helva calmly. "Vocal peculiarities often become excessively irritating during prolonged intra-stellar distances and must be eliminated. I enjoyed my lessons."

Although this was the first time that Helva had seen unshelled people, she took this experience calmly. Any other reaction would have been reported instantly.

"I meant that you have a nice singing voice . . . dear," the lady amended.

"Thank you. Would you like to see my work?" Helva asked, politely. She instinctively sheered away from personal discussions but she filed the comment away for further meditation.

"Work?" asked the lady.

"I am currently reproducing the Last Supper on the head of a screw."

"O, I say," the lady twittered.

Helva turned her vision back to magnification and surveyed her copy critically.

"Of course, some of my color values do not match the old Master's and the perspective is faulty but I believe it to be a fair copy."

The lady's eyes, unmagnified, bugged out.

"Oh, I forget, " and Helva's voice was really contrite. If she could have blushed, she would have. "You people don't have adjustable vision."

The monitor of this discourse grinned with pride and amusement as Helva's tone indicated pity for the unfortunate.

"Here, this will help," suggested Helva, substituting a magnifying device in one extension and holding it over the picture.

In a kind of shock, the ladies and gentlemen of the committee bent to observe the incredibly copied and brilliantly executed Last Supper on the head of a screw.

"Well," remarked one gentleman who had been forced to accompany his wife, "the good Lord can eat where angels fear to tread."

"Are you referring, sir," asked Helva politely, "to the Dark Age discussions of the number of angels who could stand on the head of a pin?"

"I had that in mind."

"If you substitute 'atom' for 'angel,' the problem is not insoluble, given the metallic content of the pin in question."

"Which you are programed to compute?"

"Of course."

"Did they remember to program a sense of humor, as well, young lady?"

"We are directed to develop a sense of proportion, sir, which contributes the same effect."

The good man chortled appreciatively and decided the trip was worth his time.

If the investigation committee spent months digesting the thoughtful food served them at the Laboratory School, they left Helva with a morsel as well.

"Singing" as applicable to herself required research. She had, of course, been exposed to and enjoyed a music appreciation course which had included the better known classical works such as "Tristan and Isolde," "Candide," "Oklahoma," "Nozze de Figaro," the atomic age singers, Eileen Farrell, Elvis Presley and Geraldine Todd, as well as the curious rhythmic progressions of the Venusians, Capellan visual chromatics and the sonic concerti of the Altairians. But "singing" for any shell person posed considerable technical difficulties to be overcome. Shell people were schooled to examine every aspect of a problem or situation before making a prognosis. Balanced properly between optimism and practicality, the nondefeatist attitude of the shell people led them to extricate themselves, their ships and personnel, from bizarre situations. Therefore to Helva, the problem that she couldn't open her mouth to sing, among other restrictions, did not bother her. She would work out a method, by-passing her limitations, whereby she could sing.

She approached the problem by investigating the methods of sound reproduction through the centuries, human and instrumental. Her own sound production equipment was essentially more instrumental than vocal. Breath control and the proper enunciation of vowel sounds within the oral cavity appeared to require the most development and practice. Shell people did not, strictly speaking, breathe. For their purposes, oxygen and other gases were not drawn from the surrounding atmosphere through the medium of lungs but sustained artificially by solution in their shells. After experimentation, Helva discovered that she could manipulate her diaphragmic unit to sustain tone. By relaxing the throat muscles and expanding the oral cavity well into the frontal sinuses, she could direct the vowel sounds into the most felicitous position for proper reproduction through her throat microphone. She compared the results with tape recordings of modern singers and was not unpleased although her own tapes had a peculiar quality about them, not at all unharmonious, merely unique. Acquiring a repertoire from the Laboratory library was no problem to one trained to perfect recall. She found herself able to sing any role and any song which struck her fancy. It would not have occurred to her that it was curious for a female to sing bass, baritone, tenor, alto, mezzo, soprano and coloratura as she pleased. It was, to Helva, only a matter of the correct reproduction and diaphragmic control required by the music attempted.

If the authorities remarked on her curious avocation, they did so among themselves. Shell people were encouraged to develop a hobby so long as they maintained proficiency in their technical work.

On the anniversary of her sixteenth year in her shell, Helva was unconditionally graduated and installed in her ship, the XH-834. Her permanent titanium shell was recessed behind an even more indestructible barrier in the central shaft of the scout ship. The neural, audio, visual and sensory connections were made and sealed. Her extendibles were diverted, connected or augmented and the final, delicate-beyond-description brain taps were completed while Helva remained anesthetically unaware of the proceedings. When she awoke, she *was* the ship. Her brain and intelligence controlled every function from navigation to such loading as a scout ship of her class needed. She could take care of herself and her ambulatory half, in any situation already recorded in the annals of Central Worlds and any situation its most fertile minds could imagine.

Her first actual flight, for she and her kind had made mock flights on dummy panels since she was eight, showed her complete mastery of the techniques of her profession. She was ready for her great adventures and the arrival of her mobile partner.

There were nine qualified scouts sitting around collecting base pay the day Helva was commissioned. There were several missions which demanded instant attention but Helva had been of interest to several department heads in Central for some time and each man was determined to have her assigned to *his* section. Consequently no one had remembered to introduce Helva to the prospective partners. The ship always chose its own partner. Had there been another "brain" ship at the Base at the moment, Helva would have been guided to make the first move. As it was, while Central wrangled among itself, Robert Tanner sneaked out of the pilots' barracks, out to the field and over to Helva's slim metal hull.

"Hello, anyone at home?" Tanner wisecracked.

"Of course," replied Helva logically, activating her outside scanners. "Are you my partner?" she asked hopefully, as she recognized the Scout Service uniform.

"All you have to do is ask," he retorted hopefully.

"No one has come. I thought perhaps there were no partners available and I've had no directives from Central."

Even to herself Helva sounded a little self-pitying but the truth was she was lonely, sitting on the darkened field. Always she had had the company of other shells and more recently, technicians by the score. The sudden solitude had lost its momentary charm and become oppressive.

"No directives from Central is scarcely a cause for regret, but there happen to be eight other guys biting their fingernails to the quick just waiting for an invitation to board you, you beautiful thing."

Tanner was inside the central cabin as he said this, running appreciative fingers over her panel, the scout's gravity-couch, poking his head into the cabins, the galley, the head, the pressured-storage compartments.

"Now, if you want to give Central a shove and do *us* a favor all in one, call up the Barracks and let's have a ship-warming partner-picking party. Hmmmm?"

Helva chuckled to herself. He was so completely different from the occasional visitors or the various Laboratory technicians she had encountered. He was so gay, so assured, and she was delighted by his suggestion of a partner-picking party. Certainly it was not against anything in her understanding of regulations.

"Cencom, this is XH-834. Connect me with Pilot Barracks."

"Visual?"

"Please."

A picture of lounging men in various attitudes of boredom came on her screen.

"This is XH-834. Would the unassigned scouts do me the favor of coming aboard?"

Eight figures galvanized into action, grabbing pieces of wearing apparel, disengaging tape mechanisms, disentangling themselves from bedsheets and towels.

Helva dissolved the connection while Tanner chuckled gleefully and settled down to await their arrival.

Helva was engulfed in an unshell-like flurry of anticipation. No actress on her opening night could have been more apprehensive, fearful or breathless. Unlike the actress, she could throw no hysterics, china objects d'art or greasepaint to relieve her tension. She could, of course, check her stores for edibles and drinks, which she did, serving Tanner from the virgin selection of her commissary.

Scouts were colloquially known as "brawns" as opposed to their ship "brains." They had to pass as rigorous a training program as the brains and only the top one percent of each contributory world's highest scholars were admitted to Central Worlds Scout Training Program. Consequently the eight young men who came pounding up the gantry into Helva's hospitable lock were unusually fine-looking, intelligent, well-co-ordinated and adjusted young men, looking forward to a slightly drunken evening, Helva permitting, and all quite willing to do each other dirt to get possession of her.

Such a human invasion left Helva mentally breathless, a luxury she thoroughly enjoyed for the brief time she felt she should permit it. She sorted out the young men. Tanner's opportunism amused but did not specifically attract her; the blond Nordsen seemed too simple; dark-haired Al-atpay had a kind of obstinacy with which she felt no compassion: Mir-Ahnin's bitterness hinted an inner darkness she did not wish to lighten although he made the biggest outward play for her attention. Hers was a curious courtship—this would be only the first of several marriages for her, for brawns retired after 75 years of service, or earlier if they were unlucky. Brains, their bodies safe from any deterioration, served 200 years, and were then permitted to decide for themselves if they wished to continue. Helva had actually spoken to one shell person three hundred and twenty-two years old. She had been so awed by the contact she hadn't presumed to ask the personal questions she had wanted to.

Her choice did not stand out from the others until Tanner started to sing a scout ditty, recounting the misadventures of the bold, dense, painfully inept Billy Brawn. An attempt at harmony resulted in cacophony and Tanner wagged his arms wildly for silence.

"What we need is a roaring good lead tenor. Jennan, besides palming aces, what do you sing?"

"Sharp," Jennan replied with easy good humor.

"If a tenor is absolutely necessary, I'll attempt it," Helva volunteered.

"My good *woman*," Tanner protested.

"Sound your 'A'," laughed Jennan.

Into the stunned silence that followed the rich, clear, high "A," Jennan remarked quietly, "Such an A, Caruso would have given the rest of his notes to sing."

It did not take them long to discover her full range.

"All Tanner asked for was one roaring good lead tenor," Jennan complained jokingly, "and our sweet mistress supplies us an entire repertory company. The boy who gets this ship will go far, far, far."

"To the Horsehead Nebulae?" asked Nordsen, quoting an old Central saw.

"To the Horsehead Nebulae and back, we shall make beautiful music," countered Helva, chuckling.

"Together," Jennan amended. "Only you'd better make the music and with my voice, I'd better listen."

"I rather imagined it would be I who listened," suggested Helva.

Jennan executed a stately bow with an intricate flourish of his crush-brimmed hat. He directed his bow toward the central control pillar where Helva *was*. Her own personal preference crystallized at that precise moment and for that particular reason: Jennan, alone of the men, had addressed his remarks directly at her physical presence, regardless of the fact that he knew she could pick up his image wherever he was in the ship and regardless of the fact that her body was behind massive metal walls. Throughout their partnership, Jennan never failed to turn his head in her direction no matter where he was in relation to her. In response to this personalization, Helva at that moment and from then on always spoke to Jennan only through her central mike, even though that was not always the most efficient method.

Helva didn't know that she fell in love with Jennan that evening. As she had never been exposed to love or affection, only the drier cousins, respect and admiration, she could scarcely have recognized her reaction to the warmth of his personality and consideration. As a shell-person, she considered herself remote from emotions largely connected with physical desires.

"Well, Helva, it's been swell meeting you," said Tanner suddenly, as she and Jennan were arguing about the Baroque quality of "Come All Ye Sons of Art." "See you in space some time, you lucky dog, Jennan. Thanks for the party, Helva."

"You don't have to go so soon?" pleaded Helva, realizing belatedly that she and Jennan had been excluding the others.

"Best man won," Tanner said, wryly. "Guess I'd better go get a tape on love ditties. May need 'em for the next ship, if there're any more at home like you."

Helva and Jennan watched them leave, both a little confused.

"Perhaps Tanner's jumping to conclusions?" Jennan asked.

Helva regarded him as he slouched against the console, facing her shell directly. His arms were crossed on his chest and the glass he held had been empty for some time. He was handsome, they all were; but his watchful eyes were unwary, his mouth assumed a smile easily, his voice (to which Helva was particularly drawn) was resonant, deep and without unpleasant overtones or accent.

"Sleep on it, Helva. Call me in the morning if it's your opt."

She called him at breakfast, after she had checked her choice through Central. Jennan moved his things aboard, received their joint commission, had his personality and experience file locked into her reviewer, gave her the co-ordinates of their first mission and the XH-834 officially became the JH-834.

Their first mission was a dull but necessary crash priority (Medical got Helva), rushing a vaccine to a distant system plagued with a virulent spore disease. They had only to get to Spica as fast as possible.

After the initial, thrilling forward surge of her maximum speed, Helva realized her muscles were to be given less of a workout than her brawn on this tedious mission. But they did have plenty of time for exploring each other's personalities. Jennan, of course, knew what Helva was capable of as a ship and partner, just as she knew what she could expect from him. But these were only facts and Helva looked forward eagerly to learning that human side of her partner which could not be reduced to a series of symbols. Nor could the give and take of two personalities be learned from a book. It has to be experienced.

"My father was a scout, too, or is that programed?" began Jennan their third day out.

"Naturally."

"Unfair, you know. You've got all my family history and I don't know one blamed thing about yours."

"I've never known either," Helva confided. "Until I read yours, it hadn't occurred to me I must have one, too, some place in Central's files."

Jennan snorted. "Shell psychology!"

Helva laughed. "Yes, and I'm even programed against curiosity about it. You'd better be, too,"

Jennan ordered a drink, slouched into the gravity couch opposite her, put his feet on the bumpers, turning himself idly from side to side on the gimbals.

"Helva—a made-up name . . ."

"With a Scandinavian sound."

"You aren't blond," Jennan said positively.

"Well, then, there're dark Swedes."

"And blond Turks and this one's harem is limited to one."

"Your woman in purdah, yes, but you can comb the pleasure houses—" Helva found herself aghast at the edge to her carefully trained voice.

"You know," Jennan interrupted her, deep in some thought of his own, "my father gave me the impression he was a lot more married to his ship, the Silvia, than to my mother. I know I used to think Silvia was my grandmother. She was a low number so she must have been a great-great-grandmother at least. I used to talk to her for hours."

"Her registry?" asked Helva, unwitting of the jealousy for everyone and anyone who had shared his hours.

"422. I think she's TS now. I ran into Tom Burgess once."

Jennan's father had died of a planetary disease, the vaccine for which his ship had used up in curing the local citizens.

"Tom said he'd got mighty tough and salty. You lose your sweetness and I'll come back and haunt you, girl," Jennan threatened.

Helva laughed. He startled her by stamping up to the control panel, touching it with light, tender fingers.

"I *wonder* what you look like," he said softly, wistfully.

Helva had been briefed about this natural curiosity of scouts. She didn't know anything about herself and neither of them ever would or could.

"Pick any form, shape and shade and I'll be yours obliging," she countered as training suggested.

"Iron Maiden, I fancy blondes with long tresses," and Jennan pantomined Lady Godiva-like tresses. "Since you're immolated in titanium, I'll call you Brunehilda, my dear," and he made his bow.

With a chortle, Helva launched into the appropriate aria just as Spica made contact.

"What'n'ell's that yelling about? Who are you? And unless you're Central Worlds Medical go away. We've got a plague with no visiting privileges."

"My ship is singing, we're the JH-834 of Worlds and we've got your vaccine. What are our landing co-ordinates?"

"Your *ship* is singing?"

"The greatest S.A.T.B. in organized space. Any request?"

The JH-834 delivered the vaccine but no more arias and received immediate orders to proceed to Leviticus IV. By the time they got there, Jennan found a reputation awaiting him and was forced to defend the 834's virgin honor.

"I'll stop singing," murmured Helva contritely as she ordered up poultices for this third black eye in a week.

"You will not," Jennan said through gritted teeth. "If I

have black eyes from here to the Horsehead to keep the snicker out of the title, we'll be the ship who sings."

After the "ship who sings" tangled with a minor but vicious narcotic ring in the Lesser Magallenics, the title became definitely respectful. Central was aware of each episode and punched out a "special interest" key on JH-834's file. A first-rate team was shaking down well.

Jennan and Helva considered themselves a first-rate team, too, after their tidy arrest.

"Of all the vices in the universe, I *hate* drug addiction," Jennan remarked as they headed back to Central Base. "People can go to hell quick enough without that kind of help."

"Is that why you volunteered for Scout Service? To redirect traffic?"

"I'll bet my official answer's on your review."

"In far too flowery wording. 'Carrying on the traditions of my family which has been proud of four generations in Service' if I may quote you your own words."

Jennan groaned. "I was *very* young when I wrote that and I certainly hadn't been through Final Training and once I was in Final Training, my pride wouldn't let me fail. . . .

"As I mentioned, I used to visit Dad on board the Silvia and I've a very good idea she might have had her eye on me as a replacement for my father because I had had massive doses of scout-oriented propaganda. It took. From the time I was seven, I was going to be a scout or else." He shrugged as if deprecating a youthful determination that had taken a great deal of mature application to bring to fruition.

"Ah, so? Scout Sahir Silan on the JS-422 penetrating into the Horsehead Nebulae?"

Jennan chose to ignore her sarcasm. "With *you*, I may even get that far but even with Silvia's nudging *I* never day-dreamed myself *that* kind of glory in my wildest flights of fancy. I'll leave the whoppers to your agile brain henceforth. I have in mind a smaller contribution to Space History."

"So modest?"

"No. Practical. We also serve, et cetera." He placed a dramatic hand on his heart.

"Glory hound!" scoffed Helva.

"Look who's talking, my Nebulae-bound friend. At least I'm not greedy. There'll only be one hero like my dad at Parsaea, but I *would* like to be remembered for some kudo. Everyone does. Why else do or die?"

"Your father died on his way back from Parsaea, if I may point out a few cogent facts. So he could never have known he was a hero for damning the flood with his ship. Which kept Parsaean colony from being abandoned. Which gave them a chance to discover the anti-paralytic qualities of Parsaea. Which *he* never knew."

"*I* know," said Jennan softly.

Helva was immediately sorry for the tone of her rebuttal. She knew very well how deep Jennan's attachment to his father had been. On his review a note was made that he had rationalized his father's loss with the unexpected and welcome outcome of the Affair at Parsaea.

"Facts are not human, Helva. My father was and so am I. And *basically*, so are you. Check over your dials, 834. Amid all the wires attached to you is a heart, an underdeveloped human heart. Obviously!"

"I apologize, Jennan," she said contritely.

Jennan hesitated a moment, threw out his hands in acceptance and then tapped her shell affectionately.

"If they ever take us off the milkruns, we'll make a stab at the Nebulae, huh?"

As so frequently happened in the Scout Service, within the next hour they had orders to change course, not to the Nebulae, but to a recently colonized system with two habitable planets, one tropical, one glacial. The sun, named Ravel, had become unstable; the spectrum was that of a rapidly expanding shell, with absorption lines quickly displacing toward violet. The augmented heat of the primary had already forced evacuation of the nearer world, Daphnis. The pattern of spectral emissions gave indication that the sun would sear Chloe as well. All ships in the vicinity were to report to Disaster Headquarters on Chloe to effect removal of the remaining colonists.

The JH-834 obediently presented itself and was sent to outlying areas on Chloe to pick up scattered settlers who did not appear to appreciate the urgency of the situation. Chloe, indeed, was enjoying the first temperatures above freezing since it had been flung out of its parent. Since many of the colonists were religious fanatics who had settled on rigorous Chloe to fit themselves for a life of pious reflection, Chloe's abrupt thaw was attributed to sources other than a rampaging sun.

Jennan had to spend so much time countering specious arguments that he and Helva were behind schedule on their way to the fourth and last settlement. Helva jumped over the high range of jagged peaks that surrounded and sheltered the valley from the former raging snows as well as the present heat. The violent sun with its flaring corona was just beginning to brighten the deep valley.

"They'd better grab their toothbrushes and hop aboard," Helva commented. "HQ says speed it up."

"All women," remarked Jennan in surprise as he walked down to meet them. "Unless the men on Chloe wear furred skirts."

"Charm 'em but pare the routine to the bare essentials. And turn on your two-way private."

Jennan advanced smiling, but his explanation was met with absolute incredulity and considerable doubt as to his authenticity. He groaned inwardly as the matriarch paraphrased previous explanations of the warming sun.

"Revered mother, there's been an overload on that prayer circuit and the sun is blowing itself up in one obliging burst. I'm here to take you to the spaceport at Rosary—"

"That Sodom?" the worthy woman glowered and shuddered disdainfully at his suggestion. "We thank you for your warning but we have no wish to leave our cloister for the rude world. We must go about our morning meditation which has been interrupted— "

"It'll be permanently interrupted when that sun starts broiling. You must come now," Jennan said firmly.

"Madame," said Helva, realizing that perhaps a female voice might carry more weight in this instance than Jennan's very masculine charm.

"Who spoke?" cried the nun, startled by the bodiless voice.

"I, Helva, the ship. Under my protection you and your

sisters-in-faith may enter safely and be unprofaned by association with a male. I will guard you and take you safely to a place prepared for you."

The matriarch peered cautiously into the ship's open port. "Since only Central Worlds is permitted the use of such ships, I acknowledge that you are not trifling with us, young man. However, we are in no danger here."

"The temperature at Rosary is now 99°," said Helva. "As soon as the sun's rays penetrate directly into this valley, it will also be 99°, and it is due to climb to approximately 180° today. I notice your buildings are made of wood with moss chinking. Dry moss. It should fire around noontime."

The sunlight was beginning to slant into the valley through the peaks and the fierce rays warmed the restless group behind the matriarch. Several opened the throats of their furry parkas.

"Jennan," said Helva privately to him, "our time is very short."

"I can't leave them, Helva. Some of those girls are barely out of their teens."

"Pretty, too. No wonder the matriarch doesn't want to get in."

"Helva."

"It will be the Lord's will," said the matriarch stoutly and turned her back squarely on rescue.

"To burn to death?" shouted Jennan as she threaded her way through her murmuring disciples.

"They want to be martyrs? Their opt, Jennan," said Helva dispassionately. "*We* must leave and that is no longer a matter of option."

"How can I leave, Helva?"

"Parsaea?" Helva flung tauntingly at him as he stepped forward to grab one of the women. "You can't drag them *all* aboard and we don't have time to fight it out. Get on board, Jennan, or I'll have you on report."

"They'll die," muttered Jennan dejectedly as he reluctantly turned to climb on board.

"You can risk only so much," Helva said sympathetically. "As it is we'll just have time to make rendezvous. Lab reports a critical speed-up in spectral evolution."

Jennan was already in the airlock when one of the

younger women, screaming, rushed to squeeze in the closing port. Her action set off the others and they stampeded through the narrow opening. Even crammed back to breast, there was not enough room inside. Jennan broke out spacesuits for the three who would have to remain with him in the airlock. He wasted valuable time explaining to the matriarch that she must put on the suit because the airlock had no independent oxygen or cooling units.

"We'll be caught," said Helva grimly to Jennan on their private connection. "We've lost 18 minutes in this last-minute rush. I am now overloaded for maximum speed and I must attain maximum speed to outrun the heatwave."

"Can you lift? We're suited."

"Lift? Yes," she said, doing so. "Run? I stagger."

Jennan, bracing himself and the women, could feel her sluggishness as she blasted upward. Heartlessly, Helva applied thrust as long as she could, despite the fact that the gravitational force mashed her cabin passengers brutally and crushed two fatally. It was a question of saving as many as possible. The only one for whom she had any concern was Jennan and she was in desperate terror about his safety. Airless and uncooled, protected by only one layer of metal, not three, the airlock was not going to be safe for the four trapped there, despite their spacesuits. These were only the standard models, not built to withstand the excessive heat to which the ship would be subjected.

Helva ran as fast as she could but the incredible wave of heat from the explosive sun caught them halfway to cold safety.

She paid no heed to the cries, moans, pleas and prayers in her cabin. She listened only to Jennan's tortured breathing, to the missing throb in his suit's purifying system and the sucking of the overloaded cooling unit. Helpless, she heard the hysterical screams of his three companions as they writhed in the awful heat. Vainly, Jennan tried to calm them, tried to explain they would soon be safe and cool if they could be still and endure the heat. Undisciplined by their terror and torment, they tried to strike out at him despite the close quarters. One flailing arm became entangled in the leads to his power pack and the damage was quickly done. A connection, weakened by heat and the dead weight of the arm, broke.

For all the power at her disposal, Helva was helpless. She watched as Jennan fought for his breath, as he turned his head beseechingly toward *her*, and died.

Only the iron conditioning of her training prevented Helva from swinging around and plunging back into the exploding sun. Numbly she made rendezvous with the refugee convoy. She obediently transferred her burned, heat-prostrated passengers to the assigned transport.

"I will retain the body of my scout and proceed to the nearest base for burial," she informed Central dully.

"You will be provided escort," was the reply.

"I have no need of escort," she demurred.

"Escort is provided, XH-834," she was told curtly.

The shock of hearing Jennan's initial severed from her call number cut off her half-formed protest. Stunned, she waited by the transport until her screens showed the arrival of two other slim brain ships. The cortege proceeded homeward at unfunereal speeds.

"834? The ship who sings?"

"I have no more songs."

"Your scout was Jennan?"

"I do not wish to communicate."

"I'm 422."

"Silvia?"

"Silvia died a long time ago. I'm 422. Currently MS," the ship rejoined curtly. "AH-640 is our other friend, but Henry's not listening in. Just as well—he wouldn't understand it if you wanted to turn rogue. But I'd stop *him* if he tried to delay you."

"Rogue?" The term snapped Helva out of her apathy.

"Sure. You're young. You've got power for years. Skip. Others have done it. 732 went rogue two years ago after she lost her scout on a mission to that white dwarf. Hasn't been seen since."

"I never heard about rogues," gasped Helva.

"As it's exactly the thing we're conditioned against, you sure wouldn't hear about it in school, my dear," 422 said.

"Break conditioning?" cried Helva, anguished, thinking of the white, white furious hot heart of the sun she had just left.

"For you I don't think it would be hard at the moment," 422 said quietly, her voice devoid of her earlier cynicism. "The stars are out there, winking."

"Alone?" cried Helva from her heart.

"Alone!" 422 confirmed bleakly.

Alone with all of space and time. Even the Horsehead Nebulae would not be far enough away to daunt her. Alone with a hundred years to live with her memories and nothing . . . nothing more.

"Was Parsaea worth it?" she asked 422 softly.

"Parsaea?" 422 came back, surprised. "With his father? Yes. We were there, at Parsaea when we were needed. Just as you . . . and his son . . . were at Chloe. When you were needed. The crime is always not knowing where need is and not being there."

"But *I* need *him*. Who will supply my need?" said Helva bitterly. . . .

"834," said 422 after a day's silent speeding. "Central wishes your report. A replacement awaits your opt at Regulus Base. Change course accordingly."

"A replacement?" That was certainly not what she needed . . . a reminder inadequately filling the void Jennan left. Why, her hull was barely cool of Chloe's heat. Atavistically, Helva wanted time to mourn Jennan.

"Oh, none of them are impossible if *you're* a good ship," 422 remarked philosophically. "And it is just what you need. The sooner the better."

"You told them I wouldn't go rogue, didn't you?" Helva said heavily.

"The moment passed you even as it passed me after Parsaea, and before that, after Glen Arhur, and Betelgeuse."

"We're conditioned to go on, aren't we? We *can't* go rogue. You were testing."

"Had to. Orders. Not even Psycho knows why a rogue occurs. Central's very worried, and so, daughter, are your sister ships. I asked to be your escort. I . . . don't want to lose you both."

In her emotional nadir, Helva could feel a flood of gratitude for Silvia's rough sympathy.

"We've all known this grief, Helva. It's no consolation

but if we couldn't feel with our scouts, we'd only be machines wired for sound."

Helva looked at Jennan's still form stretched before her in its shroud and heard the echo of his rich voice in the quiet cabin.

"Silvia! I *couldn't* help him," she cried from her soul.

"Yes, dear. I know," 422 murmured gently and then was quiet.

The three ships sped on, wordless, to the great Central Worlds base at Regulus. Helva broke silence to acknowledge landing instructions and the officially tendered regrets.

The three ships set down simultaneously at the wooded edge where Regulus' gigantic blue trees stood sentinel over the sleeping dead in the small Service cemetery. The entire Base complement approached with measured step and formed an aisle from Helva to the burial ground. The honor detail, out of step, walked slowly into her cabin. Reverently they placed the body of her dead love on the wheeled bier, covered it honorably with the deep blue, star-splashed flag of the Service. She watched as it was driven slowly down the living aisle which closed in behind the bier in last escort.

Then, as the simple words of interment were spoken, as the atmosphere planes dipped wings in tribute over the open grave, Helva found voice for her lonely farewell.

Softly, barely audible at first, the strains of the ancient song of evening and requiem swelled to the final poignant measure until black space itself echoed back the sound of the song the ship sang.

Introduction

Roger Zelazny

I have over the years written in occasional imitation of other authors' themes, techniques, styles—or whatever else it might be about a particular writer's stories which I felt could prove fruitful to emulate. While I am hardly above an occasional pastiche or parody, what I refer to here—and with specific regard to Rudyard Kipling—is rather of that order which Robert Lowell attempted in poetry in his 1958 collection, *Imitations:* a sequence of personal renderings of material from other writers, which amounted to variations on themes.

I have done experiments of this sort throughout my career, from points of departure as diverse as the wacky improbabilities of John Collier to the stylized colloquialisms of Damon Runyon. But I believe that the first such which I attempted was "Lucifer," which appeared in the June, 1964 issue of *Worlds of Tomorrow.* My tale of a nameless holocaust's survivor who labors mightily to jury-rig the works in a power plant for a glimpse of something lost, was directly based on Rudyard Kipling's "The Devil and the Deep Blue Sea".

There was a phase in Kipling's career comparable to Robert Heinlein's and John D. MacDonald's fascination with process, with their desire to share with the reader some fairly detailed understandings of how things work. That a didactic, engineering aspect of narrative can succeed is of no surprise to those of us in the science fiction area. That Kipling succeeded with it in such diverse tales as ".007," a story of locomotives, and "The Ship That Found Herself," a dialogue amongst the machinery in a steamship, as well as my model for this story, places him closer in spirit to science fiction than one might ordinarily realize on first regarding this amazing man's wide-ranging literary output.

Those were my feelings about twenty-five years ago when I decided to write this story and learn something about what I considered the "suspense of process." Looking over it now, I am pleased to see that I still agree with my earlier self, that I still feel it was an instructive thing to have attempted.

Lucifer

Roger Zelazny

Carlson stood on the hill in the silent center of the city whose people had died.

He stared up at the Building—the one structure that dwarfed every hotel-grid, skyscraper-needle, or apartment-cheesebox packed into all the miles that lay about him. Tall as a mountain, it caught the rays of the bloody sun. Somehow it turned their red into gold halfway up its height.

Carlson suddenly felt that he should not have come back.

It had been over two years, as he figured it, since last he had been here. He wanted to return to the mountains now. One look was enough. Yet still he stood before it, transfixed by the huge Building, by the long shadow that bridged the entire valley. He shrugged his thick shoulders then, in an unsuccessful attempt to shake off memories of the days, five (or was it six?) years ago, when he had worked within the giant unit.

Then he climbed the rest of the way up the hill and entered the high, wide doorway.

His fiber sandals cast a variety of echoes as he passed through the deserted offices and into the long hallway that led to the belts.

The belts, of course, were still. There were no thousands riding them. There was no one alive to ride. Their deep belly-rumble was only a noisy phantom in his mind as he climbed onto the one nearest him and walked ahead into the pitchy insides of the place.

It was like a mausoleum. There seemed no ceiling, no walls, only the soft *pat-pat* of his soles on the flexible fabric of the belt.

He reached a junction and mounted a cross-belt, instinctively standing still for a moment and waiting for the forward lurch as it sensed his weight.

Then he chuckled silently and began walking again.

When he reached the lift, he set off to the right of it until his memory led him to the maintenance stairs. Shouldering his bundle, he began the long, groping ascent.

He blinked at the light when he came into the Power Room. Filtered through its hundred high windows, the sunlight trickled across the dusty acres of machinery.

Carlson sagged against the wall, breathing heavily from the climb. After awhile he wiped a workbench clean and set down his parcel.

Then he removed his faded shirt, for the place would soon be stifling. He brushed his hair from his eyes and advanced down the narrow metal stair to where the generators stood, row on row, like an army of dead, black beetles. It took him six hours to give them all a cursory check.

He selected three in the second row and systematically began tearing them down, cleaning them, soldering their loose connections with the auto-iron, greasing them, oiling them and sweeping away all the dust, cobwebs, and pieces of cracked insulation that lay at their bases.

Great rivulets of perspiration ran into his eyes and down along his sides and thighs, spilling in little droplets onto the hot flooring and vanishing quickly.

Finally, he put down his broom, remounted the stair and returned to his parcel. He removed one of the water bottles and drank off half its contents. He ate a piece of dried meat and finished the bottle. He allowed himself one cigarette then, and returned to work.

He was forced to stop when it grew dark. He had planned on sleeping right there, but the room was too oppressive. So he departed the way he had come and slept beneath the stars, on the roof of a low building at the foot of the hill.

It took him two more days to get the generators ready. Then he began work on the huge Broadcast Panel. It was in better condition than the generators, because it had last been used two years ago. Whereas the generators, save for the three he had burned out last time, had slept for over five (or was it six?) years.

He soldered and wiped and inspected until he was satisfied. Then only one task remained.

All the maintenance robots stood frozen in mid-gesture. Carlson would have to wrestle a three hundred pound power cube without assistance. If he could get one down from the rack and onto a cart without breaking a wrist he would probably be able to convey it to the Igniter without much difficulty. Then he would have to place it within the oven. He had almost ruptured himself when he did it two years ago, but he hoped that he was somewhat stronger—and luckier—this time.

It took him ten minutes to clean the Igniter oven. Then he located a cart and pushed it back to the rack.

One cube was resting at just the right height, approximately eight inches above the level of the cart's bed. He kicked down the anchor chocks and moved around to study the rack. The cube lay on a downward-slanting shelf, restrained by a two-inch metal guard. He pushed at the guard. It was bolted to the shelf.

Returning to the work area, he searched the tool boxes for a wrench. Then he moved back to the rack and set to work on the nuts.

The guard came loose as he was working on the fourth nut. He heard a dangerous creak and threw himself back out of the way, dropping the wrench on his toes.

The cube slid forward, crushed the loosened rail, teetered a bare moment, then dropped with a resounding crash onto the heavy bed of the cart. The bed surface bent and began to crease beneath its weight; the cart swayed toward the outside. The cube continued to slide until over half a foot projected beyond the edge. Then the cart righted itself and shivered into steadiness.

Carlson sighed and kicked loose the chocks, ready to

jump back should it suddenly give way in his direction. It held.

Gingerly, he guided it up the aisle and between the rows of generators, until he stood before the Igniter. He anchored the cart again, stopped for water and a cigarette, then searched up a pinch bar, a small jack and a long, flat metal plate.

He laid the plate to bridge the front end of the cart and the opening to the oven. He wedged the far end in beneath the Igniter's doorframe.

Unlocking the rear chocks, he inserted the jack and began to raise the back end of the wagon, slowly, working with one hand and holding the bar ready in the other.

The cart groaned as it moved higher. Then a sliding, grating sound began and he raised it faster.

With a sound like the stroke of a cracked bell the cube tumbled onto the bridgeway; it slid forward and to the left. He struck at it with the bar, bearing to the right with all his strength. About half an inch of it caught against the left edge of the oven frame. The gap between the cube and the frame was widest at the bottom.

He inserted the bar and heaved his weight against it—three times.

Then it moved forward and came to rest within the Igniter.

He began to laugh. He laughed until he felt weak. He sat on the broken cart, swinging his legs and chuckling to himself, until the sounds coming from his throat seemed alien and out of place. He stopped abruptly and slammed the door.

The Broadcast Panel had a thousand eyes, but none of them winked back at him. He made the final adjustments for Transmit, then gave the generators their last checkout.

After that, he mounted a catwalk and moved to a window.

There was still some daylight to spend, so he moved from window to window pressing the "Open" button set below each sill.

He ate the rest of his food then, and drank a whole bottle of water and smoked two cigarettes. Sitting on the stair, he thought of the days when he had worked with Kelly and Murchison and Djizinsky, twisting the tails of electrons until they wailed and leapt out over the walls and fled down into the city.

The clock! He remembered it suddenly—set high on the wall, to the left of the doorway, frozen at 9:33 (and forty-eight seconds).

He moved a ladder through the twilight and mounted it to the clock. He wiped the dust from its greasy face with a sweeping, circular movement. Then he was ready.

He crossed to the Igniter and turned it on. Somewhere the ever-batteries came alive, and he heard a click as a thin, sharp shaft was driven into the wall of the cube. He raced back up the stairs and sped hand-over-hand up to the catwalk. He moved to a window and waited.

"God," he murmured, "don't let them blow! Please don't—"

Across an eternity of darkness the generators began humming. He heard a crackle of static from the Broadcast Panel and he closed his eyes. The sound died.

He opened his eyes as he heard the window slide upward. All around him the hundred high windows opened. A small light came on above the bench in the work area below him, but he did not see it.

He was staring out beyond the wide drop of the acropolis and down into the city. His city.

The lights were not like the stars. They beat the stars all to hell. They were the gay, regularized constellation of a city where men made their homes: even rows of streetlamps, advertisements, lighted windows in the cheesebox-apartments, a random solitaire of bright squares running up the sides of skyscraper-needles, a searchlight swivelling its luminous antenna through cloudbanks that hung over the city.

He dashed to another window, feeling the high night breezes comb at his beard. Belts were humming below; he heard their wry monologues rattling through the city's deepest canyons. He pictured the people in their homes, in theaters, in bars—talking to each other, sharing a common amusement, playing clarinets, holding hands, eating an evening snack. Sleeping ro-cars awakened and rushed past each other on the levels above the belts; the background hum of the city told him its story of production, of function, of movement and service to its inhabitants. The sky seemed to wheel overhead, as though the city were its turning hub and the universe its outer rim.

Then the lights dimmed from white to yellow and he hurried, with desperate steps, to another window.

"No! Not so soon! Don't leave me yet!" he sobbed.

The windows closed themselves and the lights went out. He stood on the walk for a long time, staring at the dead embers. A smell of ozone reached his nostrils. He was aware of a blue halo about the dying generators.

He descended and crossed the work area to the ladder he had set against the wall.

Pressing his face against the glass and squinting for a long time he could make out the position of the hands.

"Nine thirty-five, and twenty-one seconds," Carlson read.

"Do you hear that?" he called out, shaking his fist at anything. "Ninety-three seconds! I made you live for ninety-three seconds!"

Then he covered his face against the darkness and was silent.

After a long while he descended the stairway, walked the belt, and moved through the long hallway and out of the Building. As he headed back toward the mountains he promised himself—again—that he would never return.

Kipling

John Brunner

Today, Rudyard Kipling is chiefly remembered as a spokesman for imperialism and as a skilful versifier, and it is often overlooked that approximately one in six of his published short stories were science fiction or fantasy. His influence on 20th-century SF writers was probably greater than anyone else's of his generation, except Wells, and is acknowledged by writers as disparate as Poul Anderson and myself.

His formal excursions into the future are few but memorable. "With the Night Mail" describes an Atlantic crossing by airship in the year 2000, and is accompanied by excerpts from the magazine in which it was supposed to appear. Socially, little appears to have changed, but technologically this is an astounding vision; at a time when it was novel for a liner to carry radio-telegraphy equipment, and broadcasting was still experimental, Kipling envisaged the need for air traffic control and a General Communicator system. In the sequel. "As Easy as ABC," he speculated on the demise of democracy owing to its tendency to lapse into mob-rule—this may have been conditioned by his disappointment with the USA at a time when lynch-law was still common: witness the terrifying image of the memorial statue, "The Nigger in Flames"—and on a cure for over-population, a problem he had encountered during his time in India.

His other works of SF and fantasy range from the early

"The Bridge-Builders," in which a civil engineer overhears the Indian gods debating whether or not to destroy his masterpiece spanning the Ganges, through those astonishing *tours-de-force* without human characters like ".007" (steam locomotives) and "The Ship That Found Herself" (steel plates and girders and the ship's steam!), by way of speculative SF like "In the Same Boat" (a man and a woman discover that the nightmares haunting them refer to real events which happened while they were in the womb) and "The Finest Story in the World" (a City clerk remembers his previous lives, as a galley-slave and on an expedition to Vinland), right up to those complex, subtle stories when he left his readers and critics far behind, like "The Children of the Zodiac" and "The Tender Achilles."

He wrote the classic ghosts-in-reverse story, "They," and the deadpan fantasies of *Just So Stories*; in *Puck of Pook's Hill* and *Rewards and Fairies* he brought the people of past ages forward to the present to speak for themselves; and he wrote about sea-serpents and mysterious curses and the heady excitement of modern inventions—but never quite as anyone else would have handled them. For example, "Wireless" is indeed about early radio, but the narrator's experimental friend, trying to eavesdrop on the Royal Navy, fails to notice how the soul of Keats is striking an echo across time in a lovelorn, tubercular assistant pharmacist.

Kipling, who was possibly the most completely equipped writer ever to tackle the short-story form in the English language, exemplifies the fact that in our literary tradition there has never been a hard-and-fast line between realistic and fantastic. Indeed, he was a master at making the fantastic seem credible.

. . . Many years later I wrote about a medieval artist, a monastery, and the premature discovery of the microscope ("The Eye of Allah"). Again and again it went dead under my hand, and for the life of me I could not see why. I put it away and waited. Then said my Daemon—and I was meditating on something else at the time—"Treat it as an illuminated manuscript." I had ridden off on hard black-and-white decorations instead of pumicing the whole thing ivory-smooth, and loading it with thick colour and gilt.

—Rudyard Kipling, *Something of Myself* (1937)

The Eye of Allah

Rudyard Kipling

The Cantor of St Illod's being far too enthusiastic a musician to concern himself with its Library, the Sub-Cantor, who idolized every detail of the work, was tidying up, after two hours' writing and dictation in the Scriptorium. The copying-monks handed him in their sheets—it was a plain Four Gospels ordered by an Abbot at Evesham—and filed out to vespers. John Otho, better known as John of Burgos, took no heed. He was burnishing a tiny boss of gold in his miniature of the Annunciation for his Gospel of St. Luke, which it was hoped that Cardinal Falcodi, the Papal Legate, might later be pleased to accept.

'Break off, John,' said the Sub-Cantor in an undertone.

'Eh? Gone, have they? I never heard. Hold a minute, Clement.'

The Sub-Cantor waited patiently. He had known John more than a dozen years, coming and going at St Illod's, to which monastery John, when abroad, always said he belonged. The claim was gladly allowed, for, more even than other Fitz Othos, he seemed to carry all the Arts under his hand, and most of their practical receipts under his hood.

The Sub-Cantor looked over his shoulder at the pinned-down sheet where the first words of the Magnificat were built up in gold washed with red-lac for a background to the Virgin's hardly yet fired halo. She was shown, hands joined in wonder, at a lattice of infinitely intricate arabesque, round the edges of which sprays of orange-bloom seemed to load the blue hot air that carried back over the minute parched landscape in the middle distance.

'You've made her all Jewess,' said the Sub-Cantor, studying the olive-flushed cheek and the eyes charged with fore-knowledge.

'What else was Our Lady?' John slipped out the pins. 'Listen Clement. If I do not come back, this goes into my Great Luke, whoever finishes it.' He slid the drawing between its guard-papers.

'Then you're for Burgos again—as I heard?'

'In two days. The new Cathedral yonder—but they're slower than the Wrath of God, those masons—is good for the soul.'

'*Thy* soul?' The Sub-Cantor seemed doubtful.

'Even mine, by your permission. And down south—on the edge of the Conquered Countries—Granada way—there's some Moorish diaper-work that's wholesome. It allays vain thought and draws it towards the picture—as you felt, just now, in my Annunciation.'

'She—it was very beautiful. No wonder you go. But you'll not forget your absolution, John?'

'Surely.' This was a precaution John no more omitted on the eve of his travels than he did the recutting of the tonsure which he had provided himself with in his youth, somewhere near Ghent. The mark gave him privilege of clergy at a pinch, and a certain consideration on the road always.

'You'll not forget, either, what we need in the Scriptorium. There's no more true ultramarine in this world now. They mix it with that German blue. And as for vermilion—'

'I'll do my best always.'

'And Brother Thomas' (this was the Infirmarian in charge of the monastery hospital) 'he needs—'

'He'll do his own asking. I'll go over his side now, and get me re-tonsured.'

John went down the stairs to the lane that divides the hospital and cook-house from the back-cloisters. While he was being barbered, Brother Thomas (St Illod's meek but deadly persistent Infirmarian) gave him a list of drugs that he was to bring back from Spain by hook, crook, or lawful purchase. Here they were surprised by the lame, dark Abbot Stephen, in his fur-lined night-boots. Not that Stephen de Sautré was any spy; but as a young man he had shared an unlucky Crusade, which had ended, after a battle at Mansura, in two years' captivity among the Saracens at Cairo where men learn to walk softly. A fair huntsman and hawker, a reasonable disciplinarian, but a man of science above all, and a Doctor of Medicine under one Ranulphus, Canon of St. Paul's, his heart was more in the monastery's hospital work than its religious. He checked their list interestedly, adding items of his own. After the Infirmarian had withdrawn, he gave John generous absolution, to cover lapses by the way; for he did not hold with chance-bought Indulgences.

'And what seek you *this* journey?' he demanded, sitting on the bench beside the mortar and scales in the little warm cell for stored drugs.

'Devils, mostly,' said John, grinning.

'In Spain? Are not Abana and Pharpar—?'

John, to whom men were but matter for drawings, and well-born to boot (since he was a de Sanford on his mother's side), looked the Abbot full in the face and—'Did *you* find it so?' said he.

'No. They were in Cairo too. But what's your special need of 'em?'

'For my Great Luke. He's the master-hand of all Four when it comes to devils.'

'No wonder. He was a physician. You're not.'

'Heaven forbid! But I'm weary of our Church-pattern devils. They're only apes and goats and poultry conjoined. Good enough for plain red-and-black Hells and Judgement Days—but not for me.'

'What makes you so choice in them?'

'Because it stands to reason and Art that there are all musters of devils in Hell's dealings. Those Seven, for example, that were haled out of the Magdalene. They'd be she-devils—no kin at all to the beaked and horned and bearded devils-general.'

The abbot laughed.

'And see again! The devil that came out of the dumb

man. What use is snout of bill to *him*? He'd be faceless as a leper. Above all—God send I live to do it!—the devils that entered the Gadarene swine. They'd be—they'd be—I know not yet what they'd be, but they'd be surpassing devils. I'd have 'em diverse as the Saints themselves. But now, they're all one pattern, for wall, window, or picture-work.'

'Go on, John. You're deeper in this mystery than I.'

'Heaven forbid! But I say there's respect due to devils, damned tho' they be.'

'Dangerous doctrine.'

'My meaning is that if the shape of anything be worth man's thought to picture to man, it's worth his best thought.'

'That's safer. But I'm glad I've given you Absolution.'

'There's less risk for a craftsman who deals with the outside shapes of things—for Mother Church's glory.'

'Maybe so, but, John'—the Abbot's hand almost touched John's sleeve— 'tell me, now, is—is she Moorish or—or Hebrew?'

'She's mine,' John returned.

'Is that enough?'

'I have found it so.'

'Well—ah well! It's out of my jurisdiction, but—how do they look at it down yonder?'

'Oh, they drive nothing to a head in Spain—neither Church nor King, bless them! There's too many Moors and Jews to kill them all, and if they chased 'em away there's be no trade nor farming. Trust me, in the Conquered Countries, from Seville to Granada, we live lovingly enough together—Spaniard, Moor, and Jew. Ye see, *we* ask no questions.'

'Yes—yes,' Stephen sighed. 'And always there's the hope she may be converted.'

'Oh yes, there's always hope.'

The Abbot went on into the hospital. It was an easy age before Rome tightened the screw as to clerical connections. If the lady were not too forward, or the son too much his father's beneficiary in ecclesiastical preferments and levies, a good deal was overlooked. But, as the Abbot had reason to recall, unions between Christian and Infidel led to sorrow. None the less, when John with mule, mails, and man, clattered off down the lane for Southampton and the sea, Stephen envied him.

He was back, twenty months later, in good hard case, and loaded down with fairings. A lump of richest lazuli, a bar of orange-hearted vermilion, and a small packet of dried beetles which make most glorious scarlet, for the Sub-Cantor. Besides that, a few cubes of milky marble, with yet a pink flush in them, which could be slaked and ground down to incomparable background-stuff. There were quite half the drugs that the Abbot and Thomas had demanded, and there was a long deep-red cornelian necklace for the Abbot's Lady—Anne of Norton. She received it graciously, and asked where John had come by it.

'Near Granada,' he said.

'You left all well there?' Anne asked. (Maybe the Abbot had told her something of John's confession.)

'I left all in the hands of God.'

'Ah me! How long since?'

'Four months less eleven days.'

'Were you—with her?'

'In my arms. Childbed.'

'And?'

'The boy too. There is nothing now.'

Anne of Norton caught her breath.

'I think you'll be glad of that,' she said after a while.

'Give me time, and maybe I'll compass it. But not now.'

'You have your handiwork and your art, and—John—remember there's no jealousy in the grave.'

'Ye-es! I have my Art, and Heaven knows I'm jealous of none.'

'Thank God for that at least,' said Anne of Norton, the always ailing woman who followed the Abbot with her sunk eyes. 'And be sure I shall treasure this'—she touched the beads— 'as long as I shall live.'

'I brought—trusted—it to you for that,' he replied, and took leave. When she told the Abbot how she had come by it, he said nothing, but as he and Thomas were storing the drugs that John handed over in the cell which backs on to the hospital-chimney, he observed, of a cake of dried poppy-juice: 'This has power to cut off all pain from a man's body.'

'I have seen it,' said John.

'But for pain of the soul there is, outside God's Grace, but one drug; and that is a man's craft, learning, or other helpful motion of his own mind.'

'That is coming to me, too,' was the answer.

John spent the next fair May day out in the woods with the monastery swineherd and all the porkers; and returned loaded with flowers and sprays of spring, to his own carefully kept place in the north bay of the Scriptorium. There, with his travelling sketch-books under his left elbow, he sunk himself past all recollections in his Great Luke.

Brother Martin, Senior Copyist (who spoke about once a fortnight), ventured to ask, later, how the work was going.

'All here!' John tapped his forehead with his pencil. 'It has been only waiting these months to—ah God!—be born. Are ye free of your plain-copying, Martin?'

Brother Martin nodded. It was his pride that John of Burgos turned to him, in spite of his seventy years, for really good page-work.

'Then see!' John laid out a new vellum—thin but flawless. 'There's no better than this sheet from here to Paris. Yes! Smell it if you choose. Wherefore—give me the compasses and I'll set it out for you—if ye make one letter lighter or darker than its next, I'll stick ye like a pig.'

'Never, John!' The old man beamed happily.

'But I will! Now, follow! Here and here, as I prick, and in script of just this height to the hair's-breadth, ye'll scribe the thirty-first and thirty-second verses of Eighth Luke.'

'Yes, the Gadarene Swine! "*And they besought him that he would not command them to go out into the abyss. And there was a herd of many swine*"'—Brother Martin naturally knew all the Gospels by heart.

'Just so! Down to "*and he suffered them,*" Take your time to it. My Magdalene has to come off my heart first.'

Brother Martin achieved the work so perfectly that John stole some soft sweetmeats from the Abbot's kitchen for his reward. The old man ate them; then repented; then confessed and insisted on penance. At which, the Abbot, knowing there was but one way to reach the real sinner, set him a book called *De Virtutibus Herbarum* to fair-copy. St Illod's had borrowed it from the gloomy Cistercians, who do not hold with pretty things, and the crabbed text kept Martin busy just when John wanted him for some rather specially spaced letterings.

'See now,' said the Sub-Cantor improvingly. 'You should not do such things, John. Here's Brother Martin on penance for your sake—'

'No—for my Great Luke. But I've paid the Abbot's cook. I've drawn him till his own scullions cannot keep straight-faced. *He*'ll not tell again.'

'Unkindly done! And you're out of favour with the Abbot too. He's made no sign to you since you came back—never asked you to high table.'

'I've been busy. Having eyes in his head, Stephen knew it. Clement, there's no Librarian from Durham to Torre fit to clean up after you.'

The Sub-Cantor stood on guard; he knew where John's compliments generally ended.

'But outside the Scriptorium—'

'Where I never go.' The Sub-Cantor had been excused even digging in the garden, lest it should mar his wonderful book-binding hands.

'In all things outside the Scriptorium you are the masterfool of Christendie. Take it from me, Clement. I've met many.'

'I take everything from you,' Clement smiled benignly. 'You use me worse than a singing-boy.'

They could hear one of that suffering breed in the cloister below, squalling as the Cantor pulled his hair.

'God love you! So I do! But have you ever thought how I lie and steal daily on my travels—yes, and for aught you know, murder—to fetch you colours and earths?'

'True,' said just and conscience-stricken Clement. 'I have often thought that were I in the world—which God forbid!—I might be a strong thief in some matters.'

Even Brother Martin, bent above his loathed *De Virtutibus*, laughed.

* * *

But about mid-summer, Thomas the Infirmarian conveyed to John the Abbot's invitation to supper in his house that night, with the request that he would bring with him anything that he had done for his Great Luke.

'What's toward?' said John, who had been wholly shut up in his work.

'Only one of his "wisdom" dinners. You've sat at a few since you were a man.'

'True: and mostly good. How would Stephen have us—?'

'Gown and hood over all. There will be a doctor from Salerno—one Roger, an Italian. Wise and famous with the knife on the body. He's been in the Infirmary some ten days, helping me—even me!'

'Never heard the name. But our Stephen's *physicus* before *sacerdos*, always.'

'And his Lady has a sickness of some time. Roger came hither in chief because of her.'

'Did he? Now I think of it, I have not seen the Lady Anne for a while.'

'Ye've seen nothing for a long while. She has been housed near a month—they have to carry her abroad now.'

'So bad as that, then?'

'Roger of Salerno will not yet say what he thinks. But—'

'God pity Stephen! . . . Who else at table, besides thee?'

'An Oxford friar. Roger is his name also. A learned and famous philosopher. And he holds his liquor too, valiantly.'

'Three doctors—counting Stephen. I've always found that means two atheists.'

Thomas looked uneasily down his nose. 'That's a wicked proverb,' he stammered 'You should not use it.'

'Hoh! Never come you the monk over me, Thomas! You've been Infirmarian at St Illod's eleven years—and a lay-brother still. Why have you never taken orders, all this while?'

'I—I am not worthy.'

'Ten times worthier than that new fat swine—Henry Who's-his-name—that takes the Infirmary Masses. He bullocks in with the Viaticum, under your nose, when a sick man's only faint from being bled. So the man dies—of pure fear. Ye know it! I've watched your face at such times. Take Orders, Didymus. You'll have a little more medicine and a little less Mass with your sick then; and they'll live longer.'

'I am unworthy—unworthy,' Thomas repeated pitifully.

'Not you—but—to your own master you stand or fall. And now that my work releases me for awhile, I'll drink with any philosopher out of any school. And, Thomas,' he coaxed, 'a hot bath for me in the Infirmary before vespers.'

When the Abbot's perfectly cooked and served meal had ended, and the deep-fringed naperies were removed, and the Prior had sent in the keys with word that all was fast in the Monastery, and the keys had been duly returned with the word, 'Make it so till Prime,' the Abbot and his guests went out to cool themselves in an upper cloister that took them, by way of the leads, to the South Choir side of the Triforium. The summer sun was still strong, for it was barely six o'clock, but the Abbey Church, of course, lay in her wonted darkness. Lights were being lit for choir-practice thirty feet below.

'Our Cantor gives them no rest,' the Abbot whispered. 'Stand by this pillar and we'll hear what he's driving them at now.'

'Remember, all!' the Cantor's hard voice came up. 'This is the soul of Bernard himself, attacking our evil world. Take it quicker than yesterday, and throw all your words clean-bitten from you. In the loft there! Begin!'

The organ broke out for an instant, alone and raging. Then the voices crashed together into that first fierce line of the '*De Contemptu Mundi*.'*

'*Hora novissima—tempora pessima*'—a dead pause till the assenting *sunt* broke, like a sob, out of the darkness, and one boy's voice, clearer than silver trumpets, returned the longdrawn *vigilemus*.

'*Ecce minaciter, imminet Arbiter*' (organ and voices were leashed together in terror and warning, breaking away

*Hymn No. 226, A. and M., 'The world is very evil.'

liquidly to the '*ille supremus*'). Then the tone-colours shifted for the prelude to—'*Imminet, imminet, ut mala terminet*—'

'Stop! Again!' cried the Cantor; and gave his reasons a little more roundly than was natural at choir-practice.

'Ah! Pity o' man's vanity! He's guessed we are here. Come Away!' said the Abbot. Anne of Norton, in her carried chair, had been listening too, further along the dark Triforium, with Roger of Salerno. John heard her sob. On the way back, he asked Thomas how her health stood. Before Thomas could reply the sharp-featured Italian doctor pushed between them. 'Following on our talk together, I judged it best to tell her,' said he to Thomas.

'What?' John asked simply enough.

'What she knew already,' Roger of Salerno launched into a Greek quotation to the effect that every woman knows all about everything.

'I have no Greek,' said John stiffly. Roger of Salerno had been giving them a good deal of it, at dinner.

'Then I'll come to you in Latin. Ovid hath it neatly. "*Utque malum late solet immedicabile cancer*—" but doubtless you know the rest, worthy Sir.'

'Alas! My school-Latin's but what I've gathered by the way from fools professing to heal sick women. "*Hocus-pocus*—" but doubtless you know the rest, worthy Sir.'

Roger of Salerno was quite quiet till they regained the dining-room, where the fire had been comforted and the dates, raisins, ginger, figs, and cinnamon-scented sweetmeats set out, with the choicer wines, on the after-table. The Abbot seated himself, drew off his ring, dropped it, that all might hear the tinkle, into an empty silver cup, stretched his feet towards the hearth, and looked at the great gilt and carved rose in the barrel-roof. The silence that keeps from Compline to Matins had closed on their world. The bull-necked Friar watched a ray of sunlight split itself into colours on the rim of a crystal salt-cellar; Roger of Salerno had re-opened some discussion with Brother Thomas on a type of spotted fever that was baffling them both in England and abroad; John took note of the keen profile, and—it might serve as a note for the Great Luke—his hand moved to his bosom. The Abbot saw, and nodded permission. John whipped out silverpoint and sketch-book.

'Nay—modesty is good enough—but deliver your own opinion,' the Italian was urging the Infirmarian. Out of courtesy to the foreigner nearly all the talk was in table-Latin; more formal and more copious than monk's patter. Thomas began with his meek stammer.

'I confess myself at a loss for the cause of the fever unless—as Varro saith in his *De Re Rustica*—certain small animals which the eye cannot follow enter the body by the nose and mouth, and set up grave diseases. On the other hand, this is not in Scripture.'

Roger of Salerno hunched head and shoulders like an angry cat. 'Always *that*!' he said, and John snatched down the twist of the thin lips.

'Never at rest, John.' The Abbot smiled at the artist. 'You should break off every two hours for prayers, as we do. St Benedict was no fool. Two hours is all that a man can carry the edge of his eye or hand.'

'For copyists—yes. Brother Martin is not sure after one hour. But when a man's work takes him, he must go on till it lets him go.'

'Yes, that is the Demon of Socrates,' the Friar from Oxford rumbled above his cup.

'The doctrine leans towards presumption,' said the Abbot. 'Remember, "Shall mortal man be more just than his Maker?" '

'There is no danger of justice'; the Friar spoke bitterly. 'But at least Man might be suffered to go forward in his Art or his thought. Yet if Mother Church sees or hears him move anyward, what says she? "No!" Always "No." '

'But if the little animals of Varro be invisible'—this was Roger of Salerno to Thomas— 'how are we any nearer to a cure?'

'By experiment'—the Friar wheeled round on them suddenly. 'By reason and experiment. The one is useless without the other. But Mother Church—'

'Ay!' Roger de Salerno dashed at the fresh bait like a pike. 'Listen, Sirs. Her bishops—our Princes—strew our roads in Italy with carcasses that they make for their pleasure or wrath. Beautiful corpses! Yet if I—if we doctors—so much as raise the skin of one of them to look at God's fabric beneath, what says Mother Church? "Sacrilege! Stick to your pigs and dogs, or you burn!" '

'And not Mother Church only!' the Friar chimed in. '*Every* way we are barred—barred by the words of some man, dead a thousand years, which are held final. Who is any son of Adam that his one say-so should close a door towards truth? I would not except even Peter Peregrinus, my own great teacher.'

'Nor I Paul of Aegina,' Roger of Salerno cried. 'Listen, Sirs! Here is a case to the very point. Apuleius affirmeth, if a man eat fasting of the juice of the cut-leaved buttercup—*sceleratus* we call it, which means 'rascally" '—this with a condescending nod towards John—'his soul will leave his body laughing. Now this is the lie more dangerous than truth, since truth of a sort is in it.'

'He's away!' whispered the Abbot despairingly.

'For the juice of that herb, I know by experiment, burns, blisters, and wries the mouth. I know also the *rictus*, or pseudo-laughter, on the face of such as have perished by the strong poisons of herbs allied to this ranunculus. Certainly that spasm resembles laughter. It seems then, in my judgement, that Apuleius, having seen the body of one thus poisoned, went off at score and wrote that the man died laughing.'

'Neither staying to observe, nor to confirm observation by experiment,' added the Friar, frowning.

Stephen the Abbot cocked an eyebrow towards John.

'How think *you*?' said he.

'I'm no doctor,' John returned, 'but I'd say Apuleius in all these years might have been betrayed by his copyists. They take short-cuts to save 'emselves trouble. Put case that Apuleius wrote the soul *seems* to leave the body laughing, after this poison. There's not three copyists in five (*my* judgement) would not leave out the "seems to". For who's question Apuleius? If it seemed so to him, so it must be. Otherwise any child knows cut-leaved buttercup.'

'Have you knowledge of herbs?' Roger of Salerno asked curtly.

'Only that, when I was a boy in convent, I've made

tetters round my mouth and on my neck with buttercup-juice, to save going to prayer o' cold nights.'

'Ah!' said Roger. 'I profess no knowledge of tricks.' He turned aside, stiffly.

'No matter! Now for your own tricks, John,' the tactful Abbot broke in. 'You shall show the doctors your Magdalene and your Gadarene Swine and the devils.'

'Devils? Devils? *I* have produced devils by means of drugs; and have abolished them by the same means. Whether devils be external to mankind or immanent, I have not yet pronounced,' Roger of Salerno was still angry.

'Ye dare not,' snapped the Friar from Oxford. 'Mother Church makes Her own devils.'

'Not wholly! Our John has come back from Spain with brand-new ones.' Abbot Stephen took the vellum handed to him, and laid it tenderly on the table. They gathered to look. The Magdalene was drawn in palest, almost transparent, grisaille, against a raging, swaying background of woman-faced devils, each broke to and by her special sin, and each, one could see, frenziedly straining against the Power that compelled her.

'I've never seen the like of this grey shadowwork,' said the Abbot. 'How came you by it?'

'*Non nobis!* It came to me,' said John, not knowing he was a generation or so ahead of his time in the use of that medium.

'Why is she so pale?' the Friar demanded.

'Evil has all come out of her—she'd take any colour now.'

'Ay, like light through glass. *I* see.'

Roger of Salerno was looking in silence—his nose nearer and nearer the page. 'It is so,' he pronounced finally. 'Thus it is in epilepsy—mouth, eyes, and forehead—even to the droop of her wrist there. Every sign of it! She will need restoratives, that woman, and, afterwards, sleep natural. No poppy-juice, or she will vomit on her waking. And thereafter—but I am not in my Schools." He drew himself up. 'Sir,' said he, 'you should be of Our calling. For, by the Snakes of Aesculapius, you *see*!'

The two struck hands as equals.

'And how think you of the Seven Devils?' the Abbot went on.

These melted into convoluted flower- or flame-like bodies, ranging in colour from phosphorescent green to the black purple of outworn iniquity, whose hearts could be traced beating through their substance. But, for sign of hope and the sane workings of life, to be regained, the deep border was of conventionalized spring flowers and birds, all crowned by a kingfisher in haste, atilt through a clump of yellow iris.

Roger of Salerno identified the herbs and spoke largely of their virtues.

'And now, the Gadarene Swine,' said Stephen. John laid the picture on the table.

Here were devils dishoused, in dread of being abolished to the Void, huddling and hurtling together to force lodgement by every opening into the brute bodies offered. Some of the swine fought the invasion, foaming and jerking; some were surrendering to it, sleepily, as to a luxurious back-scratching; others, wholly possessed, whirled off in bucking droves for the lake beneath. In one corner the freed man stretched out his limbs all restored to his control, and Our Lord, seated, looked at him as questioning what he would make of his deliverance.

'Devils indeed!' was the Friar's comment. 'But wholly a new sort.'

Some devils were mere lumps, with lobes and protuberances—a hint of a fiend's face peering through jelly-like walls. And there was a family of impatient, globular devillings who had burst open the belly of their smirking parent, and were revolving desperately towards their prey. Others patterned themselves into rods, chains and ladders, single or conjoined, round the throat and jaws of a shrieking sow, from whose ear emerged the lashing, glassy tail of a devil that had made good his refuge. And there were granulated and conglomerate devils, mixed up with the foam and slaver where the attack was fiercest. Thence the eye carried on to the insanely active backs of the downward-racing swine, the swineherd's aghast face, and his dog's terror.

Said Roger of Salerno, 'I pronounce that these were begotten of drugs. They stand outside the rational mind.'

'Not these,' said Thomas the Infirmarian, who as a servant of the Monastery should have asked his Abbot's leave to speak. 'Not *these*—look!—in the bordure.'

The border to the picture was a diaper of irregular but balanced compartments or cellules, where sat, swam or weltered, devils in blank, so to say—things as yet uninspired by Evil—indifferent, but lawlessly outside imagination. Their shapes resembled, again, ladders, chains, scourges, diamonds, aborted buds, or gravid phosphorescent globes—some well-nigh star-like.

Roger of Salerno compared them to the obsessions of a Churchman's mind.

'Malignant?' the Friar from Oxford questioned.

' "Count everything unknown for horrible," ' Roger quoted with scorn.

'Not I. But they are marvellous—marvellous. I think—'

The Friar drew back. Thomas edged in to see better, and half opened his mouth.

'Speak,' said Stephen, who had been watching him. 'We are all in a sort doctors here.'

'I would say then'—Thomas rushed at it as one putting out his life's belief at the stake—'that these lower shapes in the bordure may not be so much hellish and malignant as models and patterns upon which John has tricked out and embellished his proper devils among the swine above there!'

'And that would signify?' said Roger of Salerno sharply.

'In my poor judgement, that he may have seen such shapes—without help of drugs.'

'Now who—*who*,' said John of Burgos, after a round and unregarded oath, 'has made thee so wise of a sudden, my Doubter?'

'I wise? God forbid! Only John, remember—one winter six years ago—the snow-flakes melting on your sleeve at the cookhouse-door. You showed me them through a little crystal, that made small things larger.'

'Yes. The Moors call such a glass the Eye of Allah,' John confirmed.

'You showed me them melting—six-sided. You called them, then, your patterns.'

'True. Snow-flakes melt six-sided. I have used them for diaper-work often.'

'Melting snow-flakes as seen through a glass? By art optical?' the Friar asked.

'Art optical? *I* have never heard!' Roger of Salerno cried.

'John,' said the Abbot of St Illod's commandingly, 'was it—is it so?'

'In some sort,' John replied, 'Thomas has the right of it. Those shapes in the bordure were my workshop-patterns for the devils above. In *my* craft, Salerno, we dare not drug. It kills hand and eye. My shapes are to be seen honestly, in nature.'

The Abbot drew a bowl of rose-water towards him. 'When I was prisoner with—with the Saracens after Mansura,' he began, turning up the fold of his long sleeve, 'there were certain magicians—physicians—who could show—' he dipped his third finger delicately in the water—'all the firmament of Hell, as it were in—' he shook off one drop from his polished nail on to the polished table—'even such a supernaculum as this.'

'But it must be foul water—not clean,' said John.

'Show us then—all—all,' said Stephen. 'I would make sure—once more.' The Abbot's voice was official.

John drew from his bosom a stamped leather box, some six or eight inches long, wherein, bedded on faded velvet, lay what looked like silver-bound compasses of old box-wood, with a screw at the head which opened or closed the legs to minute fractions. The legs terminated, not in points, but spoon-shapedly, one spatula pierced with a metal-lined hole less than a quarter of an inch across, the other with a half-inch hole. Into this latter John, after carefully wiping with a silk rag, slipped a metal cylinder that carried glass or crystal, it seemed, at each end.

'Ah! Art optic!' said the Friar. 'But what is that beneath it?'

It was a small swivelling sheet of polished silver no bigger than a florin, which caught the light and concentrated it on the lesser hole. John adjusted it without the Friar's proffered help.

'And now to find a drop of water,' said he, picking up a small brush.

'Come to my upper cloister. The sun is on the leads still,' said the Abbot, rising.

They followed him there. Half-way along, a drip from a gutter had made a greenish puddle in a worn stone. Very carefully, John dropped a drop of it into the smaller hole of the compass-leg, and, steadying the apparatus on a coping, worked the screw in the compass-joint, screwed the cylinder, and swung the swivel of the mirror till he was satisfied.

'Good!' He peered through the thing. 'My Shapes are all here. Now look, Father! If they do not meet your eye at first, turn this nicked edge here, left- or right-handed.'

'I have not forgotten,' said the Abbot, taking his place. 'Yes! They are here—as they were in my time—my time past. There is no end to them, I was told. . . . There *is* no end!'

'The light will go. Oh, let me look! Suffer me to see, also!' the Friar pleaded, almost shouldering Stephen from the eyepiece. The Abbot gave way. His eyes were on time past. But the Friar, instead of looking, turned the apparatus in his capable hands.

'Nay, nay,' John interrupted, for the man was already fiddling at the screws. 'Let the Doctor see.'

Roger of Salerno looked, minute after minute. John saw his blue-veined cheek-bones turn white. He stepped back at last, as though stricken.

'It is a new world—a new world, and—Oh, God Unjust!—I am old!'

'And now Thomas,' Stephen ordered.

John manipulated the tube for the Infirmarian, whose hands shook, and he too looked long. 'It is Life,' he said presently in a breaking voice. 'No Hell! Life created and rejoicing—the work of the Creator. They live, even as I have dreamed. Then it was no sin for me to dream. No sin—O God—no sin!'

He flung himself on his knees and began hysterically the *Benedicite omnia Opera*.

'And now I will see how it is actuated,' said the Friar from Oxford, thrusting forward again.

'Bring it within. The place is all eyes and ears,' said Stephen.

They walked quietly back along the leads, three English counties laid out in evening sunshine around them; church upon church, monastery upon monastery, cell after cell, and the bulk of a vast cathedral moored on the edge of the banked shoals of sunset.

When they were at the after-table once more they sat down, all except the Friar, who went to the window and huddled bat-like over the thing. 'I see! I see!' he was repeating to himself.

'He'll not hurt it,' said John. But the Abbot, staring in front of him, like Roger of Salerno, did not hear. The Infirmarian's head was on the table between his shaking arms.

John reached for a cup of wine.

'It was shown to me,' the Abbot was speaking to himself, 'in Cairo, that man stands ever between two Infinities—of greatness and littleness. Therefore, there is no end—either to life—or— '

'And *I* stand on the edge of the grave,' snarled Roger of Salerno. 'Who pities *me*'

'Hush!' said Thomas the Infirmarian. 'The little creatures shall be sanctified—sanctified to the service of His sick.'

'What need?' John of Burgos wiped his lips. 'It shows no more than the shapes of things. It gives good pictures. I had it at Granada. It was brought from the East, they told me.'

Roger of Salerno laughed with an old man's malice. 'What of Mother Church? Most Holy Mother Church? If it comes to Her ears that we have spied into Her Hell without Her leave, where do we stand?'

'At the stake,' said the Abbot of St Illod's, and, raising his voice a trifle, 'You hear that? Roger Bacon, heard you that?'

The Friar turned from the window, clutching the compasses tighter.

'No, no!' he appealed. 'Not with Falcodi—not with our English-hearted Foulkes made Pope. He's wise—he's learned. He reads what I have put forth. Foulkes would never suffer it.'

' "Holy Pope is one thing, Holy Church another," ' Roger quoted.

'But I—*I* can bear witness it is no Art Magic,' the Friar went on. 'Nothing is it, except Art optical—wisdom after trial and experiment, mark you. I can prove it, and—my name weighs with men who dare think.'

'Find them!' croaked Roger of Salerno. 'Five or six in all the world. That makes less than fifty pounds by weight of ashes at the stake. I have watched such men—reduced.'

'I will not give this up!' The Friar's voice cracked in passion and despair. 'It would be to sin against the light.'

'No, no! Let us—let us sanctify the little animals of Varro,' said Thomas.

Stephen leaned forward, fished his ring out of the cup, and slipped it on his finger. 'My sons,' said he, 'we have seen what we have seen.'

'That it is no magic but simple Art,' the Friar persisted.

' 'Avails nothing. In the eyes of Mother Church we have seen more than is permitted to man.'

'But it was Life—created and rejoicing,' said Thomas.

'To look into Hell as we shall be judged—as we shall be proved—to have looked, is for priests only.'

'Or green-sick virgins on the road to sainthood who, for cause any midwife could give you—'

The Abbot's half-lifted hand checked Roger of Salerno's outpouring.

'Nor may even priests see more in Hell than Church knows to be there. John, there is respect due to Church as well as to Devils.'

'My trade's the outside of things,' said John quietly. 'I have my patterns.'

'But you may need to look again for more,' the Friar said.

'In my craft, a thing done is done with. We go on to new shapes after that.'

'And if we trespass beyond bounds, even in thought, we lie open to the judgement of the Church,' the Abbot continued.

'But thou knowest—*knowest!*' Roger of Salerno had returned to the attack. 'Here's all the world in darkness concerning the causes of things—from the fever across the land to thy Lady's—thine own Lady's—eating malady. Think!'

'I have thought upon it, Salerno! I have thought indeed.'

Thomas the Infirmarian lifted his head again; and this time he did not stammer at all. 'As in the water, so in the blood must they rage and war with each other! I have dreamed these ten years—I thought it was a sin—but my dreams and Varro's are true! Think on it again! Here's the Light under our very hand!'

'Quench it! You'd no more stand to roasting than—any other. I'll give you the case as Church—as I myself—would frame it. Our John here returns from the Moors, and shows us a hell of devils contending in the compass of one drop of water. Magic past clearance! You can hear the faggots crackle.'

'But thou knowest! Thou hast seen it all before! For man's poor sake! For old friendship's sake—Stephen!' The Friar was trying to stuff the compasses into his bosom as he appealed.

'What Stephen de Sautré knows, you his friends know also. I would have you, now, obey the Abbot of St Illod's. Give to me!' He held out his ringed hand.

'May I—may John here—not even make a drawing of one—one screw?' said the broken Friar, in spite of himself.

'Nowise!' Stephen took it over. 'Your dagger, John. Sheathed will serve.'

He unscrewed the metal cylinder, laid it on the table, and with the dagger's hilt smashed some crystal to sparkling dust which he swept into a scooped hand and cast behind the hearth.

'It would seem,' said he, 'the choice lies between two sins. To deny the world a Light which is under our hand, or to enlighten the world before her time. What you have seen, I saw long since among the physicians at Cairo. And I know what doctrine they drew from it. Hast *thou* dreamed, Thomas? I also—with fuller knowledge. But this birth, my sons, is untimely. It will be but the mother of more death, more torture, more division, and greater darkness in this dark age. Therefore I, who know both my world and the

Church, take this Choice on my conscience. Go! It is finished.'

He thrust the wooden part of the compasses deep among the beech logs till all was burned.

For there is a type of mind that dives after what it calls "psychical experiences." . . . I have seen too much evil and sorrow and wreck of good minds on the road to Endor to take one step along that perilous track.

—Rudyard Kipling, *Something of Myself* (1937)

'They'

Rudyard Kipling

One view called me to another; one hill-top to its fellow, half across the county, and since I could answer at no more trouble than the snapping forward of a lever, I let the county flow under my wheels. The orchid-studded flats of the East gave way to the thyme, ilex, and grey grass of the Downs; these again to the rich cornland and fig-trees of the lower coast, where you carry the beat of the tide on your left hand for fifteen level miles; and when at last I turned inland through a huddle of rounded hills and woods I had run myself clean out of my known marks. Beyond that precise hamlet which stands godmother to the capital of the United States, I found hidden villages where bees, the only things awake, boomed in eighty-foot lindens that overhung grey Norman churches; miraculous brooks diving under stone bridges built for heavier traffic than would never vex them again; tithe-barns larger than their churches, and an old smithy that cried out aloud how it had once been a hall of the Knights of the Temple. Gipsies I found on a common where the gorse, bracken, and heath fought it out together up a mile of Roman road;

and a little farther on I disturbed a red fox rolling dog-fashion in the naked sunlight.

As the wooded hills closed about me I stood up in the car to take the bearings of that great Down whose ringed head is a landmark for fifty miles across the low countries. I judged that the lie of the country would bring me across some westward-running road that went to his feet, but I did not allow for the confusing veils of the woods. A quick turn plunged me first into a green cutting brim-full of liquid sunshine, next into a gloomy tunnel where last years's dead leaves whispered and scuffled about my tyres. The strong hazel stuff meeting overhead had not been cut for a couple of generations at least, nor had any axe helped the moss-cankered oak and beech to spring above them. Here the road changed frankly into a carpeted ride on whose brown velvet spent primrose-clumps showed like jade, and a few sickly, white-stalked bluebells nodded together. As the slope favoured I shut off the power and slid over the whirled leaves, expecting every moment to meet a keeper; but I only heard a jay, far off, arguing against the silence under the twilight of the trees.

Still the track descended. I was on the point of reversing and working my way back on the second speed ere I ended in some swamp, when I saw sunshine through the tangle ahead and lifted the brake.

It was down again at once. As the light beat across my face my fore-wheels took the turf of a great still lawn from which sprang horsemen ten feet high with levelled lances, monstrous peacocks, and sleek round-headed maids of honour—blue, black, and glistening—all of clipped yew. Across the lawn—the marshalled woods besieged it on three sides—stood an ancient house of lichened and weather-worn stone, with mullioned windows and roofs of rose-red tile. It was flanked by semi-circular walls, also rose-red, that closed the lawn on the fourth side, and at their feet a box hedge grew man-high. There were doves on the roof about the slim brick chimneys, and I caught a glimpse of an octagonal dove-house behind the screening wall.

Here, then, I stayed; a horseman's green spear laid at my breast; held by the exceeding beauty of that jewel in that setting.

'If I am not packed off for a trespasser, or if this knight does not ride a wallop at me,' thought I, 'Shakespeare and Queen Elizabeth at least must come out of that half-open garden door and ask me to tea.'

A child appeared at an upper window, and I thought the little thing waved a friendly hand. But it was to call a companion, for presently another bright head showed. Then I heard a laugh among the yew-peacocks, and turning to make sure (till then I had been watching the house only) I saw the silver of a fountain behind a hedge thrown up against the sun. The doves on the roof cooed to the cooing water; but between the two notes I caught the utterly happy chuckle of a child absorbed in some light mischief.

The garden door—heavy oak sunk deep in the thickness of the wall—opened further: a woman in a big garden hat set foot slowly on the time-hollowed stone step and as slowly walked across the turf. I was forming some apology when she lifted up her head and I saw that she was blind.

'I heard you,' she said. 'Isn't that a motor car?'

'I'm afraid I've made a mistake in my road. I should have turned off up above—I never dreamed—' I began.

'But I'm very glad. Fancy a motor car coming into the garden! It will be such a treat—' She turned and made as though looking about her. 'You—you haven't seen any one, have you—perhaps?'

'No one to speak to, but the children seemed interested at a distance.'

'Which?'

'I saw a couple up at the window just now, and I think I heard a little chap in the grounds.'

'Oh, lucky you!' she cried, and her face brightened. 'I hear them, of course, but that's all. You've seen them and heard them?'

'Yes,' I answered. 'And if I know anything of children, one of them's having a beautiful time by the fountain yonder. Escaped, I should imagine.'

'You're fond of children?'

I gave her one or two reasons why I did not altogether hate them.

'Of course, of course,' she said. 'Then you understand.

Then you won't think it foolish if I ask you to take your car through the gardens, once or twice—quite slowly. I'm sure they'd like to see it. They see so little, poor things. One tries to make their life pleasant, but—' she threw out her hands towards the woods. 'We're so out of the world here.'

'That will be splendid,' I said. 'But I can't cut up your grass.'

She faced to the right. 'Wait a minute,' she said. 'We're at the South gate, aren't we? Behind those peacocks there's a flagged path. We call it the Peacocks' Walk. You can't see it from here, they tell me, but if you squeeze along by the edge of the wood you can turn at the first peacock and get on to the flags.'

It was sacrilege to wake that dreaming house-front with the clatter of machinery, but I swung the car to clear the turf, brushed along the edge of the wood and turned in on the broad stone path were the fountain-basin lay like one star-sapphire.

'May I come to?' she cried. 'No, please don't help me. They'll like it better if they see me.'

She felt her way lightly to the front of the car, and with one foot on the step she called: 'Children, oh, children! Look and see what's going to happen!'

The voice would have drawn lost souls from the Pit, for the yearning that underlay its sweetness, and I was not surprised to hear an answering shout beyond the yews. It must have been the child by the fountain, but he fled at our approach, leaving a little toy boat in the water. I saw the glint of his blue blouse among the still horsemen.

Very disposedly we paraded the length of the walk and at her request backed again. This time the child had got the better of his panic, but stood far off and doubting.

'The little fellow's watching us,' I said. 'I wonder if he'd like a ride.'

'They're very shy still. Very shy. But, oh, lucky you to be able to see them! Let's listen.'

I stopped the machine at once, and the humid stillness, heavy with the scent of box, cloaked us deep. Shears I could hear where some gardener was clipping; a mumble of bees and broken voices that might have been the doves.

'Oh, unkind!' she said weariedly.

'Perhaps they're only shy of the motor. The little maid at the window looks tremedously interested.'

'Yes?' She raised her head. 'It was wrong of me to say that. They are really fond of me. It's the only thing that makes life worth living—when they're fond of you, isn't it? I daren't think what the place would be without them. By the way, is it beautiful?'

'I think it is the most beautiful place I have ever seen.'

'So they all tell me. I can feel it, of course, but that isn't quite the same thing.'

'Then have you never—?' I began, but stopped abashed.

'Not since I can remember. It happened when I was only a few months old, they tell me. And yet I must remember something, else how could I dream about colours. I see light in my dreams, and colours, but I never see *them*. I only hear them just as I do when I'm awake.'

"It's difficult to see faces in dreams. Some people can, but most of us haven't the gift,' I went on, looking up at the window where the child stood all but hidden.

'I've heard that too,' she said. 'And they tell me that one never sees a dead person's face in a dream. Is that true?'

'I believe it is—now I come to think of it.'

'But how is it with yourself—yourself?' The blind eyes turned towards me.

'I have never seen the faces of my dead in any dream,' I answered.

'Then it must be as bad as being blind.'

The sun had dipped behind the woods and the long shades were possessing the insolent horsemen one by one. I saw the light die from off the top of a glossy-leafed lance and all the brave hard green turn to soft black. The house, accepting another day at end, as it had accepted an hundred thousand gone, seemed to settle deeper into its rest among the shadows.

'Have you ever wanted to?' she said after the silence.

'Very much sometimes,' I replied. The child had left the window as the shadows closed upon it.

'Ah! So've I, but I don't suppose it's allowed. . . . Where d'you live?'

'Quite the other side of the county—sixty miles and

more, and I must be going back. I've come without my big lamps.'

'But it's not dark yet. I can feel it.'

'I'm afraid it will be by the time I get home. Could you lend me someone to set me on my road at first? I've utterly lost myself.'

'I'll send Madden with you to the cross-roads. We are so out of the world, I don't wonder you were lost! I'll guide you round to the front of the house; but you will go slowly, won't you, till you're out of the grounds? It isn't foolish, do you think?'

'I promise you I'll go like this,' I said, and let the car start herself down the flagged path.

We skirted the left wing of the house, whose elaborately cast lead guttering alone was worth a day's journey; passed under a great rose-grown gate in the red wall, and so round to the high front of the house, which in beauty and stateliness as much excelled the back as that all others I had seen.

'Is it so very beautiful?' she said wistfully when she heard my raptures. 'And you like the lead figures too? There's the old azalea garden behind. They say that this place must have been made for children. Will you help me out, please? I should like to come with you as far as the cross-roads, but I mustn't leave them. Is that you, Madden? I want you to show this gentleman the way to the cross-roads. He has lost his way, but—he has seen them.'

A butler appeared noiselessly at the miracle of old oak that must be called the front door, and slipped aside to put on his hat. She stood looking at me with open blue eyes in which no sight lay, and I saw for the first time that she was beautiful.

'Remember,' she said quietly, 'if you are fond of them you will come again,' and disappeared within the house.

The butler in the car said nothing till we were nearly at the lodge gates, where catching a glimpse of a blue blouse in a shrubbery I swerved amply lest the devil that leads little boys to play should drag me into child-murder.

'Excuse me,' he asked of a sudden, 'but why did you do that, Sir?'

'The child yonder.'

'Our young gentleman in blue?'

'Of course.'

'He runs about a good deal. Did you see him by the fountain, Sir?'

'Oh, yes, several times. Do we turn here?'

'Yes, Sir. And did you 'appen to see them upstairs too?'

'At the upper window? Yes.'

'Was that before the mistress come out to speak to you, Sir?'

'A little before that. Why d'you want to know?'

He paused a little. 'Only to make sure that—that they had seen the car, Sir, because with children running about, though I'm sure you're driving particularly careful, there might be an accident. That was all, Sir. Here are the crossroads. You can't miss your way from now on. Thank you, Sir, but that isn't *our* custom, not with—'

'I beg your pardon,' I said, and thrust away the British silver.

'Oh, it's quite right with the rest of 'em as a rule. Good-bye, Sir.'

He retired into the armour-plated conning-tower of his caste and walked away. Evidently a butler solicitous for the honour of his house, and interested, probably through a maid, in the nursery.

Once beyond the signposts at the cross-roads I looked back, but the crumpled hills interlaced so jealously that I could not see where the house had lain. When I asked its name at a cottage along the road, the fat woman who sold sweetmeats there gave me to understand that people with motor cars had small right to live—much less to 'go about talking like carriage folk'. They were not a pleasant-mannered community.

When I retraced my route on the map that evening I was little wiser. Hawkin's Old Farm appeared to be the Survey title of the place, and the old *County Gazetteer*, generally so ample, did not allude to it. The big house of those parts was Hodnington Hall, Georgian with early Victorian embellishments, as an atrocious steel engraving attested. I carried my difficulty to a neighbour—a deep-rooted tree of that soil—and he gave me a name of a family which conveyed no meaning.

A month or so later—I went again, or it may have been that my car took the road of her own volition. She over-ran the fruitless Downs, threaded every turn of the maze of lanes below the hills, drew through the high-walled woods, impenetrable in their full leaf, came out at the cross-roads where the butler had left me, and a little farther on developed an internal trouble which forced me to turn her in on a grass way-waste that cut into a summer-silent hazel wood. So far as I could make sure by the sun and a six-inch Ordnance map, this should be the road flank of that wood which I had first explored from the heights above. I made a mighty serious business of my repairs and a glittering shop of my repair kit, spanners, pump, and the like, which I spread out orderly upon a rug. It was a trap to catch all childhood, for on such a day, I argued, the children would not be far off. When I paused in my work I listened, but the wood was so full of the noises of summer (though the birds had mated) that I could not at first distinguish these from the tread of small cautious feet stealing across the dead leaves. I rang my bell in an alluring manner, but the feet fled, and I repented, for to a child a sudden noise is very real terror. I must have been at work half an hour when I heard in the wood the voice of the blind woman crying: 'Children, oh, children! Where are you?' and the stillness made slow to close on the perfection of that cry. She came towards me, half feeling her way between the tree boles, and though a child, it seemed, clung to her skirt, it swerved into the leafage like a rabbit as she drew nearer.

'Is that you?' she said, 'from the other side of the county?'

'Yes, it's me from the other side of the county.'

'Then why didn't you come through the upper woods? They were there just now.'

'They were here a few minutes ago. I expect they knew my car had broken down, and came to see the fun.'

'Nothing serious, I hope? How do cars break down?'

'In fifty different ways. Only mine has chosen the fifty-first.'

She laughed merrily at the tiny joke, cooed with delicious laughter, and pushed her hat back.

'Let me hear,' she said.

'Wait a moment,' I cried, 'and I'll get you a cushion.'

She set her foot on the rug all covered with spare parts, and stooped above it eagerly. 'What delightful things!' The hands through which she saw glanced in the chequered sunlight. 'A box here—another box! Why, you've arranged them like playing shop!'

'I confess now that I put it out to attract them. I don't need half those things really.'

'How nice of you! I heard your bell in the upper wood. You say they were here before that?'

'I'm sure of it. Why are they so shy? That little fellow in blue who was with you just now ought to have gotten over his fright. He's been watching me like a Red Indian.'

'It must have been your bell,' she said. 'I heard one of them go past me in trouble when I was coming down. They're shy—so shy even with me.' She turned her face over her shoulder and cried again: 'Children, oh, children! Look and see!'

'They must have gone off together on their own affairs,' I suggested, for there was a murmur behind us of lowered voices broken by the sudden squeaking giggles of childhood. I returned to my tinkerings and she leaned forward, her chin on her hand, listening interestedly.

'How many are they?' I said at last. The work was finished, but I saw no reason to go.

Her forehead puckered a little in thought. 'I don't quite know,' she said simply. 'Sometimes more—sometimes less. They come and stay with me because I love them you see.'

'That must be very jolly,' I said, replacing a drawer, and as I spoke I heard the inanity of my answer.

'You—you aren't laughing at me?' she cried. 'I—I haven't any of my own. I never married. People laugh at me sometimes about them because—because—'

'Because they're savages,' I returned. 'It's nothing to fret for. That sort laugh at everything that isn't in their own fat lives.'

'I don't know. How should I? I only don't like being laughed at about *them*. It hurts; and when one can't see . . . I don't want to seem silly,' her chin quivered like a child's as she spoke, 'but we blindies have only one skin, I think. Everything outside hits straight at our souls. It's different with you. You've such good defences in your eyes—looking out—before anyone can really pain you in your soul. People forget that with us.'

I was silent, reviewing that inexhaustible matter—the more than inherited (since it is also carefully taught) brutality of the Christian peoples, besides which the mere heathendom of the West Coast nigger is clean and restrained. It led me a long distance into myself.

'Don't do that!' she said of a sudden, putting her hands before her eyes.

'What?'

She made a gesture with her hand.

'That! It's—it's all purple and black. Don't! That colour hurts.'

'But how in the world do you know about colours?' I exclaimed, for here was a revelation indeed.

'Colours as colours?' she asked.

'No. *Those* Colours which you saw just now.'

'You know as well as I do,' she laughed, 'else you wouldn't have asked that question. They aren't in the world at all. They're in *you*—when you went so angry.'

'D'you mean a dull purplish patch, like port wine mixed with ink?' I said.

'I've never seen ink or port wine, but the colours aren't mixed. They can separate—all separate.'

'Do you mean black streaks and jags across the purple?'

She nodded. 'Yes—if they are like this,' and zig-zagged her finger again, 'but it's more red than purple—that bad colour.'

'And what are the colours at the top of the—whatever you see?'

Slowly she leaned forward and traced on the rug the figure of the Egg itself.

'I see them so,' she said, pointing with a grass stem, 'white, green, yellow, red, purple, and when people are angry or bad, black across the red—as you were just now.'

'Who told you anything about it—in the beginning?' I demanded.

'About the colours? No one. I used to ask what colours were when I was little—in tablecovers and curtains and carpets you see—because some colours hurt me and some made me happy. People told me; and when I got older that was how I saw people.' Again she traced the outline of the Egg which it is given to very few of us to see.

'All by yourself?' I repeated.

'All by myself. There wasn't anyone else. I only found out afterwards that other people did not see the Colours.'

She leaned against the tree-bole plaiting and unplaiting chance-plucked grass stems. The children in the wood had drawn nearer. I could see them with the tail of my eye frolicking like squirrels.

'Now I am sure you will never laugh at me,' she went on after a long silence. 'Nor at *them*.'

'Goodness! No!' I cried, jolted out of my train of thought. 'A man who laughs at a child—unless the child is laughing too—is a heathen!'

'I didn't mean that, of course. You'd never laugh *at* children, but I thought—I used to think—that perhaps you might laugh about *them*. So now I beg your pardon. . . . What are you going to laugh at?'

I had made no sound, but she knew.

'At the notion of your begging my pardon. If you had done your duty as a pillar of the State and a landed proprietress you ought to have summoned me for trespass when I barged through your woods the other day. It was disgraceful of me—inexcusable.'

She looked at me, her head against the tree-trunk—long and steadfastly—this woman who could see the naked soul.

'How curious,' she half whispered. 'How very curious.'

'Why, what have I done?'

'You don't understand . . . and yet you understood about the Colours. Don't you understand?'

She spoke with a passion that nothing had justified, and I faced her bewilderedly as she rose. The children had gathered themselves in a roundel behind a bramble bush. One sleek head bent over something smaller, and the set of the little shoulders told me that fingers were on lips. They, too, had some child's tremendous secret. I alone was hopelessly astray there in the broad sunlight.

'No,' I said, and shook my head as though the dead eyes

could note. 'Whatever it is, I don't understand yet. Perhaps I shall later—if you'll let me come again.'

'You will come again,' she answered. 'You will surely come again and walk in the wood.'

'Perhaps the children will know me well enough by that time to let me play with them—as a favour. You know what children are like.'

'It isn't a matter of favour but of right,' she replied, and while I wondered what she meant, a dishevelled woman plunged round the bend of the road, loose-haired, purple, almost lowing with agony as she ran. It was my rude, fat friend of the sweetmeat shop. The blind woman heard and stepped forward. 'What is it, Mrs Madehurst?' she asked.

The woman flung her apron over her head and literally grovelled in the dust, crying that her grandchild was sick to death, that the local doctor was away fishing, that Jenny the mother was at her wits' end, and so forth, with repetitions and bellowings.

'Where's the nearest doctor?' I asked between paroxysms.

'Madden will tell you. Go round to the house and take him with you. I'll attend to this. Be quick!' She half supported the fat woman into the shade. In two minutes I was blowing all the horns of Jericho under the front of the House Beautiful, and Madden, in the pantry, rose to the crisis like a butler and a man.

A quarter of an hour at illegal speeds caught us a doctor five miles away. Within the half-hour we had decanted him, much interested in motors, at the door of the sweetmeat shop, and drew up the road to await the verdict.

'Useful things, cars,' said Madden, all man and no butler. 'If I'd had one when mine took sick she wouldn't have died.'

'How was it?' I asked.

'Croup. Mrs Madden was away. No one knew what to do. I drove eight miles in a tax-cart for the doctor. She was choked when we came back. This car'd ha' saved her. She'd have been close on ten now.'

'I'm sorry,' I said. 'I thought you were rather fond of children from what you told me going to the cross-roads the other day.'

'Have you seen 'em again, Sir—this mornin'?"

'Yes, but they're well broke to cars. I couldn't get any of them within twenty yards of it.'

He looked at me carefully as a scout considers a stranger—not as a menial should lift his eyes to his divinely appointed superior.

'I wonder why,' he said just above the breath that he drew.

We waited on. A light wind from the sea wandered up and down the long lines of the woods, and the wayside grasses, whitened already with summer dust, rose and bowed in sallow waves.

A woman, wiping the suds off her arms, came out of the cottage next the sweetmeat shop.

'I've be'n listenin' in de back-yard,' she said cheerily. 'He says Arthur's unaccountable bad. Did ye hear him shruck just now? Unaccountable bad. I reckon t'will come Jenny's turn to walk in de wood nex' week along, Mr Madden.'

'Excuse me, Sir, but your lap-robe is slipping,' said Madden deferentially. The woman started, dropped a curtsey, and hurried away.

'What does she mean by "walking in the wood"?' I asked.

'It must be some saying they use hereabouts. I'm from Norfolk myself,' said Madden. 'They're an independent lot in this county. She took you for a chauffeur, Sir.'

I saw the Doctor come out of the cottage followed by a draggle-tailed wench who clung to his arm as though he could make treaty for her with Death. 'Dat sort,' she wailed—'dey're just as much to us dat has 'em as if dey was lawful born. Just as much—just as much! An' God he'd be just as pleased if you saved 'un, Doctor. Don't take it from me. Miss Florence will tell ye de very same. Don't leave 'im, Doctor!'

'I know, I know,' said the man; 'but he'll be quiet for a while now. We'll get the nurse and the medicine as fast as we can.' He signalled me to come forward with the car, and I strove not to be privy to what followed; but I saw the girl's face, blotched and frozen with grief, and I felt the hand without a ring clutching at my knees when we moved away.

The Doctor was a man of some humour, for I remember he claimed my car under the Oath of Aesculapius, and used it and me without mercy, First we convoyed Mrs Madehurst and the blind woman to wait by the sick-bed till the nurse should come. Next we invaded a neat county town for presciptions (the Doctor said the trouble was cerebro-spinal meningitis), and when the County Institute, banked and flanked with scared market cattle, reported itself out of nurses for the moment we literally flung ourselves loose upon the county. We conferred with the owners of great houses—magnates at the ends of overarching avenues whose big-boned womenfolk strode away from their tea-tables to listen to the imperious Doctor. At last a white-haired lady sitting under a cedar of Lebanon and surrounded by a court of magnificent Borzois—all hostile to motors—gave the Doctor, who received them as from a princess, written orders which we bore many miles at top speed, through a park, to a French nunnery, where we took over in exchange a pallid-faced and trembling Sister. She knelt at the bottom of the tonneau telling her beads without pause till, by short cuts of the Doctor's invention, we had her to the sweetmeat shop once more. It was a long afternoon crowded with mad episodes that rose and dissolved like the dust of our wheels; cross-sections of remote and incomprehensible lives through which we raced at right angles; and I went home in the dusk, wearied out, to dream of the clashing horns of cattle; round-eyed nuns walking in a garden of graves; pleasant tea-parties beneath shady trees; the carbolic-scented, grey-painted corridors of the County Institute; the steps of shy children in the wood, and the hands that clung to my knees as the motor began to move.

I had intended to return in a day or two, but it pleased Fate to hold me from that side of the county, on many pretexts, till the elder and the wild rose had fruited. There came at last a brilliant day, swept clear from the south-west, that brought the hills within hand's reach—a day of unstable airs and high filmy clouds. Through no merit of my own I was free, and set the car for the third time on that known road. As I reached the crest of the Downs I felt the soft air change, saw it glaze under the sun; and, looking down at the sea, in that instant beheld the blue of the Channel turn through polished silver and dulled steel to dingy pewter. A laden collier hugging the coast steered outward for deeper water, and, across copper-coloured haze, I saw sails rise one by one on the anchored fishing-fleet. In a deep dene behind me an eddy of sudden wind drummed through sheltered oaks, and spun aloft the first dry sample of autumn leaves. When I reached the beach road the sea-fog fumed over the brickfields, and the tide was telling all the groynes of the gale beyond Ushant. In less than an hour summer England vanished in chill grey. We were again the shut island of the North, all the ships of the world bellowing at our perilous gates; and between their outcries ran the piping of bewildered gulls. My cap dripped moisture, the folds of the rug held it in pools or sluiced it away in runnels, and the salt-rime stuck to my lips.

Inland the smell of autumn loaded the thickened fog among the trees, and the drip became a continuous shower. Yet the late flowers—mallow of the wayside, scabious of the field, and dahlia of the garden—showed gay in the mist, and beyond the sea's breath there was little sign of decay in the leaf. Yet in the villages the house doors were all open, and bare-legged, bare-headed children sat at ease on the damp doorsteps to shout 'pip-pip' at the stranger.

I made bold to call at the sweetmeat shop, where Mrs Madehurst met me with a fat woman's hospitable tears. Jenny's child, she said, had died two days after the nun had come. It was, she felt, best out of the way, even though insurance offices, for reasons which she did not pretend to follow, would not willingly insure such stray lives. 'Not but what Jenny didn't tend to Arthur as though he'd come all proper at de end of de first year—like Jenny herself.' Thanks to Miss Florence, the child had been buried with a pomp which, in Mrs Madehurst's opinion, more than covered the small irregularity of its birth. She described the coffin, within and without, the glass hearse, and the evergreen lining of the grave.

'But how's the mother?' I asked.

'Jenny? Oh, she'll get over it. I've felt dat way with one or two o' my own. She'll get over. She's walkin' in de wood now.'

'In this weather?'

Mrs Madehurst looked at me with narrowed eyes across the counter.

'I dunno but it opens de 'eart like. Yes, it opens de 'eart. Dat's where losin' and bearin' comes so alike in de long run we do say.'

Now the wisdom of the old wives is greater than that of all the Fathers, and this last oracle sent me thinking so extendedly as I went up the road, that I nearly ran over a woman and a child at the wooded corner by the lodge gates of the House Beautiful.

"Awful weather!' I cried, as I slowed dead for the turn.

'Not so bad,' she answered placidly out of the fog. 'Mine's used to 'un. You'll find yours indoors, I reckon.'

Indoors, Madden received me with professional courtesy, and kind inquiries for the health of the motor, which he would put under cover.

I waited in a still, nut-brown hall, pleasant with late flowers and warmed with a delicious wood fire—a place of good influence and great peace. (Men and women may sometimes, after great effort, achieve a creditable lie; but the house, which is their temple, cannot say anything save the truth of those who have lived in it.) A child's cart and a doll lay on the black-and-white floor, where a rug had been kicked back. I felt that the children had only just hurried away—to hide themselves, most like—in the many turns of the great adzed staircase that climbed steadily out of the hall, or to crouch and gaze behind the lions and roses of the carven gallery above. Then I heard her voice above me, singing as the blind sing—from the soul:

'In the pleasant orchard-closes.'

And all my early summer came back at the call.

'In the pleasant orchard-closes,
God bless all our gains say we—

But may God bless all our losses,
Better suits with our degree.'

She dropped the marring fifth line, and repeated—

'Better suits with our degree!'

I saw her lean over the gallery, her linked hands white as pearl against the oak.

'Is that you—from the other side of the county?' she called.

'Yes, me—from the other side of the county,' I answered, laughing

'What a long time before you had to come here again.' She ran down the stairs, one hand lightly touching the broad rail. 'It's two months and four days. Summer's gone!'

'I meant to come before, but Fate prevented.'

'I knew it. Please do something to that fire. They won't let me play with it, but I can feel it's behaving badly. Hit it!'

I looked on either side of the deep fireplace, and found but a half-charred hedge-stake with which I punched a black log into flame.

'It never goes out, day or night,' she said, as though explaining. 'In case any one comes in with cold toes, you see.'

'It's even lovelier inside than it was out,' I murmured. The red light poured itself along the age-polished dusky panels till the Tudor roses and lions of the gallery took colour and motion. An old eagle-topped convex mirror gathered the picture into its mysterious heart, distorting afresh the distorted shadows, and curving the gallery lines into the curves of a ship. The day was shutting down in half a gale as the fog turned to stringy scud. Through the uncurtained mullions of the broad window I could see the valiant horsemen of the lawn rear and recover against the wind that taunted them with legions of dead leaves.

'Yes, it must be beautiful,' she said. 'Would you like to go over it? There's still light enough upstairs.'

I followed her up the unflinching, wagon-wide staircase

to the gallery whence opened the thin fluted Elizabethan doors.

'Feel how they put the latch low down for the sake of the children.' She swung a light door inward.

'By the way, where are they?' I asked. 'I haven't even heard them today.'

She did not answer at once. Then, 'I can only hear them,' she replied softly. 'This is one of their rooms—everything ready, you see.'

She pointed into a heavily-timbered room. There were little low gate tables and children's chairs. A doll's house, it's hooked front half open, faced a great dappled rocking-horse, from whose padded saddle it was but a child's scramble to the broad window-seat overlooking the lawn. A toy gun lay in a corner beside a gilt wooden cannon.

'Surely they've only just gone,' I whispered. In the failing light a door creaked cautiously. I heard the rustle of a frock and the patter of feet—quick feet through a room beyond.

'I heard that,' she cried triumphantly. 'Did you? Children, oh, children! Where are you?'

The voice filled the walls that held it lovingly to the last perfect note, but there came no answering shout such as I had heard in the garden. We hurried on from room to oak-floored room; up a step here, down three steps there; among a maze of passages; always mocked by our quarry. One might as well have tried to work an unstopped warren with a single ferret. There were bolt-holes innumerable—recesses in walls, embrasures of deep-slitten windows now darkened, whence they could start up behind us; and abandoned fireplaces, six feet deep in the masonry, as well as the tangle of communicating doors. Above all, they had the twilight for their helper in our game. I had caught one or two joyous chuckles of evasion, and once or twice had seen the silhouette of a child's frock against some darkening window at the end of a passage; but we returned empty-handed to the gallery, just as a middle-aged woman was setting a lamp in its niche.

'No, I haven't seen her either this evening, Miss Florence,' I heard her say, 'but that Turpin he says he wants to see you about his shed.'

'Oh, Mr Turpin must want to see me very badly. Tell him to come to the hall, Mrs Madden.'

I looked down into the hall whose only light was the dulled fire, and deep in the shadow I saw them at last. They must have slipped down while we were in the passages, and now thought themselves perfectly hidden behind an old gilt leather screen. By child's law, my fruitless chase was as good as an introduction, but since I had taken so much trouble I resolved to force them to come forward later by the simple trick, which children detest, of pretending not to notice them. They lay close, in a little huddle, no more than shadows except when a quick flame betrayed an outline.

'And now we'll have some tea,' she said. 'I believe I ought to have offered it you at first, but one doesn't arrive at manners somehow when one lives alone and is considered—h'm—peculiar.' Then with very pretty scorn, 'Would you like a lamp to see to eat by?'

'The firelight's much pleasanter, I think.' We descended into that delicious gloom and Madden brought tea.

I took my chair in the direction of the screen ready to surprise or be surprised as the game should go, and at her permission, since a hearth is always sacred, bent forward to play with the fire.

'Where do you get these beautiful short faggots from?' I asked idly. 'Why, they are tallies!'

'Of course,' she said. 'As I can't read or write I'm driven back on the early English tally for my accounts. Give me one and I'll tell you what it meant.'

I passed her an unburned hazel-tally, about a foot long, and she ran her thumb down the nicks.

'This is the milk-record for the home farm for the month of April last year, in gallons,' said she. 'I don't know what I should have done without tallies. An old forester of mine taught me the system. It's out of date now for everyone else; but my tenants respect it. One of them's coming now to see me. Oh, it doesn't matter. He has no business here out of office hours. He's a greedy, ignorant man—very greedy, or—he wouldn't come here after dark.'

'Have you much land then?'

'Only a couple of hundred acres in hand, thank goodness.

The other six hundred are nearly all let to folk who knew my folk before me, but this Turpin is quite a new man—and a highway robber.'

'But are you sure I shan't be—?'

'Certainly not. You have the right. He hasn't any children.'

'Ah, the children!' I said, and slid my low chair back till it nearly touched the screen that hid them. 'I wonder whether they'll come out for me.'

There was a murmur of voices—Madden's and a deeper note—at the low, dark side door, and a ginger-headed, canvas-gaitered giant of the unmistakable tenant-farmer type stumbled or was pushed in.

'Come to the fire, Mr Turpin,' she said.

'If—if you please, Miss, I'll—I'll be quite as well by the door.' He clung to the latch as he spoke like a frightened child. Of a sudden I realized that he was in the grip of some almost overpowering fear.

'Well?'

'About that new shed for the young stock—that was all. These first autumn storms settin' in . . . but I'll come again, Miss.' His teeth did not chatter much more than the door-latch.

'I think not,' she answered levelly. 'The new shed—m'm. What did my agent write you on the 15th?'

'I—fancied p'raps that if I came to see you—ma—man to man like, Miss. But—'

His eyes rolled into every corner of the room wide with horror. He half opened the door through which he had entered, but I noticed it shut again—from without and firmly.

'He wrote what I told him,' she went on. 'You are over-stocked already. Dunnett's Farm never carried more than fifty bullocks—even in Mr Wright's time. And *he* used cake. You've sixty-seven and you don't cake. You've broken the lease in that respect. You're dragging the heart out of the farm.'

'I'm—I'm getting some minerals—superphosphates—next week. I've as good as ordered a truck-load already. I'll go down to the station tomorrow about 'em. Then I can come and see you man to man like, Miss, in the daylight. . . . That gentleman's not going away, is he?' He almost shrieked.

I had only slid the chair a little farther back, reaching behind me to tap on the leather of the screen, but he jumped like a rat.

'No. Please attend to me, Mr Turpin.' She turned in her chair and faced him with his back to the door. It was an old and sordid little piece of scheming that she forced from him—his pleas for the new cow-shed at his landlady's expense, that he might with the covered manure pay his next year's rent out of the valuation after, as she made clear, he had bled the enriched pastures to the bone. I could not but admire the intensity of his greed, when I saw him outfacing for its sake whatever terror it was that ran wet on his forehead.

I ceased to tap the leather—was, indeed, calculating the cost of the shed—when I felt my relaxed hand taken and turned softly between the soft hands of a child. So at last I had triumphed. In a moment I would turn and acquaint myself with those quick-footed wanderers . . .

The little brushing kiss fell in the centre of my palm—as a gift on which the fingers were, once, expected to close: as the all-faithful half-reproachful signal of a waiting child not used to neglect even when grown-ups were busiest—a fragment of the mute code devised very long ago.

Then I knew. And it was as though I had known from the first day when I looked across the lawn at the high window.

I heard the door shut. The woman turned to me in silence, and I felt that she knew.

What time passed after this I cannot say. I was roused by the fall of a log, and mechanically rose to put it back. Then I returned to my place in the chair very close to the screen.

'Now you understand,' she whispered, across the packed shadows.

'Yes, I understand—now. Thank you.'

'I—I only hear them.' She bowed her head in her hands. 'I have no right, you know—no other right. I have neither borne nor lost—neither borne nor lost!'

'Be very glad then,' said I, for my soul was torn open within me.

'Forgive me!'

She was still, and I went back to my sorrow and my joy.

'It was because I loved them so,' she said at last, brokenly. '*That* was why it was, even from the first—even before I knew that they—they were all I should ever have. And I loved them so!'

She stretched out her arms to the shadows and the shadows within the shadow.

'They came because I loved them—because I needed them. I—I must have made them come. Was that wrong, think you?'

'No—no.'

'I—I grant you that the toys and—and all that sort of thing were nonsense, but—but I used to so hate empty rooms myself when I was little.' She pointed to the gallery. 'And the passages all empty . . . And how could I ever bear the garden door shut? Suppose—'

'Don't! For pity's sake, don't!' I cried. The twilight had brought a cold rain with gusty squalls that plucked at the leaded windows.

'And the same thing with keeping the fire in all night. *I* don't think it so foolish—do you?'

I looked at the broad brick hearth, saw, through tears, I believe, that there was no unpassable iron on or near it, and bowed my head.

'I did all that and lots of other things—just to make believe. Then they came. I heard them, but I didn't know that they were not mine by right till Mrs Madden told me—'

'The butler's wife? What?'

'One of them—I heard—she saw. And knew Hers! *Not* for me. I didn't know at first. Perhaps I was jealous. Afterwards, I began to understand that it was only because I loved them, not because— . . . Oh, you *must* bear or lose,' she said piteously. 'There is no other way—and yet they love me. They must! Don't they?'

There was no other sound in the room except the lapping voices of the fire, but we two listened intently, and she at least took comfort from what she heard. She recovered herself and half rose. I sat still in my chair by the screen.

'Don't think me a wretch to whine about myself like this, but—but I'm all in the dark, you know, and *you* can see.'

In truth I could see, and my vision confirmed me in my resolve, though that was like the very parting of spirit and flesh. Yet a little longer I would stay since it was the last time.

'You think it is wrong, then?' she cried sharply, though I had said nothing.

'Not for you. A thousand times no. For you it is right. . . . I am grateful to you beyond words. For me it would be wrong. For me only . . .'

'Why?' she said, but passed her hand before her face as she had done at our second meeting in the wood. 'Oh, I see,' she went on simply as a child. 'For you it would be wrong.' Then with a little indrawn laugh. 'And, d'you remember, I called you lucky—once—at first. You who must never come here again!'

She left me to sit a little longer by the screen, and I heard the sound of her feet die out along the gallery above.

POUL ANDERSON

Poul Anderson is one of the most honored authors of our time. He has won seven Hugo Awards, three Nebula Awards, and the Gandalf Award for Achievement in Fantasy, among others. His most popular series include the Polesotechnic League/Terran Empire tales and the Time Patrol series. Here are fine books by Poul Anderson available through Baen Books:

THE GAME OF EMPIRE

A *new* novel in Anderson's Polesotechnic League/Terran Empire series! Diana Crowfeather, daughter of Dominic Flandry, proves well capable of following in his adventurous footsteps.

FIRE TIME

Once every thousand years the Deathstar orbits close enough to burn the surface of the planet Ishtar. This is known as the Fire Time, and it is then that the barbarians flee the scorched lands, bringing havoc to the civilized South.

AFTER DOOMSDAY

Earth has been destroyed, and the handful of surviving humans must discover which of three alien races is guilty before it's too late.

THE BROKEN SWORD

It is a time when Christos is new to the land, and the Elder Gods and the Elven Folk still hold sway. In 11th-century Scandinavia Christianity is beginning to replace the old religion, but the Old Gods still have power, and men are still oppressed by the folk of the Faerie. "Pure gold!"—Anthony Boucher.

THE DEVIL'S GAME

Seven people gather on a remote island, each competing for a share in a tax-free fortune. The "contest" is ostensibly sponsored by an eccentric billionaire—but the rich man is in league with an alien masquerading as a demon . . . or is it the other way around?

THE ENEMY STARS

Includes for the first time the sequel to "The Enemy Stars": "The Ways of Love." Fast-paced adventure science fiction from a master.

SEVEN CONQUESTS

Seven brilliant tales examine the many ways human beings—most dangerous and violent of all species—react under the stress of conflict and high technology.

STRANGERS FROM EARTH

Classic Anderson: A stranded alien spends his life masquerading as a human, hoping to contact his own world. He succeeds, but the result is a bigger problem than before . . . What if our reality is a fiction? Nothing more than a book written by a very powerful Author? Two philosophers stumble on the truth and try to puzzle out the Ending . . .

You can order all of Poul Anderson's books listed above with this order form. Check your choices below and send the combined cover price/s to: Baen Books, Dept. BA, 260 Fifth Avenue, New York, New York 10001.*

THE GAME OF EMPIRE • 55959-1 • 288 pp. • $3.50 ______
FIRE TIME • 55900-1 • 288 pp. • $2.95 ______
AFTER DOOMSDAY • 65591-4 • 224 pp. • $2.95 ______
THE BROKEN SWORD • 65382-2 • 256 pp. • $2.95 ______
THE DEVIL'S GAME • 55995-8 • 256 pp. • $2.95 ______
THE ENEMY STARS • 65339-3 • 224 pp. • $2.95 ______
SEVEN CONQUESTS • 55914-1 • 288 pp. • $2.95 ______
STRANGERS FROM EARTH • 65627-9 • 224 pp. • $2.95 ______

"Drake has distinguished himself as the master of the mercenary sf novel."—Rave Reviews

DAVID DRAKE

IS

ROLLING HOT

Hammers Slammers

Rolling Hot

The latest novel of Col. Alois Hammer's Slammers—Hammers Slammers vs. a 22nd Century Viet Cong.

Hammers Slammers

The new *expanded* edition of the book that began the legend of Colonel Hammer.

At Any Price

The 23rd armored division faces its deadliest enemies ever: aliens who *teleport into combat*.

Counting the Cost

The cold ferocity of the Slammers vs. red-hot religious fanaticism.

Ranks of Bronze

Alien traders were looking to buy primitive soldier-slaves—they needed troops who could win battles without high-tech weaponry. But when they bought Roman legionaries, they bought *trouble* . . .

Vettius and His Friends

A Roman Centurion and his merchant friend fight and connive to stave off the fall of Rome.

Lacey and His Friends

Jed Lacey is a 21st-century cop who plays by the rules. His rules.

Men Hunting Things
Things Hunting Men

Volumes One and Two of the *Starhunters* series. Exactly what the titles indicate, selected and with in-depth introductions by the creator of Hammer's Slammers.

To receive books by one of BAEN BOOKS most popular authors send in the order form below.

Rolling Hot, 69837-0 ✪ $3.95 . . . . ☐
Hammer's Slammers, 65632-5 ✪ $3.50 . . . . ☐
At Any Price, 55978-8 ✪ $3.50 . . . . ☐
Counting the Cost, 65355-5 ✪ $3.50 . . . . ☐
Ranks of Bronze, 65568-X ✪ $3.50 . . . . ☐
Vettius and His Friends, 69802-8 ✪ $3.95 . . . . . ☐
Lacey and His Friends, 65593-0 ✪ $3.50 . . . . ☐
Men Hunting Things, 65399-7 ✪ $2.95 . . . . ☐
Things Hunting Men, 65412-8 ✪ $3.50 . . . . ☐

Please send me the books checked above. I have enclosed a check or money order for the combined cover price made out to: BAEN BOOKS, 260 Fifth Avenue, New York N.Y. 10001.